A Midsummer Night's Kiss

The Howertys 1

Emily Morgans

MISCHIEVOUS INK

Copyright © 2024 by Emily Morgans

All rights reserved.

No part of this publication may be reproduced, distributed, or transmitted in any form or by any means, including photocopying, recording, or other electronic or mechanical methods, without the prior written permission of the publisher, except for the use of brief quotations in a book review.

The story, all names, characters, and incidents portrayed in this production are fictitious. No identification with actual persons (living or deceased), places, buildings, and products is intended or should be inferred.

Content Warning:
This book contains sexual content, and other mature themes, including an attempted SA, and mentions of suicide. Please read at your own discretion.

Language:
Please note that this book is written in British English, so you will find some extra letters, especially u's (like humour), and a distinct lack of z's (like realise), and while we're at it, some extra c's (like defence). I hope this doesn't put you off an otherwise decent story.

For Mormor

I wish you could have been here

Chapter One

Dear Diary,
 It was as if a dark angel had lain down
 amongst the crisp, white sheets.
 A very wicked angel.

London, England
April 12, 1811

Angelique Grafton had imagined several scenarios for her unexpected early arrival at her brother's London townhouse. None of them involved finding a stranger sleeping in her bed.

Hovering in the doorway to her room, she bit her lower lip while debating her options. The proper response would be to fetch her brother or the butler, and yet her feet refused to move.

Lying on his back, the man's face was covered by his arm. The white sheets pulled up to his chest only emphasised the fact that there wasn't a shred of clothing on his upper body.

It was the most bare skin she'd ever seen on a man. A quiet life in the country provided no sights like this. Overcome by curiosity, she took a few hesitant steps closer. Ignoring the fluttering of her nerves, she walked up to the bed, fully aware that she was doing something she shouldn't be.

Not even the thought of her aunt's disapproval was enough to deter her from the tantalising sight of all that bare male form. *'Angel, what are you thinking? To enter a room with a naked man inside! Are you trying to get yourself ruined?'*

With the arm over his face, she could see little of the stranger's features, but his skin was smooth and tanned, much darker than her own pale complexion. It looked utterly touchable.

She glanced at the open door and made sure she was alone before using her teeth to loosen her gloves at the fingertips. Pulling them off, she quietly put them on the nightstand by the bed and reached a hand out. Only to pull it back just as quickly. The stranger let out a small sigh.

What was she doing? She must have lost her wits. You didn't just walk into a room to touch someone simply because their skin looked warm and inviting—even if they happened to be sleeping in your bed. With a rueful smile, she shook her head and stepped back.

When the man suddenly reached out and grabbed her bare arm, she almost bit her tongue in surprise. Before she had time to react, he pulled her down onto the bed and her body collided with his.

"Don't leave, darling," he mumbled, the hoarse quality of his sleepy voice sending shivers down her back.

"I—" She did bite her tongue then, trying to keep herself from saying something inane while her mind reeled from their inappropriate closeness. "I do believe I should."

His chest was solid against her own as she lay half on top of him, and the arm not covering his face had moved to circle her waist. Oh, this was wrong. So very, very wrong. If anyone saw them like this, they would most definitely make the wrong assumption, and her reputation would be ruined. She tried to pull away, but the man's grip on her waist didn't waver.

"But we were having so much fun." His words, spoken through a yawn, made her realise he wasn't quite awake and must be confusing her with whatever dream he'd been having.

Trying to get back up, she placed her hand on his chest and was momentarily distracted by the firmness and heat of his skin against her palm. He finally appeared to stir, slowly sitting.

In fascinated horror, she watched the sheets fall from his chest and bundle around his waist, revealing a flat abdomen with sculpted muscles. A pair of dark eyes fastened on her, and she wanted to squirm. They stared at each other. Her mouth fell open. This was the most handsome man she had ever seen.

He had the perfect face one would expect on an angel, but with his tanned skin and unruly black hair, he was probably more like a fallen angel. A dark shadow of stubble covered his strong, angular jaw. While her mind swam with visions that made her cheeks burn, Angel tried to swallow, but her throat was dry.

High cheekbones, a straight nose, and black brows suited him very well. Almost too well. And then there was his mouth. Her cheeks heated even more when she realised she was staring. It was full and sensual, with a slight upward bend at the corners, giving him more the air of a wicked satyr than an angel. What was a man like this doing in her bed?

While she was busy ogling the stranger, he rubbed his eyes. Looking at her again, he took her in—top to toe—his eyes turning darker every moment until finally, something seemed to click in his sleep-addled brain. With a curse, he sat up straighter, nearly dislodging her from the bed.

"Who are you?" he demanded. "I don't know you."

"I'm well aware," she replied in an attempt to make a jest, but her voice was oddly breathless and she was alarmingly aware that he had yet to move his arm from her waist.

"Who the hell are you?"

"I... This is my room," she blurted out. Not the most eloquent thing she'd ever said, but she was quite happy to have been able to string any words together. Why had he not let go of her yet? She was certain she would be able to focus much better if only he would.

"Your room?" He frowned and looked around the room. "This isn't the guest room?" Understanding dawned on his face and he abruptly let go of her as if he'd burned himself. "You're Gowthorpe's sister!"

That didn't sound like a joyful statement by any standard. More like an accusation. She got off the bed, deeming it an excellent idea to put some distance between them.

"I marvel at your remarkable skill of deduction," she said, gaining a grim look from the stranger. "Who are you, if I may be so bold? You are, after all, in *my* room."

Judging from his scowl, he'd just as well throw her out of the aforementioned room headfirst.

"Nathaniel Howerty," he muttered after a few moments of silence. "What the h—" He cut himself short before he could curse in her presence yet again and ran a hand through his dark hair. "What are you doing here? Your brother isn't expecting you for another fortnight."

She tried to keep her eyes on his face and not the smooth, bare chest that was still visible above the sheets. "I arrived early," she said, sounding distracted even to herself.

"Yes, I gathered as much." There was no mistaking the dry tone in his voice.

Her cheeks flushed. He must believe she lived in a permanent state of reddened cheeks. "I begged my aunt to let me come sooner. We rarely see James, and I wanted some time with him in London before everyone else joined. I thought I might surprise him."

She was blathering, something she did when nervous. A naked man in her bed definitely made her nervous.

"It sure as hell surprised me," he muttered under his breath, and she was fairly certain he hadn't intended for her to hear it. "Why are you here by yourself? Shouldn't someone have shown you to your room and seen I was here?"

"I told Dobbins I could find my way. It's not like I can't find my own room." She pointedly added, "I wasn't exactly expecting to find a strange man in my bed."

He smiled wryly, raking a hand through his hair again, his dark gaze on her. "We cannot tell anyone about this. Your reputation would be ruined, even if nothing happened."

She nodded. He was right.

"I daresay this incident is best forgotten by both of us," he continued.

Forget it? She doubted her ability to. The sight of his bare chest was surely etched into her memory for all eternity.

"Good." He let out a sigh of relief despite her saying nothing. "That's decided. Now, I suggest you leave before anyone sees us together and before you see more of me than either of us would like."

At first, she wasn't sure what he meant, but when he started getting out of bed, her eyes widened and she quickly turned her back to him. There was a limit to how much naked male body she could handle in one day. She could have sworn she heard him chuckle as she fled.

Nathaniel smirked when the woman's white dress disappeared through the door. Entering a bedchamber with a man sleeping inside had been a risky move on her part.

She should know better, even if it was her room. With a huff, he dressed, thankful that no one had seen them. The last thing he needed was to be caught alone—naked—with his friend's younger sister. What had she been thinking?

Many gentlemen of the *ton* wouldn't think twice about grabbing and seducing any woman who wandered into their room. He wasn't one of those men, but she did not know that.

Once fully dressed, he went downstairs in search of something to eat. He found his friend, James Grafton, Viscount Gowthorpe, already at the table in the dining room with a cup of tea and a plate filled to the brim with eggs, bacon, and toast. His sister sat next to him, clasping a cup of tea and fastidiously avoiding Nathaniel's eyes as he walked over to them.

Gowthorpe stood, grinning widely. "I didn't expect you up yet."

"Neither did I. Nor did I expect to see you." In fairness, it was most likely approaching noon by now, but they had only stumbled home in the early hours of the morning after a night about town.

"A maid woke me to inform me that my sister had arrived. I don't believe you've met before." Gowthorpe turned to his sister. "Angel, please allow me to introduce to you Nathaniel Howerty, the Marquess of Pensington. He's a good friend. I believe I may have mentioned him to you?"

She nodded, her eyes still on the cup of tea. It must be an absolutely riveting cup of tea.

"Pensington, this is my sister Angelique Grafton. Angel to family and close friends."

She stood and demurely offered her hand. He took it and softly placed a kiss above her knuckles, then pretended not to notice that she all but snatched it back.

"We've met," he said, surprising himself as much as her. The look of panic in her wide green eyes made it all worth it. Maybe it would teach her not to walk into rooms where strange men were sleeping.

"Oh? When was that?" Gowthorpe looked between them, a line between his brows. "I cannot think when you two would have met. Angel is rarely in London."

They all sat back down at the table and Nathaniel glanced at Angel, wondering what she would tell her brother. She stirred her tea with a small frown puckering her brow while she was presumably debating what she could say without giving away too much.

"When did the two of you meet?" Gowthorpe asked again, and Nathaniel almost laughed when Angel gave him a sullen look through her eyelashes. It was wicked of him to tease her like this, but he was enjoying it far too much.

Looking at the two siblings, it was easy to see that they were family. They had the same blond hair and pale skin, although Gowthorpe's was a few shades darker than his sister's. Both had high cheekbones, a finely chiselled nose, and arched brows.

However, where Gowthorpe's eyes were a clear blue, Angel's were light green.

She may not be someone who would turn heads at first glance, mainly because with her white dress and fair complexion she seemed to fade into the surroundings, but once you paid attention, she was quite pretty. Though he was probably better off not thinking of his friend's sister as pretty.

"When I arrived, I went upstairs to my bedchamber." Angel stopped stirring her tea and looked up, a stubborn tilt to her chin even as her cheeks darkened with a blush. "I did not realise that someone else used it in my absence."

Nathaniel schooled his features when his friend turned to him with a frown. Well played, Miss Grafton. Well played.

"No one is meant to," Gowthorpe said. "You slept in my sister's room?"

"Apparently," Nathaniel replied with a wry smile. "We were both quite foxed last night. I think I fell into the first available room I could find."

His friend chuckled. "It was a rather good night, wasn't it?"

Crisis averted, and they returned to their tea. It had been a foolish thing to taunt her like that. He really needed to learn to control his impulses better. Fortunately, Gowthorpe didn't seem to suspect anything untoward had happened. Which was the truth.

As long as one ignored the fact that Nathaniel had pulled her down onto the bed. His friend might take exception to that.

In his defence, he had been half-asleep and thought he was still dreaming when the alluring scent of rosewater tickled his nose.

A footman brought over a plate for his breakfast, interrupting his wandering thoughts. While he ate, he looked over at Angel. She was focusing on her tea, but now and then he caught her throwing him a furtive glance. Maybe she was trying to discern whether he would tell her brother about their unfortunate meeting after all. He would never be so foolish, but he didn't mind watching her squirm.

Gowthorpe questioned his sister about her journey while finishing up his scrambled eggs, leaving Nathaniel to observe in silence. Why was she so eager to come to London that she'd travel without the comfort of her family?

"I assume you will be at your sister's coming-out ball tomorrow evening, Pensington?" Gowthorpe asked, stalling Nathaniel's ponderings.

"It's not like I have a choice," he said, feigning disgust. "I never thought having a sister of marriageable age would be so much work on my part."

Gowthorpe laughed. "Be glad only one of them is! Imagine if you had all three out at once."

"My aunt already has plans for the younger ones, I'm sure," Nathaniel muttered. To think he would have to go through it all two more times after this year. He didn't mind the social swirl, but the sheer number of events his aunt wanted him to join this season was beyond reasonable.

"Angel, did you bring a ball gown, or are they all coming down with our family?"

"I believe my maid packed one or two." She set down her cup of tea. "But we're not having our coming-out ball until Marie comes down with our aunt and uncle, so I probably shouldn't attend any functions just yet."

"Hogwash!" Gowthorpe exclaimed, waving away her excuses. "You've been presented at court. The ball is a formality at best, and a glorified meat market at worst. Of course, you can attend events before it."

A smile played at the corners of her mouth, and her eyes twinkled. Nathaniel swallowed hard. Angel wasn't just pretty. She was beautiful. A fact he would rather not have noticed.

"Do you think?" she said, then her face fell. "I don't know... Marie will be cross if I am allowed to attend balls without her. She was already throwing a tantrum when Aunt Christine agreed I could travel early."

"Our cousin throws tantrums about everything. Do not let it bother you. While our aunt and uncle have been taking care of you since I reside in London, I am your legal guardian, and I say you can attend this event with me tomorrow. It's Pensington's sister's ball. His family is a lot nicer than he lets on, and I'm sure you will get along splendidly."

"They aren't that bad," Nathaniel agreed. "Well, the youngest is more feral than domesticated, but she won't be allowed to attend."

Angel stared at him, and he grinned. "I beg your pardon, I make them sound terrible. Truly, they are not." *Most of the time.* He loved his family dearly but he was not blind to their faults, just like they were not blind to his.

A footman entered the dining room, presenting Nathaniel with a note on a silver tray. "My lord, this was just delivered for you."

"Thank you." He took the note and unfolded it. After quickly skimming the words, he stood. "My aunt is requesting my presence to help with preparations for tomorrow's ball. Possibly to ensure that my sister does not lock herself in the library before it is time."

"Does she not wish to attend her ball?" Angel asked.

"Probably not," he admitted with a wry smile. "My sister is what some might call a bluestocking and would rather read than find a husband."

"She sounds like a reasonable young lady to me," Angel said pertly, making him laugh.

"I do believe our sisters might get along." Gowthorpe chuckled. "We will see you tomorrow night."

Nathaniel nodded and, after a bow, he followed the footman out to the hallway. It wasn't until after he'd shrugged into his greatcoat and the butler had gone to open the front door that he realised Angel had followed him. She came up to him, staring at him with her large green eyes.

"Yes?" he prompted when she didn't immediately speak.

She cast a nervous glance towards the butler by the door, but he didn't appear to be listening. Leaning a little closer, she said quietly, "I thought we weren't telling anyone about—" Her words stalled for a moment, and her cheeks stained pink. "About this morning. And yet you told James straight away."

"I apologise for that. It slipped out."

She crossed her arms over her chest. "Can I trust you to keep it to yourself from now on? I don't wish to create a scandal on my first day in London."

He chuckled. "You won't. It won't happen again. I would be in equal trouble if your brother was to find out. Like we said, let us pretend it never happened."

There was a slight quiver of her lips as if she was holding back a smile, but she nodded. "All forgotten," she murmured, her gaze avoiding his.

Nathaniel bowed again and exited through the door the butler held open for him. His aunt had sent a carriage for him, so he jumped in and sat down on the bench.

With a last glance at his friend's London townhouse, he already knew he'd struggle to forget. He could still remember the warmth of Angel's body against his. The faint scent of roses.

Damn it. He really shouldn't be attracted to his friend's sister.

Chapter Two

Dear Diary,
    I have never had a true friend.
    Is that not sad? Marie and I may
    have grown up together, but I do
    not think anyone would call us friends.

I can do this. Angel stared at her reflection in the looking glass. They were about to leave for the Howertys' dinner and ball, and she couldn't quite swallow back the anxious energy that wanted to well up whenever she was about to be in a crowded room with people she barely knew.

Years of her aunt and cousin commenting on her pale complexion did nothing to steady her nerves while she inspected her outfit for the fifth time. Not even her maid's reassurances that she looked wonderful could silence her doubts.

Her maid had fashioned her hair in a simple style tied back in a loose bun, with a few soft tendrils framing her face. The dress was one of the few she had chosen herself. Made of white satin, with puff sleeves, and a pale-rose-coloured bodice, it complemented her fair skin rather than washed her out the way the colours her aunt usually chose for her did.

Not that she minded fading into the background. Sometimes, it was rather comforting to be invisible.

I can do this.

Taking a deep breath, she brushed a few non-existent specks of dust from one of her white, elbow-length gloves. This was her very first social event in London. She suspected it would be like nothing she had ever experienced before. Back in the country, her family did not attend any large gatherings. At most, they would visit other families in the area for a dinner or game night.

Tonight, she would attend a ball. A London ball. She would have to mingle with and speak to the fashionable people of the *ton*. When you were shy and quiet, that seemed a rather daunting prospect. She could only hope she wouldn't make a complete fool of herself by blurting out something foolish or insipid.

After a final, longing glance at her diary—writing was so much easier than speaking—she stepped out into the hallway and walked downstairs, where her brother waited for her.

"Angel, you look beautiful." He smiled and took her arm to escort her to their carriage. When he helped her into it and got a better look at her, a frown puckered his brow. "Is that dress not a little low-cut?"

She sat down on a seat in the carriage, running her hands down the skirt to smooth it over her legs. "No, it's actually quite modest for an evening dress."

Entering the vehicle, James sat down on the seat opposite hers. He was still scowling. "I suppose," he muttered. "Somehow, they seemed a lot less revealing when not worn by my sister."

His dour look made her smile. Growing up, they had never spent much time together since he was eight years her senior and had spent much of his youth away at school, and later had kept his residence in London while she stayed with their aunt and uncle in the country. His sudden over-protectiveness was rather amusing. And maybe a little endearing.

"Fret not," she said with a teasing smile. "Most ladies will have gowns like mine. Or even more revealing. Logic says their brothers must struggle more than you."

James stared at her for a moment before letting out a surprised laugh. "I believe you just ruined my enjoyment of looking at ladies' decolletages. Now, all I can think of will be their long-suffering brothers."

It was a relief to see he did not mind her teasing. Her humour was rarely appreciated back home, and she had learnt to hold back most of her comments around her cousin, aunt, and uncle.

But then, they probably preferred she speak nothing at all. The thought dampened her mood, and she leaned back against the carriage seat to look out at the passing streets.

"We're here," James said when the carriage pulled up in front of a large, whitewashed house on York Street, close by the corner of St. James Square. Lights shone in every window, making her feel oddly welcome. Maybe tonight wouldn't be so bad.

A footman opened the carriage door, and James stepped out before turning back to assist Angel. Her brother escorted her up the few steps to the entrance, where another footman held the door open for them. They were led through the house to where the family was receiving guests and offering drinks before dinner would be served.

No more than a dozen guests attended the dinner, which helped steady her nerves somewhat. She would have a brief respite before the ball—and its much larger number of guests. Even so, her face burned and she couldn't stop flexing her fingers in her silk gloves.

A pleasant-looking woman in her forties dressed in a beautiful, silvery-grey gown came towards them, with the Marquess of Pensington by her side. When Angel caught sight of his handsome face, something fluttered to life in her stomach. She took a deep breath to settle herself, while her brother greeted the woman, and tried very hard not to stare at the marquess nearby.

"Mrs Grey," James said. "I'd like to introduce to you my sister, Miss Angelique Grafton."

The older woman welcomed her with a warm smile. "It's a pleasure to finally meet you. Your brother is a dear friend to the family and always speaks fondly of you."

With warm cheeks, Angel remembered to curtsy. "Thank you, Mrs Grey. You have a wonderful home."

"Thank you." Mrs Grey smiled and motioned to the attractive man by her side. "Have you met my nephew, the Marquess of Pensington?"

This forced her to look at him—something she had studiously avoided until now, and she'd rather have continued staring at his lapels—and her throat dried. He was exceedingly handsome in his black evening clothes. The darkness of his hair and attire made her feel like a washed-out mouse next to him.

Before she could open her mouth to greet him, he caught her hand and brought it to his lips for a soft kiss. Even through the fabric of her gloves, the touch sent tingles along her arm and through her entire being, and she had to refrain from snatching her hand back. What was wrong with her?

"Good evening, Miss Grafton." He met her gaze, his dark eyes twinkling like he knew how desperately she wanted to tug her hand from his grasp. Instead, he held it a moment longer than necessary. She was certain it was only to torture her.

"Good evening, my lord." She didn't like the breathless quality of her voice.

"Please, allow me to introduce you to the girls," Mrs Grey said and then looked at James. "I hope you won't mind if I steal your sister for a moment?"

"Go ahead." He waved them off. "Take her off my hands, please."

Then he grinned at Angel, who wanted to kick him in the shins. He knew how uncomfortable she was around strangers. Unable to do anything else without appearing horribly rude, she followed Mrs Grey across the room to a group of young ladies. The two youngest extracted themselves from the others when they approached.

"Aunt Jane, who is this? I saw her arrive on Gowthorpe's arm," the youngest girl demanded. She could not be much older than fourteen years of age, with long blond hair and golden-brown eyes. Her face was pretty, with a smiling mouth and a scattering of freckles across the bridge of her nose.

"Nicola," Mrs Grey admonished. "That is no way to greet a lady. Do not make me regret talking your brother into allowing you to attend this dinner."

The girl shrugged like she didn't much care if she greeted someone the correct way or not, then followed it up with a curtsy executed well enough to have met approval at court.

"No, no, no." Mrs Grey sighed. "You haven't been introduced yet." She turned towards Angel. "I do apologise. She's a mischievous girl, and she loves to aggravate me. We normally don't allow the younger girls to take part, but they promised to behave tonight."

"Do not apologise on my behalf," Angel said, trying to hide her amusement. These antics were making her much more at ease.

"Miranda, Nicola," Mrs Grey said with a look that brokered no more silliness. "This is Miss Angelique Grafton, Viscount Gowthorpe's sister."

"I'm Nick!" the adolescent girl piped up and executed yet another smart curtsy. "It's a pleasure to meet you, Miss Grafton."

Their aunt sighed again, then made a motion to the older of the two girls. She couldn't be over fifteen years old but was already more beautiful than any woman Angel had met.

Her skin was flawless, bringing to mind a porcelain doll Angel once had, and her hair was thick and dark—nearly as dark as the marquess's—while her eyes were cornflower blue.

"Lady Miranda Howerty."

Angel curtsied. "I'm honoured to make your acquaintance."

Mrs Grey motioned towards the younger girl. "Lady Nicola Howerty."

"We usually call her Nick because she is such a tomboy," Lady Miranda said with a grin.

The little girl glared at her sister. "I am not!"

"You wear breeches at our country estate."

"That doesn't make me a tomcat!"

"Not a tomcat, you twit, a tomboy." Lady Miranda gave her sister a suffering look. "But never you mind." Turning back to Angel, she smiled. "If you are Gowthorpe's sister, you're practically family. He is a very dear friend to us. Please call us by our given names. Close friends and family call me Rain."

Nick gave Angel a thoughtful look. "So, Gowthorpe is your brother?"

"Yes."

"Very fortunate. Had you been his intended, I fear I would have had to dispose of you in a most cruel and underhanded manner."

"Nick!" Mrs Grey hissed with a look of horror on her face. "Miss Grafton, I do apologise. Again. Her sisters have been reading her too many gothic novels."

"She's planning to marry your brother," Rain confided with a wink.

Their playfulness made Angel completely forget her shyness, and she found herself grinning at them. "I see no problem there. He could use a good wife."

Mrs Grey had apparently given up hope of making the girls behave and was looking around the room with a slight frown. "Where is your sister?"

"I don't know," Rain said. "She was here not long ago."

"Please excuse me." Mrs Grey gave Angel an apologetic look before she disappeared in search of the missing sister.

"I think she's hiding out in the library," Rain admitted with a sheepish grin once her aunt was out of earshot. "She doesn't much care for balls."

"Is this not her coming-out ball?"

"Yes, it is, but not because she wanted one. Our aunt simply did not give her a choice in the matter. I heard Jessica tell Nathaniel she would happily have skipped the Season altogether. Which is incomprehensible to me. I would give anything to join the social scene." Rain sighed longingly.

Not much later, Mrs Grey returned with a young woman in tow. Like all the Howertys, she was beautiful, but she was probably the one who looked the least like her brother. She had the same blonde hair as Nick, but cornflower-blue eyes like Rain.

"Lady Jessica Howerty." Mrs Grey made the introductions. "Miss Angelique Grafton."

They both curtsied and Lady Jessica looked nearly as uncomfortable as Angel felt.

"You can call her Jessica," Nick offered helpfully, immediately breaking the awkward silence. "It's only fair since we said you could call us Nick and Rain."

Jessica raised an eyebrow, and the corner of her mouth twitched. "On such friendly terms already?"

"Yes," Nick said with a resolute nod. "She will be my sister-in-law."

The blonde woman's head pivoted back towards Angel. "You're marrying my brother? Why has no one told me?"

Angel's cheeks burned hotly for the second time that evening. The image of the marquess lying in her bed flashed through her mind, doing little to help her flushed face.

"No, I... I'm not marrying your brother," she said quickly. Maybe a little too quickly. "I only met him yesterday."

"Oh. I beg your pardon." Jessica's brows drew together while she tried to make sense of her sister's statement. "Then why—?"

"I'm marrying Gowthorpe!" Nick interjected, then added glumly, "I cannot believe you forgot already."

Jessica laughed. It was an irresistible laugh, full-throated and without false affection. It made the corners of Angel's mouth twitch as well. Soon, they were all laughing, causing several other guests to give them odd glances.

"I'm very glad to meet you, Miss Grafton," Jessica said, finally sobering up. "We've always been curious about Gowthorpe's sister."

Angel smiled. "Please, if we are to be sisters, call me Angel."

Returning the smile, the other woman said, "I'm Jessica."

Nick looked across the room to where James stood next to their brother. "Once we are engaged," she said. "I shall finally call him James. My James."

Angel and Jessica looked at each other and giggled. A warm feeling spread through Angel when she realised she might have found a kindred spirit. Perhaps even a friend.

"I saw you met my sisters."

A small shiver travelled down Angel's spine when she recognised the deep voice of the man to her left. She was standing by the wall of the ballroom, looking at the couples on the dance floor where Jessica was being partnered by a tall, handsome man.

The two youngest Howertys had been banned from the lower floor after dinner and had disappeared to their chambers in a sulk some time ago.

Turning her head slightly to the side, she looked up at the marquess. His face was impassive while he studied the dancers in front of them.

"Yes, I find your sisters charming. You are very lucky to have them."

"That I am."

"Sometimes I wish I would have had a sister." The thought slipped out before she could stop it, and she regretted it when the marquess turned his head to look at her, his dark eyes inquisitive.

"I thought you grew up with your cousin?"

She had. After her parents passed away when she was five, her aunt and uncle moved into Hefferton Place with their daughter—her cousin, Marie—to care for her. She looked down at her hands, fidgeting with the dance card attached to her wrist.

Marie was nothing like what she imagined a sister to be. There had been no sisterly moments of shared interests between them, no teasing or ribbing typical of the usual sibling rivalry. Only rivalry. Perhaps because of their opposite personalities. While Angel was shy and quiet, Marie was talkative and forward.

Sometimes, she envied her cousin's effortless charm. Marie never struggled to make conversation or spend time in a room filled with people.

"Miss Grafton?" The marquess's soft query brought her back.

"I beg your pardon, my lord." She forced a light smile. "It is not the same."

He looked like he wanted to know in what way it was different, but must have sensed her reticence since he did not ask her to explain. Instead, he changed the subject. "Why are you not dancing?"

"No one has asked me to," she replied without thinking.

With a smile, he turned towards her and bowed. "Would you please do me the honour of a dance, Miss Grafton?"

"Oh! I didn't mean…" Her mouth wasn't quite cooperating to form words. "I mean— You don't have to."

He acted like he hadn't heard her pitiful excuses. "Please do me the honour of a dance?"

For a split moment, she considered saying no. Spending time on the dance floor with someone who made your knees weak seemed like a terrible idea. But before she could open her mouth to decline, she heard herself say, "Certainly."

The first few notes of a quadrille floated out over the ballroom when the marquess offered his arm and escorted her out on the dance floor. When his strong, lean fingers curved around hers to lead her in the dance, she nearly snatched her hand back, surprised by how the mere touch made her skin burn hot.

She really had to get used to that before she made a fool out of herself. If he had noticed her reaction, there was no sign of it as he stared at the top of her head with an unreadable expression on his face.

EMILY MORGANS

They followed the intricate steps of the dance, and every time his hand touched hers, something fluttered in her stomach. It flustered her that he could affect her the way he did. She barely knew him, and she could not fathom what it was about him that made every nerve in her body tingle.

Glancing up at him, she tried to tamp down her reaction when his dark eyes briefly met hers. He was an exceedingly handsome man. Perhaps it was simply a natural response to someone so good-looking.

Guilt gnawed at her. She had never felt anything remotely similar for Philip. And if there was anyone she ought to feel such things for, surely it was the man her family wanted her to marry?

There was a commotion behind them and she turned her head to see the object of her musings coming towards them as if her thoughts had conjured him. Had the fates heard her and decided to punish her? A feeling of dread settled in her stomach when Philip came up to them.

"May I cut in on this dance?" he asked, and she could feel the marquess's fingers tighten around hers.

"Philip," she said with a weak smile, unable to put any genuine feeling into her voice, and wondering with a slight note of panic why the marquess hadn't let go of her hand yet.

Chapter Three

Dear Diary,
 I cannot help it. Sometimes, Philip
 reminds me of something slimy.
 Maybe a nasty, green toad.
 But then why doesn't a kiss turn him into a prince?

"Chettisham," the marquess said tonelessly, finally letting go of Angel even as he took a step closer.

"Pensington," Philip replied in the same even tone.

Couples continued dancing around them, ignoring the silent battle between the two men. The cheerful music filling the room seemed ill-matched to their set faces and assessing eyes.

Looking back and forth between them, a ball knotted inside her. "Do you know each other?"

"We've met." Philip took her arm harshly enough that she winced in pain. "Now, dance with me."

The marquess looked at her for a moment, like he wanted to say something. She was torn between wanting him to and not wishing him to make a scene. Then he gave a curt bow and left. Philip took her hand to lead her through the steps of the quadrille.

No longer enjoying the dance, she wished she could have left the dance floor too. But that would have been terribly rude, so she stayed.

"I did not know you had arrived in London," Philip said, his light-blue eyes cold as ice. "I thought you were arriving in a fortnight."

"That was the original plan," she admitted. "I arrived sooner. Only yesterday."

"You should have informed me."

Her answer had displeased him. She could tell by the tightening around his lips. He was quite a handsome man, really—when he wasn't angry—tall and slim with light brown hair.

Her cousin Marie always pointed out that he had an attractive face with his clean lines and straight nose. Objectively, she could agree. He was not displeasing to the eye, but something about him always made her feel awkward and uncomfortable.

Sometimes, she couldn't help comparing him to something wet and slimy. He might be considered a catch with his excellent looks and coming from a good family, but she had never felt attracted to him. Not the way her body hummed to life every time Nathaniel was near. Which was disconcerting when one considered she barely knew the man.

"I didn't realise you would be here," she said quietly, hoping to keep their discussion away from the ears of the other dancers.

"That is hardly the point. In the future, I would like to be informed of any change of plans where you are involved."

She nodded. Not arguing had been instilled in her since she was a little girl. No one ever listened to her. The music finished, and Philip led her off the dance floor.

"Would you like some punch?" he asked with a pleasant smile. His mood had turned for the better now that she was agreeable to him. Like her family, he preferred her to do as he said and stay silent when not asked for her opinion. No wonder the lot of them got on so well.

"Yes, please."

"Wait right here." He disappeared towards the refreshment table, leaving her standing alone by the edge of the dance floor. She looked after him while he made his way through the crowd. Had he left her alone on purpose? Why couldn't he have taken her back to her brother? Instead, she now stood alone in a mass of strangers.

From across the ballroom, Nathaniel watched Angel dance with Chettisham again. A sight that bothered him more than he cared to admit. Gowthorpe stood next to him, sipping on a glass of fruit punch while he eyed the ladies present.

"What is Chettisham's relationship with your family?" Nathaniel asked. "He appeared quite familiar with your sister."

"Chettisham?" Gowthorpe sounded a little distracted, tearing his eyes from the form of a beautiful lady a few feet away to look over at his sister. "Oh. He's Angel's intended."

Intended? Nathaniel frowned. The information didn't sit well with him. From the look on Angel's face when the other man had cut in, he never would have guessed it was the man she was meant to marry. She'd looked about ready to bolt and run in the other direction. "They're betrothed?"

Gowthorpe took another sip of his punch. "No, not yet. It's more of an informal understanding between our families. Nothing has been announced."

"Why him?" The thought of Angel with Chettisham… It simply felt wrong. He didn't know the man particularly well; they had attended Eton and Oxford at the same time but had never hung with the same crowds. The few times he had interacted with him, he had never quite taken to the other man.

"Our parents and his were great friends and I've been told they always wanted a union between our families." Gowthorpe shrugged. "So when our parents passed… The understanding was that Angel and Chettisham would eventually marry to honour that wish. My aunt wanted her to marry him without attending the Season, but I put my foot down there. She deserves a season in London before settling down. It also affords them a chance to get to know each other, since they have only met a few times."

Nathaniel nodded, though he wasn't sure why. It wasn't for him to get in between a planned engagement, so he would keep his mouth shut. He had no business getting involved in what Gowthorpe's sister did. Who she married. Especially when he was not on the lookout for a wife himself.

Finding her in the crowd, he discovered she was on her own at the very edge of the room. She was beautiful in a pale-rose-coloured gown, and he couldn't help but wonder why no other man had noticed yet. She should be inundated with suitors. Gowthorpe's thoughts seemed to have drifted in the same direction.

"I expected to have to fend suitors off, but it seems I will be spared the trouble since Angel is making herself invisible." He sounded amused by his sister's obvious attempts at not drawing attention to herself. The moment Chettisham had left her side, she had moved into a corner and was nearly concealed behind other guests. Gowthorpe chuckled, nodding towards the other side of the room. "You, on the other hand, are not so lucky."

Looking in the direction indicated, Nathaniel caught sight of his sister. A group of young fops surrounded Jessica, all looking at her like she was a sugarcoated treat and they had not eaten for days.

"I should have agreed when she tried begging off the season," he muttered.

His friend laughed. "Come now. It's not that bad. Your sister is a nice-looking young lady and has a sizeable dowry to boot. You knew this would happen."

"I did." He sighed. "But that does not mean I cannot wish it wasn't so. How will I ever find one that I think deserves her?"

"You won't," Gowthorpe said. "Whoever she chooses, you will simply have to accept it and move on."

"Sounds awful."

"It's the plight of us brothers." Gowthorpe grinned. "Now, if you will excuse me, I see a lady who requires a dance partner."

As his friend disappeared, Nathaniel stayed where he was so he could keep an eye on his sister and her suitors, but he could not keep his gaze from straying until he found Angel in the crowded room. Each time he saw her, he scolded himself and forced his attention back to Jessica.

Finally, he gave up and walked across the room to where Angel appeared to be hiding behind a potted tree while sipping some punch. Apparently, Chettisham had seen fit to give her something to drink but didn't bother to stick around. She looked up when he came to stand beside her.

"Are you enjoying your evening so far, Miss Grafton?" he asked politely.

"Very much, thank you," she answered, just as politely.

"Is that why you're hiding behind a tree?"

She choked on the punch she was about to swallow and coughed. "I beg your pardon?" she sputtered.

With her eyes watery from the coughing, they appeared greener than before. Framed with thick, dark lashes, they were one of her most attractive features. Her pink lips were slightly parted like she could not quite believe what he'd just said. The sudden urge to kiss those lips shocked him.

"Lord Pensington?"

Her soft query forced him to pull himself together. "It seemed to me as if you were hiding. Lurking behind plants usually is not an activity of those who enjoy a ball."

A faint blush crept up her cheeks, making her look even more adorable. "I don't know what you're speaking of," she mumbled, facing the ballroom and refusing to look at him.

"It was not my intention to embarrass you. Please accept my sincere apologies."

She gave him a quick look. "Are you making sport of me, Lord Pensington?"

"I would never dream of it," he said with a look of mock horror that made her laugh and finally relax.

"I fear I truly am hiding," she admitted with a sigh. "I'm terribly shy and all these people make me nervous."

"Where is your Chettisham?" He looked out over the crowd, trying to locate him.

"He's not my Chettisham," she muttered, only to add, "At least not yet."

"Well, if he hopes to win your hand in marriage, he should be by your side."

That made her laugh again, only it had a hollow quality to it this time. "There is no winning involved, I'm afraid. It is what it is. I am to be his wife, and that's that."

He knew he shouldn't ask. It was none of his business, but he couldn't help himself. "Do you wish to be his wife?"

She fell silent, her eyes following the dancing couples in the middle of the room. Following her line of sight, Nathaniel found Chettisham dancing with a beautiful, buxom lady. Was she jealous? He didn't think so.

"That is an awfully personal question, Lord Pensington," she mumbled. "Do you truly think we are acquainted enough to speak of such private matters?"

"I did sleep in your bed," he said with a straight face.

Gasping, she spun towards him, her cheeks red. "That is an awful thing to say to a young lady, my lord!"

"It was merely an observation." He tried to look innocent but had a suspicion he was failing miserably.

"You, my lord, are a rogue." The words were admonishing, but a smile tugged at the corners of her mouth.

"Considering that you have seen me in a state of undress that few can claim to, I believe you may call me Nathaniel."

She blushed again while nodding. "We really shouldn't, but you are a dear friend to my brother. You may call me Angel. But I thought you told me we should never mention that incident again."

"So I did," he agreed. "But that was before I realised I could not stop thinking about it."

Silence stretched out between them. She looked as shocked as he felt by the admission. That was not something he had planned to admit. Even if it was true. He wished it wasn't. He certainly shouldn't be thinking about his friend's sister in that way. But that didn't make it any less true.

Their eyes locked, and he found he could not break the contact. She, too, was unable—or unwilling—to and they continued to stare at each other. He leaned a little closer.

"I should have—"

"There you are!"

Angel abruptly turned around and took a quick step away from him. Jessica was weaving her way through the guests, waving at them. It may have been the first time in his life he was unhappy to see his sister.

"I have been looking all over for you," Jessica said when she reached them. "You left me on my own with those popinjays! Where have you been, Angel?"

"Hiding behind a potted plant," Nathaniel replied dryly.

Jessica ignored him and took her new friend's arm. "Please, walk with me. I need you to keep me company, so the bloody men will stop hounding me. Why won't they realise I'm dreadfully boring and they'd be better off chasing some other young lady with a dowry?"

"Jessica!" He stared at his younger sister. When had she begun cursing?

She rewarded him with a cheeky smile and a roll of her eyes. "Brother, you should be lucky *that* is the only word I used. What are you going to do? Punish me?"

"Just don't do it in front of others," he muttered, knowing when to admit defeat. It was clear the two women didn't need him, so he sketched a bow before going in search of Gowthorpe.

Chapter Four

Dear Diary,
   Spending time in London with only
   James has been lovely, and I rather
   wish it wouldn't end. It's been a rare freedom.

Angel's family's imminent arrival in London came sooner than she would have liked, as the following two weeks went by quicker than ever. Jessica Howerty had become a friend in a way she had never experienced before, and she loved every moment they had together.

They could easily spend an afternoon discussing books or the latest gossip making the rounds of the *ton*. There were shopping excursions with Mrs Grey and the other Howerty sisters. Lengthy rides in Hyde Park. Meetings in fashionable tea shops.

All things she had never imagined herself doing, but now found she enjoyed immensely.

Apparently, it had a lot to do with the company you kept.

Philip had called on her a couple of times but never stayed long, which was probably just as well since they had nothing to talk about. He mainly enjoyed talking about his trips to the racing course, or which balls he had attended, and which ladies he had danced with like he hoped to make her jealous.

She wasn't sure if she was meant to be, but she had to admit she couldn't muster even a sliver of the green-eyed devil.

Not wanting to anger her cousin Marie, who never liked it when Angel was allowed to do something she was not, she had not attended any more balls after Jessica's. Not being particularly fond of crowded rooms, it didn't bother her to wait a little longer, and it would keep the peace with her cousin. Sometimes it was just easier to comply, something she had learnt early on.

Jessica complained about her absence, saying the balls were all very dull without her, but they saw each other plenty. Sometimes Nathaniel joined, and even though she didn't want to admit it, those were some of Angel's favourite times.

She was waiting for just such an occasion—Nathaniel had bought a new phaeton and had promised to take her and Jessica for a ride in Hyde Park—when she heard some commotion in the entrance hall. Thinking it might be her friends, she went to see why the footman had not come to inform her. When she entered the hall, she stopped, her stomach tying itself into a hard knot.

"Non, non, non!" Her aunt, Christine Brown, gestured wildly at a footman carrying some of their luggage. "Not that one!"

The entrance hall was full of heavy trunks and footmen preparing to take them to their rooms. Both large in stature, Mr and Mrs Brown filled the room, their shadows blocking the light and leaving the room darker and heavier than usual. Aunt Christine always used her size to her advantage, since it allowed her to appear quite domineering when she wanted to be. Which was usually always.

"Angel!" Her cousin Marie caught sight of her, and when she noticed Angel's jacket, her blue eyes narrowed. "Where are you going?"

Angel took a few steps into the hallway. "I'm going for a ride in the park with some friends."

"Which ones?" The tone of her cousin's voice implied she didn't think she had any.

"Lady Jessica Howerty and her brother, the Marquess of Pensington." Angel wasn't proud of it, but she enjoyed the look of astonishment and vexation that came over Marie's pretty face.

"How did you get to know them?"

"The marquess is an old friend of James's."

"I see." Marie watched her with unbridled envy. It was no secret that she was hoping to marry a titled gentleman this season. The higher ranked, the better. Her cousin had never set her expectations low, but Angel didn't think it was an impossible goal. Despite her hate for Angel, Marie was a good-looking young woman with her chestnut-brown hair and voluptuous body, and she could be charming to those she deemed worthy.

"Angel!" Aunt Christine called out. "Come over here so I can look at you."

Dutifully, Angel walked over to the older woman. Aunt Christine had been beautiful once. She probably still was, but bitterness had edged deep lines into her face that could not be erased. Even so, one could see where Marie had got her looks. Compared to the dark-haired, well-bred Browns, Angel couldn't help but feel like a pasty plank. Flat and colourless.

"I heard you say you're going for a ride in the park." Her aunt looked her over with a critical eye. "Mon Dieu! Pinch your cheeks, girl. You look like a ghost!"

Before Angel could step out of reach, her aunt pinched her cheeks a little harder than necessary. "There! Much better. Where is your bonnet? You cannot go outside without it or you will freckle."

"It's in the drawing room."

"Well then, go get it. Allez! You can't seem unprepared if you're going riding with a marquess."

There was no point arguing with her aunt, so Angel turned around and trudged back to the drawing room where she'd left the bonnet on a small table. When she returned to the entrance hall, she could hear her aunt's voice coming down the hallway.

"My lord, why don't you take my lovely daughter with you as well?"

Hurrying her steps, Angel reached the hall in time to see Nathaniel and Jessica being courted by her aunt.

Marie was practically devouring Nathaniel with her eyes, something she supposed she couldn't blame her for since she'd done the same. He looked splendid in a black cutaway coat, a starched white cravat, and a pair of dove-grey pantaloons tucked into Hessian boots. His dark hair and eyes stood in stark contrast to the white of his shirt.

"My apologies, Mrs Brown," Nathaniel said politely, "but my phaeton can only fit three people, and even that is a bit of a squeeze."

Aunt Christine looked like she wanted to suggest that he take Marie instead of Angel, but even she could not be that forward. "Very well. I am sure you will have time to be properly introduced another time."

Standing behind Nathaniel, Jessica caught Angel's eyes and waved, an amused smile playing at her lips since she too must have realised what Aunt Christine was hoping. As Angel walked into the entrance hall, Nathaniel caught sight of her and she could see him visibly relax.

"Ah, here is Miss Grafton! I fear we must be off then or we shall be late for the... eh... fashionable hour in Hyde Park." He bowed towards the Browns and then ushered Jessica and Angel outside to his carriage. After assisting the women into the phaeton, he took the reins from a waiting footman and climbed in to sit between them.

"I thought your aunt would make you stay home and have us take your cousin instead!" Jessica laughed while Nathaniel set the carriage in motion. "The poor girl couldn't stop staring, and her mother looked like she saw the words 'eligible bachelor' stamped on his forehead."

"Lord save me from marriage-minded mothers," Nathaniel muttered.

"Surely you must be used to them by now," Jessica teased. "They must have been after you for years, handsome devil that you are."

He let out a very ungentlemanly snort.

"Well, I suppose your wealth and title add to the attraction." Jessica grinned, obviously enjoying her ability to rib her older brother.

"At least I can console myself by knowing you have the same problem." He glanced at his sister, a grin of his own spreading across his face. "You've captured the interest of quite a few gentlemen since your coming out."

"Please, don't remind me." She made a face. "I don't even wish to be married." She grumbled something unintelligible and then gave him a hopeful look. "Can't we simply skip the Season and return to Davenhall?"

"Certainly not. I want you married and off my hands."

"You shouldn't say such things to your beloved sister." Jessica glared at him in mock anger and hit him on the shoulder with her small reticule.

Angel smiled at their banter. She loved spending time with the Howerty family, even if she didn't always take part in the conversations. Watching them interact with each other was a pleasure since it was so unlike anything she had ever experienced growing up with the Browns.

"Are those your relatives?" Jessica asked, leaning forward so she could speak to Angel on the other side of Nathaniel. "They look nothing like you and your brother."

"We take after our father. Aunt Christine is my mother's sister."

"Oh, I forgot that you're half-French. We always call you Angel, so it's easy to forget your name is Angelique. Would you prefer to be called by your full name?"

"No, Angel is fine. I've grown used to it, and while I don't remember myself, James says that's what our mother called me." There was a small twinge in the region of her heart. If her parents had still been alive, would she have felt less like an outsider in her own home?

"They're both beautiful. At least your parents didn't name you after Shakespeare characters," Jessica said with a rueful smile.

"Oh, I had not realised. Are all your names from Shakespeare?" She had to admit that she didn't know the writings well enough to remember all the names.

"Yes." Nathaniel's lips curved into a bemused smile. "Some characters are more obscure than others. There's no Nicola. She was meant to be a Nicholas, from some side characters."

They reached Hyde Park, and as usual in the afternoon, the park was full of the fashionable people of the *ton*. Carriages, people on horseback, and men and women taking a stroll filled the paths through the park.

No one could say a trip to the park was a swift ride, but then that was never the intention. One went to get some fresh air and exercise, but most of all, one went to see and be seen. Angel enjoyed her time with the Howertys and didn't mind the slow pace. The longer she was away from home now that the Browns had arrived, the better.

Jessica jerked upright. "Angel, isn't that your cousin over there?"

Looking in the direction her friend indicated, Angel caught sight of Marie sitting next to Philip Chettisham in a sporty curricle. She groaned inwardly. "Indeed, it is."

"I thought they had only just arrived from the country." A slight frown creased Jessica's brow. "I'm surprised she's up for a ride in the park so soon."

Saying nothing, Angel watched Philip's curricle come up next to theirs.

"Miss Grafton," Philip said, his voice deceptively soft. "I did not expect to see you here."

It was a blatant lie since surely Marie and Aunt Christine would have told him where she was. Forcing a smile, Angel nodded towards him. "Mr Chettisham." She turned her head to her cousin. "Marie."

Once greetings had been extended, Marie smiled, not without glee. "Mr Chettisham came by the house soon after you left. He had hoped to take you for a ride in the park. Since you were not available, I agreed to go in your stead, but now that we've caught up with you, we can switch places."

"I would be much obliged if you would join me for a ride through the park," Philip said, his lips tightening slightly as he glanced at Nathaniel.

Angel swallowed. She wanted to say no so desperately, but there was no polite way to deny his request. Philip was the man her family intended for her to marry and she ought to spend time with him. Giving Nathaniel and Jessica an apologetic look, she made to leave the carriage. Nathaniel stopped her with a hand on her arm.

"Allow me," he said, stepping out of the phaeton. Reaching up, he helped her down and then turned away to assist her cousin down from Philip's curricle.

Once Marie sat securely next to Jessica with a smirk on her lips, Nathaniel took Angel's hand to help her into the seat of Philip's curricle.

She could feel the heat of his grip even through the layers of both of their gloves and while it made her hand tingle, it was also oddly comforting. Maybe she imagined it, but she could have sworn his hand lingered on hers a moment longer than necessary. She glanced up to meet his dark gaze, but his face was nothing but a polite mask.

Her bottom had barely touched the seat when Philip said a curt farewell and set the vehicle into motion.

"Why do I keep seeing you in the presence of that man?" he asked irritably once they were out of earshot.

She stared at her hands in her lap, subconsciously rubbing the hand Nathaniel had touched. "Lady Jessica is my friend and occasionally her brother joins us for an afternoon in the park."

"Then why were you dancing with him at the ball two weeks ago?"

A spark of anger glowed hotly in her stomach. She had sensed he didn't like her dancing with Nathaniel when he had found her at the ball, but this was the first time he had mentioned it in a fortnight. "He was the only one kind enough to ask me to dance." She could not keep a note of irritation out of her voice.

"You should not have been at that ball to begin with," Philip spat. "While a respectable gentleman, your brother is a poor substitute for a chaperone, and you should have waited for your aunt to arrive."

She squeezed her fingers and counted to ten to subdue her temper. Years with the Browns had taught her she would get nowhere by arguing. Keeping her voice calm, even while her insides vibrated with suppressed anger, she said, "My apologies. You are right, of course."

He nodded, and she could see his shoulders sagging as the tension left his body. Like the Browns, Philip preferred her quiet and mellow. Whenever she showed any sign of spirit, he immediately wanted to quench it.

Looking over her shoulder, she tried to catch sight of her friends, but they were too far ahead by now. Her hand tingled when she remembered Nathaniel's lingering hold when assisting her into the carriage. There was something dark and dangerous, and oh so tantalising, that bubbled up inside her whenever she was near the handsome marquess.

Something unlike anything she had ever felt around Philip. But her late parents had wanted her to marry Philip. The last thing she wanted was to let them down by not fulfilling their wish. And yet... She wanted to explore these novel feelings. Would that be so bad of her?

Chapter Five

Dear Diary,
   Sometimes I wish I could say what's on my mind.
   That I could speak up for myself.
   But what good has wishing ever done anyone?

"How was your ride in the park?" Aunt Christine asked the moment Angel entered the drawing room.

"Very pleasant, thank you." She smiled, determined not to rise to the bait. Sitting down on the sofa opposite her aunt, she took a biscuit from the plate set out on the table and poured herself a cup of tea.

The older woman remained quiet for a short while. "Did they catch up with you?"

She gave her aunt an innocent look. "Who?"

"Nothing." With a sigh, her aunt lifted her tea to her lips.

Angel did the same so she could hide her smile. Making her aunt believe her scheme had failed, even for a brief moment, was a petty—but sweet—revenge. Unfortunately, it didn't last nearly as long as she would have liked, since Marie returned not much later.

"Oh, Maman!" Her cousin sank down on the sofa next to her mother with a dreamy sigh. "Lord Pensington is the most handsome man I've ever seen. Those dark eyes!"

Aunt Christine threw an annoyed look in Angel's direction when she realised she'd been deceived, but turned to her daughter. "He is very handsome, indeed. We must ensure that we invite him to your coming-out ball, and you shall look your very best."

"The marquess and his family are already invited," Angel muttered, receiving glum stares. "As he is an old friend of James's, he would have been included in the first set of invitations sent out."

"Very well then," Aunt Christine said. "Tomorrow we are due at the modiste. We must find an exceptional dress for Marie to wear to the ball." After a derisive look in Angel's direction, she added, "And something for you too."

The cousins' coming-out ball had been planned for quite some time already, with only the final preparations to be done now that the Browns had arrived in London.

Angel rather dreaded the occasion since the idea of having everyone's attention on her nearly made her break out in hives.

At least in this, Marie's need to be the centre of attention worked in her favour. She could hide behind her cousin and everyone would be happy.

"I do believe Lord Pensington might have taken a fancy to me," Marie gleefully said. "I would be a perfect marchioness, don't you think?"

After listening to her aunt and cousin discuss the merits of catching a wealthy and titled husband for some time, Angel excused herself and retired to her room. One could only listen to their chatter for so long without contracting a headache.

Maybe she would have felt differently if she had her own mother here for the season. Perhaps then she would have sat in the drawing room discussing the handsome marquess over a cup of tea and biscuits.

A pang of longing shot through her at the thought of a world she would never experience. With both her parents gone, she would never have anyone other than the Browns and her brother.

Picking up her diary, she sat down on the window seat where she could look out over the garden behind the house. Once she married Philip, she would have her own family. Children to fill the void. She'd always wanted a big family, and getting married would give her that chance. So why did the thought not make her happy?

The next day, Angel found herself inside the shop of a modiste—a Madam Beauvain—on Bond Street together with her aunt and cousin. An assistant to the modiste was showing them the latest fashion plates and fabrics.

While Aunt Christine and Marie excitedly discussed the possibilities for the dresses with the assistant, Angel was bored to tears. Her aunt had suggested a horrible pastel lemon-coloured fabric for her dress and would not hear her protests that the colour made her look positively sickly.

"Nonsense! Marie looks wonderful in yellow, and so will you," had been her aunt's reply, which was all very well since Marie had the complexion to wear yellow. With her pale skin, Angel usually looked like a person risen from their deathbed when wearing the particular light pastels her aunt wanted to buy for her.

"Oh, Maman! That dress," Marie suddenly exclaimed, pointing at one of the fashion plates.

Angel peered around her aunt's imposing form to have a look, only to see an overdone dress that had more details than it knew what to do with. She supposed it would serve Marie's purpose in catching a husband. A man would only need to look at that dress before fainting from the horror. Then Marie could marry him while he was still lying unconscious on the floor.

Mumbling an excuse, which probably no one heard, she left them discussing the atrocious dress and stepped outside the shop onto Bond Street to get some fresh air. Her mood had been rather foul since the previous day and she needed a moment away from her relatives. A stroll down the street ought to be just the thing to ease her mood.

She turned around, only to bump into someone's hard chest and almost lost her balance. She would have fallen had the man she bumped into not caught her elbow and steadied her.

"Angel!"

Looking up, she stared into Nathaniel Howerty's dark eyes. Jessica stood next to him, and she was the one who had called out her name.

"My apologies." Angel carefully extracted her elbow from Nathaniel's grip, since he hadn't deemed it prudent to release her. "I am so very clumsy sometimes. I really ought to look more carefully before I walk."

"It's those damned bonnets." Nathaniel motioned towards her quite fashionable headwear. "They're just as effective as blinders on horses."

"Cursing in front of ladies?" Jessica raised a brow but wasn't able to hide a teasing grin. "What has happened to your manners?"

"My apologies." Nathaniel executed an elaborate bow. "I did not mean to offend your delicate ears."

She ignored her brother's sarcastic apology and looked at Angel. "Are you here alone?"

"No, my aunt and cousin are at the modiste."

Jessica peered inside. "What are they doing? Buying more bonnets to keep us from seeing what's around us?"

"We're looking for something to wear at our coming-out ball."

"Then what are you doing outside on the street?" Nathaniel asked with an amused twinkle in his dark eyes. "I don't believe they have a lot of dresses out here."

Her cheeks heated. "I needed some fresh air. It is very stuffy inside."

Neither of the Howertys looked like they believed her. She sighed. "Very well. Their chattering was giving me a headache, and my aunt is determined to see me in a lemony pastel dress."

"Lemon?" Jessica's nose scrunched up as if she smelled something foul. "That wouldn't suit you at all."

"I know. I suspect that is why she wants me to wear it."

A smile spread over Jessica's face and her eyes took on a dangerous light.

"Oh no." Nathaniel groaned. "That's how they all look when they have some mischief in mind."

"Let your aunt buy you that dress," Jessica said. "Then you and I will go shopping tomorrow to find you something you like. Tell your aunt you're invited to tea at my house, and then we will go to another modiste together."

She wanted to shout yes, but the thought of her aunt's rebuke tempered her words. "I... I'm not sure. Aunt Christine will be so mad if I show up at the ball in the wrong dress."

"So?" Jessica shrugged, apparently caring little for her worries. "What is she going to do? Boot you from the house?"

The idea was incredibly tempting. She hated wearing the unflattering dresses her aunt put her in. And Jessica was right, there wasn't much Aunt Christine could do to her. At least not while in London in the presence of James. In the country, she could make Angel's life hell, but here? She wouldn't dare to cause too much unpleasantness when James had the power to throw her out on her rear if he so chose. He was the title holder. The viscount.

She nodded. "Let's do it."

"Wonderful!" Jessica beamed at her. "I shall see you tomorrow."

"Yes, thank you. I had better go back inside before they miss me."

They made quick farewells before Angel entered the modiste's again. Her heart felt lighter, and she allowed her aunt to have her fitted for the lemon-coloured dress she had no intention of ever wearing. Guilt niggled at her for letting the modiste sew up something she wouldn't use, but she could probably give it to Marie. Her cousin would hardly say no to another piece of clothing.

"I think maybe this one," Jessica said the next day when they stood inside Madame Dautry's popular shop looking at fashion plates.

Mrs Grey picked up the plate and shook her head. "No, I don't like the neckline."

The Howertys' lovely aunt had heard about Angel's dilemma and agreed to come along to help the two young ladies find a suitable dress for the ball. Something Angel was grateful for since the older woman's taste in clothing was impeccable.

"I would prefer a neckline that isn't too scooped," Angel said from her vantage point on top of a stool where an assistant was taking her measurements. "I don't have enough to fill it out."

"But you want to be dazzling gentlemen with your charms," Jessica quipped, somehow able to keep her face straight.

"Not those charms," Mrs Grey said with a bemused smile. "Miss Grafton has so many other charms, and we don't want the gentlemen to miss those because they were too busy staring at her bosom."

"Why not? All the other young ladies seem to do so."

"That's because they have no other charms," Mrs Grey muttered, only to look startled when Jessica laughed. A look of dismay crossed her face. "Did I just say that out loud?"

"I'm afraid so." Jessica grinned.

Mrs Grey sighed and shuffled some fashion plates around on the table. "Well... Oh! This one." She pulled a plate out from underneath a pile and showed it to Jessica, who nodded her approval.

"May I see?" Angel stepped down from the stool. She looked at the image Jessica brought over to her and smiled. That was exactly the dress for her.

They proceeded to pick out the fabrics and then they returned to Pensington House, where tea and biscuits were quickly served to them in the drawing room.

"Are you excited about your coming-out ball?" Mrs Grey asked when they were sipping their tea.

"Dreading it is probably more accurate," Angel admitted with a sheepish smile. "I'm rather shy and large crowds make me anxious. The thought of everyone being there to see me and Marie is terrifying."

"You will do fine." Mrs Grey gave her an encouraging smile.

"Just make sure there are no potted plants nearby or she might disappear." She recognised the droll voice instantly and focused on her tea to keep her head from whipping around to stare at its handsome owner.

"Nathaniel." Jessica smiled. "Why don't you join us for some tea and biscuits?"

"Don't mind if I do." He sat down on a chair, surveying the offerings on the table.

A maid brought in another teacup and an additional plate of biscuits. He patiently waited for his aunt to pour him the tea and add a lump of sugar before he took a biscuit.

"What is this about plants?" Mrs Grey asked, refilling her cup.

Angel threw Nathaniel a threatening look, but he paid her no heed.

"Our young friend, Miss Grafton, has an uncommon urge to hide behind potted plants during balls."

"Really?" Mrs Grey gave her a curious look. "Is it truly that bad?"

"I wasn't hiding," Angel muttered. "I was merely—"

"Concealing yourself?" Nathaniel supplied helpfully, which made Jessica choke on her tea.

"No." Angel glared at Jessica, who was trying to hide her mirth. "I was enjoying a spot of privacy."

"Ah. Well, you had me fooled." Nathaniel took a sip of his tea, then made a face and added another lump of sugar.

Mrs Grey frowned. "Your teeth will rot if you keep on doing that."

"Teasing innocent young ladies?"

"Drinking tea with more sugar than tea." She gave him an exasperated look. "But refraining from the other would do you good as well."

"But how else am I to amuse myself?"

"I'm sure you can find a way," Mrs Grey remarked dryly.

He grinned, showing without a doubt that there was nothing wrong with his teeth. When Angel saw the teasing look in his dark eyes, something lurched inside her. A dozen butterflies fluttered around without direction.

She'd heard he was one of the most sought-after bachelors in London, and she could well believe it. Ladies must be falling at his feet, begging for his attention.

"We picked out a wonderful dress for Angel today," Jessica said with a smile. "She will have to fend suitors off at her ball."

"I'm sure she will," Nathaniel agreed with an unreadable look in Angel's direction.

Her cheeks heated and for a moment, their eyes met and the butterfly wings inside froze as if they too were mesmerised by this man. She nearly jumped out of her seat when Mrs Grey cleared her throat.

"More tea, anyone?"

Nathaniel was on his way to the library, which also served as his study, when he heard steps following him down the hallway.

"Do you have any designs on my friend?"

Stopping dead in his tracks, he turned around to face his younger sister. "What are you talking about?"

"Angel and the way you were looking at her." Jessica crossed her arms, looking at him like he was a naughty schoolboy.

"I don't know what you're talking about." It sounded false, even to him, and his sister was no fool.

"Ha!" she scoffed, and taking him by the arm, she dragged him into the library, where she closed the door behind them. This did nothing to make him feel less like a schoolboy about to be scolded. "You do have feelings for her!"

"Don't be ridiculous," he snapped. "She's the sister of one of my best friends."

"That's a terrible excuse," Jessica muttered. "Who someone is related to or friends with has no bearing on how you feel about them. And you were staring at her."

"Jessica." He sighed. "This may come as a surprise to you, but I am not blind. Angel is pretty. I'm a man. Surely you didn't expect me not to notice?"

And he certainly had noticed. Angel Grafton wasn't someone who turned heads. With her pale skin and blonde hair, she easily blended into the background, especially when wearing light or muted colours. *Or hiding behind potted plants.* But if one paid attention and actually saw her... She was quite beautiful. And once you noticed, it was impossible to ignore.

Even if he wished he could. It wasn't as if he wanted to be attracted to his friend's sister.

"Of course not."

"And even if I took an interest—" He held a hand up when Jessica opened her mouth. "And I'm not saying I have. But even then, I would never act upon it. She's Gowthorpe's sister and, as such, I would never think to touch her. She's the kind of girl you marry, and I'm of no such inclination."

His sister looked him straight in the eyes. "Good. Because Angel has become a dear friend to me and I will not allow anyone to hurt her. That includes you."

"Your protectiveness of your friend is commendable but misguided." He smiled wryly. "She's a sweet girl, and that's all. You don't touch your friend's sisters."

Jessica grinned. "I suppose Nick has no chance with Gowthorpe, then?"

He chuckled. "I believe our sister has decided on that match more out of stubbornness than a genuine interest in Gowthorpe. That said, I would probably kill any of my friends if they were to touch one of my sisters." They might frustrate him daily, but he loved his sisters fiercely and would defend their honour until his dying breath.

Jessica laughed but didn't meet his eyes. "Well, that's settled then."

With that, she finally left him alone. He stared at the closed door with a frown. It was disconcerting to see that his sister had noticed him looking at Angel. What he told her was true. More or less. He would never court Angel.

Marriage was not something he was ready for, and she was definitely someone you had to marry. He would never touch her or risk her reputation. But that didn't mean he didn't want to. It frustrated him how attracted he was to her.

When he would finally settle down to marry, he had no intention of marrying someone he cared for. He had seen first-hand how devastating love could be, and he wanted none of it.

He imagined he would marry some pleasant enough chit that he could stand to be around enough to sire some heirs. But romance and love? No, thank you. And that was exactly why he would stay away from Angel. Because she interested him too much already, and the idea of coming to truly care for someone terrified him. He never wanted to end up like his father.

Walking over to his desk, he pulled out a drawer and retrieved a glass and a bottle of brandy. He poured himself a drink before sitting down in his comfortable old chair and had a sip.

It didn't matter if he found Angel attractive. She was meant to marry Philip Chettisham. Though that seemed like a bloody waste. Chettisham wasn't fit to kiss the hem of her dress. But if Chettisham was who Angel wanted, then Nathaniel certainly would not stand in their way.

A discreet knock on the door, and Aunt Jane entered. After closing the door behind her, she sat down on the chair on the opposite side of the desk, giving his brandy glass a look, but making no mention of it.

"So what brings me the honour of your company?" he asked when she said nothing. "You never disturb me in the library unless you have something you wish to discuss. I doubt you're here to judge me for having a glass of brandy."

His aunt gave him an odd look he couldn't quite read. "It's about Angel."

He groaned. "Et tu, Brute?"

"Too?"

"Jessica was in here earlier, warning me to stay away from her friend." He drained his glass and immediately refilled it. Lord save him from meddling women.

"And?"

"And what?" His aunt's one-word questions were grating on his already frayed nerves.

She sighed. At least he thought it was a sigh. It could equally be a frustrated huff. "What did you tell her?"

"That she has nothing to worry about, of course. I have no designs on Angel Grafton."

"No?" His aunt's knowing gaze searched his face and he could not meet her eyes.

"Why is everyone insisting that I have an interest in this girl?" Exasperation and irritation mingled in his voice.

"Probably because you look at her like she's some delectable dessert that you wish to devour," Aunt Jane replied dryly.

He stared at her.

"Well, you do."

"She's a beautiful woman."

"There are many beautiful women out there, Nathaniel. I've never seen you look at any of them the way you look at this one."

"Maybe it's because I can't have her?" he suggested, then added in an annoyed tone when the words struck too close to home, "I don't know, but rest assured that I have no intention of seducing an innocent. I'm no rake."

"Of course. I would never think that of you," Aunt Jane said softly. "But she's a lovely girl and mistakes have been made with less."

"I can assure you, Madam," Nathaniel said, his words clipped. "That I am a fully grown man and have no problems controlling any urges where young ladies are concerned."

"I'm not worried about you. I'm worried about her."

He blinked, his anger evaporating like water on a hot plate. "Pardon?"

"Well..." Aunt Jane hedged. "You're an attractive man. You know this. Women are always chasing after you. They always have. What if she falls in love with you?"

"She has no reason to." He frowned. "I am not courting her or encouraging her if that's what you're worried about."

"That's the thing. You don't have to encourage anyone. They fall for you anyway because of your natural charm."

"Don't be ridiculous." The tips of his ears felt hot as embarrassment washed over him. He knew women found him attractive, but no one had ever stated it quite so plainly before. "Besides, Angel is practically betrothed to Philip Chettisham."

"Oh, I didn't know." Aunt Jane's brows rose. "She's never mentioned him. But that's good then. Maybe I'm imagining things. I simply know how charming you can be and I have yet to see a young lady spend more than a quarter of an hour in your company without fancying herself in love with you."

He scoffed. "Angel is far too sensible to take a fancy to a man she barely knows." He wasn't entirely sure if he was trying to convince himself or his aunt at this point. Because they had spent a fair bit of time together in the past fortnight, and he certainly did not think of her as a stranger.

"You're right." Aunt Jane smiled. "I don't know what made me worry. She has shown no inclination to fall at your feet at the barest hint of a smile."

"Go away," he said, but smiled. "You're embarrassing me. I do not make young ladies swoon at the sight of me."

"No, but at the sight of your smile." She winked and left the library.

For the second time, Nathaniel was left staring at the closed door. What was it with his female relatives and their meddling?

Chapter Six

Dear Diary,
 I don't see why I must have a coming-out ball.
 Surely a dinner with our closest friends
 would suffice? Or, even better, a simple note.

"Oh, Miss! You must stop touching your hair or we will have to do it all over again." Agnes, the lady's maid Angel shared with her cousin, walked over to correct two curls that had escaped the elaborate hairdo.

Angel stared at her reflection in the mirror, trying to ignore the tendrils of unease crawling along her skin at the thought of having to go downstairs to face a ballroom full of people. People that would look at her and judge her, and quite possibly find her wanting. She fiddled with the few wayward curls her maid had artfully arranged to frame her face, only to have her hand swatted away by Agnes.

Flashing the maid a sheepish smile, she picked up the dance card her aunt had dropped off earlier and rotated it between her fingers. Would it remain empty? Part of her hoped it would, while another desperately hoped she wouldn't be a complete failure.

The dress Mrs Grey and Jessica had helped her pick out was prettier than any dress she had ever owned. Made in the popular high-waisted fashion with a green bodice of figured satin formed close to the bosom, it was beautiful, and the colour made the green of her eyes more vibrant. Short, white puff sleeves and a skirt of white crepe, trimmed at the bottom with lace, matched her pearl earrings and necklace.

"Miss," Agnes said, startling her away from the mirror and nearly making her drop the dance card. "It's time to go downstairs. The ball will begin soon."

She nodded jerkily. Not at all debating if she could lock the door and feign a headache. Not even a little.

The maid helped her tie the ribbons of the card around her wrist and gave her an encouraging smile. "You will be a great success, Miss."

"Thank you, Agnes."

Picking up a fan of carved ivory and clutching it tighter than necessary, she entered the hallway. There was no one else around. She was the last to get ready, and everyone would already be downstairs. Most of the guests wouldn't arrive for a little while longer since they would want to be fashionably late. She didn't have that luxury as much as she would have liked to.

Arriving late enough, one might avoid being noticed, but it would be difficult to avoid attention during one's official coming-out ball. No, there was no escaping this. Tonight she would be introduced to London's society and what her brother termed 'the marriage mart.'

She took a deep breath before walking the length of the hallway and down the stairs. Her family waited in the drawing room where they would stand to greet the arrivals in a receiving line. Then the guests would continue to the ballroom at the back of the house.

"Angel! There you are." James smiled and walked over to her when she entered. "I feared you might not be joining us."

Returning her brother's smile, she neglected to say that she would have loved that. As nervous as she was, she appreciated that he had insisted on her having a season instead of marrying Philip straight away as her aunt had suggested. If she had not been allowed this slight reprieve, she never would have met Jessica, her new best friend. *Or Nathaniel.* Her cheeks heated when his name came unbidden to her mind.

"You look beautiful tonight," James said with an appreciative nod as he escorted her to stand next to him at the front of the receiving line. A fact she knew annoyed Marie, who had to stand last according to rank.

She glanced over at her cousin, who stood with her mother, speaking quietly. Marie looked amazing in a dress made of marigold silk, with a scooped neckline and style that flattered her curvy body in a way that many would envy. They had apparently decided against the monstrosity of a gown they had initially looked at in the shop, instead going for something more understated that showed off her beauty rather than overpowered it. Angel was just about to compliment her cousin on her appearance when Aunt Christine finally looked at her.

"What are you wearing?" she burst out, staring at Angel's new dress.

"Oh. The dress you ordered, unfortunately, had a tear," she lied smoothly. It was something she had practised with Jessica ahead of time, and she was pleasantly surprised that her voice didn't waver. "So I picked this one instead."

"You should have worn the other one," Aunt Christine muttered, possibly unhappy that her niece didn't look like a wrung-out dishcloth for the evening. "It would have looked much better on you."

"I think Miss Grafton looks fetching," a deep voice said.

Looking up at Nathaniel, Angel's heart skipped a beat. He stood just inside the door with Jessica and Mrs Grey, and she had never been happier to see them. Dressed in the formal black evening wear he seemed to favour, he was exceptionally good-looking. His dark gaze held Aunt Christine's, silently daring her to disagree with him in front of everyone. She was not up to the challenge.

"Naturally," she murmured. "It's just such a pity. It was a lovely dress."

Nathaniel nodded, then turning to Angel, he took her hand. Bowing formally, he placed a soft kiss above her knuckles. "Miss Grafton, good evening."

"My lord." She curtsied, cursing the breathlessness of her voice. Trying not to let her eyes linger on the handsome marquess, she collected herself and smiled at Jessica as she came to see her while Nathaniel greeted the rest of the family.

"We're early since I didn't want to leave you alone in the lion's den," her friend said with a grin, giving her a quick hug.

"Thank you. It's much appreciated." Angel rubbed the hand Nathaniel had touched. Why was it tingling? She was wearing gloves. His lips hadn't even touched her skin.

Next, Mrs Grey came up to greet her with a kiss on the cheek. "You look wonderful," she whispered with a conspiratorial wink.

Sometime later, Angel and her family could finally break up the receiving line and enter the ballroom to mingle with their guests. The butler and two footmen remained in the hallway to guide any late arrivals. Angel immediately searched the room for her friend, and once she found Jessica, she walked across the floor to see her.

"Thank you for arriving unfashionably early," she said. "It helped settle my nerves."

"Oh, it was no problem." Jessica smiled, handing her a glass of lemonade. "We thought you might need to see a friendly face or three."

"You arrived at the right moment." Angel laughed softly. "Aunt Christine was just about to berate me for wearing the wrong dress."

"You're wearing the perfect dress." Jessica nodded towards a group of men looking in their direction. "Once the first one dares to approach, suitors will crowd you."

"Don't be ridiculous." Angel laughed, but it sounded rather hollow since the very idea of that much attention made her feel lightheaded.

"You'll see. Mark my words."

Unfortunately, Jessica was right. It didn't take long before gentlemen surrounded them both, trying to get their attention or steal a dance. Angel wasn't sure whether she was elated that she wasn't a failure or terrified by the number of eyes on her.

"She's looking beautiful tonight."

Nathaniel tore his eyes away from Angel—she was dancing with one of the young fops that hadn't left her side the entire evening—to look down at his aunt.

"Yes, she is."

"I knew she would be popular." A smug smile played on Aunt Jane's lips.

"What's your point?" He had a suspicion he wouldn't like it, whatever it was.

"Oh, nothing." She smiled blithely, then nodded towards the other side of the room. "Your sister is having quite some success as well."

As usual lately, Jessica was surrounded by a gaggle of men vying for her attention. It amused him to know she would have much preferred an evening curled up with a book to this, and none of the gentlemen knew. Whoever caught his sister's eye would have to be someone special, indeed.

"I'm certain she will make a good match," Aunt Jane said beside him. "All of your sisters will once it's their time. They're too wonderful not to."

"Wonderful?" He huffed a laugh. "While I'm their brother and will agree to some extent, let's not pretend that whoever marries Nick will have to have the patience of a saint."

"She's only young. She will calm down."

He wasn't as certain as his aunt sounded, but he didn't argue. "I bet you didn't consider the hassle of finding suitable matches for three girls when you agreed to take care of us after Mother passed away."

The ghost of a smile crossed Aunt Jane's lips. "Admittedly, it was not my first thought. But I have never regretted my decision. You're all my late sister's children, and your father needed help. He wasn't capable of raising you."

A pang of grief made Nathaniel look away. The day his mother died, his father had lost his will to live. Love had destroyed him, and Nathaniel had sworn that it would never happen to him. He would never allow himself to have such deep feelings for a woman.

"And we can never thank you enough for stepping in," he said, and he meant it. While he would always miss his mother, Aunt Jane had been everything he and his sisters needed.

Aunt Jane looked up at him and nodded, a suspicious glittering at the corners of her eyes. Then she looked away, perhaps wanting a change of topic as much as he did.

Suddenly, she chuckled. "Is that Miss Grafton's supposed betrothed? He doesn't look pleased."

He followed her gaze to Philip Chettisham standing at the refreshment table, glaring daggers at Angel and her admirers. Somehow, that improved his mood substantially.

"I don't doubt he's furious." He almost grinned. "From what I've heard, he does not enjoy sharing."

"He should be proud that his future wife is so admired."

"Maybe that's how women feel about men." He shrugged. "But men would much rather lock their women away somewhere only they can enjoy them."

"But that's ridiculous!"

"We're very territorial."

Aunt Jane caught sight of his grin and whacked him on the shoulder with her fan. "I don't appreciate it when you pull my leg."

"But what a beautiful leg it is," a smooth voice said behind them.

Turning around, Aunt Jane smiled. "Lord Wortham! I didn't know you'd be here tonight."

"Ah, I could not possibly miss an evening with my favourite lady." The handsome man who had just joined them bowed and placed a kiss on Aunt Jane's gloved hand before turning to Nathaniel. "And a good evening to you, Pensington."

Jacob Hurst, the Earl of Wortham and future Duke of Ashbrook, was one of Nathaniel's oldest and best friends. The Ashbrook estate was close to Nathaniel's own, and Wortham had been his friend since they both attended Eton as young boys.

"I didn't realise you were back in London," he said. "I haven't seen you in an age."

"Arrived back the other day," Wortham admitted while his blue eyes scanned the crowd. "I saw an invitation from Gowthorpe and thought it would only be polite of me to make an appearance. Where is the old geezer?"

"Last time I saw him, he was taking a lady out into the garden."

"Trying to live up to my reputation?" Wortham grinned.

"I doubt that's possible," Nathaniel remarked dryly. "Though he is doing an excellent job of trying."

Someone cleared their throat, and he gave his aunt a guilty look. "I beg your pardon, Aunt Jane. I forgot you are here."

"Obviously." Aunt Jane turned to Wortham. "It was lovely seeing you again, Wortham. You should come calling on us soon."

"I wouldn't miss it for the world." With a graceful bow, Wortham placed yet another kiss on her hand, which had her blushing prettily.

"Must you flirt with my aunt?" Nathaniel asked with a grimace once she had left to seek out some friends.

"Why not?" A wide grin split Wortham's face. "She's a charming lady, and I'm not one to discriminate."

Nathaniel decided to change the subject. He had learnt early on that it was the easiest way to deal with his friend. "Where have you been this time? You've been gone quite some time."

"I spent a few weeks at a friend's estate up in the Lake District. London bores me and I have no interest in spending time in the country with my father and his condescension." Wortham's gaze went back to scanning the crowd. He nudged Nathaniel, nodding towards the group of people dancing. "I say, who is the beautiful lady dancing with Chettisham?"

Nathaniel knew the answer before even looking. "She's off limits."

Wortham chuckled. "No one is off limits."

"She's an innocent, and I believe you stay as far away from them as I do."

"Well." Wortham glanced at him before looking back in Angel's direction. "I might make an exception."

"She's off limits," Nathaniel reiterated, sickness twisting his gut at the obvious interest displayed by his friend. Not that he should care. He didn't care. But Angel was young and innocent. She didn't stand a chance if a rake like Wortham targeted her.

"She looks available to me," Wortham argued. "Especially if she's dancing with that bounder Chettisham."

"She's Gowthorpe's sister, Angelique Grafton."

"Really?" A twinkle of something Nathaniel couldn't quite read glinted in his friend's eyes. "And is that why your eyes keep straying to her?"

Taken aback, he stared at Wortham. "What? Why... No, I've..."

It was a lie. He could not keep himself from finding her in the crowd all night. She couldn't hide tonight, and no one had escaped the fact that there was another beautiful lady available to court. Well, two, he supposed. Her cousin Marie appeared to be quite popular too, but Nathaniel only had eyes for Angel.

"I don't blame you," Wortham said. "She's beautiful."

"She's our friend's sister."

"Is that meant to mean something to me?"

"Remind me to keep you away from my sisters," Nathaniel muttered.

Wortham scoffed. "Please. I may be debauched, but I don't court children."

Giving his friend a look from the corner of his eye, Nathaniel kept his voice even. "What you do is hardly courting. And Jessica is eighteen, just a year younger than Angel, whom you're ogling like she were a cherry tart. You missed Jessica's coming-out ball a few weeks ago."

A frown puckered Wortham's brow. "Eighteen, really? I could have sworn she was younger. Fifteen at most."

"Rain is fifteen, and I want you to stay at least ten yards away from her at any given time."

Wortham chuckled. "Time flies. I never realised. Jessica Howerty, eighteen years old and out for her first season. Imagine that!" He grinned and turned his head to look at Nathaniel. "Is she here tonight? Does she still hate my guts?"

"Probably. And yes, she is, but don't even think about it." That his sister despised Wortham was something that seemed to amuse the earl more than anything else, and Nathaniel didn't want his friend ruining her evening.

"I just want to reintroduce myself." Wortham was still grinning. "I've not seen her for an age. Has she stepped on anyone's toes yet? Spilt lemonade on someone's new dress?"

Nathaniel glared at his friend. "My sister is not clumsy." Only ever when she was around the earl. Maybe he annoyed her so badly that she couldn't focus on where her limbs were. She wouldn't be the first. Wortham revelled in annoying people.

"If you say so," Wortham agreed easily while searching the crowd. "Now, where is your sister?"

"You had better behave if you want me to bring you to her. Or I will have your head on a platter."

"I always behave," Wortham said, but the look on his face quite betrayed his words.

Nathaniel wasn't too worried. Having grown up together, it wasn't likely that his friend would entertain the notion of seducing any of his sisters. He was much more likely to annoy them until they threw him out of the house.

"The evening has been quite a success." Jessica smiled at Angel while they had a brief respite from their admiring suitors. After Jessica mentioned that they were parched, all the men had offered to get them refreshments simultaneously and then rushed off to get some.

"I can scarcely believe it," Angel admitted. "I have danced almost every single dance tonight."

"Believe it! You're a tremendous success!"

Her cheeks heated. "Philip doesn't like it."

"Philip can sod off," Jessica said vehemently, making Angel burst into laughter. Her friend smiled sheepishly. "I know he's your intended, but he seems rather disagreeable."

"He is unhappy with me." Despite the topic, Angel couldn't stop smiling. Her mood was too good to let Philip's foul temper bring it down.

"Oh lord." Jessica stiffened, staring at something across the room.

"What is the matter?" Her friend was usually so relaxed, that Angel wasn't sure what to make of the quick change in her demeanour.

"Nothing!" With flushed cheeks, Jessica moved in front of her, turning her back towards the crowd. "Is Nathaniel coming this way?"

Angel peered around her friend to see Nathaniel winding his way between the guests. "Yes."

"Is he alone?"

"No, there is another man with him." It wasn't anyone she recognised from introductions, and she wondered who it might be. Jessica obviously knew them.

Her friend let out a groan before turning back to face the approaching men, muttering something under her breath. A moment later, Nathaniel and his companion reached them. Both men towered over Angel, and she noted that the newcomer was nearly as handsome as Nathaniel. His dark brown hair was unruly, swept back from his brow in a style that seemed careless but probably took a fair amount of preparation. They made introductions. He was Jacob Hurst, the Earl of Wortham, and apparently an old friend of the Howerty family.

Angel curtsied. "It's a pleasure to meet you, my lord."

"The pleasure is all mine," Lord Wortham dazzled with his smile, his blue eyes glittering.

There was a clattering noise by her side, and she realised Jessica had dropped her fan. Lord Wortham quickly bent to pick it up and handed it to her friend with a teasing grin.

"I believe you dropped this."

Jessica all but snatched the fan out of his hand with a terse, "Thank you."

The gentlemen who had been hovering around them most of the evening chose that moment to return with refreshments, making Angel feel like they were beset by a murder of crows flapping their tailcoats in the wind. Her throat dry, she accepted a drink from one man. The ballroom was hot and crowded, even with the doors to the terrace and garden wide open. Nathaniel and his friend remained in the group, joining in the conversations.

It was interesting to see the change in her usually graceful friend as Jessica dropped her fan several times, almost spilt the contents of her glass over her dress, and stepped on the toes of several gentlemen.

There were too many people gathered in too small a space, and after a short while, Angel excused herself and walked out onto the terrace for some fresh air. It was wonderful to step outside, where a light breeze played with the leaves of the trees growing in the garden.

"I don't like what you're doing."

She spun around at the terse voice, coming face to face with Philip. With his brow knotted and his eyes dark, he looked far from pleased.

"Pardon?" She backed away from the doors leading to the ballroom. If he was about to cause a scene, she'd rather not have an audience.

"You are flirting with every man in attendance!" he snapped, following her until they stood by the terrace railing.

"That's rather unfair. I am merely enjoying myself and dancing. There is no flirting involved."

"Don't try to fool me. You are hoping to make a more advantageous match. I knew it was a mistake for you to have a season."

He pushed his face close to hers. He was so close she could feel his sharp breath on her face, and it made her skin crawl. "You are mine, Angel, and don't you forget it."

He leaned forward to kiss her, but she turned her head to the side so his lips landed on her cheek. He took a step backwards.

"You never let me kiss you."

"It's not proper," she mumbled. "Not until we're married."

"No one will say anything if we steal a kiss or two before the wedding."

He was just about to attempt another when voices drifted through the air. Someone was coming out onto the terrace. With a curse, he stepped away from her. A moment later, a small group came outside, probably in search of the same reprieve from the heat inside. With a disappointed grunt, Philip turned around and went back inside. Drawing a shaky breath, Angel silently thanked the small group for arriving and sending him away. She ought to return to the ball, but she wanted a moment of peace, so she remained on the terrace.

He should stay inside. Nathaniel knew this. And yet he found himself drawn outside to the terrace where he'd seen Angel disappear. She had been outside for quite a while now without returning. At first, he thought she might have intended to sneak a kiss with her betrothed since Chettisham had followed closely behind her, but the man had returned shortly after without her.

I just want to make sure she's all right. She's a family friend.

It rang untrue even to him, but he refused to consider any other possibilities. Making his way outside, he was so busy scanning the terrace for Angel that he didn't notice the woman on her way inside, and they bumped into each other. He recognised her as Lady Amelia, considered by many the most popular young lady of the season. They had danced on a few occasions and he quite liked her, but tonight he did not have time for pleasantries.

Lady Amelia curtsied. "My lord."

"Lady Amelia." He sketched a bow even while his eyes strayed behind her to search for the one he truly wished to see. Fortunately, she appeared as disinterested in having a conversation as he was and she quickly slipped inside.

"Nathaniel?" Angel's soft voice was a siren's call from the other side of the terrace and his feet steered him towards her. "Did you need a spot of air too?"

She stood by the edge of the terrace, her hands on the balustrade. Coming to stand next to her, he leaned his hips against the railing, wondering what he had planned when coming out here. Nothing. He had planned nothing. When she had not returned inside, he had worried about her. Chettisham wasn't known to be the most pleasant of men. That the man was intended to marry Angel left a sour taste in his mouth. It wasn't right. She deserved better.

"You didn't return inside," he said.

Her head tilted to the side, allowing her to look at him. "You knew I was here?"

"I saw you leave the ballroom earlier. You've been out here for quite some time. People might begin to wonder where you are if you don't return soon."

"I needed some fresh air." Her finger drew circles on the balustrade, a small crease appearing between her brows. "Philip followed. He's not thrilled about the attention I've received tonight."

"He's probably worried you will find a better match."

She let out a small, humourless laugh. "He did say something along those lines. I don't know why he would worry. My family is quite adamant this match is happening. It was my late parents' wish and we all want to honour it."

He said nothing. It was not his place, even if he wanted to shout out that Chettisham was a terrible match. If her parents had actually met him as an adult, he doubted they would have still wanted her to marry the man. Maybe he ought to speak to Gowthorpe about it. Her brother must know Chettisham's reputation.

Angel sighed, her bosom rising slightly against the fitted, green bodice. The pale moonlight streaked her blond hair with silver, and she looked almost ethereal where she stood with her gloved hands on the railing.

"I never expected to receive this much attention." A slight smile played at the corners of her mouth. "I can scarcely believe it."

"You're beautiful, and not a man in there could escape noticing." He winked. "As long as you're not hiding behind potted plants."

Her head turned, and her gaze met his. "Could you?"

The bright green of her eyes drew him towards her. "Could I what?" he asked softly.

"Escape noticing."

"I told you," he whispered as he leaned closer. "Not one man could."

Another moment passed while they stared at each other, so close their breaths mingled.

The laughter from someone down in the garden made him regain his senses, and he quickly pulled away. "We had better return inside."

"Yes," she agreed breathlessly, leaving him alone on the terrace while she hurried inside like she had the devil snapping at her heels.

As she slipped through the open doors, he cursed and raked a hand through his hair. What was he thinking? He'd just been about to kiss his friend's sister.

Chapter Seven

Dear Diary,
 Balls aren't so bad after all. Who would
 have thought? I should, however,
 remember to stay off moonlit balconies.
 They're bad for my composure.

Angel flicked her ivory fan open and used it to cool her flushed face. Had Nathaniel been about to kiss her? For a moment, she had thought he was, and when he didn't, there had been an undeniable stab of disappointment. She must have misread the situation. Nathaniel Howerty—one of the season's most eligible bachelors—would not want to kiss her. And even if he did, she didn't want him to. Or did she?

The realisation that she most definitely did made her cheeks burn hotly. Which was odd, since she knew from experience that she didn't enjoy kissing. Philip had kissed her a handful of times, and she had not appreciated it in the least. To the point where she had avoided his kisses ever since.

Moving further into the ballroom, she caught sight of her cousin chatting with two gentlemen. Marie had been a great success that evening and had danced with several suitable gentlemen. Noticing her attention, Marie's eyes narrowed. Extracting herself from her admirers, she came up to block Angel's path.

"Where have you been?" she asked. Had she seen her on the terrace with Nathaniel?

"I was getting some fresh air."

"Alone?"

"Yes." Angel prayed she wouldn't blush. Remembering how close Nathaniel had been as he leaned in set off a fluttering of butterflies inside her, and she didn't want her cousin to have any reason to suspect anything. Marie had a nose for sniffing out anything Angel enjoyed and always found a way to destroy it. When James had brought her a kitten once, Marie had suddenly developed allergies, despite having had a cat herself in the past.

"Is no one else on the terrace?"

"There have been others coming and going. It's hot in here and I imagine everyone needs a reprieve." Angel forced a smile and lifted one shoulder in a shrug. "I didn't speak to anyone. You know I prefer to be alone."

Marie smiled, but there was no warmth in her eyes. "That's true. You've never been a skilled conversationalist."

Angel's smile wavered slightly at the thinly veiled barb and her fingers tightened around the handle of the fan.

Noticing her reaction, her cousin's smile widened. "I'm surprised you've been as popular as you've been tonight. I suppose they will soon realise you're a quiet mouse who can't hold their interest."

The words struck true. Marie knew exactly what to say for the biggest impact. She was well aware of Angel's insecurities and how concerned she was about her shyness. Turning her head, Angel caught Jessica looking at her. Seeing her friend's face filled her with strength, and she raised her chin and met Marie's gloating eyes.

"Surely you wish to return to your adoring crowd, so perhaps you could refrain from insulting me and leave?"

Marie's blue eyes narrowed. "I hope you realise none of these gentlemen are interested in you," she spat. "They are probably only hanging around you to get to know your friend. She's the popular one."

"Perhaps," Angel allowed. "If that's the case, I do not mind. I'm meant to marry Philip, aren't I?"

"Yes. He's the only one who will have you. As bound by his parents' promise as you are by yours." Marie pushed an errant lock of dark hair behind her ear. "You should be grateful Maman agreed to carry out your parents' wish, or you would have ended up a spinster."

Content that she had knocked Angel down enough pegs, she left. Angel stared at her slipper-clad feet as a hollow feeling spread through her chest. It was easy to give in to the whispers of her inadequacy. She had heard them for years. Swallowing back the knot in her throat, she looked up when she heard movement next to her.

"What was that about?" Jessica asked, handing her a cup of lemonade.

"Cousinly concern?" she suggested with a wry smile, trying not to let her emotions show.

"I doubt it." Jessica let out an unladylike snort. "But if you do not wish to speak about it, I certainly will not force you." She took Angel's arm and smiled. "Now come, let's dance with some dashing gentlemen and forget all about family and other dreadfully boring things."

"Are you enjoying the evening, my lord?"

Nathaniel whipped around to discover Angel's cousin Miss Marie Brown standing behind him. A little closer than necessary. He was relieved when a quick glance confirmed that a few more people had joined them on the terrace. After Angel left, he'd been lost in thought and hadn't noticed.

"I'm enjoying it very much, indeed." Why had she sought him out? They had barely exchanged two sentences since she'd been foisted on him in Hyde Park. "And you, Miss Brown? Are you enjoying your coming-out ball?"

She moved to his side by the railing, her eyes settling on him, and there was no mistaking the flirtatious quality of her smile.

"I love it," she admitted, her smile widening. "The dancing. The music. The company."

Discreetly moving to put a little distance between them, Nathaniel returned the smile. "Is this your first ball?" he asked politely.

She nodded. "I have attended a few country dances, but nothing compares to a London ball." She gave him a conspiratorial wink. "I must say that the company in London is much more pleasant."

"If nothing else, there's a lot more of it," he agreed, not allowing her to bait him. "I am certain that you and your cousin will be invited to several more balls following this one. You've both had great success."

A shadow passed over her face at his last words. "I suppose," she said slowly. "I fear it may not last, though. Angel is terribly shy and reserved. The *ton* will soon realise she has nothing to offer."

She moved a step closer, her face schooled into something that must have been meant to look sympathetic. "Poor thing really struggles around people," she said with an exaggerated sigh. "It cannot be easy being so... dull."

It was rather amazing how skilled this young woman was at making her cousin sound like a completely different person from the one Nathaniel had come to know the last few weeks. Yes, Angel was shy, but she had shown plenty of spirit. If anything, her family exacerbated her shyness. He had noticed a remarkable difference in her when around them.

It reminded him of the roses his aunt grew on his estate Davenhall. They had not grown well for years when she first moved in, stuck in an area of the garden that didn't get much sun. Once she removed the shade and ensured they got all the sunlight they required, they flourished.

Listening to Marie, the changes in Angel suddenly made sense. If Marie was comfortable enough to speak about her cousin like this to him, what did she say to Angel's face?

"I don't believe I would use the term 'dull' for your cousin," he said.

There was a flash of annoyance in Marie's pretty blue eyes, but it was soon hidden behind a charming smile. "I feel sorry for her," she said. "It's fortunate that she's bound to marry Mr Chettisham. She doesn't have to worry about finding a match this season."

Chettisham. He swallowed back the urge to deny her claim. No one should have to marry that man. But who was he to tell Angel whom she could and could not marry? No one. He had no claim to her, and he had no plans to make one. She was exactly the type of woman he didn't want to marry. Someone he might come to care for.

Not sure what to say, he mumbled something unintelligible before sketching a bow. "If you will excuse me, I should return to the ballroom."

He left before she could reply, having had enough of listening to her disparaging Angel. Scanning the ballroom, he found Jessica still surrounded by admirers. Angel stood a short distance away, speaking with Philip Chettisham. He scowled when Chettisham bent down to whisper something in her ear.

"I must say that Gowthorpe's sister has grown up to be quite a beautiful young lady."

He turned his head to glare at Wortham. His friend always knew to show up at the worst possible moment. It was a hidden, and not particularly appreciated, skill. "Do you have to sneak up on me?"

"I wasn't sneaking." Wortham chuckled. "You were simply too busy spying on that chit to hear me approach." When Nathaniel didn't offer a reply, Wortham smirked. "Does he have a legitimate claim on her? Or why are you glaring?"

"There's nothing official, but from what I know, there is an understanding between their families that it will happen."

"So she's still available," Wortham said with a satisfied grin. He might as well have been rubbing his hands together like a villain at the theatre.

"I didn't say that."

"You might as well have."

"She's still Gowthorpe's sister."

"That may stop *you*."

"Say what you will, Wortham, but I know you too well. You'd never ruin an unmarried woman. Especially not if she's your friend's sister."

Wortham grunted. "I suppose you're right. If only I could dispose of my conscience."

"What's left of it," Nathaniel muttered dryly, eliciting a chuckle from his friend.

Chapter Eight

Dear Diary,
   I never before appreciated quite how
   captivating Shakespeare's writing is.
   Who knew?

A few days later, Angel sat alone in the drawing room waiting for Philip to take her for a carriage ride in Hyde Park when a footman entered to tell her that the Marquess of Pensington and his sister had come to call. Giving the servant a surprised look, she stood and smoothed the skirt of her simple, white walking dress.

"Please, show them in."

The footman nodded and disappeared towards the entrance hall. A few moments later, Jessica and Nathaniel entered the room. Taking one glance at all the bouquets and flowers filling every available surface, Jessica laughed a little.

"Is this the new conservatory?" she asked with twinkling eyes. "Did I enter the wrong room?"

Angel grinned sheepishly, her cheeks heating. She had never expected to have this much attention. "Don't be silly."

Her friend walked along one of the long tables, inspecting the many beautiful and extravagant flowers. She reached out to touch some exotic bloom as she looked back at Angel. "Are they all for you?"

"Not at all. At least half, if not more, are for Marie."

Nathaniel picked up a crisp white card that had arrived with a group of exquisite orchids. "To Miss Grafton. Shall I compare thee to a summer's dawn?" He grimaced in disgust. "Surely they must be jesting. Misquoting Shakespeare? Not very romantic."

Jessica laughed. "It does quite ruin the moment, but not everyone knows Shakespeare inside out. You know, some people did not grow up with a parent obsessed with his writings. They also might not have your impeccable memory."

"Then they should do their research better," he muttered, putting the offending card back in the bouquet.

"I can't imagine it being romantic having Shakespeare quoted to you anyway," Angel said. "Don't misunderstand," she quickly added when both siblings turned to stare at her. "I love Shakespeare, but I think it would make me laugh if someone started quoting it to me."

"Do you think so?" Nathaniel asked.

The hint of a smile playing on his lips made her insides flutter. "Yes, I do believe so."

"Would you care to place a bet on that?"

"I... I don't know."

He moved over to stand in front of her, a little closer than was strictly proper, his dark eyes glittering. She stared up at him, unable to tear her gaze from his. For a man, he had beautiful eyes, so dark they were almost black and framed by thick, sooty eyelashes that would make most women envious. He leaned in a little closer, making her breath catch in her throat.

"Doubt thou the stars are fire," he recited slowly, the words a soft caress. "Doubt that the sun doth move."

The rich cadence of his voice and the wicked glimmer in his dark eyes were mesmerising, and even if she'd wanted to, she couldn't have moved away from him. Not that she wanted to. She was utterly spellbound by their proximity.

"Doubt truth to be a liar." He leaned in close enough that she could feel his warm breath on her face. "But never doubt I love."

Swallowing with some difficulty, she tried to move, but her feet didn't obey. They stood so close that she could smell the crisp, clean scent of his newly pressed clothes, and something darker, manlier. Was it sandalwood?

"There are at least as many flowers for you as for Marie," Jessica muttered from the other side of the room, the reminder of her presence breaking the spell.

Angel drew a deep breath and stepped away from Nathaniel. Her head was foggy, and she struggled to piece two thoughts together. "Perhaps," she said. "I haven't read every card."

Turning around from a display of bouquets, Jessica looked over at them. Seeing her brother, her eyes narrowed for a second before she moved along to another table. "Do you like flowers?" she asked over her shoulder.

"I suppose." Angel smiled apologetically. "I suppose it would be considered dull, but I prefer roses. There is no need for all these exotic and expensive flowers."

"It livens up the room at least," Jessica said with a teasing smile. "We came by to ask if you wanted to join us for a ride in the park."

"I would have loved to, but I have promised this afternoon to Philip. He should be here any moment to pick me up."

"Pity." Jessica gave her a hopeful look. "I suppose we can't abduct you?"

Angel laughed. "I fear not." She frowned. "Didn't you agree to go for a ride with that gentleman? Mr Merriweather, wasn't it?"

The wide-eyed shock on Jessica's face was a little too innocent to be genuine. "Oh, no..."

Nathaniel groaned. "You cannot stand suitors up like this, Jessica. And you definitely cannot allow me to be your accomplice in doing so."

"Of course, I can," she muttered.

He let out a long-suffering sigh before bowing towards Angel. "Miss Grafton, we shall see you tomorrow evening at Lady Yates's musical evening, I hope." Throwing a sardonic look in his sister's direction, he added, "I must take my sister home to see her suitor."

Jessica muttered something under her breath, gave Angel a quick hug, and then the two siblings left.

Smiling to herself, Angel sat down on the sofa to wait for Philip. He arrived not much later. When he saw the number of bouquets in the room, a scowl settled on his face.

"Where did all these flowers come from?" he asked abruptly, without even extending a greeting.

She looked around the room. There really were a lot of them. "Most are for Marie," she said. "She has been quite popular since the ball."

He appeared to accept the explanation and offered his arm. Picking up her rose-coloured cashmere shawl and her bonnet, she took it and allowed him to lead her outside to the waiting carriage. They spoke little during the ride to the park, so she occupied herself by watching the people walking along the streets. Once they arrived, he had to slow their speed to manoeuvre the crush of the park, but when they reached a less busy part, he finally relaxed. It was a beautiful, sunny day and Angel couldn't resist turning her face up towards the sun.

"You shouldn't do that," Philip said disapprovingly. "You might tan. Or get freckles."

She refrained from telling him she never tanned, only burned, but bowed her head so her bonnet protected her face from the warm sunlight.

"I was hoping to speak with you regarding a matter." He turned his head to look at her and her stomach plummeted.

"Oh?"

"When will we announce our betrothal?"

Never. The word came unbidden to her mind. Unable to meet his eyes, she looked out over the park, noticing that they were close to The Serpentine, its water sparkling in the sun. She felt nothing for this man that her family wanted her to marry. It wasn't something she had paid too much attention to until meeting Nathaniel. Her reactions to the two men were like night and day.

Around Philip, she always felt uncomfortable and awkward, and she had assumed it was simply because of who she was. But when she was with Nathaniel... Well, she was still awkward. But she enjoyed his company, and he made her smile. Philip never made her smile.

Not that she ever believed a popular bachelor like Nathaniel would ever look twice in her direction—as Marie was all too happy to remind her of any chance she got—but it was proof that there was something else out there. More than what she could have with Philip. A future different from the dreadful one her family offered. But her parents had wanted this...

"Angel?" he said when she still said nothing.

"I... I don't know," she said. "Didn't James say I could have this season?"

Philip let out a puff of air. "It's only a formality. You are not here to see what else is available to you. We are still meant to marry, and I am not unreasonable. We can wait to get married until after the end of the Season, but that doesn't stop us from announcing our betrothal sooner."

No. She didn't want that. Not yet. She wanted more time. More time for what, she wasn't sure, but she knew she wasn't ready to agree to become his wife. "We don't know each other well enough yet. James said we should use this season to become better acquainted, and I think that is a good idea."

"Many couples get married who barely know each other." He shrugged dismissively.

"I just don't know if we're a good match." The words slipped out before she could stop them and she almost slapped a hand over her mouth.

His cold eyes bore into hers. "Are you saying you don't wish to marry me?"

She could sense his anger in the way his fingers tightened around the reins and the jerky movements of his head. Not wanting him to lose his temper, she tried to placate him. "No... No, I'm not saying that. But I don't want to rush into this."

"We're hardly rushing. You are nineteen, a year older than most for their first season. I think we've waited long enough."

"Surely a little longer doesn't make much difference in the whole scheme of things?" she said, trying to keep her tone light.

His nostrils flared. "I don't understand why this is so difficult. Our parents arranged this match and we should honour their wishes."

She looked down at her glove-clad hands in her lap, nervously wringing a piece of her dress. For as long as she could remember, her aunt had talked about this match, but in the last couple of years—as the time drew nearer—it had become something Aunt Christine constantly reminded her of. It was the only thing her parents could ever ask of her, and she wanted to honour their wishes. But why was it so hard?

"I know," she mumbled. "And I want to. But I worry we will not be happy together. I'm not sure we even like each other."

"We'll like each other well enough." His lips were a thin line on his face, and she wondered what he was thinking. Did he struggle with this decision as much as she was? He certainly didn't give her the impression of a man in love. Then, without warning, he turned to her and pressed his mouth roughly against hers.

She pushed him away, the panic bubbling up inside making her rash. "Don't kiss me!" she whispered urgently, looking around to see if anyone had seen them. "I don't like it."

"You don't like it?" The icy quality of his voice was far scarier than if he had shouted at her. "You don't like being kissed?"

"No," she admitted miserably, wishing she was anywhere but there, having any conversation other than this one.

He turned his face to look at her, and the cold fury in his eyes made her shiver. "I don't enjoy kissing you either," he spat.

"It's like kissing a dead fish. Since you find my company so distasteful, you can walk home."

Her eyes widened. "What?"

"Get out of my carriage. Now!" He almost yelled the last word, and she quickly scrambled out of the carriage. She'd barely reached the ground when he set the horses in motion and left her standing alone on the road, staring after him.

She stood stunned for several moments until there was no longer any sight of the carriage or Philip. Dejected, she looked around the park. She had to get home. On foot. Fortunately, it wasn't too far to Berkeley Square from Hyde Park, but it was still some distance without proper walking boots. With a sigh, she started moving towards the other side of the park.

She was humming to herself and had not walked far when someone called her name. Turning around, she caught sight of Jessica sitting in a nice open carriage together with a good-looking young man. Next to them, Nathaniel rode on a bay horse. Mortified that they had found her alone, she wished she could sink through the earth. The last thing she wanted was to let anyone know she had displeased a man so much he'd evicted her from his vehicle.

The carriage moved up alongside, and Jessica looked down at her with a worried look on her face. "Angel, what are you doing alone in the park? I thought Mr Chettisham was picking you up?"

"I..." She desperately wanted to come up with a plausible excuse. Nathaniel stared darkly at her, his brow furrowed, making it harder to think. Looking back at Jessica, she mumbled something non-committing.

"I beg your pardon? I couldn't hear you." Nathaniel dismounted his horse and moved closer.

"Philip cancelled. I still wanted some fresh air and decided to go for a walk."

Nathaniel's eyes narrowed. "You walked all the way here from Berkeley Square. Alone. Without a chaperone?" There was a distinct note of disbelief in his voice.

"Yes," she said stubbornly, meeting his angry gaze without flinching.

"And are you planning to walk home?"

"I... Yes, of course."

"Surely we cannot allow Angel to walk the distance home," Jessica interrupted. "We will take her in the carriage."

"It's not big enough," Nathaniel said. "Are you still maintaining that you walked here, Miss Grafton?"

She nodded, but she could tell he didn't believe her, and from the pitying looks from Jessica, neither did she.

"Why don't you take my carriage and bring Miss Grafton home?" Mr Merriweather, Jessica's suitor, said helpfully. "Lady Jessica and I can stroll through the park in the meantime."

"Yes," Jessica quickly agreed. "Please, Nathaniel. Will you do it?"

He said nothing, but nodded tersely and waited while Mr Merriweather and Jessica stepped down from the carriage.

Handing the other man the reins of his horse, he then climbed up and sat down.

"I'm sorry we had to meet again under these circumstances," Mr Merriweather said with an apologetic smile while he helped Angel into the carriage.

"Thank you, Mr Merriweather." She didn't want to meet anyone's gaze. The whole situation was humiliating.

Jessica waved when the carriage lurched into motion, and Angel waved back before turning forward. Nathaniel remained silent, and she decided it was wise to follow suit. Especially considering that he was gripping the reins with such force, she wondered if he imagined it being her neck. Once they left the park behind them and were driving along a quiet street, he turned to look at her.

"He left you there, didn't he?" he asked directly.

She stared straight ahead, refusing to meet his eyes, lest he read the answer in hers. "No."

"Please don't lie to me. Chettisham doesn't deserve you protecting his unacceptable behaviour."

Smoothing out an invisible crease on her dress, she pondered his words. She wasn't protecting Philip. She was protecting herself. No one wanted to admit to being so disagreeable that their intended future husband didn't want to see them. Aunt Christine always said she ought to consider her words before speaking, and now she could see why. There had probably been a better way to discuss matters with Philip, but he had put her on the spot and she had panicked.

"Miss Grafton?"

"I've said you can call me Angel," she muttered, glancing up at him. He was such a handsome man with his olive-tinted skin and black hair that it almost hurt her to look at him. With his marked cheekbones, straight nose, and slashed dark eyebrows, he had something of a wicked look.

When she had first seen him and compared him to a dark angel, it seemed rather apt. His mouth was wide, and there was something sensual about it, especially when he smiled at her the way he did now. Tearing her gaze away from his lips, she stared straight ahead again.

"Angel." He sighed softly. "What am I to do with you?"

"You need not do anything with me at all. I'm not your responsibility."

"You're my best friend's sister." The words caused a stab of disappointment. "I can't ignore it when I see you being mistreated by the man they're planning to marry you off to."

"I'm not being mistreated!" Why was she arguing with him? Pride?

"I am no fool, Angel. Chettisham left you in the park."

She didn't reply. What could she say?

"I should tell your brother what happened."

"No!" She whipped her head around to give him a pleading look. She couldn't bear it if James found out what a failure she was. Who couldn't even go for a simple carriage ride without angering Philip. "Please don't tell him. It was my fault."

Nathaniel's eyes glittered dangerously. "No gentleman leaves a lady alone in the park. No matter the reasons."

"I... I angered him," she admitted. "I should have kept my mouth shut."

"It's no excuse."

"Please don't tell James." She put her hand on his dark-clad arm.

He looked at her hand for a moment, then sighed. "Very well. But it's against my better judgement."

"Thank you."

"Don't. I'm doing you a disfavour."

A short while later, he stopped the carriage outside Gowthorpe House and turned to look at her. "I won't follow you inside since it would raise questions."

Jumping down from the carriage, he assisted her down. She looked up at him with a slight smile. "Thank you for being my friend and for not telling my brother."

"A true friend would save you from yourself."

"I can take care of myself quite well."

The look on his face clearly showed he didn't agree, but she decided not to take him to task about it. Especially since today hadn't exactly been a stellar show of her independence. Bidding him a quick farewell, she hurried up the steps to the house and entered as she heard the carriage pull away. The footman who opened the door didn't comment, and she was happy that no one in her family was around. Not in the mood to speak to anyone, she went upstairs to her room and closed the door behind her.

Untying her bonnet, she threw it on the bed. Her gloves followed suit. The room was pleasantly warm from the afternoon sun shining through the tall windows. She sat down in her favourite spot; the window seat where she could look out over the garden. The grassy area was currently empty, but she found it soothing to sit and watch the flowers and plants. With a sigh, she leaned her head against the cool glass of the windowpane and closed her eyes.

She didn't know what to do. Philip obviously wished to go ahead with their betrothal, despite their lack of interest in one another. Was it strange that she didn't enjoy kissing him? Everyone always talked about kissing like this wonderful—and forbidden—thing, but she didn't enjoy it in the least.

Was there something wrong with her? She'd always been distant and quiet, even as a child. Maybe love and passionate kisses just weren't for her?

'Your parents so dearly wanted this.' The words her aunt so often used to remind her echoed through her mind. She remembered little of her parents. Any memories she had were faint, like thin gossamer threads in the far reaches of her mind. She could only remember her mother's soft hands and French accent, and the way she had tucked her into bed herself rather than letting the nanny do it. She remembered even less of her father, only that he'd been tall and blond, and smelled of fine cigars.

Would they have wanted this for her had they still been alive? She did not know. Maybe if she could bring herself to be more pleasant to Philip, he would return in kind. They would meet at the musical evening tomorrow night, and she would make an effort to please him. She would give this her best effort. Her parents deserved that much.

Chapter Nine

Dear Diary,
  I cannot understand the obsession
  with kissing. After having tried it,
  I find it decidedly <u>un</u>pleasant!

Having made a conscious effort to enjoy herself, the evening was turning out much better than Angel had feared. The musical evening was a pleasant affair with a skilled Italian singer visiting London. During a brief break, while they served refreshments in a nearby receiving room, Angel savoured a moment of alone time as the other guests had left the music room.

After spending a good hour in an overcrowded room, being able to sit by herself was pure bliss. The light-green walls gave the room a light feel, and with one wall covered by tall windows facing the garden, it didn't make her skin crawl the way some enclosed spaces did. Especially now, when she was alone rather than stuck in there with everyone else. A pianoforte stood before the window, facing the chairs and small sofas that had been carried into the room for the audience to sit on.

Even Philip had been pleasant that evening, which she considered a small victory and proof that if she was polite and kind to him, he would return the favour. On her insistence, he had gone with the other guests to get some refreshments, and he had promised to bring her back a glass of lemonade. All too soon, everyone started pouring back into the room, signalling that the intermission was coming to an end.

A moment later, Philip returned with her promised lemonade and sat down on her left. James, who had come in with him, sat down on her right. Taking the glass from Philip, she thanked him before taking a sip. She made a face since it wasn't lemonade at all but punch.

She never drank alcohol, but her throat was dry, so she continued sipping the drink. Her brother and Philip discussed some matter she had no interest in over her head, so she watched the guests trickling back into the room. It was always interesting to observe people. Much more preferable to interacting with them.

Jessica, Nathaniel, and Mrs Grey entered the room. Her friend caught sight of her and gave her a quick wave. Soon, the lights in the back were extinguished to give more effect to the singer who had returned to finish her performance. Angel enjoyed the show, captivated by the woman's beautiful, rich voice.

The punch made her head feel pleasantly tingly. During the show, she felt Philip's hand on her knee in the semi-darkness, and she slowly and discreetly moved it back to his own lap. It was highly improper for him to be touching her, especially in public.

She glanced around to make sure no one had seen the inappropriate display, and her eyes met Nathaniel's where he stood to the side. His eyes glimmered darkly in the light from the candles in the front of the room, and her face heated. Had he seen Philip touching her? Staring straight ahead, refusing to look at Nathaniel, she could still sense his intense gaze on her, and the knowledge that he was looking made her stomach do an awkward somersault.

Once the singer finished her set, everyone left the music room to enjoy some social mingling in the receiving room, where more refreshments were being served. Angel followed James and Philip but hung back when they went to speak to the Italian singer.

Jessica caught sight of her and left her aunt and brother to come over, handing her another glass of punch. "That was an excellent performance, was it not?"

"Yes, I thought it was wonderful." Angel smiled, fanning herself with her carved ivory fan. The room was sweltering from the considerable amount of people squeezed into such a small space. She took another sip of the drink, quite enjoying the buzz it had brought on. "It's the first time I've heard a professional singer."

"Really?" Jessica looked up from digging through her reticule.

"You must remember that I have only been in London on brief visits before. No time for the opera or anything such."

"I keep forgetting that you've spent your entire life holed up in the country," Jessica said with a teasing grin, then made a little sound of triumph when she pulled a fan out.

"From what I've heard, you've spent most of your time on your family's country estate as well. So no pointing fingers," Angel replied in mock offence.

"She certainly should not. I remember the days when she would run barefoot over the estate with no regard for decency."

Angel looked up to find that Lord Wortham had joined them, a charming smile on his lips. While she doubted anyone could be as handsome as Nathaniel, she had to admit that the earl was very attractive with his dark brown hair and clear blue eyes. He had a roguish charm that was difficult to resist.

"Lord Wortham," Jessica muttered in greeting, flicking her fan open and hiding her face behind it.

"Lady Jessica," he replied smoothly, executing a smart bow. Turning to Angel, he smiled. "Miss Grafton. It's a pleasure to meet you again. May I say that you look stunning as usual?"

Her cheeks warmed. As if she wasn't feeling hot enough already. "Thank you, my lord." She turned to Jessica, her interest piqued. "Barefoot?"

"I certainly never did," Jessica said with a huff, but she wasn't looking at Wortham.

He chuckled. "I distinctly remember it. Surely you are not implying that I'm a liar?"

Jessica sighed in exasperation. "It was once. One. Single. Time."

"Then I'm glad I crossed your path that day," Wortham said teasingly. "You have very adorable feet."

For the first time that Angel could remember, she saw Jessica's face flush red while she stared at Wortham.

"Are you bothering my sister again?"

The earl turned his head to grin at Nathaniel. "Yes, but it is so enjoyable."

"I'd rather you didn't."

"You never let me have any fun," Wortham complained.

"Not at my sister's expense, no."

"I shall look for entertainment elsewhere then." With a grin, Wortham bowed and left them, walking over to speak to the beautiful Italian singer.

"He's such a rake," Jessica said in disgust, watching him flirt with the woman.

Nathaniel narrowed his eyes at his sister. "What do you know about rakes?"

"Please. I'm eighteen years old, Nathaniel, not eight."

"I'd rather you were eight," he muttered.

Angel excused herself and made her way outside onto the terrace at the back of the house. Her fan did little to cool her down from the stifling heat from the crush of people, and the evening air felt good against her face. Tall windows covered most of the house, allowing her to see what was going on inside. Having little interest, she moved away from the windows to a part of the terrace outside some unused, unlit rooms.

Walking up to the terrace railing, she looked out over the garden, remembering another evening not too long ago on a similar terrace. The butterflies in her stomach fluttered to life at the mere memory, even though nothing had happened. Nathaniel might have looked like he was about to kiss her, but she couldn't imagine that he ever would. And she shouldn't want him to. Based on her experience, kisses were not for her. And yet...

A noise behind her made her turn around, and the fluttering inside increased for a moment as a tall shape moved towards her. Her heart plummeted when Philip came out from the shadows.

"Philip," she mumbled. "I went outside for a spot of fresh air."

He nodded silently and came over to stand beside her. There were a few moments of silence as they both stared out over the garden. They had not spoken since he had left her in the park the previous day.

"I wanted to apologise," he said quietly.

Her eyes widened. He had never apologised to her before, and she wasn't quite sure how to react. Usually, whenever his temper made him say something unpleasant, he would simply act like it had never happened. Maybe he realised this time had been worse than most.

"For what happened in the park," he qualified. He turned to face her. "It was wrong of me to leave you the way I did. You made me so angry when you first said you didn't think we are a good match, and then that you don't enjoy kissing me."

She nodded slowly, and he continued. "I came back for you a short while later, intending to apologise and bring you home. But you were gone."

"Lord Pensington took me home."

"So I heard." There was a distinct tone of dislike in his voice, but he didn't make an issue out of it. "I hope you can forgive me."

He reached out to touch her face, and she had to fight the immediate urge to flinch. "I forgive you," she said, though she wasn't sure she truly did. But her family expected her to marry this man, so she must do her best to keep their relationship pleasant.

Smiling, he bowed his head to place a kiss on her lips. She stood still, keeping herself calm. Surely she would feel something if only she tried? Everyone obsessed about kissing, so it couldn't be all bad.

The kiss was hard, crushing her lips against her teeth. The grip on her arms was almost painful. Suddenly, she felt the tip of his tongue tap insistently against her closed mouth, and she took an involuntary step away from him.

"What's the matter?" he complained.

"I... I don't enjoy that," she whispered miserably.

"Then there is something wrong with you," he snapped. "You must be made of ice. I would get more response from a statue."

"That's not very fair of you." Her lower lip quivered. She tried to calm herself, but his words stung. Especially since she had just worried about the same thing. What was wrong with her?

He looked at her with narrowed eyes. "If you cannot learn to accept a man's kisses, you will never find a husband. You're a cold fish, Angel. It's not very attractive."

With those parting words, he turned on his heel and left her alone. She stared after him with his words still ringing in her ears. Why didn't she enjoy kissing? Taking a shaking breath, she left the terrace and stepped into the unlit garden where she could be alone with no one seeing her. She found a stone bench and sat down with her hands clasped in her lap, while a few errant tears trickled down her cheeks.

She was such a failure. Her parents would be so disappointed in her. They had wanted the two families joined through marriage. Aunt Christine always reminded her of how her parents and the Chettishams had been the best of friends. Even if she could learn to accept his advances, Philip didn't seem to enjoy kissing her, either.

What kind of woman was she if she couldn't even entice the man she was meant to marry? Maybe her aunt was right. Maybe she truly was strange.

"Angel?"

Quickly wiping the tears off her face, she looked up to see who had called her name. Nathaniel stood in the middle of the garden, his gaze searching for her, but the shadows of the two trees by the bench hid her from view.

"Angel?" he repeated quietly. "Are you here?"

"I'm here," she replied just as quietly and stood.

The movement caught his eye, and he walked over to her. He looked down at her in the semi-darkness with a slight frown. Before she could say anything, he reached out and touched her cheek with the pad of his thumb.

"You've been crying. What did he do?"

She gave him a wry smile. "Nothing. Are you always going to come charging to my rescue?"

"It would appear I'm your knight in shining armour." He chuckled, the warm sound soothing her.

"I couldn't imagine a better one." She regretted the words as soon as they left her mouth.

He fell silent, taking in her appearance. "Why are you sad?"

"It's silly, really."

"Tell me."

She looked up at him, her eyes watering despite her attempts to hold back. "I'm a failure," she blurted out.

He frowned. "Why would you think that?"

"No man will ever want me." She turned her back to him while wiping a few tears away from her face. Crying in front of others wasn't exactly on her list of favourite things to do. "Philip said I'm like a cold fish."

"Chettisham's the cold fish," Nathaniel muttered. "But why would he say that of you?"

Her cheeks heated. "I..." She gave him an embarrassed glance over her shoulder. "I don't enjoy it when he kisses me. I think I might be broken."

His immediate chuckle rankled her, and she turned around to glare at him. He held his hands up. "I beg your pardon," he said, still smiling. "But, Angel... I can assure you that you're not broken."

"You cannot know that," she pointed out. "Philip doesn't seem to enjoy kissing me, either. It's not right. Something must be wrong with me."

Nathaniel shook his head. "I'm certain there is nothing wrong with you, Angel. You shouldn't worry. I don't see how Chettisham could elicit a response from anyone, he—"

"He's quite handsome," she cut in. "Several ladies have told me so. Saying how lucky I am."

He snorted. "I suppose he's not ugly, but it's not all about looks. His personality leaves much to be desired."

"You do not like him?" She'd sensed it before, but this was the first time he'd said something outright.

"It's not my place," he muttered. "But no, Chettisham and I do not get along. However, I know you intend to marry him, and you make your own choices."

"It's hardly a choice."

They stared at each other for a moment, neither speaking. There was a part of her that wished he would tell her not to marry Philip. Everyone in her life was so set on this match, it would have been nice to have someone who wasn't as keen. Jessica was the only one who had spoken against the match, believing she could do better.

"In any case." Nathaniel cleared his throat and ran a hand through his dark hair. "What I was going to say was that I am certain nothing is wrong with you. I imagine Philip is the only man you've kissed, so you have nothing to compare to. It truly might be that the issue lies with him."

"That's it!" she exclaimed, making him raise his eyebrows at her outburst. "I must kiss another man to know if Philip is the issue, or if I don't enjoy any kisses."

"I don't think that's a good idea." He sounded hesitant, but with her head buzzing from two glasses of punch, she rather thought it was a brilliant idea. "It's not very proper for a young lady to go around kissing scores of men."

"Of course not. I would only need to kiss one other man."

"Even that has the potential to ruin you."

Her mood dropped. "I did not think of that."

"Good. I'm glad we've put that idea behind us." He smiled.

"Unless..." An idea had taken root in her mind.

"Unless what?" He narrowed his eyes suspiciously as she gave him an imploring look.

"You could kiss me," she quickly blurted out before she lost her nerve. How she could be so brazen, she wasn't sure. Maybe it was the punch. But at that moment, it felt imperative that she find out if there was something wrong with her, or if she just couldn't bring herself to accept Philip. She needed to know if she was broken.

Nathaniel stared at her like she had sprouted two heads, making her doubt the wisdom of her plan.

"I beg your pardon?" he finally choked out.

"It's not such a terrible idea." She wasn't sure if she was trying to convince herself or him. "We are friends, are we not?"

"Yes," he hedged. "But—"

"And as my friend, you would never dream of ruining my reputation by telling anyone. And I trust you."

He raked a hand through his hair again, mussing it up. No longer looking at her, he was focusing on a spot somewhere two feet above her head. "I can't kiss you, Angel."

Her face fell. "You can't?"

Of course not. What had she been thinking? He was one of the most handsome men she had ever seen and one of the most sought-after bachelors in London. He could have his pick of ladies to kiss. He wouldn't want to kiss her. She was a country bumpkin. Her aunt was right. She was a nobody who should be so lucky if the match her late parents had made for her would deign to marry her.

"Of course you can't," she said, more to herself than to him. It had been a spur-of-the-moment idea, and she felt foolish for even having suggested it. What must he think of her? "You would never kiss someone like me. I'm not popular enough. Not attractive enough."

"I did not say that." Nathaniel gave Angel a frustrated look. Did she not understand what she was asking of him? Did she not know how desperately he wanted to do exactly what she asked?

"You did not have to." She looked so sad and dejected that it nearly broke his heart.

"You're my friend's sister." It was a reasonable excuse, and at least partly why he could never kiss her.

"I'm not asking you to ruin me," she muttered, kicking at a tuft of grass with the toe of her slipper. "All I'm asking for is a single kiss."

He knew he was staring, but he wasn't sure how to get out of this situation without hurting her feelings. His gaze darted to her lips, and he mentally kicked himself. That did nothing for his resolve.

There were few things he wanted more than to oblige her request. He had wanted to kiss her for some time now, but he was an honourable man, and he'd never kiss a friend's sister. Especially not someone he might catch feelings for.

"I just need to know," she pleaded. "If I feel nothing when you kiss me, then I know it's me. Everyone else seems to enjoy kissing, but I don't."

"Who is everyone?" he grumbled. "Your friends are all innocents, like you, as far as I'm aware."

She waved a hand in the air. "Everyone. The world in general." Her shoulders sloped and her gaze dropped to her feet. "I just want to know if I'm broken."

Bloody hell. He raked a hand through his hair. Again. At this rate, he'd go bald soon.

"Angel, I can't." There was a note of desperation in his voice as his resolve quickly withered in the face of her utter dejection. Her argument even started sounding logical. It was only one kiss. What harm could it do?

She tilted her head to look up at him, her large eyes catching the moonlight filtering through the leaves of the trees, making the tears gathering in the corners glitter. He fought back the desperate urge to bend down and kiss her right then. What he should do was run in the opposite direction, away from temptation.

He took one step away from her, but when her eyes lowered in wounded silence at his retreat, there was no turning back.

With a groan, he took the two steps separating them. One kiss. He could do one kiss. Stopping right in front of her, with only a scant foot separating their bodies, he gazed down at her.

"I'll do it," he said hoarsely, hoping he wouldn't regret it. "One kiss. And you have to tell me to stop if you don't enjoy it."

She nodded, her face blank. Then she closed her eyes, her lashes resting against her pale cheeks. He watched her for a moment and her rosy lips parted slightly, her breath coming in quick puffs. When he leaned closer, she shivered and her eyes squeezed shut tightly. She must expect an onslaught.

"Open your eyes," he ordered grimly. She did, blinking to focus, and her eyes widened when she discovered him only a few inches away from her face.

"Have you changed your mind?" Her voice was little more than a whisper.

He shook his head. "No." It was the truth. Now that he'd decided that he would be allowed one kiss, nothing could stop him.

"Then why did you ask me to open my eyes?"

"You looked like you were awaiting the hangman's snare." He chuckled.

"Oh." Her cheeks stained red. "I'm sorry."

"That's all right."

He cupped her cheeks and wiped his thumbs over her skin to remove the stains left by her tears. Then he traced the outline of her eyebrows, followed by the shape of her nose, to finally softly caress her lips with the pad of his thumb. During the entire time, he held her gaze, and she seemed unable to look away.

When he leaned in a little closer, her eyes fluttered close, and she took a shaky breath. He whispered, "I'm going to kiss you now."

Chapter Ten

Dear Diary,
I was wrong... So very, very wrong.

The moment his lips brushed against hers, Angel knew that kissing Nathaniel Howerty would be nothing like her previous experiences. Even though their lips were barely touching, her entire body hummed in sudden awareness.

She leaned into the kiss, raising her hands to bury her fingers in the soft hair at the back of his head. With a groan, he moved his hands away from her face and slid them down along her back to pull her closer, pressing her intimately against his lean frame. Her soft curves fit perfectly against the hard planes of his body, and the closeness sent heat coursing through her.

When his tongue gently caressed her lower lip, she allowed him entry without hesitation. He took immediate advantage, deepening the kiss, igniting something that had lain dormant deep inside. It was intoxicating and frightening at the same time. She'd never felt like this. This need to be close to a man, to feel his lips on hers. His hands. She never wanted it to stop. Timidly, she tried to return the kiss, causing a low sound at the back of his throat, and he pulled her even closer, grinding his hips against hers.

A spear of pure pleasure shot from the junction of her thighs throughout her body, and the force of it surprised her so much that she tore her mouth from his and opened her eyes to stare at him. He stared back, still holding her close, his eyes impossibly dark in the dusk. His breath was laboured, just like hers, and for a moment she could do nothing but stare at the man who had just given her the best kiss of her life. So this was what everyone raved about. Now, she finally understood.

When he released her, she stumbled back. Touching her lips with trembling fingers, she marvelled at the contrast of the cool silk of her gloves compared to the hot pressure of Nathaniel's kiss.

"I beg your pardon," he mumbled, his eyes not leaving her.

He was so handsome, the semi-darkness of the evening making him seem like some dark, sensual spirit of a maiden's dream. Her body still hummed from the unfamiliar sensations and feelings, and she could not find her voice. The silence seemed to frustrate him, and he ran a hand through his black hair, mussing it up even more than before.

"Christ," he muttered. "I never meant to..." He groaned. "I'm so sorry, Angel. That went too far."

"I... It's fine," she whispered.

"I don't know what came over me." He sounded angry with himself. "I was only going to give you a quick peck."

"It's fine," she said again, her voice a little louder this time.

"No, it's not. I frightened you."

She smiled wryly. "No. You just surprised me a little."

He reached out to touch her face. "Even so, I apologise. I took advantage of the situation when you had asked me for a simple favour."

"I didn't mind," she admitted, and somehow managed to meet his eyes without blushing.

They stared at each other for a moment, and she wished he would kiss her again. She wanted to experience it one more time. When he leaned closer, she thought she'd got her wish, until he quickly pulled away and took a few steps away. With a curse, he turned his back to her.

"Nathaniel?"

"Please go back inside," he said, his voice hoarse.

"Are you all right?" She wasn't sure what was happening. Why wouldn't he look at her? Standing straight as a board, he looked uncomfortable, and she wanted to ease his tension. Torn between wanting to go to him and wanting to run from the unfamiliar sensations he provoked in her, she moved towards him and reached her hand out to touch his arm. He whirled around and stared at her, his dark eyes burning.

"Angel, go inside. Please." There was a tone in his voice she couldn't quite place. She swallowed, then with a quick nod, she turned on her heel and hurried back to the house.

Nathaniel watched Angel slip back into the ballroom. He was the worst kind of cad. Kissing her had not been the sensible thing to do, but then he had quite obviously lost anything even resembling common sense where Angel Grafton was concerned. He had only meant to give her a quick kiss on the lips, as chaste as possible, but she'd felt so good in his arms that he couldn't resist pulling her close, and then he'd been lost.

The kiss had turned more passionate than he intended, and his body still yearned for her. It amazed and frustrated him how a kiss alone affected him more than he could remember anyone ever having done before. He had forced himself to send her back inside before he reached for her again.

She was meant for another man, yet his body wanted nothing more than to keep kissing her until she forgot everything about Philip Chettisham. Nathaniel would not get between them. It was not his place since he had no intentions of courting Angel himself. She was too dangerous. Too easy to like.

Running a hand through his hair, he sighed and willed his body to calm down. He couldn't very well return to the house in his current state. That would certainly set some tongues wagging. He sat down on the stone bench where Angel had been sitting earlier and rested his face in his hands as he wondered how sinful it was to desire your friend's younger sister. Surely it was mentioned in the good book somewhere. *'Thou shall not covet your best friend's sister.'*

He needed a stiff drink.

This was why Gowthorpe found him sitting at White's the next day with a half-empty bottle of brandy on the table next to him. His friend raised his eyebrows but said nothing about it. Instead, he sat down in one of the comfortable leather chairs and motioned for a footman to bring him a glass.

"I'm not used to seeing you indulge like this so early in the day," Gowthorpe finally said, filling his glass with brandy.

"I usually don't." Nathaniel refilled his glass, not in the mood to discuss his inner turmoil. Especially not with Angel's brother.

His friend seemed to accept his unwillingness to talk and turned his attention to the other guests in the room. "Oh, have you heard? Leighton seduced Lady Amelia Warble. Adrian Warble is furious. I cannot blame him. I don't know what I would do if one of my friends seduced Angel." He took a sip from his glass. "I'd probably have to kill him."

Nathaniel groaned and emptied his glass in one swift motion.

Gowthorpe frowned at him. "What's the bloody matter with you, man?"

"I'm a bloody fool, that's what the matter is," he muttered. "Fools are allowed to drink themselves into oblivion."

"I don't pretend to know what's going on, but surely it cannot be that bad."

Nathaniel let out an inelegant snort. "Bad doesn't even begin to describe it."

What had he been thinking, kissing Angel like that? Now he couldn't get the memory of her lips against his out of his mind. The way her body had felt pressed against him. He wanted to kiss her again. He definitely could never kiss her again.

"It's not one of your sisters, is it?" Gowthorpe asked carefully. So carefully that Nathaniel almost laughed.

No, his sisters were all safe. It was his friend's sister who had attracted the attention of a bounder. He had turned into one of those men he so despised, the kind of man who would prey on the young, innocent ladies who needed a proper marriage. It may have been only a kiss, but his thoughts had been anything but honourable.

"Pensington?"

"No. It's not one of my sisters." If anything, his friend's concern only made him feel worse since he did not deserve it.

Gowthorpe shrugged, obviously willing to let it go since it was clear Nathaniel didn't wish to speak about it. "Shall we continue all day, then? You have a head start." He emptied his glass and grinned.

Nathaniel grimly lifted his own in a toast. From now on, he would stay away from Angel. He obviously could not be trusted near her.

Chapter Eleven

Dear Diary,
 I have made a decision and there
 is no going back. I can only pray
 my family will accept my decision.

"I do believe the marquess quite fancies me."

Angel ignored her cousin's chatter while she stared out the carriage window. They were on their way to a weekend party on the estate of Lord and Lady Kilkenny, which was only half a day's journey from London.

According to James, the party was a yearly tradition since Lady Kilkenny was desperate to marry her son off. They had tragically lost their eldest son a few months ago, and their younger son had been called home from the war to take his place as the heir to the Kilkenny title. Lady Kilkenny had always tried hard to marry off her sons, but apparently, she was trying even harder now that she only had one.

The entire Grafton and Brown family were joining for the weekend, but James had elected to ride a horse outside the carriage, leaving Angel inside with her aunt, uncle, and cousin. Marie and Aunt Christine sat opposite her, while Uncle George shared her seat. The man always smelled faintly of sour sweat, so she wasn't sure if she had the better deal or not. Marie, on the other hand, liked to 'accidentally' elbow her, so maybe the slight smell of sweat was better after all.

"Oh, I don't see how any man could not fancy you," Aunt Christine crooned with a proud smile.

"He is so handsome. We look very well together." Marie's gaze strayed across the carriage, and her lips twisted into a smirk. "Do you not think so, Angel?"

She forced a smile. "Very well, indeed."

As Marie continued chatting about Nathaniel and how well-suited they were, Angel stopped listening. Turning her head, she looked out over the landscape passing by outside the carriage. It had been nearly a week since the embarrassing evening when she'd lost her head and asked Nathaniel to kiss her.

Every time she remembered, she blushed from the mere memory, and she couldn't believe she'd had the audacity to ask such a thing of someone. Least of all Nathaniel Howerty, the Marquess of Pensington. The most handsome man she knew.

It had been a foolish thing to do. The kiss must not have affected him nearly as much as it had her because he had avoided her ever since. She worried she might have ruined their friendship by asking for that kiss. He had not shown up when she visited Jessica and had not accompanied his sister to the Grafton house or outings as he had before. The few times they had attended the same events, he had not once approached her to wish her a good evening. He had spent more time talking to Marie than her.

She could handle him avoiding her but in favour of Marie? That one stung.

She threw her cousin a glance. Did he fancy Marie? The thought made her feel sick. Her cousin had always been popular, and no one could deny that she was a beautiful, young woman. It had only been a matter of time before Nathaniel realised it too. But that thought did nothing to improve her mood. She sighed inwardly.

If nothing else, at least the kiss had proved one thing. She was not broken. She could enjoy kisses. It was the ultimate proof that she and Philip were a terrible match and should not get married. Now she only had to work up the courage to tell him so.

The opportunity might come this weekend at the Kilkenny's. She didn't look forward to it since she doubted he would take it well, but she refused to spend her life with someone she had no feelings for. It broke her heart that she would not fulfil her late parents' wish, but she liked to think they wouldn't have wanted her to marry a man she didn't love—didn't even like. They had loved her dearly, and surely they would have wanted her to be happy?

They arrived at the Kilkenny estate a couple of hours later and were greeted by Lady Kilkenny herself. A formidable woman of considerable height, with greying blond hair and green eyes, she showed the family to their rooms. They were all in the same corridor, and she explained that the Howertys were on the same floor as she knew the families were close. Entering her room, Angel was glad for some privacy and happy they had not made her share with her cousin. The room was small but well-kept and comfortable with a marvellous view of the front of the estate so she could watch everyone arriving while she sat with her diary in her lap.

In the early evening, everyone gathered on the extensive lawn at the back of the house for a garden party. Tables had been set up with a large buffet, and there were plenty of chairs and benches placed throughout the garden for the guests. Coloured lanterns created a cosy atmosphere. Further back from the house, a large hedgerow maze ruled a vast expanse of land. She wanted to explore it, but preferably in broad daylight.

She spent most of her time on James's arm and found it a pleasure to be with her brother. They shared jokes, and James gave her tidbits of gossip about the other guests. There were more unmarried women than men, which made sense considering the primary aim of the event.

The hostess herself walked around with her son in tow to ensure he met every single one of the unmarried ladies. Since Angel was not officially connected to Philip, she was one of the women Lady Kilkenny made sure her son greeted.

Gabriel Winter was a pleasant man with ruffled blond hair and green eyes who seemed to put up with his mother's matchmaking with remarkable patience. Now that she was determined to call things off with Philip, she figured that a man like Gabriel Winter was what she should look to for marriage. He was soft-spoken and nice-looking without being so handsome that women would trip over their feet to catch his attention.

Unlike Nathaniel.

She winced at the treacherous thought before throwing a quick look over her shoulder to see what the marquess was doing. As one would have expected, with so many single young ladies present, a fairly large number of giggling females surrounded him.

If Lady Kilkenny was serious about wanting to marry her son off, she should probably stop inviting men like Nathaniel, since most would choose the handsome marquess over the pleasant future earl any day. Even James had received a fair bit of attention. But she supposed her brother was a good-looking man, and while his title wasn't as high as Nathaniel's or the one Lord Winter would eventually have, a Viscount was nothing to scoff at.

"Are you having a good evening?" James asked, bringing her back from her thoughts.

"Very much so, thank you. This is a beautiful estate."

"Yes, the Kilkennys are a good family." He nodded. "Had you not been promised to Philip, I think I may have tried to match you with Winter."

"Even though you think him rather dull?" she teased, even while guilt niggled at her. She ought to tell him that she didn't want Philip, but fear of his reaction kept her quiet. What if James insisted she follow through on the agreement?

"I never said that!" James stared at her with wide eyes, bringing her back from her straying thoughts.

"You did. I heard you talk about him with your friends."

"Well..." He made a face. "Winter may not be the sharpest tool in the shed, but he's a pleasant fellow who would treat a wife well."

She laughed quietly and gave her brother's arm a reassuring pat. "Not to worry. I won't tell anyone you said so." Winking at him, she was amused to see James's bewildered look.

"I'm not used to you teasing me. I'm beginning to think I've not spent nearly enough time with you," he muttered. "It's a regret of mine that we never saw much of each other growing up."

She smiled wistfully. "Indeed, we didn't, and it would have been nice to have you around more. But you were in school and you had your own life. You were too young to take care of me by yourself." Her smile widened. "But you can spend more time with me now."

"I intend to." He returned her smile. "Before you are married and Philip whisks you away."

"Of course," she mumbled, unable to meet her brother's eyes. A familiar knot tightened in her stomach. He deserved to know that she would not fulfil their parents' wish, but how could she tell him?

They had spent their life with the understanding that she would honour this last thing their parents had wanted. And now she would no longer do it. The weight of disappointing not only James but the memory of their parents as well weighed on her shoulders.

But she had to tell him. The thought of a future with Philip made her feel like a hollow shell.

"James?" she said quietly, staring down at her feet, her heart pounding so loudly she was sure he could hear it. "What if... What if I don't want to marry Philip?"

Her brother stopped walking and turned to her. When she still refused to look at him, he put his finger under her chin and nudged her face up. His eyes searched hers and she wished she could tell what he was thinking. Was he angry? Disappointed? Waiting for him to respond was almost unbearable.

"Do you not want to, Angel?" The question was softer and less confrontational than she had expected. Had it been Aunt Christine, she would have been yelled at by now.

She shook her head, feeling as if she were standing on the edge of a cliff. "I don't. I wanted to honour our parents by following through, but James..." Her voice hitched, working around the lump in her throat. "No matter how much I try, I cannot bring myself to care for Philip. Not the way one should care for their spouse."

Now that she had started talking, she couldn't stop. The words poured out of her in a stream. "I'm so sorry to disappoint you. I know we both wanted to do what our parents wished. But, James, I just cannot... I cannot marry him."

James shook his head, a tender smile playing on his lips. "Angel," he said, stopping her word barrage. "It's absolutely fine. You don't need to keep justifying it to me. If you don't want to marry Philip, I would never ask you to."

"You... You wouldn't?" She blinked, struggling to process his reaction. It was so different to what she had expected. She was so used to her family ignoring her feelings and asking her to do what they wanted, that she hadn't even considered the possibility of her brother simply accepting her decision. A wave of relief washed over her, so powerful it made her knees weak.

"Of course not." James smiled wryly. "I only went along with this arrangement because you seemed to not mind. You know, this is the first time you've voiced your feelings about it?"

"I... I'm sorry." She didn't have to marry Philip. As the realisation hit her, joy bubbled up, threatening to overflow. "I was so worried you wouldn't understand."

He smiled down at her and squeezed her shoulder. "I know I haven't always been around, but please know that all I ever want is for you to be happy."

There was a suspicious burning feeling behind her eyes, and she blinked quickly to remove it. "Thank you, James."

"No need to thank me."

He offered her his arm again, and they continued walking. She felt lighter somehow, like a weight had fallen from her shoulders, each step a taking her closer to a future of her own choosing.

"Do you need me to tell Chettisham?" James asked while he nodded his greetings to a passerby.

"Thank you, but no. I feel it's only fair that I tell him myself." She owed him that much, at least. They might not really like each other, but he had spent most of his life in the belief they would marry just like she had, and she could at least do him the honour of letting him down gently. The thought of that conversation filled her with dread, but also a strange sense of anticipation. It would be the final step in taking control of her life. Of freedom from the expectation to marry a man she would never love.

"If that's what you want. If you change your mind, do let me know. I have no issues telling him to bugger off."

Her eyes widened and she stared at her brother, scandalised but secretly amused. "James! Language."

He chuckled. "Sorry, but I'm actually quite relieved you don't want to marry him."

"Really? You never said." She glanced at her brother who smiled down at her.

"Like you, I think I was just going along with what everyone expected of us, but I have no fondness for Chettisham."

To think she had worried so much about telling James when he was so understanding. No matter what, her brother was in her corner, and it felt amazing. Warmth spread inside her, a sense of security she hadn't felt in years. Now she just needed to find the courage to tell Philip.

The chance came sooner than she would have wished when Philip came up to them and asked if James would allow him to take her for a stroll around the garden. Her brother graciously agreed and with a look at her that seemed to say 'good luck', he went in search of his friends.

Looking down at her, Philip noticed her flattering white silk dress. "You look nice tonight," he commented as he offered her his arm.

"Thank you." She placed her hand at his elbow and followed when he walked between the other guests gathered on the lawn. Steeling herself, she forced the words out before she could lose her nerve. "Philip, I would like to speak with you in private."

He smiled. "I wish to see you in private as well."

As he walked them towards the large hedgerow maze, she had the distinct feeling they were not thinking the same thing. Before she could object, he had pulled her behind the first hedgerow, blocking them from view. When he bent his head to kiss her, she quickly sidestepped. His brow furrowed.

"What's wrong?" Irritation laced his voice. "You said you wanted to go somewhere private."

"Yes. To speak."

"We can talk later." He reached for her and she backed away again.

"No. I want to speak now."

He narrowed his eyes and crossed his arms. "So speak."

Thinking about breaking things off with him was much easier than actually doing it. She stared up into his forbidding face, and her throat closed up, rendering her unable to speak. This was the man that should have become her husband.

"Well?" His impatience didn't help her nerves.

"I don't wish to marry you!" The words burst out before she could stop herself.

Ominous silence spread between them, making her fidget. It had not been the best way to tell him. She probably should have tried to ease into it, but his presence made her nerves knot into a hard ball in the pit of her stomach, and she just... blurted it all out. Why wasn't he responding? She yelped when his hands shot out and grabbed her arms, pulling her close so he could stare into her face. His blue eyes flashed with anger, making her regret not telling him in plain view of the other guests.

"You can't break it off with me," he hissed angrily.

"But I am," she whispered. Her throat was dry, and her pulse raced, but she had to finish this. She could not marry this man. "I don't love you and I don't want to marry you. And in all honesty, I doubt you want to marry me."

"You were promised to me!" He pushed her away, and she stumbled back. "You can't do this to me."

"I'm sorry, Philip." She hugged her arms around herself as if it could somehow protect her from his ire. "But we both deserve better. We don't love each other, and I hope for more than that in a marriage. You should too."

He glared at her. "No one will ever love you. You're made of ice."

That stung. She had never been one for emotional displays, and sometimes she wondered if something was wrong with her. But no, she was not made of ice. Nathaniel's kiss had proved that much. Even if he had avoided her since. It seemed neither he nor Philip enjoyed kissing her. Still, she would rather spend her life alone than with Philip.

"Leave me alone," she said coldly. If he thought her made of ice, then she would act like it.

His eyes widened and his nostrils looked white and stiff as he stared at her, his mouth a thin line. For a brief moment, she feared he might strike her. "You will never be rid of me, Angel," he vowed. "You will be my wife. Just wait and see."

Turning on his heel, he left her alone in the maze. She let out a breath when the tension left her body. The man made no sense. Why did he still want to marry her? He obviously didn't like her and was surely not lacking in other prospects. It was a mystery, but not one she had the energy to deal with at that moment.

The brief encounter with Philip had left her feeling drained and not up to rejoining the party just yet, so she walked further into the maze. Lanterns along the hedges gave enough light to move around without too much trouble, and the reassuring sounds of others talking on the other side of the hedges kept her ambling along the pathways. Every few turns there were marble benches, and after a while, she chose one close to what she calculated to be the middle of the maze and sat down.

She was so deep in thought that she didn't realise she had company until a man suddenly sat down next to her and put his arm around her shoulders.

"Hello, luv," he said, leaning closer and treating her to a nice dose of alcoholic fumes.

"Good evening," she mumbled and tried to scoot further away. He was sitting much too close and most definitely should not take the liberty of putting his arm around her shoulders. It was highly inappropriate.

She remembered seeing him at a few balls before, but could not remember his name. From what she remembered, he was a nice enough man, but he had clearly imbibed too much, and some men could become unreliable when drunk.

"What's such a lovely young lady doing out here by herself?" he asked with a crooked smile. He leaned a little closer with a conspiratorial grin, swaying unsteadily in his seat. "Are you waiting for your lover?"

"Certainly not." She wasn't sure whether to be alarmed or amused. The man was obviously inebriated but seemed relatively innocent. "Could you please remove your arm?"

"Oh please, just a kiss before you leave, fair maiden." He hiccoughed before puckering his lips.

She stared at him. Surely he must be jesting.

"Just a tiny kiss. Save me from the evil dragon." He pulled back for a moment, consternation crossing his face. "No, wait. I save you from the dragon."

How much had this man been drinking? She tried to pull away again. "I beg your pardon, Sir. But I really must be going."

Getting out from under his arm, she stood to leave. He followed suit, probably a bit too quickly, as he oscillated on the heels of his shoes.

"Don't leave yet, fair maiden!" he complained and reached for her, but the movement was too much for his compromised balance, and with a groan, he stumbled forward. In a futile attempt to stay upright, he grabbed hold of her shoulders, and with a distressed yelp, she fell, landing heavily on the ground with the man on top of her.

"Get off me," she muttered, trying to shove him off, but he was too heavy for her to budge.

He moved his head to sniff at her neck. "You smell good," he mumbled drunkenly. "The dragon must not have gobbled you up yet."

"Sir," she tried again. "You must get off me."

"Oh, but we're in a perfect position for a kiss!" the man exclaimed happily. He glanced around, then leaned closer, whispering loudly, "As long as we're safe from the dragon?"

"I don't want to kiss!"

This was getting bothersome. The man seemed fairly harmless, even if too amorous for her comfort, and it frustrated her she could not get off the ground. Couldn't the lout stand up?

Just as she was about to remind him to do just that, he was lifted off her and tossed to the side.

Her stunned gaze met Nathaniel's, and before she could say anything, he pulled her to her feet. After a glance to make sure she didn't look any worse for wear, he strode over to the man who sat on the ground a few feet away, rubbing his head.

"Get out of here," Nathaniel growled.

The man's eyes widened. "Dragon!" He winced and rubbed his head again. "We were having such an enjoyable time. It's rather rude to interrupt."

Nathaniel reached down and pulled the man up by his coat lapels to stare him straight in the face. "The lady is spoken for. So you better get your arse out of here before I have my foot assist you."

The man blanched and nodded. "Of course. Naturally. Didn't realise she was attached to you, Pensington."

Before anyone could correct him, the man scampered off and disappeared around a corner. Angel breathed a sigh of relief. Walking up to Nathaniel to thank him for his help, she stopped dead in her tracks when he pivoted to stare at her with dark, flashing eyes.

"What the hell do you think you're doing?"

Chapter Twelve

Dear Diary,
　Men can be so daft.

Angel stared at Nathaniel. How could he possibly be angry with her? He was an impressive sight when in a high temper, with his hair on end from having raked his hand through it one time too many, and his dark eyes glittering.

"Pardon?" She frowned up at him, not sure what this was about. It surprised her she wasn't more worried in the face of his displeasure. She had always tiptoed around Philip, always making sure she didn't anger him, but with Nathaniel, she felt safe. Even when he glared at her.

"What are you doing walking around a hedgerow maze at night without an escort?"

"I wanted a moment alone."

"Well, you managed really well with that," he remarked sarcastically.

Crossing her arms, she glared back at him. She was getting mightily fed up with people telling her what she could and could not do. "You have no right to be angry with me."

He dragged his hand through his hair, but his eyes didn't leave hers. "I am not angry with you," he drawled, though his tone certainly suggested otherwise. "When I saw Chettisham return without you, I got worried. I thought he'd abandoned you again and that you couldn't find your way out."

"I know exactly where I am." There was no need for him to come to her rescue. Even if it was sort of sweet. He had seen her leave with Philip? It warmed her to think he noticed.

"I didn't know that," he muttered. "But if you know your way out, you should have left the maze the moment he left you alone. It's not safe for a young lady to walk around alone at night."

"There was no danger."

"I beg your pardon? Was there not a man lying on top of you just a moment ago?"

They stared at each other for a moment. The corners of her mouth twitched, and then a giggle burst forth. Nathaniel's anger seemed to vaporise as he reluctantly smiled.

"I'm sorry," she said when she finally sobered up. "I just wasn't ready to rejoin the party, but you're right that I probably shouldn't have been alone out here."

Running a hand through his already mussed-up hair, he shifted from one foot to the other. "I'm sorry for yelling at you. Seeing that man on top of you…"

She smiled wryly. "He was fairly harmless. Just incredibly drunk."

He gave her a dark look. "Even harmless-looking men can cause problems."

"Of course. I didn't mean—"

"What was he doing on top of you, anyway?" he interrupted with a frown. "You seem very calm about it."

"He tripped and fell. Then he didn't want to get up."

"Bastard," Nathaniel muttered, then ushered her towards the exit of the maze.

They walked a few turns, Angel a few steps in front of him, before she blurted out, "I'm not spoken for anymore."

"What do you mean?"

She stopped and turned around to look at him, nearly causing a collision since he was closer than she'd realised.

"You told that man that I'm spoken for." She took a step back and craned her neck so she could meet his eyes. "But I'm not anymore."

A line appeared between his brows. "I don't understand."

"I called everything off with Philip."

There was a moment's silence while he considered her words, and then he quietly asked, "Why?"

"I... I don't love him. Never will." She tried to put her feelings into sentences but wasn't sure she was successful. "And I don't think he would treat me well."

"He wasn't treating you well now," Nathaniel remarked pointedly. "You can make a much better match."

"Can I? Every man I kiss wants nothing more to do with me." That was blatantly untrue. She was being dramatic. Philip may have said she was made of ice, but he obviously wasn't ready to let her go.

Nathaniel quirked an eyebrow. "Every man?"

"I know I haven't kissed scores," she muttered, her cheeks heating. "But Philip always said I was cold and unfeeling, and after you kissed me, I've barely seen you."

His eyes on hers were dark and impossible to read. He sighed. "I know I've avoided you since..." He cleared his throat. "Since our last meeting. It has nothing to do with the kiss."

"Really?" Even she could hear the scepticism dripping off the one word. "The timing does seem awfully suspicious."

He closed his eyes for a moment, and she wondered what he was thinking. Was he trying to come up with an excuse? Reliving the awful kiss they had shared? Well, not awful for her. The memory of his lips against hers made tiny butterfly wings flutter to life in her stomach.

"Angel, I—"

"You don't need to make excuses." She didn't want or need to hear his apology. "You didn't enjoy kissing me. Let us not make a big thing out of it. What hurts the most is that you've given more attention to Marie than me. I did not think you got along with her that well, but she seems quite taken with you, and..."

The corners of his mouth twitched, making her stop her blathering. She always said too much when nervous. Too much or nothing at all.

"Angel," he said softly. "Did it never occur to you that your cousin seeks me out, not the other way around? I am a gentleman, and I will be polite, but that's the extent of our conversations."

"I... Oh." Her cheeks burned when she realised how irrationally jealous she had been for no reason.

"And also..." He tucked his finger under her chin and raised her face to meet his gaze. The fluttering in her abdomen intensified and her skin tingled from the simple touch. "I enjoyed kissing you. Very much so. Too much."

She wanted to say something—anything—but no words could make it past the dryness of her throat. When his hand dropped and he took an almost imperceptible step away from her, disappointment stabbed her.

"Which is why," he continued. "I can never do so again."

Any sign of the fluttering of wings instantly stopped. She shouldn't be surprised. Kissing before marriage was highly improper, and Nathaniel would never risk her reputation. However, that didn't keep her body from wanting nothing more than to kiss him again. Foolish, treacherous body.

He smiled wryly. "You're the sister of one of my best friends. Even if I had been in the habit of kissing innocents—which I am not—I could never do that to him. Now that you're free of Chettisham, you should find a nice man to marry."

"Of course." She nodded jerkily. He might as well have said he had no interest in her beyond kissing. No desire to court her. Or her being his friend's sister would have mattered little. "I had better return to the others before someone misses me."

She turned around and walked away before he could see the moisture gathering in her eyes. The only man she wanted was the one standing behind her.

The next day, the guests split up into groups depending on who wanted to do which activity. Some men disappeared to do some hunting, while most women took a trip to a nearby village. Angel's family, the Howertys, and a few other guests stayed behind on the estate for a picnic on the grass by a small pond.

It was a pleasant afternoon, and they had spread out large blankets on the ground where people sat in small groups and chatted while eating some cold fare that the kitchen staff had prepared and sent out in wicker baskets.

Angel sat with her brother, Nathaniel, Jessica, Mrs Grey, and the Earl of Wortham, while her aunt, uncle, and Marie sat with another family a short distance away. Every so often, she caught her cousin glaring at them, supposedly because Angel was lucky enough to sit with the handsome marquess and earl, while Marie was stuck with the dull Lyttletons.

"I say," Wortham said. "Isn't that Chettisham over there, flirting with young Ellie Featherstone?"

Jessica put down her book of poetry and had a quick look. "I do believe it is."

"What a bounder," the earl scoffed. "It's insulting to Miss Grafton. Maybe you ought to go over there and speak to him, Gowthorpe."

Having been watching Philip and the pretty, dark-haired Ellie Featherstone, Angel's cheeks heated. "Oh, no, that won't be necessary."

"Why not?" Jessica asked. "He's been telling everyone that you're practically his betrothed, and then he goes off to court some other woman? It reflects badly on you."

"I... I called everything off yesterday."

"Finally!" Jessica grinned. "I'm so pleased for you. What made you change your mind?"

Sensing everyone in the group watching her, waiting for her answer, Angel fidgeted. "I realised he wouldn't make me happy."

"Well, may I say that it was probably for the best," Wortham said. "You're too good for Chettisham, Miss Grafton."

She looked down at her hands in her lap, her cheeks burning from the compliment. The earl was a good-looking man, and she wasn't used to receiving attention. It didn't escape her notice that Nathaniel had remained quiet throughout the exchange. Sitting on the opposite side of the picnic blanket, he looked very interested in the piece of cheese he was eating.

Closing her book and standing up, Jessica smiled down at Angel. "Come," she said. "Walk with me."

Angel stood, and they linked arms while they walked along the edge of the small pond. Now and then, Jessica glanced over at Philip and Miss Featherstone.

"I think he's trying to make you jealous," she said as soon as they were out of earshot of their families.

"What makes you think that?"

"You broke things off yesterday, and today he is courting another woman in plain sight? It's obvious he wants you to notice. Are you jealous?"

"Not in the least. But it does feel a little odd. Everyone thinks he's my future husband. Have you not noticed their pitying looks?"

"I did, but I think you are better off without him. Let them pity you if they wish. Now we can focus on finding you a decent husband. I can think of a few suitable ones already."

"Match-making now, are you?" Angel smiled at her friend.

"I've never tried before, but it could prove entertaining. I'm sure I could do a better job than most. Some people just need to be saved from themselves."

"Shouldn't you match yourself first?"

"Heaven forbid!" Jessica said in mock horror.

"Don't you want to get married?" She realised she had never asked. Her friend always made a show of disliking the season, the balls, and the attention of eligible bachelors. But she had never figured out if it was entirely genuine or something she did to amuse herself.

Jessica shrugged. "I don't know. It's supposed to be every woman's dream, but I just can't imagine myself being someone else's wife."

"How come?"

They continued their walk around the lawn while Jessica pondered the question. She glanced back at the blanket where their families sat before shrugging again. "I just never felt inclined," she said. "I'm sure one day I will have to find a husband. My aunt will not allow me to become a spinster if it can be avoided. She is convinced we all must find true love and live our happily ever afters." She scoffed. "As if it were that easy."

There was more to this story. Angel was sure of it. But she would not pressure her friend if she didn't want to divulge anything further. Jessica would tell her when she was ready. Instead, she smiled and teasingly said, "You sure don't lack suitors to choose from."

Jessica made a face. "They're just not who I want. I mean, what I want." Clearly ready to change the subject, she squeezed Angel's arm. "What about you? Any of the gentlemen tickle your fancy?"

The question immediately brought back memories of the kiss she'd shared with Nathaniel, and her cheeks heated. She couldn't very well admit her thoughts were all so occupied with her friend's brother that she'd had no time to consider any other men. Did she even want to consider any other men?

She nearly tripped on a piece of uneven ground, but Jessica steadied her. That was a disturbing thought. Nathaniel was the last person she should set her sights on, but her body and emotions didn't care. No other man could ever live up to the marquess. Ever since that fateful morning when she first found him sleeping in her bed, she could not stop thinking about him. Dreaming about him.

There was no other man like Nathaniel Howerty. At least not to her. He was intelligent and kind, and he made her laugh with his droll humour. His mere presence made her entire body tingle from wanting to be near him. And he had a wonderful family. The kind of family she had always dreamed of. Not perfect, but loving and accepting.

Unfortunately, practically every unmarried woman in London knew he was a catch, and he was one of the most sought-after bachelors. She didn't stand a chance. He could have his pick, and she was not exactly a diamond of the first water.

As they neared the blanket where their families chatted amicably, she felt a stab of panic. How could she interact with Nathaniel without him realising how she felt about him? She blushed the moment he laid eyes on her. The last thing she wanted was for him to pity her.

When they reached the others, she quickly excused herself, claiming a headache, and left them before anyone could object. Cursing herself for acting foolish, she walked back towards the large manor house, wanting some time alone to think. To sort out her twisted and knotted feelings. She was following a pebbled path around the house when someone caught up with her. Turning around, she suppressed a groan when she saw Philip looking at her with a triumphant smile.

"It got to you, didn't it?" he gloated.

"What did?" she asked impatiently, crossing her arms. All she wanted was to be left alone.

He scowled. "Me courting another woman."

"Oh." She'd forgotten about that. Trying to sound sincere, she put a hand on his arm. "You can court whoever you please, Philip. I have no claims on you, and I hope you will find someone who makes you happy."

"You're lying!" He grabbed her upper arms like he wanted to shake her. "It did bother you!"

"It didn't." She tried to wrench free, but his grip was too tight. "Let me go!"

He bent his head to kiss her as if that would somehow prove his point, but she turned her head to the side and his lips touched her cheek instead.

"You're mine," he hissed close to her ear, making her shudder. Then he abruptly let go of her and disappeared.

Wanting to get away in case he came back, she hurried inside to her room. Philip's reaction to her cancelling their union seemed disproportionate to his lack of feelings for her. There was no reason for him to be so intent on marrying her when there were so many other single ladies available. Many of them prettier and with larger dowries. He might be used to getting what he wanted, but there was no reason for him to want her.

The whole situation was giving her a headache for real, so she decided to rest for a few hours before dinner. By now, she just wanted the weekend party to be over so she could return to London, but they weren't leaving until the next day. Maybe she would be lucky and not see Philip, or Nathaniel, any more that weekend.

Luck was not on her side. At dinner, she found herself seated between Philip and Nathaniel. It was miserable. Custom demanded that she spend equal amounts of time speaking to both of her seating partners and she wasn't sure who she wanted to speak to the least. No, that wasn't true. Speaking with Nathaniel was always a pleasure. She just wasn't sure if she knew how to anymore. What if he could tell how she felt about him? What if she blurted it out like the ninny she was?

"How is your head?" Nathaniel asked conversationally.

"Oh, much better. Thank you." Maybe she could do this. "Did I miss anything?"

"Not much. Aunt Jane berating Jessica for avoiding her beaus. Wortham annoying everyone. In other words, the usual."

"I like Lord Wortham," she admitted with a smile. The earl might enjoy ribbing people, but he was a charming man with a lot of wit.

"I'm not surprised," Nathaniel replied dryly. "Most women do."

Relieved to find that she could still carry on a conversation with Nathaniel, she steeled herself to deal with her other seating companion. If only she could have ignored Philip, but that would be terribly rude. She plastered a fake smile on her face and turned around.

"I hope you have no designs on Pensington," Philip said rudely, but quiet enough not to be overheard. "He would never look at someone like you."

"I can assure you that I have no such aspirations," she replied stiffly, her smile fading. "He is the brother of a dear friend, and that is all. Not that it concerns you."

"Everything regarding you concerns me."

"Not anymore."

His eyes flashed with anger, but he quickly tamped it down. Taking a few morsels from his plate, he ate in silence for a few blissful moments.

"I don't think you understand," he eventually drawled. "You were promised to me, and I have every intention of marrying you."

"You are being unreasonable," she whispered, not wanting anyone else to hear. "I do not wish to marry you and I will not."

"We'll see," he said calmly before proceeding to ignore her throughout the rest of the meal.

Feeling miserable, she excused herself from that evening's entertainment to stay in her room. She didn't venture outside for the remainder of their stay, despite Jessica's attempts otherwise.

Chapter Thirteen

Dear Diary,
Sometimes Aunt Christine reminds me
of a dog with a bone. Once she's dug
her teeth into something, she just won't let go!

Angel pressed her fingertips against her temples and massaged gently, hoping to relieve the headache she'd had for the past few days.

It didn't help that her aunt was pacing the room, lecturing her on how foolish she was. James had broken the news to the other family members of her decision not to marry Philip once they all returned from the Kilkenny estate, and to say her aunt was not taking it well was quite the understatement. While

James had no compunction about calling off the agreement, her aunt acted like Angel had committed a cardinal sin.

"What would your poor parents say?" Aunt Christine questioned—not for the first time—as she strode from one side of Angel's room to the other. "Disappointment! Disrespect! To go against their wishes when they are not here to tell you otherwise. And you certainly cannot hope to do any better!"

Staring at her reflection in the mirror, Angel rolled her eyes while Agnes finished her hair for the evening's ball. The maid gave her an encouraging smile, which made her feel a little better. Her hair had been pulled back in a topknot with a few loose curls to frame her face, and she wore a creamy white dress with a pink silk ribbon tied at the high waistline. It was a simple getup, but she rather liked it.

"Mr Chettisham is a prime catch. Set to inherit a nice estate from his father. You should count yourself lucky that your parents arranged this for you." Aunt Christine would not stop, and by now Angel doubted she ever would. It had been like this for two days. "It is not like you could have caught the attention of such a handsome man by yourself."

Why was her family so convinced that she could not find a decent man to marry her? He didn't even have to be handsome, as long as he was a good man. Surely there must be some of those around, and she could not be so distasteful that not a single one would have her. Right?

Grimacing at her reflection, she tried not to let her aunt's words get to her. But they were only a variation of what she had heard her whole life and were like tiny barbs pricking her skin repeatedly until she bled.

"I can only hope that Mr Chettisham will take you back once you realise how foolish you are." Aunt Christine finally stopped pacing and talking to catch her breath, allowing Angel to turn around on the low stool to look at her.

"Aunt," she said slowly, done with people telling her how to live her life. "I will not change my mind about this."

The older woman stared at her, obviously not used to being contradicted. "Of course, you will," she blurted out.

"No. My mind is set. I feel no affection for Philip, and I do not believe I ever will. I wish to marry a man who I will at least think somewhat fondly of."

"What would your parents say?" Aunt Christine snapped angrily. "You would break their hearts! They always hoped to join their family with the Chettishams."

Trying not to take the words to heart, Angel stood and squared her shoulders. "I am sure my parents would understand." She was glad her voice did not waver. "My parents loved me, and I am certain they would not have wanted me to marry a man I do not even like."

Her aunt's face took on a rather nasty shade of purple. "I don't know what's come over you," she spat. "You are so difficult to deal with lately. I hope you remember it's your parents' last wish you are denying."

Turning on her heel, she stormed out of the room, nearly colliding with Marie, who stood outside with her hand outstretched to reach the handle. Marie stared after her mother for a moment and then entered the room, giving Angel a shrewd glance.

"What was that all about?"

"Your mother and I did not agree on something," Angel muttered before nodding towards the maid. "Thank you, Anges. I think I'm done for the evening."

"Yes, miss." Agnes curtsied and quickly left.

"Was it about Mr Chettisham again?" Marie walked over to a small table where Angel kept a few porcelain figurines. Picking them up one at a time, she inspected them and then put them down again, in a different order.

"Yes. It's always about him lately."

"Well," Marie said with a nonchalant shrug of her shoulders. "It was rather foolish of you to call it off."

"I do not believe it was." Walking over to her cousin, Angel moved the porcelain figurines back into their original positions.

"You're hoping to snare Lord Pensington now, aren't you?"

Angel's hand froze on the head of a small shepherdess. Turning to Marie, she shivered at the look of pure malice that met her. "No," she said slowly. "I am well aware that I do not stand a chance with the marquess."

"Good," Marie snapped. "Because he's going to be mine, and I won't let you steal anything else that's mine."

"Anything else?" What was she on about? Angel moved backwards when Marie took a step towards her. "I've never taken anything from you, Marie."

The other woman sneered. "No? You stole my parents! You lost yours and selfishly took mine. They used to only have eyes for me, and suddenly we were taking care of you."

Angel took another couple of steps backwards as Marie advanced on her, worried that this conversation was quickly getting out of hand. "I was a child," she said. "There was no one else to take care of me and James. And you came to live at Hefferton Place with us."

"Of course, you throw that in my face!" Marie pushed her backwards, making her stumble. "How you belong at a fancy estate like Hefferton Place while my family comes from a small house in the Midlands."

"I... That was not my intention." Angel shook her head, frantically trying to understand what was happening. She'd known Marie was jealous of her, but not to this degree. To actually blame her for stealing her parents. It was almost laughable. Mr and Mrs Brown had taken care of her but had hardly given her any of the love and attention they lavished on their daughter.

"Of course not. Perfect Angel that does nothing wrong," Marie said sarcastically. "Perfect Angel that gets everything she wants."

Angel could do little but stare. Were they speaking about the same world? Her experiences were so different to her cousin's, it didn't seem real.

The vitriol in Marie's eyes made her take another step backwards, and she whelped when her foot caught on something and she lost her footing. Falling backwards, she hit the floor with a dull thud. Looking down, she saw the pair of shoes she'd tripped on. She'd fallen into the small dressing room attached to her room, where Agnes kept her clothes and accessories on shelves in neat boxes. Probably another source of contention for Marie, since her room did not come with one.

"Enjoy your evening." Marie's words made Angel whip her head up to see her cousin's smirk before the door slammed closed.

The silent 'click' of the lock sliding into place sent an icy shiver of fear down her spine. Unlike her dressing room at Hefferton Place, this one was smaller and did not have any windows, leaving her in darkness. The only light was a thin sliver from the small gap under the door. Tiny tendrils of panic nibbled at the edges of her consciousness.

"Marie?" she called out, hoping her cousin was only playing a cruel joke, but no reply came. She drew a quick breath as the tendrils pushed deeper inside. "Marie! Let me out!"

The walls closed in on her, and she took another quick gulp of breath but didn't couldn't get enough air in her lungs. Panic spread through her every fibre and she crawled over to the door, trying desperately to keep the terror of being in an enclosed space at bay. She pounded on the door, but it wouldn't budge.

"Marie!" The shrill desperation in her voice made her pound the door even harder as the darkness encroached on her mind.

Not this. Please, not this.

Nathaniel moved through the crowded ballroom towards his sister. Jessica was under siege by a group of young fops, all vying for her attention. No one had quite anticipated how much of a success she would be this season, except possibly Aunt Jane, who would look just a little smug every time they discussed it. He supposed he should have foreseen it, seeing as she was the daughter and sister of a marquess, beautiful, and with a decent dowry. To think he had to look forward to this two more times... He groaned inwardly.

"Nathaniel." Jessica smiled when he pushed his way past her bevy of suitors. "What brings you to my side?"

"I thought perhaps you would like to take a walk about the room with me."

The group of men surrounding them glared daggers at him for disturbing their time with his sister. He didn't particularly care, and from the relieved look on Jessica's face, neither did she. She looped her hand around his arm.

"Always, Brother." She smiled at her suitors. "Please excuse me, gentlemen. The marquess requires my presence."

A murmur of polite agreement followed them when he turned to walk the edges of the ballroom with Jessica next to him. He considered how to phrase the question he wanted to pose to her. The question he shouldn't even be asking.

After kissing Angel, he had done his best to stay away from her, and he'd managed rather well. It was all he could do since he didn't trust himself around her. One taste of her lips, and it was all he could think about. No other woman had occupied his thoughts like this. He didn't like it.

Since returning from the Kilkenny weekend party, he had not even had to put any effort into avoiding her. He had made it clear he was not looking for a wife, and now Angel seemed determined to stay away from him. Which should make him happy, since it made his life easier. But it was doing the opposite. At every social function, he found himself searching the crowd for her face, and once he found her, he spent the remainder of the evening fighting the urge to bring her somewhere secluded to kiss her until she could think of no other man. It was a fool's game, but one he could not stop playing.

Angel Grafton was not for him. She was too dangerous. His reaction to that kiss made that clear. And yet here he was, keeping his sister from her suitors because he could not stop scanning the room for a certain young lady.

"Have you seen Angel?" he asked.

"You want to know if I've seen my friend?"

"Have you?"

"No." She lifted a shoulder in a shrug. "I spoke briefly to Gowthorpe earlier, and he mentioned she begged off with a headache." Her eyes narrowed. "Why are you asking?"

"I merely wondered." He was rather proud of how disinterested he sounded, though he wasn't sure his sister believed him. "I saw her family arrive and noticed she wasn't with them."

Jessica opened her mouth to say something, so he quickly bowed and left her before she got the chance. He had a feeling he didn't care to hear whatever it was she wanted to tell him. Wanting a moment of privacy, he stepped out onto the terrace and into the garden. He stopped by a small fountain and stared up at the night sky above. What was he doing? He should stay as far away from Angel as possible. But she was a fever in his blood ever since that kiss, and he wanted—no, craved—more.

"Lord Pensington?" a soft voice queried behind him.

He whipped around to find Marie Brown standing a little too close for comfort. Lately, she kept seeking him out, and he knew she had her sight set on making a good match this season. He had no intention of being that match.

"Miss Brown," he said with a quick bow. "I hope you are well."

"I was hoping to speak with you, my lord." A crease marred her otherwise perfectly smooth brow while she looked from side to side. "It's about Angel."

He frowned, a tingle at the back of his neck telling him to watch out. They were alone in the garden with no chaperone. But the possibility of hearing news of Angel kept him where he was.

"What about Miss Grafton?" he said, taking a careful step away from Marie.

She glanced towards the house before giving him a hesitant smile. "Are you enjoying the evening? The weather has been lovely lately, hasn't it?"

"It's pleasant enough. What did you wish to tell me about Miss Grafton?" he asked impatiently.

"I'm concerned about her," she said, casting another glance to the side. "Something must be wrong for her to call everything off with a man like Mr Chettisham."

He rather disagreed on that one. Getting rid of Chettisham might be the best decision Angel had ever made. With a frustrated sigh, he ran a hand through his hair. "I do not know why you are telling me about this, Miss Brown."

"Oh, I thought you were friends, and..." She looked away again and then, before he had a chance to react, she threw herself at him, slid her arms around his neck, and pressed her mouth against his. Shocked, he put his hands on her waist to push her away just as he heard a gasp from somewhere a few feet to their side.

"Get your hands off my daughter!"

Wrenching free, he took two steps away from Marie. The little brat looked at him with a triumphant glow in her eyes before turning to her mother.

Running into her arms, she wailed. "Oh, Maman! He just started kissing me. I didn't know what to do!"

Mrs Brown stared at him, and he glared back, daring her to speak. "Is this true?" she finally choked out.

"No." Reining in his temper, he kept his voice even. "Your daughter threw herself at me."

"Well, I never...!" Mrs Brown sputtered.

"He's lying, Maman!"

The older woman looked from her daughter to Nathaniel, obviously uncertain about what to do. One did not easily accuse a marquess of lying. "How am I to know that my daughter is not ruined?" she finally asked irritably.

"You have my word of honour." His patience for this situation was quickly waning. He had little tolerance for scheming chits.

"What if word gets out that you kissed her?" she insisted, either unaware of his rising temper or deciding the potential win was worth the risk.

"I did not kiss your daughter!" he snapped, finally losing the tenuous grip he had on his irritation. "She came here with the intention of you finding us. The moment she saw you approach, she attacked me. You should count yourself lucky I didn't throw her in the fountain."

"But what if word gets out?" She was tenacious. He had to give her that. "It would ruin my daughter."

He crossed his arms over his chest. "The only ones who know of this incident are the three of us, and I certainly won't tell anyone. I would assume that you feel the same way since it's your daughter's reputation on the line."

Mrs Brown nodded jerkily. "Yes."

"But if people find out, you will have to marry me!" Marie piped up but went silent when he levelled her with a disdainful look.

"Trust me, young lady," he said coldly, not appreciating having been set up. "If I hear any rumours about myself making any advances towards you, I will confirm them. Then refuse to marry you. That would ensure that no other proposals would be forthcoming. At least none that I think you would consider."

Marie blushed furiously, but Mrs Brown appeared to understand his meaning and quickly ushered her daughter back into the house. Nathaniel stayed where he was, still seething from the incident. The conniving woman had tried to trick him into marriage! He exhaled slowly, trying to get his temper under control. The mere thought of her audacity made him want to go back inside and tell her exactly what he thought of her plan.

"Enjoying some solitude in the garden?" Wortham came down the few steps from the small terrace, a smirk on his lips. "Or are you waiting for someone?"

"Not quite. I'm restraining my urge to wring someone's neck."

"Oh? Who's the lucky person?" his friend asked with mild interest while he withdrew a cheroot from his pocket and lit it.

"Miss Marie Brown."

"And what has she done to deserve this honour?"

"She tried to trick me into marriage."

"Well, I'll be damned!" Wortham laughed. "I'm impressed. The chit has guts."

Nathaniel grunted. "Did you want something?"

The earl sat down on the side of the fountain, taking a puff from his cheroot. "I thought maybe you'd gone outside with some ravishing beauty and would like to share her." He grinned.

"You're despicable."

"Thank you. I do try."

"Why did you come out here? Really."

"I heard something odd in the ballroom." Wortham took another puff of his cigar.

"Yes?"

"Our very own Miss Brown said something to her mother, which I overheard. Her mother asked about Miss Grafton, and Miss Brown said she had made sure she wouldn't show up tonight."

Nathaniel frowned. That comment, combined with Marie's attempt to trap him in a scandalous situation, did not sit well with him.

"Where is Gowthorpe?"

Wortham chuckled. "Without his sister in attendance, he felt quite happy leaving with a buxom lady a short while ago. Are you going over to Gowthorpe House to check up on Miss Grafton?"

Nathaniel shifted from one foot to the other. He shouldn't. But something about this whole thing left a sour taste in his mouth.

"I can't leave Jessica and Aunt Jane here. They would have no way of getting home if I am not back in time."

"I can bring them home in my carriage," Wortham offered, being uncommonly helpful.

"Thank you. Most likely, I will make a big fool out of myself, finding her sitting peacefully reading a book." He walked away, then stopped and turned around to look at his friend. "Why did you tell me this?"

"Because I knew you'd make an arse of yourself and wanted to see it."

"What do you mean?"

Wortham raised a dark eyebrow, his blue eyes mocking. "You know what I mean. Now go make sure the chit is safe. She is Gowthorpe's little sister, after all."

"Thanks for the reminder," Nathaniel grumbled.

"My pleasure, as always." As Nathaniel left the garden, he heard his friend's mocking voice. "Being honourable is overrated, you know!"

Chapter Fourteen

Dear Diary,
Marie can be so hateful sometimes.
I still remember when we were children
and she locked me in a closet.

As he reached Gowthorpe House, Nathaniel hesitated for a moment. Was he making a fool out of himself like he had said to Wortham, coming charging like a battalion at the slightest suggestion of something being wrong? But he couldn't quite shake the feeling of something being wrong, so he left the carriage and went up the front steps. A footman opened the door and let him in before he could knock.

"Is Miss Grafton available?" he asked immediately.

The footman closed the door and turned around. "I have been informed that Miss Grafton is not receiving any visitors."

"Has anyone seen Miss Grafton?"

"No, she has been in her room all evening. No one else is at home at present. Would you like to wait in the upstairs drawing room for someone, my lord?"

Nathaniel nodded. "Please. I can see myself there."

The footman gave a curt nod before walking off. The staff was probably so used to Nathaniel visiting Gowthorpe at all hours that they allowed him freedoms normally frowned upon. Taking the steps two at a time, he went upstairs, but instead of going to the drawing room, he walked down the hallway to the room he knew belonged to Angel. Staring at the closed door, he lifted his hand. This was the moment he would find out if he was a complete idiot.

"Angel?" He knocked carefully.

There was no response, so he tried again. Nothing. Maybe she was sleeping. If she had begged off with a headache, it was not impossible. He should leave. And yet, the uneasy tingle at the back of his neck wouldn't allow him to turn around. Hoping he would not come to regret it, he slowly opened the door and looked inside. The room was dim, with only a lone oil lamp lit on a table by the window seat. He couldn't see anyone in the bed, so he stepped inside.

Where was she? Finding some matches, he lit a few candles.

"Angel?" He wasn't sure why he called her name, since she obviously wasn't there. It wasn't as if she would hide under the bed. Could she have gone out somewhere?

Then he heard it. An odd muffled sound came from the other side of the room, like something scratching against wood. He turned around but couldn't see anything in that part of the room. There was nothing but a bureau with porcelain figurines, a small vanity table, and a door to what he assumed was a dressing room. The sound came again, fainter this time, but appeared to be coming from the other side of the door. Frowning, he walked over and turned the key, hoping that Gowthorpe didn't have rats in his house.

The door swung open, and at first, he couldn't see anything inside the dark space, but when his eyes adjusted, he caught sight of a small form in a white dress and his heart skipped a beat.

"Angel?"

Other than a slight jerking movement, there was no response. She sat on the floor with her arms tightly around her, rocking back and forth while she stared unseeingly into space. The haunted look in her eyes sent apprehension down his spine. Taking the steps separating them, he hunched down before her, but she still didn't react.

Not knowing what to do, he scooped her up from the floor and carried her out. She was limp like a rag doll in his arms, and he could see tear stains on her cheeks. Her knuckles and hands were bruised and bloodied from where she must have been pounding on the door.

Bringing her over to the bed, he sat down with her in his lap. She felt small and fragile in his arms, and so incredibly cold. It was as if she didn't register his presence, or that she was out of the dressing room, instead staring at something no one else could see. Feeling helpless in the face of her unusual state, he sat there with her in his arms while stroking her hair with his hand, mumbling incoherent words of comfort. Hoping that, somehow, it would be enough to bring her back.

Eventually, her body trembled and tears streamed down her cheeks. She blinked once, twice, and then her eyes seemed to focus on him.

"N... Nathaniel?" she sniffled. "What are you doing here?"

Taking her face in his hands and wiping the tears away with his thumbs, he shook his head slightly. "What happened to you?"

"I..." Her voice broke, and she started crying in earnest. Violent sobs shook her body and her breath came quickly and irregularly. He held her close while she cried with her arms wrapped around his neck and her face buried against his shoulder.

"Someone locked me in the closet," she finally managed, as her sobs melted away and she relaxed against him.

"I figured as much. Who was it?" He was fairly certain he knew the answer to the question. It was rather obvious when one looked at the events of the evening. When she said nothing, he held her away from him so he could see her face. The evident pain and exhaustion made him want to go back to the ball and drag Marie out of there. Not for a moment did he think anyone else had locked that door. "Angel?"

Her eyes wouldn't meet his. "It doesn't matter," she mumbled, wiping a few tears from her cheeks.

"It does matter," he retorted. "They cannot expect to get away with something like this."

"You'd be surprised," she mumbled, and he suspected he wasn't meant to have heard it. Finally, she looked up and met his gaze. "It's not the first time. She always gets away with everything she does, and the only one who ends up getting in trouble is me." Seeming to realise she had said too much, she made a wry face. "Please. Can we not talk about it?"

"If that is what you wish," he said, even as his insides seethed. But he didn't want to upset her further, so he would leave it. For now. "Is there anything I can do for you?"

"Could you please keep holding me for a moment?" Her cheeks tinted pink. "I don't want to be alone just yet."

He nodded and allowed her to lean her head on his shoulder, her body flush against his. She still sat on his lap with her legs to one side like a child, but she did not feel like a child in his arms, and it was starting to affect him. But he couldn't ask her to move just yet, not when she so obviously needed some human contact.

"I've been afraid of closed spaces for as long as I can remember," she told him, forcing him to rein in his wayward thoughts. Her voice was calmer now. "I panic and think I will die if I don't get out immediately."

"I've heard of people who have that problem. It must be awful."

"Even being inside a closed carriage makes me uncomfortable," she confessed with a brittle laugh. "But I'm fine as long as I keep looking out the window."

"What about rooms?"

"If they're large, I don't have any problems. Especially if they have big windows. Small rooms, especially without windows, cause it though..." She shuddered slightly, and he pulled her a little closer. "Sometimes when a room is too crowded, I feel uncomfortable as well. Even if it's a large ballroom."

"That's why you so often go out on the terrace." It wasn't a question as much as a statement.

"Yes."

"Do you know when it started?"

"No. I suppose I was born this way." She adjusted her head to look at him, a small smile playing on her lips. "Thank you for helping me tonight."

"I'm glad I came. I wouldn't have wanted you to stay locked up in that room."

"What brought you here?" she asked. "I didn't think James was home."

"He's not. I came by to check on you when you didn't show up at the ball."

Her eyes widened slightly at the admission. "W... Why?"

Damned if he knew. He couldn't seem to leave her alone, even if he knew he ought to.

"In any case." She smiled. "Thank you. That was very sweet of you."

He chuckled. "Men don't want to be sweet. We want to be dashing and handsome."

"You are that too."

Finding her faint blush too adorable, and her body against his too enticing, he lifted her off his lap and sat her down on the bed. "I should leave. It's not proper for me to spend time alone with you in your bedchamber. I'll return to the ball before anyone misses me."

He leaned down and placed a quick kiss on her forehead before leaving.

Angel looked after Nathaniel as he walked across the room. When he reached out to open the door, she called out before she could stop herself. "Don't leave!"

He turned around and looked at her quizzically, making her feel foolish, but the thought of being alone just then terrified her.

"Why not?"

"I just..." She tried to hold back the burning feeling behind her eyelids, but she could feel tears trickling down her cheeks again. "I don't want to be alone right now."

He seemed to understand because he came back to sit down next to her on the bed. Before she really knew what she was doing, she was clasping his shirt lapels and crying against his shoulder again. It amazed her how safe she felt with him. For most of her life, she'd shied away from the touch of others, and no one had ever really offered to hug her or hold her since she lost her parents. Being close to Nathaniel was different. Instead of avoiding his nearness, she craved it.

The fear and panic from being locked in the dark dressing room had dissipated, and she wasn't even sure why she was still crying. Maybe it was the aftershock. Nathaniel kindly held her close and stroked her back while uttering words of comfort.

As her tears abated, he placed a soft kiss on her temple, and without thinking, she turned her head and kissed him. He stilled when her lips touched his, as shocked by her forwardness as she was. But after the cold, isolating darkness of the dressing room, she needed his warmth. She needed to not be alone. Holding her breath, she waited to see how he would react.

"Angel, I…" He closed his eyes for a moment, a shadow passing over his face. Then he groaned and pulled her closer, returning the kiss with fervour.

There was no longer anything comforting in his touch as he buried his hand in her hair and kissed her deeply. It was a soul-stirring kiss that made her entire body tingle and her knees weak. Fortunately, they were both sitting on the bed, because she doubted she would have been able to remain standing. His hot mouth moved away from her lips, and he placed a trail of fervent kisses along her jawline until he reached her neck. When he kissed and nibbled gently, she couldn't contain a small gasp. She'd never considered the possibility of her neck being so sensitive.

His lips found hers again for a long drugging kiss that scattered every thought. She barely registered when he lay her down on the bed, half covering her with his body. His hand found her breast and massaged it gently through the fabric of her dress, causing her nipples to turn into hard peaks. A moan broke free of her throat. Her body felt hot and sluggish, and she didn't want him to stop. The urge to touch him was overwhelming, so she slid her arms over his shoulders to caress the warm skin on his neck.

When that wasn't enough, she undid a few of the buttons at the front of his shirt so she could slide a hand underneath. His skin was unbelievably hot and smooth against her cool hands, but he seemed to enjoy her touch, making a low sound at the back of his throat. When his lips left hers, she wanted to complain. Raising himself up on his arms, he looked down at her with dark eyes.

She felt wanton with her hair in disarray and the skirt of her dress slid up to her knees. Surely her face was a mess, with puffy eyes from crying and lips bruised by kissing. He moved his hand to touch her mouth gently with his thumb as he smiled wryly. "I seem doomed to lose my composure around you."

"You can lose it again any time," she replied shyly, making him chuckle.

"I wish I could, Angel. I really do." He rolled away from her to lie on his back next to her, just far enough so that their bodies weren't touching. Turning his head to look at her, he gave her a half-smile. "But you're still reeling from tonight's ordeal, and I would be a cad if I took advantage of that."

"No." She shook her head. "I enjoy being close to you. It has nothing to do with tonight."

He sat up and ran a hand through his hair. "I can't do this. You may not realise it, but you're in shock and you need human contact. Anyone would. It would be despicable of me to take advantage of you while you're so vulnerable."

Watching him, she said nothing. Maybe she had not entirely recovered from the experience of being locked in a dark room, but she also knew that her need to be close to him had nothing to do with it.

"Very well," she mumbled. As much as she might want him to continue kissing her, she was fully aware of how scandalous it would be if anyone found them, and he had made it perfectly clear he was not looking for a wife. "You better leave before my family returns home."

"Yes, I ought to." He got off the bed after a final look at her. "I will make sure a maid comes upstairs to keep you company."

"Thank you." She couldn't look at him. Now that they were no longer touching, the embarrassment of having been so forward threatened to overwhelm her.

"I will come to call on you tomorrow to ensure that you're well."

Not trusting her voice, she nodded. He was quiet for a moment, and there was no sound of him making a move to leave. She had a feeling he was watching her, but she still couldn't bear to look at him. Then he sighed, and she heard him exit the room, leaving the door open behind him. A short while later, a maid arrived and began helping her prepare for bed while chatting lightly.

Angel stared at her reflection in the mirror while the maid brushed her hair out from the hairdo she had been meant to wear to the ball. Was it her imagination, or were her lips slightly swollen? Whatever had possessed her to kiss Nathaniel? He must think her very wanton indeed.

Nathaniel didn't leave the house. He stayed in the library downstairs, waiting for Gowthorpe to arrive. Since the viscount wasn't one to return home early—especially not after having left the ball with a woman—Nathaniel had plenty of time to curse himself to hell and back for his own stupidity. It was one thing to desire your friend's sister; it was another altogether to take advantage of her in her own bed when she was in shock from a terrifying experience.

Finding a bottle of brandy and a glass in a cupboard, he settled down in Gowthorpe's chair and made himself comfortable. With his feet on the desk, he took a sip of brandy, counting himself lucky that his friend had good taste in spirits if not in women.

That was where Gowthorpe found him several hours later. The viscount stared between him and the bottle, obviously not sure what to make of the situation. It probably didn't help the man's agility of mind, being still quite foxed after his night out.

"My butler said you were waiting in here." Gowthorpe walked over to his cupboard to grab another glass. Coming to the desk, he poured himself some brandy before looking at Nathaniel. "What I can't understand is what could be so important that you'd wait until three in the morning for me."

Sitting up straight, Nathaniel rolled his shoulders after spending so long in one position. "Do you know where I found Angel this evening?"

His friend frowned, taking a sip from his glass. "She was at home with a headache. Why would you have found her at all?"

"I came here to check on her."

"Why?"

"Not important."

Gowthorpe raised an eyebrow. "You are saying I should not be bothered by my friend calling on my sister late at night without my knowledge?"

"Let me get to the bloody point!" Nathaniel snapped, startling his friend and making him spill brandy on his hand.

"Get to it then," Gowthorpe grumbled as he wiped the brandy off with a handkerchief. "I will ignore the obvious questions for now."

"She was locked in her dressing room. In the dark. Alone."

"What?" The shout reverberated through the silent house.

"Quiet down. You'll wake everyone."

"I bloody well should," Gowthorpe grumbled. "My sister was locked in."

"She's all right now, but when I found her she was quite upset... Shocked. I've never seen anyone like that." The memory of the haunted look on Angel's face flashed before him, and he closed his eyes for a moment. "She's sleeping now."

"I'm not surprised." Gowthorpe sank down in a chair. "She's had problems with small, closed-in spaces since..." He trailed off and finished the remaining brandy in one sweep. "How did it happen? How did she get locked in?"

"She won't tell me, but I have my suspicions."

"Why wouldn't she tell you?"

He had wondered the same thing. The only reason he could think of was that she was afraid of retribution from Marie. He shrugged.

"You said you had suspicions." Gowthorpe motioned with his hand to get on with it.

"I think it might have been your cousin."

"Marie?" Gowthorpe frowned. "There's always been rivalry between them, but to actually lock Angel away?"

"I suspect it was to keep your sister out of the way while Marie tried to trick me into marriage." The thought brought back his anger at her audacity, but he tamped it down to focus on his friend, who was staring at him.

"Pardon?" Gowthorpe let out a guffaw. "She what now?"

"Marie found me outside in the garden, and when she heard her mother approach, she threw herself at me and kissed me." He glared at his friend when the other man chuckled.

"I'm sorry," Gowthorpe said. "But the visual of that..."

"Fortunately, the only one who saw it was her mother. I think I convinced her to keep it quiet."

"Amazing." Gowthorpe stood. "I must speak to Angel. Find out if it was Marie."

"Now?" Nathaniel asked while his friend walked towards the door. "It's half three in the morning. Let the poor girl sleep."

"Oh, right." Turning back, Gowthorpe sat down again. "I will speak to her first thing in the morning."

"Good. Marie should not get away with this."

"Agreed. Now." His friend looked at him with narrowed eyes. "What made you think you could walk into my sister's bedchamber?"

Nathaniel buried his face in his hands and groaned. "For the love of... Gowthorpe, you're such an arse when you're drunk. Does that truly matter now? I found her. I let her out. She's resting now."

A grumble was his only reply. Which was probably for the best. He didn't exactly want to share the particulars of what had happened that evening. How he had been unable to resist Angel—yet again. No one needed to know that. Least of all her brother.

Chapter Fifteen

Dear Diary,
Is it normal to be unable to stop thinking
of someone? All I can think about these
days is a certain man. It's quite disconcerting.

When Angel left her room the next morning, she stopped short when she came face to face with her brother, who stood leaning against the door on the opposite side of the hallway with his arms crossed over his chest. She had never seen him out of his bed this early, so this could not be a good sign. His blond hair was unruly like he had done nothing to tame it, and his clothes looked as if they'd been slept in.

She frowned. "James, are you wearing yesterday's clothes?"

"Yes," he admitted, then abruptly took her arm and unceremoniously dragged her into his bedchamber opposite hers.

As he let go of her in the middle of the room and closed the door behind him, she could do nothing but stare. This was not the good-natured brother she was used to. His countenance was dark and forbidding, his lips pressed tightly. Had Nathaniel already told him? But when?

James strode past her, pacing back and forth across the floor.

"You smell," she pointed out, wrinkling her nose at the distinct odour of alcohol that wafted over her when he moved closer. He stopped pacing to stare down at her. It didn't seem like her attempt to distract him had worked.

"We're not here to discuss my smell."

"Well, we should be," she muttered.

"I want to know who locked you in the dressing room last night." His voice was low, but the tense set of his shoulders gave away his anger.

She should have known Nathaniel would find a way to tell him. Needing a moment to collect her thoughts, she sat down on James's bed and rested her hands on her lap. It wasn't that she hadn't planned to tell him. No, that wasn't true. She had not planned to tell him because, in her experience, Marie always got away with every petty, hateful thing she did to her. While James might actually punish their cousin—unlike Aunt Christine—once the Season was over, Angel would still have to return to Hefferton Place and live with them. And Marie was not exactly the forgiving type.

"I take it you've spoken to Lord Pensington?"

"Yes. Who did this, Angel?"

She looked up at her brother. He stared back at her with his hair on end, ready to pounce. Ready to protect her. Warmth surged through her at the realisation that he cared. She knew he loved her, but having been apart more than together the last few years, she had never thought he would be this protective.

"It... It doesn't matter," she whispered.

"It bloody well does matter," he snapped. "Was it Marie? Pensington seems to believe it was, and I am rather inclined to believe him unless you tell me differently."

There seemed to be no point in denying it any longer, so she nodded. James let out a string of expletives before taking a deep breath to calm himself.

"Why would you try to protect her?" he muttered as he moved across the room to call for a servant.

"I wasn't," she said. "Not exactly. I was trying to protect myself. Unlike you, I have to live with them when I leave London."

He jerked on the cord that would make a bell go off in the servants' quarters. "You can live with me from now on if you prefer. I thought you preferred the countryside, but you are old enough to come live with me here if you'd like."

Yes. She nodded, unable to get the words out through the knot in her throat. The thought of no longer having to live with the Browns felt like the light at the end of a dark tunnel. *Yes. Yes. Yes.* Especially since if she went ahead with this accusation,

Marie would never forgive her. And neither would Aunt Christine.

"You already have your room here, as long as you don't mind living in a bachelor's residence," James said, and having decided that the servants were taking too long, he opened the door and shouted his butler's name down the hallway. Closing the door again, he continued like nothing had happened, "Though Hefferton Place belongs to me and not our aunt and uncle. I could always send them back to the Midlands, and you can live there by yourself. We could get you a lady's companion. The only reason they have been living there is to care for you, and you're old enough now not to need them."

"That... That seems harsh." No matter what, the Browns had left their own house and their own lives to come to Hefferton Place when her and James's parents died. They had not been the best caretakers, but they had been there when no one else had been available. It had to count for something.

"Very well, I won't. As long as they behave," James grumbled, resuming pacing the room.

There was a light rasp on the door, and he quickly pulled it open to find the butler on the other side.

"You called, my lord?" Dobbins said calmly, as if the viscount hadn't just been shouting his name down the hall, and looked like he'd just walked through the fires of hell with a bottle of brandy as his only companion.

"I would like you to inform Miss Brown that I should see her in the library in an hour," James said.

"Certainly, my lord. Right away."

"You may wish to take a bath," Angel suggested helpfully.

Her brother let out a long-suffering sigh. "And please have a bath drawn."

"I will have it done immediately," Dobbins agreed with a glitter of amusement in his eyes before quickly leaving the room to do as he'd been told.

"What are you planning to say to Marie?" Angel asked once the door shut.

"I don't know yet," James admitted, scratching his head.

"Try not to lose your temper." She stood. "It's going to be a difficult discussion either way."

"I will try." He made a face. "I've never been particularly good at speaking to Marie. She always seems to step around the subject."

Knowing her cousin, Marie would claim it was all a terrible misunderstanding. Hopefully, her brother would not fall for the innocent act that Aunt Christine happily believed every single time.

Giving James a reassuring smile, she bid him farewell and left the room. No matter the outcome of his confrontation with Marie, he had offered her to live with him, and that knowledge lent a fresh spring to her step as she walked back to her room. She tried to keep busy by rearranging her porcelain figurines and writing in her diary but eventually gave up since she could not stop worrying about what was about to happen. Deciding to distract herself with a book, she left again—after making sure there was no sign of Marie in the hallway.

She'd reached the library and was halfway across the room to the shelves of books before she realised she was not alone. Nathaniel lay on a chaise longue, fast asleep. That would explain how James had found out so soon. The marquess must never have left. She shifted from one foot to the other as she watched his sleeping form. It did not escape her that this was the second time she'd walked in on him sleeping in her brother's house.

Lying on his back with his face turned to the room, he looked relaxed with a hand on the floor where his arm had fallen off the chaise. He had removed his waistcoat and cravat, leaving him in only his black trousers and white shirt.

Taking a few steps closer, she noticed that the top buttons had been undone, leaving a deep V of smooth, tanned skin visible. The temptation to touch him was ever-present, and she had to clasp her hands behind her back to ensure she did not reach out towards him. He was always handsome, but when asleep and relaxed, he was simply beautiful. Surely it must be sinful for a man to be so good-looking?

Dark eyelashes rested lightly on his cheeks, the tanned skin a darker olive hue than what was common in England, making her wonder if perhaps he had ancestors from southern Europe. His mouth was sensual, with a full lower lip and a little upward bend at the corners, giving him a slightly wicked look.

He stirred, mumbling something unintelligible under his breath, making her smile. Then he blinked a couple of times before his dark eyes focused on her. Newly awake, his gaze was unguarded, and the heated hunger in it made her skin tingle. She couldn't help but imagine that he was undressing her in his mind. Or was she undressing him in hers? She wasn't entirely certain, only knew that she was suddenly very hot.

Nathaniel sat up and ran a hand through his hair. When he looked at her again, the heat had left his eyes. "Good morning," he said hoarsely.

"Good morning," she replied, happy to hear that her voice sounded normal. Nodding towards the chaise, she gave him a mischievous grin. "Sleep well?"

"Not particularly. I haven't been asleep long, and that chaise is not comfortable," he admitted with a wry grin as he stood. Even without his boots on, he towered over her, and she had to crane her neck to meet his eyes. A look of concern crossed his face. "How are you feeling?"

"Well enough that I did not enjoy being ambushed outside my room first thing in the morning."

"Ah, Gowthorpe has spoken to you then." He didn't look surprised. With a yawn, he lifted his arms and stretched. The motion made his white shirt stretch taut over his chest, showing more of his tantalising skin.

Her fingers itched to touch that alluring piece of skin, so she forced herself to keep her eyes on his face. It wasn't much better, but it helped a little.

"Yes." She barely remembered what they were talking about. Memories of last night flashed before her. How hot and smooth that skin had felt against her hands. The slow, drugging kisses.

The object of her feverish thoughts seemed to sense her heightened emotions but attributed it to the wrong thing. He reached out to gently touch her face, his gaze searching hers. "Are you sure you're all right?"

She nervously wet her lips with her tongue, making his eyes drop to her mouth. The hand on her cheek twitched, and her breath hitched.

With a groan, he bent his head and his lips were a mere breath from hers when they heard voices out in the hallway. *James!* Her brother was planning to meet Marie in the library soon. Nathaniel's hand fell to his side, quickly as he stepped away from her. They both turned to the door as it swung open and James came inside after making a final comment to his butler down the hall.

When he caught sight of them, he froze for a moment. She imagined he would have had a similar expression had he walked in on a group of kelpies dancing a jig on his desk. It didn't look great, she had to admit that. She was alone in the library with his friend, who was far from properly dressed.

Not looking at either of them, James continued into the room and stopped at his desk. For a moment, it looked like he wasn't sure what to do. Then he turned around to look at them, leaning his hips against the wooden surface. She fought the urge to touch her hair to make sure it hadn't somehow come out of its coiffure. They hadn't even kissed. *Not today.* If James noticed her cheeks heating, he didn't say.

"I'm sorry about this morning," he said. "I slept little and my mood was rather foul after finding out about what happened."

His eyes searched hers, and her stomach dropped. Did he know about her and Nathaniel? "N... No apology needed," she stammered.

"Are you all right?" James dragged a hand through his still-damp hair. After a bath and with a fresh set of clothes, he looked infinitely more presentable than he had not that long ago.

The same could not be said for Nathaniel, whose dark hair was ruffled from sleeping, his clothes wrinkled, and a dark shadow of stubble covered his jaw. Walking over to the chaise longue, he shrugged into his waistcoat. When he buttoned up his shirt, she couldn't help but feel deprived. Remembering that her brother had asked her a question, she guiltily looked back at him. His brows were knotted as he stared at her.

"I am now," she said. "But I will admit to not handling it well last night."

"You've always had problems with small spaces."

She looked down at her feet. Embarrassed about how violently she reacted to being locked in. "I don't know why I'm like that. It feels like I can't breathe, and I panic until I just... blackout."

James ran a hand over his face. "I'm sorry, Angel. I never realised it was this bad."

"How could you? It's not exactly something I tell everyone."

"You've been like this since you were a child. When you were little, you would refuse to even ride in a closed carriage. We couldn't even have you in a small room if the door was closed."

She thoughtfully chewed on her lower lip while she tried to remember any of the things her brother was talking about, but nothing came to mind.

"You were probably too young to remember," James continued. "It got better after a while. You didn't always have this problem. Only after our parents died."

"Carriage accident, wasn't it?" Nathaniel asked, coming closer while he pulled on his tailcoat. "Does that have something to do with her fear? Did she hear about it and it made her frightened of carriages?"

James sighed. "I'm afraid it's worse than that." He met Angel's gaze, and she almost shouted for him to stop. A sudden fear of knowing the truth gripped her. Maybe she was better off not knowing what triggered her fear. "When our parents' carriage slid off that road and toppled over, you were in there too."

She opened her mouth to speak, but no sound came out. Closing it, she shook her head. *No.* She'd remember something like that, wouldn't she? "I... I don't remember."

"It's probably better that you don't. You were only five years old." James's hands reached down to grip the edge of the desk as if he needed to ground himself in the face of the memories. She might not remember much of their parents or their demise, but he had been thirteen and must remember it all.

"Please, James... What happened?" Now that the box was open, she wanted to know. There was no hiding, and maybe if she knew why she reacted the way she did, she could somehow stop it from happening again.

"We—" He stopped and took a deep breath. "We don't know how you survived. The carriage must have turned around several times as it went down the hill. Both our parents died, but somehow you came away with only a few bruises. With our parents and the driver dead, there was no one to help you. We found the carriage lying on its side, and you were too small to reach the door above you. So you were stuck inside with..." He fell silent again, his blue eyes meeting hers, and the sadness etched on his face stole her breath away.

Stuck inside with their parents' dead bodies. He didn't say the words aloud, but they both knew it was the truth. *No.* It couldn't be. *How?* A coldness had seeped into her bones, making her shiver. "I don't remember any of this."

"No one knows how long you were there." James's lips flattened into a thin line as he thought back to the day they had found her. "We don't know exactly when the accident happened. By the time we found the carriage, you were completely silent. Just sitting there, staring into the distance. Staring at nothing. You didn't react to anything, and you wouldn't speak. It took months before you uttered a single word. The only sound I heard from you for what felt like an eternity was your screams and panicked crying whenever we tried to put you in a carriage, or someone left you alone in a room."

A warm hand clasped hers, startling her. Glancing down, she saw Nathaniel's tanned hand embracing her cold fingers. The simple touch comforted her, returning some of the warmth to her limbs. Turning back to James, she noted his frown as he stared at their linked hands, but he said nothing.

"Then what happened?" she asked, strengthened by Nathaniel's presence.

"I don't know," James admitted. "I had to go back to school. The next time I came home, you were speaking again. Though I will admit you were never much of a chatterbox." The shadow of a smile played across his lips. "You never spoke about what happened in that carriage, so we assumed you had forgotten. You were so young."

"I suppose you were right because I still don't remember. At least now I know why I react the way I do. Thank you for telling me."

"Maybe I should have told you sooner, but I didn't want to bring back any terrible memories that you were better off forgetting. But if your fear is this strong still, you deserve to know."

Walking up to her brother, she touched his face with her hand. "It's all right," she said with a smile she hoped was reassuring. "You did what you thought was best for me."

"It's all I've ever wanted to do," he muttered. "I realise I've failed at times. Especially if this is the type of treatment you've had to deal with from Marie. I never realised. You've never mentioned anything."

"It's..." She pursed her lips, considering her answer. "Most of the time, the best course of action has been to step away and not engage. Maybe it's not always served me, but it's been the easiest way."

"Easiest is not always the best," James pointed out as he moved around the desk to sit down in his chair.

He was probably correct there. She had become so used to the way her aunt and cousin treated her that she had stopped fighting. Maybe it was time to take a stand. She had done it with Philip. She could do it with them.

James moved a few letters around on his desk before casually looking over at his friend with a hard glint in his eyes. "Should I be concerned about repeatedly finding you alone with my sister, Pensington?"

"Repeatedly?" Nathaniel scoffed. "You found us together just now, and I told you I had been alone with her yesterday."

"That makes twice. Which is more than once. That is repeatedly."

Nathaniel gave him a dark look. "Don't be an arse."

"I didn't come here to see him. I just wanted to get a book," she blurted, hoping to avoid a conversation she wasn't sure anyone wanted to have. Moving over to a bookshelf, she quickly grabbed the first book she caught sight of. "Since you're meeting Marie soon, I will leave now."

Before her brother could object, she darted out of the library to take refuge in her room. To her dismay, she noticed that the book she'd brought with her was *'Debrett's Peerage'*. It was probably for the better. After finding out about the origin of her fear of closed-in spaces, she doubted she had the presence of mind to read anything. It was strange to think she had forgotten something like that, even if young. But it appeared her body had not forgotten since it reacted instinctively every time she was in a small room.

Throwing herself on the bed, she stared up at the ceiling while she absent-mindedly rubbed the hand Nathaniel had held. He had made it perfectly clear he did not want to court her. So why had he nearly kissed her? Again.

Inside the library, Nathaniel stood still as Gowthorpe stared at him for what seemed like an eternity before his friend spoke again.

"Surely you can see why I would be concerned?" he said. "Despite the circumstances, you were alone with Angel in her room last night. Some men would force you to marry for that. It's hardly proper."

"I would never do anything to compromise your sister." It was a blatant lie. Had anyone seen them, they would definitely have been on their way to the altar right now. "I have more honour than that. After all, I am not the rake here."

He wasn't sure that was at all relevant to the discussion, but something about the situation just made him want to be difficult. Gowthorpe wasn't falling for it.

"Perhaps," he allowed. "But you don't see me alone with any of your sisters, do you?"

Touché. Nathaniel was far from innocent. Despite his vow to stay away from Angel, he seemed unable to. But he'd be damned if he was going to admit to kissing his friend's sister.

"When she came into the library, I was still asleep." At least that much was the truth. "Not one of us got much rest this night. While you had a bed to spend a few hours on, I've been in here. She came in, I woke up. We shared a few words, and then you arrived. Nothing untoward happened here."

Unlike her room the previous night. He prayed his friend would not ask more about it. Gowthorpe seemed to sense his frustration with the topic because he nodded tersely. Maybe he had decided to trust him, which was ironic since he apparently could not be trusted around Angel any further than Gowthorpe could throw him.

"Angel admitted it was Marie who locked her in," Gowthorpe said, changing the subject.

"Damn. I knew it!" Nathaniel exploded, followed by a few less-than-exemplary words. "What are you going to do?"

"I'm meeting the girl shortly, and I will tell her that if she ever does anything like that again" —Gowthorpe's brow lowered over his eyes— "I'm throwing her and her parents out on the street, and they can return to their old homestead in the Midlands."

"Sounds fair to me." He ran a hand through his hair. "I had better return home. Aunt Jane will have my head for not returning last night."

Moving to pull on his boots, he could feel his friend watching him silently. As he tied his cravat loosely without Gowthorpe having uttered a single word, he finally snapped, "Spit it out!"

The viscount narrowed his eyes. "Are you certain I have nothing to worry about regarding Angel?"

"Nothing at all," he replied in clipped tones. Lying to his friend was not his finest moment, but what could he possibly say? *I can think of nothing these days but how good your sister feels in my arms.* Gowthorpe certainly would not appreciate hearing that.

"Very well then." Gowthorpe stood. "Will I see you at White's this afternoon?"

He nodded, then left the library before his friend could read the truth in his eyes. There was most definitely something to worry about.

Chapter Sixteen

Dear Diary,
 Everyone always seems to take Marie's
 word over mine. Sometimes I wonder
 if James would too, but I hope I never have to find out.

Angel was sitting in her usual spot in the window with her diary when Aunt Christine burst into the room like a Fury from the old Greek myths. Though one of the Greek deities with serpentine hair might have been a more welcome sight.

"How dare you accuse Marie?" she shrieked.

Closing the diary and putting it to the side, Angel inhaled deeply, steeling herself for the inevitable confrontation. She stood when James and Marie entered the room in Aunt Christine's wake, and her brother gave her an apologetic look.

Why had she not foreseen this? Marie would never go down without a fight. To keep her hands from shaking, she clasped them in front of her, gripping her fingers tightly.

"Answer me!" her aunt snapped when she said nothing.

Forcing a calm voice, she looked at the older woman. "What would you like me to say?"

"I want to know what possessed you to accuse your dear cousin of locking you in your dressing room last night!"

She almost backed down. She always backed down. But not today.

"The fact that she did?"

"Outrageous lies! My daughter would never do something like that." Aunt Christine huffed, waving her hands in the air as if the mere movement would make her words true.

"So I locked myself in the dressing room?" Angel asked dryly. It wasn't the wisest idea to goad her aunt, but she was tired of cowering before them. Tired of being the obedient one who always did what she was told. She had a will of her own and she was ready to exert it.

"Maybe someone else did it," her aunt pushed on, unwilling to consider Marie's guilt. "Or it could have been a misunderstanding."

"Pardon?" Angel almost laughed. A misunderstanding? Was she to think that Marie had somehow believed she *wanted* to be locked up?

Aunt Christine must have taken the question as an invitation to go on, her words coming out in a rush. "The door could have closed on itself. Marie admits to seeing you in your room but says she didn't close the door. Maybe it swung shut when you were inside, and she never realised you were trapped."

"Angel?" James looked at her, his face unreadable, and for a moment she faltered. Did he not believe her? Even the possibility of him not believing was like a stab in the gut. She glanced over at Marie, and the gloating look on her cousin's face strengthened her resolve.

Lifting her chin defiantly, she met her brother's eyes. "It was not a misunderstanding. Marie physically pushed me and stalked me until I fell back into the dressing room. Then she closed and locked the door. I don't believe I could have misunderstood that."

Satisfaction washed over her when Marie's smirk faded from her pretty face and her eyes widened as she realised Angel had finally stood up to her. "You're lying!"

The accusation hung potently in the air between them for a moment while everyone waited for James to react. She breathed a sigh of relief when her brother whirled around to face Marie with a dark look in his eyes. Their cousin shrank away from him when he took a step towards her.

"She's lying," she tried again, a desperate note in her voice.

"Quiet," James growled. "Don't you ever again dare suggest that Angel is a liar."

He might as well have slapped her. Marie looked so shocked at being told off. Her mouth was shaped into a perfect o as she stared at James.

"Get out of my sight!" he snapped. "And make sure I don't see you again for the next few days, because right now I want to toss you out of the house."

With a whimper, Marie dashed out of the room. Aunt Christine opened her mouth to speak, but one look from James changed her mind, and she left with a disapproving huff. She'd barely made it out the door before James slammed it shut behind her. Turning back to Angel, he dragged a hand over his face.

"Dear lord," he groaned. "I am so sorry. I never realised what you had to put up with living with them."

A tentative smile pulled on her lips. She had stood up to Marie, and the world had not ended. "It's not been so bad," she said, trying to comfort her brother. "I've been here from time to time to visit you."

"Well, from now on you will live with me full-time, like we discussed."

"I look forward to it."

"Are you certain you do not wish me to kick them out of Hefferton Place?" he asked, sounding almost hopeful.

"Yes. If you do, I am sure they would find a way to blame me."

"They will have to go eventually, anyway. When I marry, I imagine I will take up residence there when Parliament is not in session, and I am not willing to share the house with them."

"Marry, James?" She grinned at him, enjoying being able to tease him. "I thought you were a confirmed bachelor."

"I am, but sooner or later, I suppose I will have to." He made a face.

"You don't have to sound so pained about the fact. I hear it's not so bad."

"Maybe not if you find the right person," he muttered, a shadow crossing over his face, but it was gone before she could ask him about it, replaced by a wry smile. "I will let them stay at Hefferton Place for now. I'm not likely to marry soon, and I suppose they've deserved it for taking care of you these years."

He surprised her by hugging her. "I'm glad you will stay here for a while," he admitted. "I've realised I don't know you as well as I should."

Hugging him back, maybe a little tighter than necessary, she smiled. "I'm glad too."

After a hot bath and changing into clean clothes, Nathaniel felt remotely human again. Walking downstairs, he had to step over a litter of kittens his sister Rain had rescued from the gutter. His house was being overrun by wounded birds, cats, puppies, and even a squirrel, thanks to his soft-hearted sister, who could not see an injured or abandoned animal without bringing it home. He supposed he should be thankful that her charity didn't extend to reptiles or rodents. Or did it already extend to rodents? He frowned. Was a squirrel a rodent?

Still pondering the question, he nearly knocked over his aunt coming out of the library.

"Oh, there you are!" She smiled up at him, not even mentioning how he'd left her and Jessica at the ball the previous night.

"Aunt Jane." He nodded in greeting. "What can I do for you?"

"You have a visitor in the library."

"Who?" He had no meetings scheduled today and wasn't expecting anyone for a social call.

"The Earl of Wortham."

Naturally. He groaned inwardly. Wortham loved to watch his misery. The man had obviously noticed Nathaniel's interest in Angel and knew him well enough to know he would never take advantage of their friend's sister. With his twisted sense of humour, Wortham doubtlessly enjoyed the situation as much as if he were watching one of Shakespeare's plays. Probably more.

"Thank you. I will see him now." With a sense of going to his funeral, he sketched his aunt a bow before entering the library, where he found Wortham perusing some titles on a bookshelf.

"You must have been early out of the house this morning," Nathaniel said in ways of a greeting.

His friend turned to look at him with a smirk. "Oh, I never returned home. Your aunt kindly offered me a bed for the night."

"Of course she did. She doesn't know you as well as I do."

"She loves me."

"Only because she doesn't know you too well." He sat down in the chair behind the desk while Wortham casually sauntered over to sit on the opposite side.

"So, what happened last night?"

Debating if he wanted to confide in his friend, Nathaniel leaned back and ran a hand through his hair.

"Miss Brown had locked Angel in the dressing room." For once, he had the pleasure of seeing his friend surprised as Wortham straightened in the chair to look at him. He quickly explained what had happened—carefully leaving out the part where his comforting Angel had turned into something else entirely. Unfortunately, it was difficult to hide things from Wortham. The man had an unerring sense of when someone was withholding information.

"I'm amazed Gowthorpe didn't kick them out head first. I would have."

"He's soft," Nathaniel muttered.

"That he is," Wortham agreed, then casually glanced across the desk. "So when are you going to tell him you seduced his sister?"

"I... What?" Nathaniel swallowed back the futile denial when his friend watched him with twinkling eyes. "I have not."

"No?" A raised eyebrow indicated his friend was not convinced.

"Not entirely at least." There was no point in denying anything. Wortham never let anything go. He'd poke and prod until you spilt every detail.

"I'm sure Gowthorpe will appreciate the distinction." Chuckling, Wortham got up from his chair and found a bottle of brandy and two glasses.

"You bloody well know he'd kill me if he found out I had so much as an improper thought about her."

"I trust you've had plenty of those." Wortham put the glasses on the desk and poured them a finger each.

Nathaniel narrowed his eyes at him. "You're not helping."

"I beg your pardon," Wortham said with feigned innocence, bringing his glass to his lips. "I wasn't aware I was meant to."

"Oh, spare me friends like you," Nathaniel grumbled, grabbing his glass despite not wanting a drink. Instead, he moodily swirled the liquid around, following it with his eyes.

"Why don't you just marry the chit?"

Nearly spilling the brandy, he stared at his friend. "And this from a man who's sworn he will go to the grave before he gets married?"

Wortham scoffed. "I've merely said I'm having too much fun as a bachelor. That doesn't mean others can't get married and enjoy it."

"You know why I don't want to marry."

"I do," Wortham said slowly. "But you're not your father."

"I know that." Setting the drink down on the desk, Nathaniel kept his hands around the glass as he stared into the amber liquid.

Everyone knew how much his parents had loved each other. The villagers still spoke about it when he visited Bridlewood.

But after his mother died, his father was never the same. Four years after her passing, he'd died in what had been labelled a hunting accident. As much as Nathaniel preferred to believe it had truly been an accident, he knew the truth; his father simply could not go on living without the woman he loved.

His father's inability to move on had marred his view of love. Everyone had always compared him to James Howerty, saying how alike they were, and he feared they were right. What if he would react the same way if he fell in love and subsequently lost the woman he loved? What if love would destroy him too?

"Do you really?" Wortham's question brought him back to the present.

Nathaniel looked up at him, having forgotten the original question. "Do I what?"

"Do you really know that you're not your father?"

"I'd like to believe so. But I will never know, and I won't risk it. I'll marry someday, but I will steer clear of anyone I could fall in love with."

Wortham strummed his glass with a finger as he watched him shrewdly. "So you won't marry Gowthorpe's sister because...?"

Glaring at his friend, he tried not to rise to the bait. Wortham was goading him on purpose. "Because she is Gowthorpe's sister. I doubt he'd want her married to his friend. Lord knows I wouldn't have either of you marrying any of my sisters."

"Better you marry her than seduce her."

It was a fair point. Marrying her was the only way he could do all the wicked things he imagined when he lay in bed late at night since he would never compromise her. He groaned inwardly. "I will not marry her," he repeated slowly. "And I will definitely not seduce her."

"You're too bloody honourable sometimes. It makes me sick. You want the girl, so put yourself out of your misery and marry her if you can't bring yourself to seduce a friend's sister."

"How about I do neither?" Nathaniel suggested grimly, taking a sip of the brandy. No matter how much he wanted Angel, he could not seduce her. And he certainly could not marry her. She was far too dangerous for that. He never should have agreed to that first kiss. Once he had tasted her lips, he could not banish her from his mind. And last night...

Last night. If she had not been in an emotional state where he felt like he was taking advantage of her, he wasn't sure he would have had the presence of mind to stop. She melted into his arms every time they touched, and she felt amazing. Felt *right*. He rested his face in his hands and groaned. Damn it all to hell.

"Yes, you're clearly handling this brilliantly." Wortham's sarcastic voice made him look up to glare at his friend.

"Don't you have anywhere to be?" he asked pointedly.

"As a matter of fact, I do." Putting his now empty glass down, Wortham stood. "I will see you at White's this afternoon."

Nathaniel watched his friend leave, happy to see the door close behind him. Running a hand through his hair, he vowed to stay away from Angel. Again. She was not someone you could have an affair with and then forget. She was someone you had to marry. Had to love. And romance was not for him. Not now. Not ever. And definitely not with Angel Grafton.

Bloody hell.

Angel flicked her fan open to cool herself while walking along the edges of the ballroom. It was a hot evening, and the ballroom was suffocating even with the terrace doors wide open. Many guests had moved out to the garden, where a faint summer breeze provided a small amount of relief from the heat. The hostess, Lady Bates, had ordered servants to light small lanterns in the trees and bushes, which made the garden look as if filled with tiny faerie lights.

Or will-o'-the-wisps hoping to lead us astray. The thought made her smile. She'd had enough of the stifling ballroom and was on her way to enjoy some fresh air outside. Jessica had spoken to her earlier and shared some rather expressive nouns describing Marie after finding out about the incident. Then a suitor had asked her friend to join him outside, and she'd had to leave.

Coming through the doors and entering the garden, Angel took a deep breath, enjoying the slightly cooler air. It had been an odd evening, with several people giving her strange looks and whispering between themselves. Unsure of why, she had looked to make sure her dress wasn't on backwards, just in case. But no, she looked perfectly presentable. Had they somehow found out about her kissing Nathaniel in her room? It seemed unlikely since the only ones who knew were her and Nathaniel, and he certainly would not spread any rumours, since it would most likely force him to marry her.

She caught sight of Jessica standing a short distance away speaking to Viscount Leighton. Making her way through the crowd spread across the lawn, she reached her friend's side and greeted Lord Leighton with a smile.

"Congratulations on your engagement, my lord."

"Thank you, Miss Grafton." Leighton bowed, but couldn't hide a cheery grin. Rumours said he had compromised Lady Amelia, and that was why they had to marry, but neither party would confirm the gossip and acted like it was a regular engagement. Since Lady Amelia was the daughter of a duke, no one dared to question them.

A moment later, the viscount disappeared in search of his new fiancee, and Jessica turned to Angel. "Have you seen my brother?"

Not since our near-kiss in James's library. She fought back the heat threatening to fill her cheeks and shook her head. "No, and not mine either. I think they may have abandoned us."

"That would not surprise me at all." Jessica laughed and took her arm. "I hear that Lady Bates has a beautiful conservatory. While almost everyone is outside, shall we go inside and take a look?"

They strolled through the garden, which was extensive for a London townhouse. A fortunate thing on an evening like this, when most guests preferred the open air to the hot rooms of the house. When they passed two gentlemen, she again noticed the strange looks she was getting.

"Have you noticed that I'm receiving more looks than usual tonight?" she asked her friend.

"You do look lovely this evening," Jessica replied, always her biggest supporter.

"No, not in that way." She wasn't sure how to explain the phenomenon, but it was making her skin crawl. A feeling of unease had settled low in her stomach and would not go away.

Back inside, they went straight to the conservatory on the other side of the house. When they reached it, Jessica smiled. It was beautiful, filled with exotic flowers and plants of all shapes and sizes. A heady smell permeated the room and tickled their noses as they walked further between the rows of flowers.

"Beautiful," Jessica murmured, reaching out to touch a large bloom.

Angel walked ahead of her but halted when she heard some angry voices coming from an area hidden behind a tall trellis of clinging roses. Was that Nathaniel and James? Waving for her friend to join her, they moved closer so they could glance around the side of a rose wall and hear what was being said. Their brothers stood facing each other, their faces grim.

"I'm telling you," Nathaniel said. "He's been spreading rumours."

"He would never do such a thing." James shook his head dismissively.

"He most certainly would," the marquess snapped. "And he has. Lady Belmont told me herself, and Lord Croft confirmed it!"

Angel and Jessica shared a quizzical look. What on earth were they talking about? Looking back at the two men, the stricken expression on James's face made something lurch inside Angel.

"But..." He stared at Nathaniel, his blue eyes wide. "If Chettisham claims he's spent the night with Angel, that means she's ruined."

She gasped. *Philip had said what?*

Both men whipped around to stare at her.

"Angel!" James took a step towards her. "You shouldn't have heard that."

"She had to find out eventually," Nathaniel said grimly.

"But not like this."

Jessica took Angel's hand and dragged her out to their brothers. Numb from the shock, she had no words. *Ruined.* The future she had finally dared to envision for herself was crumbling before her very eyes.

Ruined.

"Angel?"

She looked up to meet James's concerned eyes. Her tongue didn't want to cooperate and all she could do was stare.

Ruined.

"Please tell me it's not true," he said.

Pulling back like he'd slapped her, she gaped at him. How could he believe such a thing?

"Of course, it's not true. I would never." Her voice came out sharper than she had intended, but it hurt her that he'd asked.

"Good. I didn't believe so, but I needed to hear it from you directly." James rubbed his neck with one hand while groaning. "This is such a headache. The bloody bastard."

"But since Chettisham is lying, then everything is fine... Isn't it?" Jessica asked hopefully.

Nathaniel's face was impassive as he answered, his voice tempered. "No. I'm afraid it's not that simple."

"Why not?" Angel watched him, trying to discern if he believed the rumours, but his face gave nothing away. "It's not true."

"We know that, but no one else does."

"Can't we just tell them?" She was grasping at straws. She knew what a claim like this would do to her reputation. Philip had effectively ensured that no one would offer for her hand in marriage. At least no one respectable. She would be a social pariah, shunned from finer establishments and looked down upon for supposedly giving herself to a man before marriage. Even if it was all lies.

The unfairness of it all made her eyes burn with tears threatening to spill. It wasn't right that Philip could steal her future so easily.

"I cannot believe this," Jessica said, shaking her head. "It's so unfair that a man can ruin a woman simply by spreading a rumour. If a woman did the same, the reaction would be far different."

"In either case, the woman would be ruined, not the man," James agreed. "It's wholly unfair."

A dreadful realisation hit Angel. "This is why everyone has been staring at me tonight," she whispered. "They were all speculating on whether or not Philip has spent the night with me."

"Vultures. That's what they are," her brother sneered.

"Why would he do this?" Jessica asked. "Is it pure revenge, or does he stand to gain anything?"

"I imagine he's hoping that Angel will be forced to marry him to save her reputation," Nathaniel said. "Her reputation would still suffer, but not as bad as if she refuses."

"I knew he needed to get married to get him out of debt." James groaned. "But I didn't think he was desperate enough to go this far. There are still plenty of other young ladies with sizable dowries. Several with better ones."

"He's in debt?" That was the first Angel was hearing of this. "Why did you not tell me?"

He made a face. "Honestly? I did not think it mattered. The understanding between our families was there. At the time, you didn't seem opposed to the idea of marrying him, so I didn't think it made much difference." He sighed, looking over at his friend. "I don't know what to do. No one will marry her now."

Jessica's hand squeezed Angel's in silent compassion, and she turned her head to give her a half-smile.

"I'll marry her."

Everyone stared at Nathaniel. He looked nearly as shocked by the statement as everyone else. Angel's heart beat wildly in her chest, so much so that she feared they could all hear it. Why would he offer to marry her? He didn't want to.

"You'd do that?" James asked. "It would certainly help. No one would dare to speak too badly of a marquess's wife."

"Exactly," Nathaniel agreed, and Angel noticed he wouldn't look at her. "And we can't allow her to marry Chettisham. The man's a right knob."

Her brother chuckled darkly. "True. He burned every available bridge with me the moment he started this rumour. Are you sure? I know your stance on marriage."

Nathaniel's dark gaze flickered to hers before returning to James. "Yes. I have to get married eventually anyway, and Angel is an excellent match. Anyone would be lucky to marry her."

It was obvious what he was doing. She swallowed back a panicked laugh. He was coming to her rescue again as her self-appointed knight in shining armour. But she didn't want him like this. Didn't want to be saved. She wanted him to want to marry her. *Her.* But she held her tongue because she also knew this was her only option. And she loved him. She'd be a fool not to accept a proposal from the man she loved. Even if it came about for all the wrong reasons.

"Angel," James said. "Is this agreeable to you?"

She looked over at Nathaniel again, but his face remained impassive as he stared back at her, waiting for her answer. What was he thinking? That he was sacrificing himself for her honour? Swallowing back the lump in her throat, she nodded.

"Brilliant!" James said, clapping his hands. "We will discuss this more tomorrow. I think it's best if I take Angel home and away from the gossip tonight."

After a quick goodbye to her friend, Angel followed her brother out to their carriage, feeling somewhat dazed after the events of the evening. What had happened? Was she truly engaged to Nathaniel?

Chapter Seventeen

Dear Diary,
  A reputation is a fragile thing. A few
  words alone shattered mine. But my
  saviour stepped up, sacrificing himself for me.

"I hear congratulations are in order."

Nathaniel groaned when Wortham threw himself into the upholstered chair next to his, where he sat at White's nursing a glass of brandy. His plan to stay away from Angel had gone up in flames the moment he uttered those fateful words.

'I'll marry her.'

Angel was the last person he should marry if he wanted to ensure he stayed emotionally detached. He already liked her far too much. But Chettisham had forced everyone to reevaluate when he spread those vile rumours. The idea of Gowthorpe being forced to marry her off had made his insides lurch.

Angel married to someone else? No. It felt wrong. And who would offer for her when they all believed a bounder like Chettisham had compromised her? No one respectable.

What he had done was the honourable thing. The respectable thing. And he had to marry eventually, anyway. So why not her? It was the perfect solution for everyone. It saved her from social ruin and he could seduce her without guilt. The memories of her pliable body under his in her bedchamber consumed him. He would never seduce an innocent, but if she was his wife...

Remembering his friend's presence, he grunted. "How did you find out? It's not common knowledge yet."

"I met Gowthorpe on my ride in the park this morning. Chettisham truly is an arse." Wortham motioned for a footman to bring him a drink before looking at Nathaniel, and there was no mistaking the amusement glittering in his eyes. "How fortunate that she has her very own knight in shining armour."

"I'm hardly that," he muttered.

A footman brought over a glass of brandy for Wortham before disappearing again. The earl picked it up and thoughtfully tapped the glass with a finger. "Glad you took my advice."

"What?"

"I told you to marry her and now you are." His friend grinned. "A regular cupid, that's what I am. I should offer my services to the masses."

"Bloody hell, never suggest such a thing. Who knows what havoc you would wreak." Nathaniel shook his head and took a sip of his brandy. "My decision to offer for Angel had absolutely nothing to do with your suggestion. I am helping her out of a terrible situation. And yes, it has the advantage that I can finally seduce her."

Maybe bedding her would finally get her out of his system. It could be all he needed to rid himself of this obsession. After that, she might become exactly the type of woman he had planned to marry all along. Pleasant enough to be around and have a family, but no threat to his heart. He buried the immediate and instinctive denial of that line of thought deep in the recesses of his mind, refusing to consider any other reason for wanting to marry her.

"That shiny armour is looking a little tarnished," Wortham remarked with a wry smile.

"What do you want from me?"

"I just want to know when you're going to admit to yourself that you love the chit."

He turned his head sharply to stare at his friend. "Pardon?"

Wortham only grinned and shrugged. "Point taken," he said with an amused look. "You don't love her. Keep telling yourself that."

With a chuckle, Wortham finished his drink and left to speak to another friend, leaving Nathaniel to glare after him. Few people were as annoying as the earl when he thought he knew something you didn't. He loved ribbing his friends and making insinuations. The more annoyed they got, the more he enjoyed it. It would be a good day when the earl could be fed some of his own medicine.

One day, Wortham would find a woman he could not resist, and no matter how long and hard he fought to avoid marriage, he would find himself in love and unable to resist. And when that day came, Nathaniel would be right there with him. Laughing.

Draining the remains of his drink, he stood. The afternoon was drawing to a close, and he had promised to come to Gowthorpe House to discuss the engagement to Angel in more detail. The idea didn't bother him as much as he had expected. Imagining Angel as his wife filled him with a bubbly warmth, and he quickly pushed it away. He was happy he could seduce her soon. That was all. It had to be.

Angel stared into the tea inside the cup in her hands, wishing she could block out her aunt and cousin the way her uncle seemed to. Uncle George sat on the other side of the drawing room, apparently deeply concentrating on the newspaper in his lap. If only she could do the same.

"There is nothing to it. You must marry Mr Chettisham." Aunt Christine nodded to herself like the matter was settled.

Her aunt had returned from the ball last night, having heard the rumours, and this morning it was all they could talk about. There was no discernible doubt in her aunt's mind that Angel was guilty and that Philip spoke the truth. It probably shouldn't surprise her. The Browns had never had a high opinion of her, and her aunt in particular had never seemed to warm to her.

"I most certainly will not marry him." Angel had not told them about Nathaniel's proposal because, in truth, she wasn't entirely sure it had actually happened. Or that he had not already changed his mind. It had obviously been a spur-of-the-moment decision, and he might very well have returned home and realised he made a mistake. Saving her was an honourable thing to do, but in doing so, he would shackle himself to her for the rest of their lives. It was a big step for anyone.

Aunt Christine's eyes widened. "But you must! Your reputation. You are ruined now and have no other choice."

"In name only." She set her teacup down on the table. The discussion was giving her a foul taste in her mouth. "It is all lies and I refuse to give Philip what he wants. Such behaviour should not be rewarded."

"Zut! No one cares if it's true. You have no choice."

"Exactly." Marie popped a biscuit in her mouth. "You should just marry him. There is nothing wrong with Mr Chettisham, and now you have little hope of catching any other respectable man."

"She's right, you know." Aunt Christine nodded. "It is the right thing to do."

Her cousin was enjoying this far too much. Giving her a feline smile, Marie asked, "What if there is a child? You can't very well raise a bastard."

"There won't be," Angel said slowly, carefully enunciating every word to make sure they heard her. "Because it's all lies."

"Even so," her aunt said with a stubborn tilt of her jaw. "There is no use fighting this. We are out of options and you must marry Mr Chettisham or the whole family risks social ruin."

"That won't be necessary. Miss Grafton is marrying me."

The dark, smooth voice made everyone look to the door where Nathaniel stood, hat in his hands, his face a perfect mask of pleasantness. But Angel could see the anger simmering in his eyes, and it warmed her to know it was on her behalf. He was as handsome as always, dressed in his usual black with a dove-grey waistcoat. Since he was such a regular visitor in the house, the footmen didn't even announce him anymore.

"What?" Marie's shriek cut through her thoughts.

Nathaniel sauntered across the room while everyone stared. Stopping in front of Angel, he picked up her hand and placed a soft kiss above her knuckles.

"Miss Grafton," he said and gave her a conspiratorial wink. Her insides immediately fluttered to life.

"Apologies, Lord Pensington," Aunt Christine said, her voice unusually meek. "We did not know. Come, Marie. We are expected at the modiste."

"We are?"

"Yes. George!" Aunt Christine's voice raised an octave, trying to get her husband's attention. "We require your presence too."

Before Angel knew it, she was alone with Nathaniel as the Browns disappeared. It was a strange occurrence lately how her aunt and cousin would disappear whenever Nathaniel came around.

"Why do they always flee your company?" she asked. "Only a week ago, Marie would have done anything to spend a few moments with you."

"There was a minor incident," he admitted but didn't offer any further detail.

"I see." She didn't, but she didn't want to push it.

"I'm here to see Gowthorpe. Is he not at home?"

"He's gone to see his solicitor and should be back shortly. Could I offer you a spot of tea?" She motioned to the teapot, cups, and biscuits on the small table in front of them.

"Please."

He sat down next to her on the sofa, and she poured him a cup of tea, remembering to add two spoonfuls of sugar. She could feel his eyes on her the entire time, making the butterflies in her stomach flutter wildly and her cheeks heat. Questions burned on her tongue but she could not bring herself to ask. It was far too embarrassing. W*hy are you marrying me?*

The teacup rattled on the saucer, and she realised her hand shook. Nathaniel's hand covered hers, stilling it, his palm warm against her skin.

"How are you?" he asked gently.

"Dazed," she admitted with a half-smile. "Everything is happening so quickly."

He nodded. A muscle in his jaw twitched. "All thanks to that bastard, Chettisham," he muttered. "If I see him, I might—"

"Oh no, please don't get into an argument with him!" She turned to him and moved her hand out of his grip to rest it on his arm as if that would keep him from doing so.

"Why not? He deserves it."

"That may be so. But I rather not cause any scenes. There is enough gossip involving me."

A smile tugged at the corners of his mouth and his face softened. "That's fair."

"I'm sorry you have been dragged into this mess." Realising her hand was still on his arm, she pulled it back to rest it on her lap. She shouldn't be touching him, no matter how much her fingers itched to do so. Or could she? If they were truly engaged, the rules might not be as strict.

His low chuckle sent goosebumps across her skin when he leaned a little closer. "Some might say I volunteered."

The heady smell of sandalwood and something she could not name, but that was so intrinsically *him,* tickled her nose. Her eyes met his dark ones, sending the butterflies inside into a frenzy. Taking a shaky breath, she wet her lips with her tongue, and his gaze dropped to her mouth. Somehow, he was closer still, his body crowding hers on the couch. His hand came up to cup her cheek.

"How do you feel about it?" he asked quietly. "No one has asked you if you are willing to marry me."

She almost laughed. Who would not want to marry this dark, wicked angel? While she didn't want him to marry her out of obligation, she would be lying if she said she didn't want him. Her entire being craved his touch. His kisses. She loved how he always listened to her—even when her family did not—and appeared to actually care about what she thought. She loved how he made her laugh. She loved him.

"My options are severely limited," she muttered, not wanting to accidentally pour her heart out to someone who had previously made it very clear he had no intention of pursuing her.

"Is that a yes? You will marry me? Your enthusiasm is extraordinary." He laughed quietly when she made a face.

"Apologies. I appreciate your offer, I really do—"

His face grew serious, the corners of his mouth dropping. "But?"

Pushing away from the sofa, she walked over to a table with a bouquet of roses in a vase. Touching the velvety petals, she considered her words, how to explain her twisted feelings. She heard Nathaniel move behind her and nearly jumped when his voice appeared behind her ear.

"Do you like my flowers?"

Glancing over her shoulder, she realised he stood behind her, closer than was appropriate, with his body nearly touching hers. If she leaned back just a little, she could have leaned her head on his chest.

"You sent these?" She looked back at the flowers, too embarrassed to meet his eyes. No one had told her they were from him and there was no card amongst the blooms.

"Yes." His hand came up to rest on the bare skin of her shoulder above her dress, making her shiver. "I remembered you saying you preferred roses."

"I do," she mumbled, touched that he had recalled that small piece of information.

Sliding his hand to her neck, Nathaniel rubbed gently at her nape with his thumb, sending warm waves through her body and making her relax against him. When he took the step separating them, she automatically tilted her head to the side to accommodate him, and he bent down to place a soft kiss on her neck.

"My offer is not entirely unselfish," he mumbled against her skin. "One day I would have to marry anyway, and the two of us get along well. And..." His lips kissed a fiery trail along her neck that made her tingle in awareness until he reached her ear and she could feel his hot breath against her temple. "It means I can kiss you as much as I want. And bloody hell, do I want to kiss you."

As if to demonstrate his words, he tilted her head up and to the side so he could place a searing kiss on her lips. Her body instantly ignited, and she pressed herself closer to him, wanting more.

"What the hell?" an angry voice exclaimed behind them.

Nathaniel quickly stepped away and let go of her, making her feel oddly bereft. It took her another moment to realise they were no longer alone. A feeling of foreboding settled low in her gut, and she turned around to find her brother standing in the doorway, staring at them. Judging from his frown, he was not happy.

"I'm marrying her," Nathaniel reminded him.

"You're not married yet," James growled, striding across the room. "So you had better keep your greedy paws off my sister until the wedding night. Preferably longer."

"It... It was only an innocent kiss," she stammered, her cheeks burning hotly.

"Didn't look particularly innocent to me." James levelled Nathaniel with a glare. "You lied to me. How long has this been going on?"

"It hasn't," Nathaniel said, and she was rather impressed by how easily he lied. Judging from James's glaring, it was probably the best approach, since she doubted he would appreciate hearing about the times they had kissed before. "We only kissed just now since we are to be married."

James rubbed his face with a hand and groaned. "I agreed to you marrying her," he said, "only because we are desperate for a good match. That does not mean I condone you touching her before you are actually married. Understood?"

"It is not unheard of for engaged couples to be given some time alone now and then," Nathaniel pointed out.

"I don't care," James snapped. "She's my sister and you're one of my best friends. You are not to touch her."

"You're being unreasonable about this."

Her brother crossed his arms over his chest. "How would you feel if Wortham or I courted one of your sisters?"

Nathaniel sighed. "I'd hate it."

"Exactly. While this is the best solution to Angel's situation, it doesn't mean I have to like it. I always imagined she would marry some decent bloke, and I would visit every so often and never see much of her husband. Now her husband will be right in front of me all the time. You had better never speak of my sister when we are amongst male friends, like some of them do." James's nose crinkled as if he smelled something foul.

"I never brag about my affairs," Nathaniel said, only to lift his hand in surrender when James's eyes narrowed. "Fine. I promise I will never speak of her."

"Good." James sat down on a sofa and poured himself a cup of what must be lukewarm tea by now, and downed the liquid in one large gulp. Looking back over at Nathaniel, he said calmly but seriously, "You are not to be alone with her at any time before the wedding. I want a chaperone with you at all times."

"As you command," Nathaniel muttered dryly.

Angel was back in her room, writing in her diary when the door suddenly burst open and Marie barged inside. Her cousin was livid and must have run up the stairs after returning to the house because her hair had loosened and hung across her face in thick strands, while her breath came out in hard pants.

"You cannot marry the marquess!" she yelled. "He's meant to be mine!"

Putting her diary aside, Angel stood. She probably should have expected this reaction, but it didn't make it any less frustrating to deal with. But her days of being pushed around by her cousin were over.

"I'm afraid I am," she said calmly.

"He doesn't want to marry you. I'm sure he only does it out of obligation." Marie pointed an accusatory finger at her. "What did you do? Did you get yourself compromised by him too?"

Anger, hot and burning, shot through Angel and she raised her chin, meeting her cousin's eyes squarely. "I have told you repeatedly that Philip is spreading lies."

"There is no other way the marquess would have chosen you over me." There was a desperate quality to Marie's voice. "You always get everything I want. It's not fair!"

It was difficult, but Angel somehow tempered her voice as she slowly said, "Please take your offending presence out of my room."

Aunt Christine appeared at the door, taking the situation in. "Marie," she said, uncommonly calm. "Come out of there."

Marie let out a loud shriek of frustration and stormed out of the room. Angel met her aunt's eyes and was surprised when the other woman looked away.

"I'm sorry about that," she said, closing the door behind her.

Angel stared at the door as if it would suddenly morph and reveal that she had entered a dream world where everything was reversed. As far as she could remember, her aunt had never apologised for anything Marie had done or said ever. Should she pinch herself to check if she was in fact asleep? Maybe being engaged to a marquess had more advantages than she had realised.

Chapter Eighteen

Dear Diary,
 James is more overbearing than I remember from when we were children. Is that something that happens to men when they grow up?

The next ball Angel attended had people staring at her and whispering among each other again, but for a different reason. Or for a partially different reason, at least. Aunt Jane had placed an ad in the newspapers about the engagement, and after Philip's vile lies, the *ton* was excited about the drama unfolding in their midst.

No one dared to suggest the Marquess of Pensington's future wife had been compromised by another man, but she suspected at least a few of them believed so.

"Let them stare." Nathaniel leaned a little closer as they wound their way between the other guests. "They will soon tire when they realise nothing exciting is happening."

She smiled up at him, grateful for him spending the evening with her. The glances and titters were a lot less daunting when on his arm. "Or the next scandal happens."

"Or that."

Reaching the refreshment table, Angel gratefully accepted a glass of lemonade, enjoying the cool liquid in the stifling ballroom. Using her other hand, she flicked her fan open. Nathaniel noticed and smiled.

"Shall we go outside?" he asked. "It's awfully crowded here."

"Please."

The idea of fresh air was a welcome one. At least now she knew why busy rooms never agreed with her. And so did Nathaniel. That he so thoughtfully suggested they go outside warmed her heart.

James stepped into their path, halting their progress.

"Where do you think you're going?" he asked with a scowl.

Nathaniel's eyes narrowed. "We wanted to get some fresh air."

"Where's your chaperone? I believe I specifically told you not to be alone with my sister."

"You're her chaperone," Nathaniel snapped. It had always been Aunt Christine, but after recent events, James had taken it upon himself even if it was generally preferred to be a lady. "We're only going out in the garden. I don't know what you expect me to do to her out there with all the other ladies and gentlemen trying to escape the crush of the ballroom."

James crossed his arms over his chest, a stubborn tilt of his jaw. "There are plenty of things one can do in a garden, as you well know."

She looked between the two men, not entirely sure what they were talking about, but she was fairly certain she ought to be embarrassed. What did James think? That she would allow herself to be ruined in the middle of a ball? Glancing up at Nathaniel's handsome profile, her cheeks heated. If he pulled her into a dark corner of the garden, she certainly would not say no.

"You are not leaving this room without a chaperone," James insisted.

Nathaniel sighed. "Very well."

As they turned around and walked back into the throng of guests, she asked, "Are you and James still at odds after...?" She trailed off when memories of their kiss a few days ago made her lips tingle in awareness. It had been far too short, interrupted by her brother, and she desperately wanted to feel Nathaniel's mouth on hers again.

"No. He's only worried about another scandal."

"But we were just going outside?"

"Yes. So I could kiss you."

She missed a step and almost stumbled. She stared up at him. "I beg your pardon?"

His eyes met hers, a fire burning in their dark depths. "I want to kiss you."

"I... We... You do?"

"You're to be my wife," he said. "I can't think of a single person I'd rather be kissing."

She smiled. Whether or not he married her to save her, he appeared to enjoy kissing her. It was something.

"But Gowthorpe seems to have us under surveillance, so I suppose I shall have to wait."

"I'm afraid so," she said and then, before she could stop herself, she added, "Or we could try to sneak out."

His eyes widened. "Really?"

She nodded, but before they could move, Wortham strolled over with a smug look on his face.

"I beg your pardon," he said to Nathaniel. "But Gowthorpe has given me explicit orders to steal Miss Grafton from you for a dance."

"You don't have to enjoy it so much," Nathaniel muttered.

Wortham grinned. "Oh, but I do."

"It is a sad day when Gowthorpe believes a woman to be safer with you than me."

"Indeed, it is. Perhaps I should be insulted." Wortham chuckled, then turned to Angel. "If you would please do me the honour, Miss Grafton?"

She took his offered hand and gave Nathaniel an apologetic look. Who could have known that her brother would turn into Mother Superior? It was ironic, considering his own reputation. Or perhaps that was exactly why he wouldn't allow her to be alone with a man.

The Earl of Wortham was an excellent dancer and led her through the steps of the cotillion without hesitation. Now and then he glanced in Nathaniel's direction and seemed to enjoy that his friend was standing alone, glaring at them.

"He's causing a scene," he mused when Angel passed him in the dance.

"You're baiting him," she replied, making him grin.

"Naturally."

After the dance, Wortham led her over to where Nathaniel stood next to Jessica, who was speaking to a friend. Angel couldn't remember the name of the young lady, but when the friend saw them approaching, she quickly excused herself and disappeared. Jessica—who had been in the middle of a sentence—stared after her friend for a moment before turning to them, her brow furrowing as she saw the earl. Then she smiled and gave Angel a quick hug.

"Are you having a good evening?" she asked.

"Perfectly pleasant. But James has become rather overbearing." Angel laughed quietly, finding her brother's behaviour rather amusing.

"Brothers are like that," her friend agreed. Turning to the man by Angel's side, she greeted him stiffly, "Wortham."

Something glittered in the earl's blue eyes, and he sketched a quick bow. "Lady Jessica."

The Earl of Wortham really was quite a handsome man, something Angel could appreciate even if her heart was fully occupied by Nathaniel. There was something raw and dangerous about Wortham that seemed to make ladies either fall at his feet or run the other way. Which was why her stomach lurched when he suddenly turned to her with one of his most charming smiles.

"But where are my manners?" he exclaimed. Taking Angel's hand, he bent to place a kiss on top of it. "My congratulations to the beautiful bride-to-be." Straightening, he glanced at Nathaniel. "How about a kiss for the future bride?"

"There will be no kissing of my future wife." Nathaniel scowled, unamused by his friend's antics.

"Pity." Wortham chuckled, relinquishing the hold on her fingers.

"Don't you have somewhere you need to be?" Nathaniel asked pointedly.

"As a matter of fact, no." Wortham grinned and leaned casually against the wall with his shoulder. "I'm feeling rather parched, though. Would you mind fetching us a drink?"

"Oh yes, please. I could really do with another glass of lemonade." Angel smiled up at Nathaniel. He groaned but nodded.

She watched his tall form when he wound his way between the guests towards the refreshment table. He towered over most of them, and combined with his black hair, he was always easy to spot in a crowd. Was she truly marrying this handsome man? It didn't seem real.

"Why are you always ribbing my brother?" Jessica asked Wortham.

He raised his eyebrows at her sudden question. "It amuses me."

"And it drives everyone else mad."

"I have little other amusements in my life." He shrugged. "Teasing people eases my boredom slightly."

Jessica snorted. "Boredom? I've heard you have quite a few amusements in your life."

Wortham gave her an unreadable look and came away from the wall to take a step closer. Jessica backed away, almost walking into a potted tree behind her. When the handsome earl leaned in, Angel heard her friend draw in a sharp breath. Feeling like they had forgotten her presence, she wished she could disappear, but there was no quick way to leave without interrupting their awkward exchange.

While his words were whispered in Jessica's ear, they were loud enough that Angel could hear them, too. "There are different kinds of boredom, my lady."

Then he walked away, leaving Jessica staring after him for a moment, shaking her head as if to clear it.

"Are you all right?" Angel asked, not entirely sure what she had just witnessed.

"Yes," Jessica muttered, then added vehemently, "He's just such a... such an arrogant arse!"

"Mind your language, young lady!" Nathaniel admonished, handing Angel her drink. He chuckled. "Though arrogant arse describes him perfectly."

Later in the evening, once Nathaniel had left to take Jessica home after she claimed a headache, Angel slipped out onto the terrace to escape the crush of the ballroom. A cool breeze caressed her heated skin, and she raised her head to the pale moon hanging above the garden painting the flowerbeds and bushes in silver. The buzz of guests indoors and the murmur of couples walking in the dark garden relaxed her and she let out a deep breath.

James had tried to remain by her side after Nathaniel left, but some men discussing politics and the latest bill to come up in parliament had taken him hostage. Having no interest in their discussion, she had excused herself to go outside. The terrace was almost empty. It was bliss.

"I suppose I'm meant to offer my congratulations." Philip's derisive voice cut through her calm, making her spine stiffen.

Turning to face him, she shook her head. "No, that is quite all right. It is not needed." Crossing her arms over her chest, she steeled herself to stand tall in the face of his vitriol. "You have done quite enough lately. I cannot believe you would spread such awful lies about me."

"I was trying to make you see reason," he said like it was the most obvious thing in the world. "We are meant to be together. No matter what."

She groaned. "Oh, Philip. You must stop this. We cannot and will not ever marry. I'm engaged to someone else now. Please see reason and stop this pursuit."

"Pensington?" he sneered, and his blue eyes travelled over her in a way that made her skin crawl. "You do realise he is only marrying you to play the hero? He's saving his friend's sister, and one day he will regret it. He doesn't love you."

Trying to hide the sting of his words, she shook her head. "Whether he does or not matters little. You forced this when you ensured my ruin by your lies."

He took the steps separating them, his hands coming up to grab hers, and his words tumbled out in a rush. "It's not too late! You can still call it off and marry me instead. The way it was always meant to be."

"What?" She pulled her hands out of his grip and took a step backwards. "No, Philip. I will never marry you. No matter what."

"We'll see."

Turning around, he disappeared inside again, leaving her staring after him. The man would not give up, despite her being engaged to another man. What would it take for him to back off? At least the wedding was not too far off now, and once she was married to Nathaniel, Philip would have no recourse but to give up this ridiculous obsession with marrying her. He didn't even like her!

The banns would be read for the first time this Sunday, and Nathaniel had insisted they get married as soon as they had been read the three times required. While she was nervous about the idea of becoming his wife, she was almost equally excited.

'He is only marrying you to play the hero.'

Philip's words echoed through her mind. It wasn't news to her, but the reminder was another stone added to the guilt of letting Nathaniel sacrifice himself by marrying her. Maybe it wasn't enough that she loved him. He was trying to save her from social ruin, but at what cost? His own happily ever after with another woman he could love?

Chapter Nineteen

Dear Diary,
 I have heard of wedding jitters, but is
 there such a thing as engagement jitters?
 I feel like I am walking around with
 my nerves twisted in knots.

Angel nervously bounced her fist against her thigh while she stood in front of Pensington House a few days later. No matter how hard she tried, she could not get Philip's words out of her head.

The engagement ball was only a week away, and she desperately wanted to speak to Nathaniel. They had not seen each other for what felt like ages, having been dragged into a frenzied whirlwind of wedding preparations and dressmaker appointments. Apparently, she needed a whole new wardrobe for life as a married woman.

The butler let her inside and brought her to the private drawing room upstairs, where he announced her to Nathaniel, Mrs Grey, and the Howerty sisters. Seeing them all staring at her unplanned appearance at their home, she clasped her hands in front of her and prayed to steady her racing heart. Nathaniel stood, a line between his brows as he must wonder what she was doing there.

Mrs Grey put her cup of tea down and motioned to the spare seat on the sofa Nathaniel had vacated. "Miss Grafton," she said. "I wasn't expecting you today. Did I forget an appointment?"

"No, not at all," Angel assured her. "I only came because I hoped to speak to Nathaniel."

The older woman nodded. "I see. Why don't you join us for a cup of tea and some cake?"

Sitting down next to Nathaniel, Angel gratefully accepted a teacup. Her hands trembled while she stirred the spoon and she cursed her nerves.

Nick reached across the table to grab a bread roll before plopping back down in her seat. Looking at Angel, she leaned forward slightly, her brown eyes glittering. "I heard your wedding dress is absolutely beautiful."

"It is," Angel agreed.

"When I get married, I want to wear trousers," Nick continued. "Dresses are in the way when you climb trees. They're such a nuisance."

"Nick!" Aunt Jane admonished while she buttered a piece of bread. "You will wear a dress at your wedding and any other day that I deem appropriate. Which would be every day. You are too old to be allowed to wear trousers. Not that we ever should have indulged it."

"But how am I going to climb trees?" Nick complained.

"A proper young lady does not climb trees."

"Then I don't want to be a proper lady!" Nick crossed her arms, her chin jutting out stubbornly.

"Don't worry," Rain teased. "No one would mistake you for a proper lady."

Jessica rolled her eyes at her younger sisters. "You better behave," she said. "Or Angel might change her mind and no longer wish to become our sister."

Nick let out a horrified gasp. "No! She has to!"

Angel smiled, watching the siblings interact. The tension left her shoulders and she relaxed. Simply being with the Howertys was some of her favourite times, and despite her reason for coming today, she enjoyed every moment with them.

Nathaniel leaned a little closer. "Don't mind them. They're always like this."

She turned to him, trying to keep her voice calm. "Do you think I could speak to you in private?"

The line was back between his brows. "I'm afraid I have strict orders from your brother to never be alone with you, but we could walk to the other side of the room."

"Yes, please."

He stood and assisted her up. They mumbled an apology to Mrs Grey before he brought Angel to the other side of the drawing room, where a window faced the back garden. The room was large enough to keep them out of earshot, as long as they didn't raise their voices. His hand rested gently on her upper arm while he studied her.

"What is wrong?"

Looking into his dark eyes, her words stalled. "I... I..." She took a deep breath and tried again. "I don't want you to feel like you have to marry me. We could cancel. I could live out my life alone in a cottage somewhere."

He shook his head slightly, like he couldn't quite believe what he was hearing. "Don't you want to marry me?" he asked, his voice oddly stiff.

Desperately. She looked out over the garden below, trying to find the right words to explain her thoughts. "It's not that I don't appreciate what you're doing," she said slowly. "But you never wanted this. You never wanted to marry me. It's unfair to expect you to go through with this only to save your friend's sister."

Glancing back at him, his frown had deepened. He opened his mouth to speak, and then something across the room caught his eyes. She turned and found Nick holding a small butter knife with both hands, moving it slowly through the air.

"What are you doing?" Nathaniel snapped.

"I'm cutting the tension," Nick replied with an innocent grin.

Aunt Jane stood, having seen the thunderous look on her nephew's face. "I believe it is time for us to go on a shopping trip," she said and ushered all the girls out of the room. The door closed, leaving Angel and Nathaniel alone inside.

"Angel..." He raked a hand through his hair and sighed. "Despite what you might think, I'm not doing this entirely unselfishly. I would have to marry eventually, and I do believe we are a good match."

"But you don't love me." The words spilt out before she could stop herself and she wished she could take them back, but they hung between them like dirty laundry on a clothesline.

"Nor do you love me," he said. "This marriage isn't about love, but that doesn't mean it can't be a good one. We enjoy each other's company, which is more than you can say for many people."

His words pricked her heart, but she nodded. It might not be love for him, but it certainly was for her. "I just don't want you to marry me, only to fall in love with someone else down the line and regret it," she mumbled.

"Love has never been part of my plan. But we are friends, and that is better."

"I feel like I have everything to gain from this and you have nothing."

A lopsided smile touched his face. "I gain a beautiful and intelligent wife."

Heat flooded her cheeks. He said all the right things, and yet it didn't feel right. They both knew he would not have married her if it wasn't for Philip's lies. She moved over to the couch and ran her hand over the backrest while she debated what the best course of action would be. How could she selfishly allow him to marry her when she was the only one in love?

"Tell me what you're thinking."

His soft voice behind her made her whirl around to stare into his dark eyes, much closer than she had expected. He had followed her across the room. Near enough that she could smell his sandalwood soap, but not near enough to touch.

"I don't want to trap you in a marriage you never wanted."

He took a step towards her, wedging her between the sofa and his body. Reaching out to cup her cheek, he flashed a wry smile. "If anyone here is being forced, it's you. It's your reputation at stake. I offered for you because I am quite content to marry you. Unless you don't want me."

She drew a shaky breath. Oh, she definitely wanted him. There was no question about that. He watched her carefully, as if trying to discern her feelings. When she made no attempt to leave, he leaned a little closer and she could feel his hot breath on her face.

"We will have a good marriage," he promised. "Surely you are not ignorant of the attraction between us?"

Considering how her body tingled from his nearness, she could not deny such a thing. She shook her head. A grin spread over his face before he captured her mouth. Her desire instantly ignited, and she wrapped her arms around his shoulders. He teased and nibbled until she opened up and he could deepen the kiss, stoking the fire within her even higher.

No matter what, they were an excellent match in this, at least. Never before had she felt the way she did when she was in his arms. One of his hands roamed over her body, sending trails of fire from every point of contact. When he brushed over a breast, she let out a small moan, which only spurred him on further. His knee wedged in between hers, causing her skirt to rise, but right then she didn't care. Straddling his thigh, she tightened her grip around his neck. The position made the sensitive spot between her legs rub against him, and her head lolled back when a jolt of pure desire reverberated through her.

Nathaniel put an arm around her back to support her as he kissed a trail down her throat, chasing fire across her skin. Slipping a hand under her raised skirt, he pulled it up further, caressing along the outside of her thigh. His fingers reached the bare skin above her stocking, his hand hot against her. Wrapping his hand around her leg, he lifted it slightly and moved his hand to support its weight under her knee. The position allowed him to lean her backwards with his other arm for support, giving him better access to her breasts, something he took immediate advantage of by pressing a kiss against one of the soft mounds through the fabric of her dress.

She thought she might combust. Every touch and kiss stoked the fire between them higher. How would this feel if they did not wear clothes? The indecent thought scattered the moment his thigh rubbed against her again and she moaned.

With a groan, Nathaniel reluctantly pulled her back up and gently set her back down on the floor, untangling his leg from her skirts. After a last, passionate kiss on her lips, he cupped her cheek and met her dazed eyes.

"Now do you believe I have no qualms about marrying you?" he asked, his voice hoarse.

She nodded, uncertain if her voice would hold.

Letting go of her, he took a step back and cleared his throat. "If you wish to be an innocent until your wedding night, I would suggest you leave now," he said with a wry smile. "That was a lot further than I had planned to take that kiss, and I am sorely tempted to keep going. However, I don't think either of us wants our first time together to be in a drawing room."

Her cheeks heated when she realised what he was saying. She opened her mouth, but he silenced her with a deep kiss that made her toes curl.

Finally, he mumbled against her lips, "Leave now, darling."

She almost stayed. Her body still burned, and while she wasn't entirely sure what she wanted, she knew she wanted more of it. But he was right. They should wait until the wedding night. Shyly, she pressed a quick kiss on his mouth before she extracted herself from his arms and escaped. Walking down the hallway, she touched her glove-clad hand to her tingling lips and smiled. Nathaniel could be quite convincing when he wanted to be.

Nathaniel took a sip of brandy before putting the glass down on the round table he shared with his friends. They had brought him to White's, saying that they wanted to play a few games of whist before the engagement ball. It was a poor excuse for them to try to get him foxed. To their dismay, he had caught on early and was drinking at a more leisurely pace than any of them had hoped for.

"Refill, Pensington?" Wortham asked pleasantly when he noticed that his glass was empty.

"Please," he said with an amused glance in his friend's direction. "But I should warn you that you will not be drinking me under the table this evening. Aunt Jane will have my head if I arrive at my engagement ball stinking of brandy."

"You wound me." Wortham poured a good amount of brandy into the empty snifter. "Would I do such a thing?"

Nathaniel's snort was answer enough.

"When does the ball start?" Gabriel Winter asked while he moved the cards around in his hands. "Mother has told me I have to attend. There might be some unfortunate lady who catches my interest."

Wortham chuckled. "Are those your words or hers?"

"A bit of both," Winter admitted with a brief grin.

Gowthorpe flicked open his pocket watch. "We still have some time before we have to get home and make ourselves presentable."

"Your days of freedom are limited." Wortham grinned at Nathaniel. "Are you sure you don't want to hurry the drinking along a little?"

"I'm fine, thank you," he replied dryly. "Feel free to drink a little extra on my behalf, though."

Wortham laughed. "Tempting, but no. I think your lovely aunt would have my head too."

Taking another sip from his snifter, Nathaniel looked down at the cards in his hand. It was only his second glass, and they had already been there for a couple of hours. He knew it frustrated Wortham that he wouldn't drink more, but that just made it easier to resist. It would be much too satisfying for Wortham to see him make an arse out of himself at his engagement ball. The event was scheduled for that evening at Pensington House, arranged by his aunt, who loved such things.

Both Aunt Jane and Gowthorpe had wanted a long engagement of several months to stave off any rumours of anything untoward having happened between Angel and Chettisham, but Nathaniel had refused. Four weeks from the day he asked Angel to be his wife and no more. His excuse had been that it was better to get it done instead of letting people gossip for the next few months. The sooner they married, the sooner the *ton* could grow bored with the news and start looking for something else to talk about.

Which was all true. But mostly, he just wanted her to be his wife. He didn't trust himself to stay away from her for longer than that. Any time they were together, he wanted to drag her into a dark corner and kiss her senseless. No, that was a lie. He wanted to do a good deal more than kiss her. And once they were married, he could.

Every night, he lay in bed thinking of Angel and their impending vows. For someone who had no interest in marriage only a couple of months ago, he had to admit that his tune had changed. The moment he blurted out his offer of marriage—the moment he'd decided he wanted Angel for his wife—he had known he wanted it to be as soon as possible because every day he could not be with her was agony.

"Pensington?" Wortham was looking at him with an amused grin playing on his lips.

"What?" The disgruntled tone made his friend grin even wider.

"It's your turn to deal."

"Right."

"I wonder if Lady Garland will be at the ball tonight," Gowthorpe said aloud while waiting for him to finish shuffling.

"The widow?" Winter asked.

"Exactly the one." Gowthorpe smiled. "We had a nice meeting last week and I wouldn't mind seeing her again."

"It's your sister's engagement ball," Winter remarked hesitantly. "Should you be seducing women?"

Wortham chuckled. "There is no time or place that is not for seducing women."

"And she is a nice-looking woman," Nathaniel agreed.

"Not that you should notice anymore," Gowthorpe said stiffly, causing Wortham to burst out laughing again.

"God, Gowthorpe," he said as his laugh abated to a chuckle. "Give the man some rest. I know he's marrying your sister, but he's not blind."

Ignoring the earl—which was usually the best tactic to use—Gowthorpe turned to Winter. "Have you met Lady Garland? She's a few years older but absolutely stunning. Cherry lips. Chocolate brown hair. Skin like rich milk."

"Bloody hell," Wortham burst out with a disgusted look at his friend. "Must you compare all your women to food?"

"Why not?" The viscount shrugged. "I love both."

Nathaniel finished dealing the cards and looked down to see what he'd received when Wortham nodded to something across the room.

"I see Chettisham has no qualms about showing his face at the club after spreading those rumours," the earl said.

Looking up, seeing the other man instantly ignited something inside Nathaniel as he watched him laugh with some friends. What he had done to Angel was unforgivable. Pushing her into a corner she could only escape by marriage. Chettisham's plan had obviously been to make her marry him, but it had backfired, and now she was marrying Nathaniel. He hoped the other man hated it. He hoped Angel would never have to see his face again.

Rising from his chair, he felt Wortham's hand on his arm and looked down at his friend. "Don't do this, Pensington. You will make a scene and you have your engagement ball to get to."

"I just want to talk to him," Nathaniel said, pulling his arm free. "Make sure he knows not to show up anywhere Angel is."

"Give him my regards," Gowthorpe suggested coolly. "I'd go myself, but I know that if I do, I will start punching."

Nathaniel nodded and walked across the room. Wortham followed a few paces behind, obviously not trusting him to go alone. They neared the group of men where Chettisham stood, only to hear the man brag loudly.

"Oh yes, she sure spread her legs wide for me."

"Bloody hell," Nathaniel cursed and forcefully grabbed the other man's shoulder to spin him around. At the sight of him, Chettisham blanched but had no time to react before Nathaniel's fist connected solidly with his jaw. The impact surprised him enough to make him stumble back a step, trip on a rug, and fall flat on his arse.

"What happened to talking?" Wortham asked dryly, looking down at Chettisham, who wisely made no attempt to stand.

"I changed my mind," Nathaniel growled.

"Obviously." His friend chuckled. "I think it's time you return home to prepare for your engagement party instead."

With a hand on Nathaniel's shoulder, he guided him back to their table, where Winter sat with his mouth wide open while Gowthorpe looked oddly satisfied. Finishing the remaining brandy in his glass in one sweep, Nathaniel shook his head.

"What was that about?" Winter asked.

"He still hasn't stopped spreading lies." He flexed his hands, fighting the urge to go back for another round.

Gowthorpe seemed to share his thoughts as he grunted. "Should have given him a few more for good measure."

"Another time," Wortham said. "Time to get ready for the ball."

"Fine," Nathaniel muttered. "But if anyone sees that bastard anywhere near Angel in the future, let me know."

Chapter Twenty

Dear Diary,
 Who would have thought I would end up
 enjoying balls? I, who normally spend
 most of my time in solitude.

Mrs Grey had outdone herself with the preparations for the engagement ball. Angel would have to remember to thank her. Again. The crowded ballroom at Pensington House was dotted with large flower arrangements featuring plump damask roses and peonies, and after finding out that Angel liked ivy, Mrs Grey had fashioned long ivy garlands that hung above every entrance. White silk cloths with rose petals sprinkled over them covered the refreshment tables.

Because of the summer heat, the large doors to the garden were wide open, allowing the faint breeze inside. Out in the garden, differently shaped lanterns lit a path between the flowers and trees. A string quartet sat at the upper side of the room, providing music for the dancers.

Guests had already proclaimed the ball a squeeze, which was high praise in London circles. It was amazing how quickly the Howertys' aunt had planned the ball and still done such an amazing job. Two weeks to plan an event of this scale was quite impressive.

It had been a lovely evening so far with everyone coming forth to offer congratulations after an initial toast to the engaged from Mrs Grey. At the moment, Angel and Nathaniel were mingling separately, but now and then he would seek her out in the crowd and impart a few teasing words or share what he had been told during congratulations. She was in great spirits, and not even Marie glaring daggers at her from across the room could spoil her good mood.

She was marrying one of London's most sought-after bachelors. It didn't seem real. When she first arrived in London, she had been resigned to marry the man her parents had chosen for her, and even after turning Philip down, she had never truly considered the possibility of marrying a man like Nathaniel. But here she was. About to marry the man of her dreams. If only he could love her too.

"You look happy," James muttered. He'd not left her side the whole evening and had glared at Nathaniel every time he approached. Apparently, he was serious about not wanting to see them together until the marriage.

"I am happy," she admitted. "It's been a lovely evening."

He grunted his reply while his eyes swept the room.

She smiled. "James, you don't have to nanny me."

"What do you mean?" he asked defensively.

"I know you've been staying near me all night to make sure I don't spend time alone with Nathaniel," she said with a small laugh. "But you don't have to."

"I think I do."

"This is our engagement ball," she reminded him. "It's not as if we could sneak off to Gretna Green with no one noticing us leaving."

He grunted again while looking across the room before looking back at her. "Are you certain?"

"Yes. I can take care of myself this evening."

After a moment's silence, he nodded, but he didn't leave. Instead, he stared at her and opened his mouth before closing it again.

When he said nothing, she asked, "Was there something else?"

"I do want you to be happy, you know." He made a face and the tips of his ears reddened. "I've not always been there for you in the past, but I want you to be happy."

She reached up on her toes and placed a kiss on his cheek. "Thank you, James. I know you do. And I am happy."

"I'm glad," he mumbled. Then he smiled and touched her cheek gently. "Play nice tonight."

He disappeared into the crowd and she looked after him for a moment with a smile tugging on her lips. As she had suspected, he made his way to a nice-looking woman with brown hair. Alone for the first time that evening, she glanced towards the tempting doors to the garden. There were other people outside, so it wouldn't be improper for her to enjoy the evening breeze. Moving in that direction, a rich voice behind her brought her up short.

"I thought he'd never leave you alone."

Turning around, she smiled at Nathaniel, who stood a little too close for propriety.

"He will be back soon if you don't keep your distance," she teased.

"Point taken." He grinned and reversed a couple of steps. "Would you care to join me for a stroll in the garden?"

"I would love to. I was just about to go out there on my own."

He smiled. "I knew you wouldn't last an entire evening in an overcrowded ballroom. Wait here." Before she could say anything, he disappeared for a few moments, only to return a short while later, carrying two glasses of champagne and a small crystal bowl of strawberries. "Something for the road," he said, offering her a glass.

Taking the champagne from him, they walked out onto the terrace and down the few steps into the garden. A few more couples followed the lit path Mrs Grey had arranged while others stayed on the terrace. They strolled along the path in companionable silence until Nathaniel stopped, turning his head to see if anyone was looking at them. Then he quickly ushered her off the path and in between some trees towards one of the garden's corners where it was darker.

"What are you doing?" she whispered frantically, even while her pulse raced in anticipation.

"I thought we should have a private celebration of our now very official engagement." The look he gave her was so sensual she might have stopped breathing.

"Are you out of your mind?" she asked, but couldn't help smiling. "What if James sees us?"

"I'm just taking you for a stroll in the garden. Besides, no one can see us."

He was right. The faint light filtering through the branches of the trees obscured them from the sight of everyone walking on the brighter path.

"He will come looking for us." It was meant as a warning, but she could not hide the breathless quality of her voice.

"Gowthorpe is busy with Lady Garland." Nathaniel grinned. "And we won't stay long. Just share a glass of champagne and some strawberries with me."

The idea of hiding from everyone was more exciting than she wanted to admit. It was only for a few minutes. What harm could there be? Nathaniel took a sip from his glass and she did the same. Finding a suitable branch on one tree, he put the small bowl of strawberries down before taking another sip. The spot he'd brought them to wasn't large, and he stood much too close. She need only reach her hand out and she'd touch him.

"Here." He took a strawberry from the bowl and held it out in front of her mouth. "Taste it."

Hesitating only for a moment, she leaned forward to take the small berry in her mouth. It was ripe and juicy, but before she could bite into it, Nathaniel pressed his lips to hers, sharing the taste of it. Then he pulled back, taking the berry with him and swallowing it.

"Delicious," he mumbled before bending down to kiss her.

Caught in the passion of his hot mouth against hers, Angel dropped her glass when she wound her arms around his neck. When she returned the kiss with equal fervour, he groaned low in his throat and pulled her body close to his. Unlike her, he somehow still held on to his glass, spilling none of the champagne. He trailed kisses along her cheek and down her neck, groaning against her skin. "God, I can't wait until the wedding is over and done with."

"So we can do this whenever we want to?" she whispered while burying her hands in his soft, dark hair.

He straightened a little so he could look at her with a wicked smile. "That," he said. "And so I can do everything I've been wanting to do to you since that morning you found me in bed."

Warmth spread through her as she stared up at him. "There's more?"

He chuckled. "Most definitely."

"Oh." She wasn't sure what to expect. There had never been a time for her mother to tell her about what happened between a husband and wife since she'd been so young at the time of her passing, and Aunt Christine had never thought it necessary to discuss such matters.

"Don't worry," Nathaniel mumbled, bending his head to kiss her again. "I will enjoy showing you everything."

His tongue slipped past her lips to explore her mouth, replacing her anxiety with a fiery heat that allowed no other thoughts. Without breaking the kiss, he put his glass away, leaving both hands free. Something he took immediate advantage of by caressing her from the shoulders down to her derriere. Pressing her close, she could feel something hard pressing against her stomach, and her body tingled as heat rushed between her thighs.

A cough behind them made Nathaniel step away from her.

"I hate to break this little party up," a male voice said. "But I'm under strict orders to make sure the two of you return to the ballroom. Preferably separately."

"Damn it, Wortham!" Nathaniel snapped, still holding her in his arms, even if their bodies were no longer pressed together. "Have you no decency?"

The glimmer of Wortham's white teeth flashed in the semi-darkness. "Of course not. I expected you to know better."

With a sigh, Nathaniel leaned his forehead against Angel's, meeting her eyes. But his words were for his friend. "Could you give us a moment to recover?"

"Afraid not," Wortham said but didn't sound the least bit contrite. "If you need a moment, you better let Miss Grafton head back inside on her own."

Reluctantly, Nathaniel let go of her and moved a little further away with a glare in Wortham's direction. "Since when do you run Gowthorpe's errands?" he asked tightly.

"Since they allow me to ruin your evening," his friend replied smoothly.

She watched the exchange even while her head spun, almost like she'd drunk too much. Whenever she spent time in Nathaniel's arms, her good sense seemed to flee the scene, replaced by nothing but the need to be close to him. And it took a moment for the escaped sense to return. Her cheeks heated. Wortham had seen them kiss! It was mortifying.

"I suppose you had better go inside to show your face before Gowthorpe comes to your rescue," Nathaniel said dryly. Giving her a quick once-over, he nodded. "You look respectable enough."

"Are you not coming inside?"

"Not yet. I need a moment to calm down." He placed a quick kiss on her lips.

She frowned. Why could he not come now? If she had calmed down enough to go back inside, then surely he must too? Wortham seemed to notice her confusion because he chuckled and offered his arm.

"Come with me, sweet," he said. "Your future husband needs a moment alone."

Taking the earl's arm, she let him lead her back towards the lit path in the garden. Before taking her out from behind the trees, he made sure no one was looking in their direction.

"I wouldn't want anyone to think I've been seducing the bride-to-be," he said with a wink, bringing her with him onto the path, walking as if they had been there all along.

"Would they think that?"

"If I came out from behind some trees with you?" He chuckled. "Most likely. I'm not known to hide between trees with women to play chess."

She blushed but dared to tease him back. "Are you known to skulk between trees at all, then?"

The question made him laugh, and she could see how so many women found him attractive. Of course, he could never measure up to Nathaniel, but his devil-may-care charm, title, and fortune would make him a prime target for any other woman looking for a husband. Though she heard some unmarried ladies weren't allowed anywhere near him because of his reputation. Apparently, there was some scandal in his past involving a young lady, but she had never heard the particulars.

"I'll admit that I prefer to bring my conquests to other places," he said with a charming grin. "Now, let's find your brother so I can show him you are still wearing all of your clothes."

Her cheeks burned. Could the man say nothing without deliberately causing embarrassment?

The ballroom was empty of people except for the small group sitting on some chairs. Without the sizable crowd that had been there until half an hour earlier, the room looked exceptionally large and empty, even with the chairs and tables along the walls. With a smile, Nathaniel crossed the room after having seen the last few guests off and came to a stop before the gathered few.

"It was a good evening," Aunt Jane said before trying to hide a yawn behind her gloved hand.

Angel smiled. "You did a wonderful job."

"We should probably head home." Gowthorpe stood and rolled his shoulders. Once he realised the Browns had gone home without them, he had given up his pursuit of Lady Garland—who had left with Wortham instead—and stayed with his sister.

"You could sleep here tonight if you wish," Nathaniel suggested.

"And allow you the chance to slip into my sister's room?" His friend wrinkled his nose as if smelling something foul. "I think not."

"James!" Angel gasped, her face flushing red.

"I can provide Miss Grafton with a key." Aunt Jane appeared more amused than shocked by Gowthorpe's comment. Nathaniel probably shouldn't be surprised. She had known his friends for years, and if one got used to the crassness of Wortham, one could handle most indelicate subjects.

"Very well." His friend nodded. "It's late, and I imagine our driver is probably already asleep somewhere. Maybe have a footman tell him so he can find an available bed."

Crossing his arms over his chest, Nathaniel met his friend's eyes. "I do have more honour than seducing your sister when you're both guests under my roof."

"I know. My apologies." Gowthorpe sighed. "It's just difficult to digest the idea of my sister with my best friend."

"You mean it's difficult to digest that your lady sweet left with Wortham," Nathaniel said dryly.

"That too."

"Gentlemen," Aunt Jane interrupted. "May I remind you that there are ladies present?"

"Beg your pardon, Aunt."

She looked out over the ballroom and smiled. "It was a lot of work, but it was worth it." Turning her head back towards Nathaniel, she continued, "I will send someone to Davenhall tomorrow to ask them to pack my and the girls' things."

He nodded, having expected this, but the statement made Angel straighten in her chair.

"Why are you packing?" she asked with a small frown puckering her brow.

Aunt Jane smiled at her. "Now that Nathaniel is taking a wife, I know he wishes to spend more time at Davenhall out of the Season, so the girls and I will move out."

"Oh." Angel worried her bottom lip with her teeth while she took in the information. "But I don't want to push you out of your own home."

"It's Nathaniel's house, not ours. And it's customary that the siblings move out of the ancestral home when the man takes a wife. But don't worry, we won't be moving far. Nathaniel owns another smaller estate only a day's ride away."

Angel was quiet for a moment before she looked up at him. "Do they have to move?"

The question surprised him. "I assumed that's what you wanted. It's customary like Aunt Jane said."

"It's just… I never had a large family," she said, looking between him and Aunt Jane. "I would much rather you stay at Davenhall together with me and Nathaniel."

His aunt smiled and took Angel's hand. "You are too sweet. If that is what you wish, then we will. At least to begin with. After a while, you might grow tired of having us about."

"I doubt it," Angel said, returning the smile before turning to him. "You don't mind, do you?"

She looked so anxious and adorable that he would have been hard-pressed to say no even if she'd asked him to cut off his right arm.

"Of course, they can stay," he mumbled. "For as long as they want. You might regret it, though. My sisters can be quite a handful."

"We're a handful?" Jessica scoffed. "That is nothing compared to what you are."

Angel beamed. "I think I will love it."

Aunt Jane leaned over and gave her a hug. "I know it's not official until you've declared yourself before a priest," she mumbled. "But welcome to the family."

"Thank you," Angel whispered, her eyes moist.

He was glad his family liked her as well as they did. Contrary to many of his acquaintances, he was actually quite close to his family, and that they liked the woman he was marrying made his life a lot easier. Things were turning out well. If only time would speed up so he could get married already, everything would be perfect. The interlude in the garden had only reminded him of how desperately he wanted Angel, and it had taken him quite a while to calm the fire raging in his body after she left with Wortham. As much as he was loath to admit it, it was probably a good thing that the earl had interrupted them because he wasn't entirely sure he would have had enough sense to stop kissing her.

When he'd brought her outside, it hadn't only been to kiss her. There was something he wanted to give her, but she had looked so lovely and delectable that he couldn't keep his hands off her. Just like Gowthorpe had feared. The irony. But that reminded him he still hadn't given her the gift.

His aunt stood, hiding another yawn. "I believe it is time for us to retire," she said before walking out of the ballroom.

Everyone fell into step behind her, but at the foot of the stairs, Nathaniel placed a hand on Angel's arm to detain her. Gowthorpe scowled.

"I only wish to speak with her for a moment," Nathaniel snapped impatiently. "You may sit outside her room and wait for her to come if you wish. It will not take long."

Gowthorpe nodded and continued up the stairs after Aunt Jane and Jessica, leaving Nathaniel and Angel alone downstairs. His first impulse was to take her in his arms again, but he resisted since he knew he very well might not let her go if he did, and his friend would soon be downstairs again if she didn't make it upstairs soon.

"Outside in the garden," he began, but stopped with a grin when she blushed. "No, I mean, I brought you outside for a different reason. Or rather, for a second reason. I definitely wanted to kiss you."

"I wanted to kiss you too," she admitted shyly, her cheeks staining prettily, and he almost reached for her again.

Forcing himself to remember the purpose of keeping her downstairs, he fished something out of his pocket and offered it to her. "I just wanted to give you this."

Lying in his palm was a gold ring. She let out a small gasp and hesitantly reached out to take it. Twirling it between her fingers, she stared at it for a moment. It was a beautiful gold ring with a band of diamonds and emeralds. Looking up at him, her eyes were moist again.

"You didn't have to get me a ring," she mumbled.

"I wanted to," he said and leaned forward to place a kiss on her lips, but straightened immediately afterwards so he wouldn't be tempted to prolong it. Taking her hand in his, he took the ring from her and carefully slipped it on her finger. "It suits you. The colour compliments your eyes."

"Thank you," she whispered.

"My pleasure." He stole another kiss. How could he resist when she looked so adorable? "We had better go upstairs now before your brother comes running to retrieve you."

She laughed. "Yes, I suppose we better."

Placing her hand on his arm, he lead her up the stairs and down the hall to a guest room. As he had expected, Gowthorpe stood in the hallway leaning against the door. Feeling slightly wicked and only wanting to irritate his friend, he bent down to give Angel a last kiss.

"A good night to you," he mumbled.

She smiled and went into her room as her brother moved away from the door.

"I really wish you wouldn't do that," Gowthorpe muttered when the door closed behind her.

"What?" Nathaniel asked innocently.

"Kiss my sister in my presence."

"You had better get used to it, old friend. In two weeks, she will be my wife."

Gowthorpe shuddered. "Please. Don't remind me."

Nathaniel laughed at his friend's disgusted expression. "Good night, Gowthorpe."

Chapter Twenty-One

Dear Diary,
 I always believed Aunt Christine's
 greatest crime was negligence
 but I'm coming to realise she did
 more damage than I ever thought possible.

The drawing room was still filled with bouquets when Angel entered a few days later. Congratulatory flowers for the newly engaged. She smiled as nervous excitement made her stomach flip. Her engagement to Nathaniel. Without thinking, her fingers automatically touched the ring on her left hand. It was such a sweet gesture. He wasn't marrying her for love, but he was still proving to be a thoughtful man. Maybe love wasn't so important after all. A particular new bloom caught her eye; in a tall, thin vase stood a single deep red rose. Walking over to it, she carefully touched its soft petals.

"That one came today without a card," Marie said when she noticed her looking. "I don't know who it's from."

Angel did. That Nathaniel remembered her bit of nonsense about preferring roses to other flowers made her feel better about their impending nuptials. He cared enough to make sure she knew he remembered. One could do a lot worse for a husband. She was still smiling when she sat down on the sofa to share tea and biscuits with her aunt and cousin, eliciting some odd looks from the two women.

"It's such a pity you didn't accept Mr Chettisham as your husband," Aunt Christine said while she put three pieces of sugar into her small teacup.

How were they back to that again? They had all literally attended her engagement to another man the other night. She had believed her aunt would give up promoting Philip when the engagement became known, but her aunt was nothing if not persistent. Taking a sip of her tea, she pretended not to have heard her aunt's comment. Naturally, that didn't dissuade the older woman.

"Mr Chettisham is such a nice-looking man," she continued. "Of course, nothing like your marquess, but he is quite popular among the ladies. Without the reputation that follows the marquess."

"Nathaniel's reputation is hardly bad," Angel cut in, unable to keep silent. "He's an honourable man."

Aunt Christine looked at her and shook her head, making a clucking sound. "He is known to be quite favoured by the ladies, you know. Any man with his looks and fortune would be. Though, naturally, he doesn't have a reputation anywhere near that of his friend, the earl. Now, that one is a true rake. But you should be careful nonetheless, Angel. When a man is used to his pick of all the ladies, he might not settle for only one woman. Even if he is married."

Flexing her hands around her teacup, Angel tried to tamp down the anger her aunt's words provoked. How dare she insinuate Nathaniel might not be faithful? Many men kept a mistress, but that was something between her and Nathaniel, and not something her aunt should discuss with her.

"I think that is something for me to worry about, and not you," she said stiffly.

"Yes. That is true, of course." Aunt Christine took a sip of her tea and glanced towards the clock on the mantelpiece. "I only want you to go into this marriage with your eyes wide open."

Seething, Angel remained silent, staring into her tea. This had always been how her aunt behaved around her. She would never outright be rude, but she would make little comments here and there that stuck in Angel's mind and made her question her own beliefs. She vaguely registered that the butler came in to announce a visitor.

"Oh, how lovely," Aunt Christine said cheerily. "Please show them in."

Not having paid attention, Angel nearly choked on her tea when Philip walked through the door a few moments later. It had been a while since she last saw him, but he looked the same as she remembered. His tall form was clad in grey with a white neckcloth.

When he sat down next to her, she moved a few inches to the side, not wanting to sit too close. What was her aunt thinking to invite him into their house after what he had done? He had single-handedly nearly brought her to social ruin.

Her aunt suddenly stood. "Oh, Marie, look at the time. We have an appointment at the... uh, modiste. If you'll excuse us."

Before Angel could react, her aunt ushered her cousin out of the room, closing the door behind them. Staring after them, Angel didn't quite understand what had just happened. What was her aunt thinking, leaving her with Philip? It was highly inappropriate for her to spend time alone with a man behind a closed door.

She quickly got up and moved towards the exit, but Philip hindered her by jumping up and blocking her path. She gave him an icy look. "Let me pass, Mr Chettisham."

Annoyance rippled over his face at the formal use of his name, but he quickly hid it. "I only wish to speak to you," he pleaded. "Please spare me a few moments of your time."

Since he was still blocking her path to the door, she took a few wary steps back into the room.

"What are you doing here?" she asked, crossing her arms.

"I wanted to apologise for my behaviour," he said, taking a hesitant step closer. "I realise that it wasn't very well done of me to spread those rumours, but I was desperate."

"Why?" She narrowed her eyes. He sounded sincere, but she couldn't help being suspicious of his intentions.

He took another few steps closer but stopped when he saw her cold look. "Have you not understood yet that I love you?" he beseeched her. "The thought of losing you is unbearable."

"So you spread lies to besmirch my good reputation." There was no mistaking the icy quality of her voice. He had accused her of being made of ice before, and she was more than happy to embody that sentiment. "Not a great way to show your affection."

A flicker of annoyance broke through the mask of sincerity he was trying to project. He reached out towards her, but she backed away another step, out of reach. "I came here today, hoping to make amends. I would still like you to be my wife."

She couldn't help the panicked laugh that escaped her, and she quickly clapped a hand over her mouth. It was just so preposterous. When his visage visibly clouded over in anger, she pulled herself together.

"I'm sorry, but it is far too late for us. I'm engaged to Nathaniel. And I do not wish to marry you," she said, trying to be direct but not unkind. "You know this, so why do you persist?"

"He's only marrying you to save your reputation. You and I... We were meant for each other, Angel. And you know it." He could no longer hide his anger and frustration. It oozed out of every pore as he stared at her. Everything she said to contradict him seemed to fuel his temper, but she was no longer the same woman who had shrunk away from every confrontation.

These last few weeks, she had not only found a new family in the Howertys, but she had found her voice, and she would no longer automatically defer to everyone else's wishes. She had her own wishes and wants and she finally felt secure enough to stand up for them.

"No, Philip. Our parents wished for us to marry, but there was no love between us. No attraction." She let out a small, helpless laugh. "For God's sake, Philip, we don't even like each other!"

"But you have to be my wife!" he snapped, which sobered her instantly. He was rarely pleasant to her, but he could be outright cruel when in a foul mood.

"No, I don't." She glanced at the closed door, debating if she could dash past him and leave before he could catch her. The way his eyes gleamed with anger and desperation made her skin crawl. Why had Aunt Christine left them alone?

"I thought the rumours would be enough to force you to marry me," he burst out, throwing an arm out in frustration. "But you fooled that idiot Pensington into marrying you instead. I guess I will have to make the rumours reality to make you mine. Do you think he will want you when I've defiled you?"

Icy fear slowed her movements even as she continued edging away. "What are you talking about?"

"I think you know." A cold sneer touched his otherwise handsome face.

"Are you daft? We're in my brother's house!" Still backing away from him, she added, "I will scream."

"In case you haven't noticed, your brother is not at home and most of your servants have their day off. The only ones in the house who will hear you scream are your aunt and cousin. Do you really think they will help you? Who do you think told me the best time to visit?" He smiled coldly.

The reality of what was happening hit her like a punch in the gut. Aunt Christine had planned this with him? The house was practically empty on a Sunday, with most of the staff visiting family. James was at his club and her uncle—though she doubted he would have helped—was in his.

Why, Aunt Christine? Why?

In a desperate attempt to reach the door, she tried to dash past him, but Philip caught her around the waist and pulled her close. Clasping a hand over her mouth to make sure she couldn't scream, he leaned close and whispered in her ear. "I told you that you're mine. You should have listened."

A spear of pure terror shot through her body and she tensed in his arms. Before she could react, he slammed her against a wall, making her lose her breath. She panicked, fighting for air with his body pressed close. He was strong and didn't seem to mind her hands trying to shove him away. When his dry lips touched her neck, she wanted to cry.

This isn't happening.

"My ice queen." He moved a hand to her breast to squeeze it hard. "Not so unaffected now, are you?"

She wanted to scream that he disgusted her, but his hand still covered her mouth. When his knee wedged itself between her legs, she began struggling in earnest and grabbed a handful of his hair with her hand. All that got her was a hard slap, which made her cheek sting and her eyes water.

He grabbed her wrist roughly and pressed it against the wall. A lascivious grin spread over his face. "If I'd known you would be this fiery, I might have tried to seduce you sooner."

It was futile, but she screamed anyway, the sound muffled by his hand.

"Scream all you want," he hissed in her ear. "It won't save you. You'll be mine soon, and your brother will make you marry me."

She shoved at him, resulting in little but a slight movement backwards. He was delusional. The grip on her face was bruising, and she could feel her cheeks getting wet from tears. She didn't even know when she had started crying. Philip pushed himself closer, crowding her against the wall. There was a strange noise, and it took her a moment to realise it was the sound of her muffled screaming.

Philip froze. She blinked. Had he changed her mind? Then, in the corner of her eye, she caught sight of the door swinging open. A moment later, her brother stepped inside. A wave of relief crashed over her, leaving her weak and sobbing.

"What the hell?" James cursed. "Get off her!"

"I can explain!" Philip blurted out. Letting her go, he stepped away from her, and she sank to the floor with her hands covering her mouth to hold back the hysterical sobbing.

"What's going on?" Nathaniel appeared behind James. Taking one look at Angel sobbing on the floor, his eyes widened and his gaze flew to Philip. "You bastard," he growled, leaping towards the other man.

Philip scrambled to get away, but Nathaniel caught him and delivered a right hook that had him sprawling on the floor. While Nathaniel was pulling him up by the front of his coat, James came over to Angel and helped her up. Hot tears streamed down her face, but her body was no longer wracked by the crying. Grateful for his arrival, she buried her face in his shoulder when he took her in his arms.

Her brother might not always have been there growing up, but he had been doing his best as a young man, and he was trying to do better. Since coming to London, her life had become better in many ways, and he was one reason. He was the safe harbour her aunt and uncle had never been.

She could hear the sounds of a scuffle behind them and the unmistakable sound of bone hitting flesh. James's stance was tense even while he held her close, like he was restraining himself from joining in.

"That's enough, Pensington," he finally said. "Throw the bastard out of the house."

"Gladly," Nathaniel's voice said, and two sets of footsteps receded.

He was gone. Philip was gone. She was safe. Suddenly she was crying again from sheer relief. When Nathaniel returned, he held his arms open and, without thinking, she moved from her brother to him. The warmth of his embrace when he wrapped his arms around her calmed her somewhat. He stroked her hair and back soothingly while she cried against his shoulder.

"How did he get in here?" he asked James over her head, his voice laced with barely suppressed anger.

"I don't know, but I intend to find out."

Lifting her head, she choked back the tears, not wanting to cry anymore. Philip didn't deserve her tears. "Aunt Christine let him in. Then she and Marie left and closed the door."

James let out a stream of curses before bellowing his butler's name. Being one of the few servants in the house that day, Dobbins arrived a short while later and was ordered to bring Mrs Brown to the drawing room immediately. While waiting for her to arrive, her brother paced the room impatiently while Nathaniel continued to hold Angel in his arms.

No longer crying, she felt weak and shaky, and in desperate need of a bath. Fortunately, Philip had not got far, but she wanted to wash the feeling of his hands and lips on her with scalding water and a lot of soap. Both Nathaniel and her brother were still seething. Philip might have been lucky to leave in one piece.

Taking her gently by the shoulders to hold her out in front of him, Nathaniel looked her over. "Are you all right?"

She nodded, and he bent his head to place a tender kiss on the top of her head. Bringing her over to the sofas, he sat down with her and poured her a fresh cup of tea. When he gave it to her, she almost spilt the contents since her hands were shaking so badly. A spark of anger flashed in his eyes at the sight, but he put the teacup back on the table and took her shaking hands in his own.

"Would you rather not be here when Gowthorpe confronts your aunt?" he asked gently.

She shook her head. "I want to be here. I need to know what she says."

"I understand." He turned her hands over and placed a kiss on the inside of one wrist. His brow creased as he saw the red mark from where Philip had grabbed her. It looked like it might turn into a bruise, and she couldn't help but wonder if the same would happen to her face.

"Bloody hell," he growled. "I'm going to kill the bastard."

"You can't tell anyone what happened here today." She wiped at her eyes. "It would shred the last remnants of my reputation. It's already in jeopardy after his vile lies."

"It's his reputation that should suffer. And it will," he vowed. "We found things out today that will make most people turn their backs on him."

"What's that?"

James gave up on his stalking and walked over to them, but remained standing. "I already knew he was in financial trouble, but it's a lot worse than I believed. His father has gambled away most of the family fortune. Once that's known, no one will marry into that family. He wanted to marry you and marry you quickly before anyone found out."

"When you broke off the engagement, he must have panicked," Nathaniel said. "He had counted on your dowry to dig him out of the hole all this time, and when that was no longer an option, he realised his bad finances make him a rather unappealing match to most families."

"Exactly." James nodded. "When you're looking for someone to marry, you either look for someone with money or a good title. He has neither. And why would he settle for just anyone when he was so close to getting you?"

"And he's a terrible human being," Nathaniel muttered.

"Well, I didn't know that." James rubbed the back of his neck. "If I'd known what scum he is, I never would have agreed to honour our parents' wish for him to marry Angel."

"None of us knew how low he would sink." Nathaniel squeezed Angel's hand. "Had I suspected anything like this might happen, I would have told you not to let him near her."

She leaned her head in her hand. It was aching from the barrage of information, but she refused to leave before they spoke to Aunt Christine. This was a confrontation she could not–would not–back down from.

"Where the hell is she?" James complained just as the woman arrived in the doorway.

"You wished to see me?" she said stiffly, with a glance in Angel's direction.

"Yes. Please take a seat."

Angel watched while Aunt Christine warily moved into the room to sit on the sofa furthest away from James, who had resumed pacing the room with restless energy. Her aunt kept her hands in her lap but nervously tugged at a small handkerchief as she watched her nephew move from one side of the room to the other.

When James whipped around in a burst of anger and levelled the older woman with a glare, they all jumped. "What the hell was going through your head to leave Chettisham alone with Angel?"

Her face blanched, and she gave Angel a desperate look as if hoping to find out what had happened. "He... He said he wanted to convince her to marry him," she said hesitantly before looking back at James. "I swear that is all he said."

"Why would you let him inside in the first place?" He scowled. "Angel is engaged to Pensington now. There was no way she would accept Chettisham's suit again."

"I wanted her to marry him," Aunt Christine admitted reluctantly, finally seeming to realise she would not get away with some poor excuse.

Angel leaned forward, and she could feel Nathaniel's hand grip hers a little harder. "Why?" she asked, unable to understand why her aunt wanted her to marry the man who had treated her so badly.

The other woman turned back to her. "I knew the day would come when we would no longer be welcome to live at Hefferton

Place. Once you married, we would be asked to move back to the Midlands." She looked at James again and said forcefully, "I hate the Midlands! I always did. The thought of returning there made me sick."

"I don't understand." James raked a hand through his blond hair. "What does this have to do with Angel marrying Chettisham?"

"There is a small estate included in Angel's dowry," Aunt Christine explained. "A lovely little house in Kent. Mr Chettisham promised me that your uncle and I would get it once he married Angel and could give it to us."

The admission was like a punch to the gut. Angel had to hold back a wave of nausea at the realisation of how little her aunt cared for her. She had always known her aunt didn't love her—certainly not the way she loved her daughter, but that her aunt could use her like this... It was beyond anything she had ever believed her capable of.

"So you were willing to sacrifice my sister so you wouldn't have to move back to the Midlands?" James's voice was dangerously calm and measured.

"You don't know what it's like!" Aunt Christine snapped. "Can you imagine what that is like for me after having lived for years in a house like Hefferton Place? My sister married a viscount while I got stuck with a man with no title. We live in a small house with barely a handful of servants! Why should I suffer when my sister's offspring gets everything served on a platter just because my sister got lucky in marriage? It's not fair!"

Angel inhaled sharply. It suddenly made so much sense why her aunt had never cared for her. She's been jealous of her sister, and Angel was an extension of that. It was both sad and something of a relief. Nothing she could have done would have changed how her aunt felt about her. It wasn't her fault.

"Did you know Chettisham was planning to force himself on Angel?" Nathaniel asked.

Her aunt looked down at her hands. "He did mention that it would be the last resort. If he ruined her, then you would no longer want her, and she'd have to marry him."

"You disgust me," James said coldly. "Get out of my sight. I want you and your family out of this house by nightfall and on your way to the Midlands. You had better pray that I never catch sight of you again."

"No!" Aunt Christine gasped. "You cannot do that!"

"Watch me," James growled.

Nathaniel watched Mrs Brown stand stiffly and leave the room in a huff. He was of two minds to follow her to make sure she packed up her belongings and vacated the premises at that minute. Coming into the drawing room after Gowthorpe to see Angel sobbing on the floor with Chettisham stepping away from her had been awful. He flexed his free hand. It still smarted after the punches he'd aimed at the other man. Chettisham should be grateful he could still walk.

With a weary sigh, Gowthorpe sank onto the sofa his aunt had vacated and ran a hand over his face. There was a haunted quality to his eyes.

"I should have thrown them out long before." Shaking his head, he looked at Angel. "I'm so sorry. This would never have happened if I had tossed them out on their arses after Marie locked you in the dressing room. I never understood how awful they were to you."

"I'm the one who asked you not to. None of us thought Aunt Christine would go this far." She looked down at her hand in her lap. The other was still in Nathaniel's.

"Still..." Gowthorpe gave his sister a helpless look. "It makes me feel horrible to imagine what you must have gone through. I should have been there for you, but I left you with the Browns, thinking you'd be better off with a family than with a scoundrel like me."

"It's all right, James." Angel managed a wobbly smile. "You didn't know. It wasn't the best childhood, but... it's over now. I never have to see them again."

Gowthorpe swallowed visibly. "Damn right. All I want is for you to be happy."

"I've been happy here with you." She reached out with her free hand and squeezed her brother's arm. Nathaniel pretended not to see when his friend blinked rapidly.

"They will never set a foot near you again," Gowthorpe vowed, his voice thick with emotion. "Aunt Christine may be our mother's sister, but she is dead to me."

Angel nodded slowly, her eyes welling up again. "I knew she cared little about me, but to finally hear how little I mean to her for her to be willing to put me in a room alone with Philip, I—"

Her voice broke on a sob, and anger rushed over Nathaniel. If he didn't think Angel needed him close, he would happily have found Chettisham for another round. Or her aunt. Anyone. He needed to hurt someone for the anguish he heard in Angel's voice. Pulling her into his arms, he let her cry against his shoulder while he looked at Gowthorpe over the top of her head.

"Make sure everyone knows of Chettisham's finances," he said coldly, and his friend nodded.

"All of London will know before the day is over." Gowthorpe glanced at his sister in Nathaniel's arms, then he sighed and stood. "I will find a servant and have them draw her a bath. It might help her relax."

Nathaniel remained on the sofa with Angel after Gowthorpe disappeared. She continued crying. Not knowing what he could do to help, he sat still and stroked her back, murmuring nonsense words of comfort, until she finally quieted. Pulling back slightly, she looked up at him with the shadow of a wry smile.

"I beg your pardon," she mumbled, drying her eyes. "I seem destined to cry and wet your coats."

"You can wet any coat of mine any time." Reaching out, he tucked a finger under her chin and gave her what he hoped was an encouraging smile. He wasn't sure he managed, since the signs of her struggle with Chettisham made his blood boil.

She stroked a lock of hair out of her face to fasten it behind her ear. Some of her hair had come loose, and her topknot hung off to the side. A red mark covered her cheekbone where she must have been slapped. He tamped down his fury. Angel needed him. This was not the time to run off in a hot-headed rage, no matter how tempting.

"How are you feeling?" he asked gently.

"In desperate need of a bath." She sighed. "I'm just sad to realise how little I mattered to Aunt Christine after all. It's no wonder I've always felt unwanted."

"You are wanted now." The words left him before he could stop them, and her gaze flew to his. He quickly added, "My aunt and sisters love you and cannot wait for you to be a part of our family."

A shadow of disappointment crossed her face, and he felt like an arse, but he didn't want to give her false hope. It was important to remember that while he liked her, and was quite content to take her as his wife, their relationship would never go beyond that. Could not go beyond that. He would never love anyone. Would never risk finding out if he would break the way his father had.

"I look forward to that, too. Your family is lovely. I will see if my bath is ready."

She stood and walked across the room. He wanted to call out. To tell her... he wasn't sure what. Something—anything—to make the sadness radiating from her evaporate. But he remained silent, watching her leave the room and close the door behind her.

He'd do well to remember he only desired her. Friendship was the extent of his feelings towards her. He flexed his hands. It was getting more and more difficult to convince himself of his lack of feelings. And that terrified him.

After her bath, Angel felt somewhat better. Wearing a simple dress, she stood in the upstairs drawing room window. Outside on the street, Aunt Christine, Uncle George, and Marie were getting into a carriage to finally depart from her life. She wouldn't miss them, but it still saddened her that it had come to this. They were meant to be her family.

Marie lifted her face, and their gazes met for a moment. The pure hatred in her cousin's blue eyes made her take a step back. It shouldn't have surprised her that her cousin would blame their eviction on her. According to Marie, every bad thing that happened was usually because of Angel. With a sigh, she walked away from the window. She would never have to worry about keeping her cousin happy again.

"Did the bath help?"

She looked up to see Nathaniel at the door to the hallway. Her skin still crawled when she thought of Philip, but she felt better, so she nodded. "I was just watching the Browns leave."

"Good riddance," Nathaniel muttered as he came over to her. Taking her hands in his, he lifted them to his mouth and placed a soft kiss on each. "I hope we never see them again."

"We shouldn't unless you're planning a trip to the Midlands." She smiled faintly. "I thought you'd returned home."

"I wanted to see you again before I left. Don't tell Gowthorpe. I think he might have my head if he sees me alone with you. He's gone to spread the information about Chettisham's finances. Soon everyone will know, and no one will want anything to do with him."

"I just want to forget about the whole ordeal. I want to think about pleasant things."

"Kittens and rainbows?" The corners of Nathaniel's mouth twitched.

"That's a start. I'm sure your sister Rain could help with at least one of those."

He chuckled and pulled her into his arms for a hug. His enveloping warmth chased away the chill of the day's events even better than the hot bath had, and she relaxed in his embrace. Resting her head on his chest, she could hear the steady beating of his heart.

"How many kittens would you like?" he mumbled against her hair. "I'm sure Rain could supply you with any number."

She stood silently in his arms for a moment before she took a step back to look up at him. "What if Philip returns?" she asked, her voice wavering. "I can't stop worrying about it, even if it seems unlikely."

"The servants have all been informed that he is never to be allowed entry to this house again." Nathaniel squeezed her arms, his eyes meeting hers. "He will never get you. And in less than two weeks, you will be my wife. If he has not admitted defeat before, he must at that point."

It was true. She would be Nathaniel's wife in less than two weeks. It still didn't seem real.

"And until then"—he bent down and placed a tender kiss on her lips—"we will keep you busy with visits to the modiste and wedding preparations. My sisters and aunt won't leave you alone. You will pray for some peace."

"I quite look forward to it. Your family is wonderful." A slight smile broke through her worries.

"They are," he agreed. With a mock frown, he wryly asked, "You're not marrying me just to get my family, are you?"

She laughed quietly, secretly loving how he tried so hard to make her relax. She winked. "Maybe just a little."

"I'm sure they would happily adopt you and toss me out." Nathaniel chuckled. "They love you."

"I love them too." *And you.* She didn't say the last words since she knew he didn't want her love. Nor had he mentioned any for her, only from his family. But she would not dwell on that. Not right now. Not with less than two weeks before their wedding.

Chapter Twenty-Two

Dear Diary,
 I wish I knew what to expect on the
 wedding night. I'm not sure if I'm
 more nervous about the wedding
 or the night to come.

Angel twirled the ring on her finger while she looked out the window of the carriage nearly two weeks later. A tight knot in her stomach reminded her of the impending wedding. *Tomorrow.* She could scarcely believe it. In only a day, she would be Nathaniel's wife.

The ceremony would take place at a church in the small village of Bridlewood to which parish Davenhall belonged. Both Nathaniel's estate and that of Wortham's family bordered the village on opposite sides. The decision had been made for most of them to stay at Wortham's estate Holcombe Hall the night before the wedding, while Mrs Grey had travelled to Davenhall a few days earlier to prepare for the wedding breakfast.

It was a kind gesture from Wortham's father, the Duke of Ashbrook, to allow them to stay. And necessary, since James had blankly refused to let her sleep in Nathaniel's house before they were married. Which was unreasonable, but that was James these days. Unreasonable.

They had set off from London the previous morning in two carriages. She with her brother, Jessica, and Wortham while Nathaniel rode with his other two sisters. He would bring them to Davenhall and their aunt before joining the wedding party at Holcombe Hall.

The Duke of Ashbrook was fond of Nathaniel and had offered his estate for any guests coming from London and needing a place to stay for the night. There shouldn't be too many, since it would be a small wedding. Angel barely knew anyone other than the Howertys, and Nathaniel had only invited his closest friends. If she was honest, she was quite relieved about the smaller size. She didn't think she would have been comfortable with a grand London wedding.

Bridlewood and the two estates surrounding it were two days' ride from London, and they had spent last night at an inn along the way. It hadn't been bad, but she looked forward to sleeping in a proper bed without having to hear people walking through the hallway at all hours of the night. And the following night, she would sleep in a new bed. *Her marriage bed.* The thought made her shiver. The idea of sharing it with Nathaniel was both terrifying and enticing, partly because she didn't know what to expect. But if it was anything like what she had experienced so far, she was rather certain she would enjoy it.

Jessica put down the book she was reading and looked outside. They'd been in the carriage for several hours already, and Angel hoped they would reach the Holcombe estate soon because her bottom was sore from the long journey.

"I think we're at the edges of the estate now, aren't we?" Jessica asked.

Wortham, who sat on the opposite seat next to James, leaned forward to have a look. "Yes," he agreed. "We should come up around the lake soon."

"There is a lake?"

"A lovely lake," Jessica said with a smile. "When there's a hot summer, the water is warm enough to swim in."

"It's not a big one," Wortham said before giving Jessica a teasing glance. "That it's placed on the Holcombe estate and not Davenhall stopped none of the Howertys from making use of it."

"The duke said he didn't mind," Jessica defended herself.

"Did he?" Wortham raised a dark eyebrow.

"Well. He never said he did mind."

Angel frowned, confused. "I thought you all knew each other as children? Surely the duke didn't mind his son's friends making use of the lake?"

Wortham chuckled. "I doubt he knew they used it. But I'm certain he wouldn't have minded, seeing as they're of noble blood and not miserly children from the village. His words, not mine."

"Pensington and Wortham didn't meet until they were at Eton together," James said. "They never knew of each other's existence before then. It's where we all met and became friends."

"My father wasn't one to take part in the social swirl." Wortham shrugged. "The first decade of my life I spent together with nursery maids and tutors."

"Poor little Wortham," Jessica teased. "All alone with no one's braids to pull."

"I never pulled your braids."

"No, you set them on fire."

Wortham shifted in his seat with a grimace. "That was an accident."

Angel couldn't help staring. "He set your braids on fire?"

"I did not," Wortham said, crossing his arms over his chest while glaring at Jessica. At that moment, he reminded Angel very much of a petulant four-year-old.

"I'm sure he didn't mean to." Jessica chuckled. "We were all playing with candles and he got too close to me."

"Not as smooth with the ladies back then as you are now, eh?" James grinned.

Wortham let out a dramatic sigh and held up his hands. "I concede. I did set your braids on fire, but it certainly wasn't intentional."

"I forgive you," Jessica said with a little laugh. "Just don't do it again."

"It's what, almost ten years ago?" Wortham said with a dark look at her. "I assure you that my finesse has quite improved."

The comment made Jessica blush, and she quickly turned her head towards the window. Nudging Angel with her elbow, she pointed outside. "Look, there's the lake."

Leaning across her friend to look outside, there was indeed a small lake with its blue water sparkling in the summer sun. She could easily imagine the Howertys as children running into it, splashing each other and having swimming contests.

"The weather has been good so far this summer," Jessica said. "I bet the water is warm enough for us to swim."

"I'll warn my father so he can post guards," Wortham muttered.

"Do you swim, Angel?" Jessica asked, ignoring the earl.

"No, I never learnt how."

"You didn't?" James stared at her.

She shrugged. "No one was there to teach me."

"Don't worry. We'll teach you," Jessica promised.

"Pensington can provide private tutoring," Wortham said, making both Angel and Jessica blush and James glare. "What?" he said innocently. "I'm sure he could."

"I think Pensington and I should reconsider allowing our sisters to be in your presence," James muttered.

Wortham laughed. "I'm not that bad."

"No comment."

Turning to Jessica, Wortham gave her one of his most charming smiles. "You don't mind my company, do you, sweetheart?"

Jessica's cheeks stained pink as she stared at the roguish earl. "I... Well..." She stopped herself short and scowled when Wortham winked at her. "You are a scoundrel, Jacob Hurst, and you know it."

"You wound me, my lady." He touched his chest above the heart. "I am merely misunderstood."

A very unladylike snort was the only response to that statement.

"Ah, we're finally getting close," James said, sounding relieved when the carriage turned around the lake.

Angel looked outside and was astonished by the beautiful mansion that came into view. It was huge. She'd known that Wortham's family was old and wealthy, but she hadn't realised he'd grown up in such a splendid place. They came around the lake, and the front of the manor came into view; a beautiful construction of red brick and limestone with curved Dutch gables and turrets, and two service wings, all framed by massive yew hedges.

"Lovely, isn't it?" Jessica said. "Holcombe Hall is one of the most breathtaking places I've seen."

"It's beautiful," Angel breathed, unable to take her eyes off the manor.

"Quite a large estate, if I remember," James said.

"Nearly three thousand acres," Wortham replied, sounding bored. "With twenty-odd farms supporting the great house."

"Davenhall is only a few hundred," Jessica said. "But I think that's more than enough."

"My family bought up or married into most of their surrounding land," Wortham said with a self-mocking tone. "We've sure done well for ourselves."

"When were you last home?" Jessica asked shrewdly.

He looked outside, his eyes on the house as they approached. "Five years ago."

The carriage brought them up to the entrance, where a footman came forward to open the door for them. Wortham looked like he was about to face the executioner, then he sighed and exited the carriage right after James. After helping the ladies down, they all walked towards the house.

Curious, Angel leaned a little closer to Jessica and quietly asked, "Why has Wortham not been home for so long?"

"I heard that he and his father had a falling out," her friend told her. "But I don't know the details."

They entered the manor into what Jessica said was The Great Hall, and the name certainly suited. It was a large hall spanning two floors, with a beautiful marble floor and a grand staircase at the far wall leading up and splitting in the two directions of the house. Above the staircase, a large window of stained glass demanded one's attention, allowing an abundance of afternoon light into the hall.

"What a spectacular house," Angel mumbled.

"It's a bloody mausoleum," Wortham muttered. "It's impersonal and made only to impress others. I always preferred Davenhall, it's much more personal."

"He's right," Jessica agreed. "This is a beautiful house, but Davenhall is a home."

"I can't wait to see it." Angel really looked forward to seeing the Howertys' home. Nervous jitters travelled over her skin at the realisation that it would be her home too after tomorrow. Like any young lady of her age and background, she had received schooling in how to run a household, but it wasn't the same as actually standing at the precipice of having to do it. Fortunately, she would not be alone, since Mrs Grey and all of Nathaniel's sisters would live with them. The thought made her slightly less nervous.

An older gentleman came walking down the stairs and it was easy to see that he was Wortham's father. They were quite similar both in build and looks. However, where Wortham's hair was still fully dark brown, his father's was sprinkled with salt, and his eyes seemed grey rather than blue.

"Welcome to Holcombe Hall," the duke said as he reached the floor of the entrance hall. Moving between them, he greeted his son with a certain stiffness, then moved to greet James and place a kiss on Jessica's cheek, to finally reach Angel.

"I don't believe we have been introduced," he said, prompting James to do so.

"Angel, please let me introduce the Duke of Ashbrook. Your Grace, this is my sister, Miss Angelique Grafton."

"Pleased to meet you, Your Grace," she said shyly and curtsied.

"The pleasure is all mine." The duke took her hand and bowed slightly over it. "I'm glad to see that Pensington has found himself such a lovely young lady to take as his wife. I can only wish that Jacob will be so lucky."

A groan could be heard from a few feet away. "And it starts already."

The duke ignored his son and placed Angel's hand on his arm. "Please allow me to escort you to the guest rooms. I'm certain you're all tired and would like to rest before supper."

"You have a wonderful house, Your Grace," Angel timidly told him while they walked through the richly decorated hallways to get to the west wing where the guest rooms were located.

"Thank you, Miss Grafton." The duke bestowed her with one of his rare—if one was to listen to Wortham—smiles, which took ten years off his face. "Holcombe has been in the family for three hundred years and I hope it will remain so for many more to come."

"I'm sure you must be proud of it."

"I am indeed. Hopefully, I will eventually get a grandson who can continue the family line. Since I was only ever blessed with one son, Jacob needs to find a wife soon to make sure our line doesn't die out."

"And people wonder why I never visit," Wortham muttered behind them, again being ignored by his father.

When they reached a place where two hallways met, the duke turned to Wortham for a moment. "I believe you will go in that direction"—he nodded towards one hallway—"to find your room. I will bring our visitors to theirs in the guest wing."

"Of course, Father." Wortham executed a mocking bow before walking away towards the private family quarters.

The manor house itself seemed built more or less like a square with the south front the tallest and the other sides a little lower, giving the slight impression of a castle. The two service wings, the duke told Angel, had been added at a later stage to house the kitchen and the servants' quarters. Every part of the house she saw was decorated with fine silk wallpapers and polished wood or marble floors. Anyone could see that the Duke of Ashbrook was a wealthy man.

Finally, having reached the guest bedchambers, the duke bid them a good afternoon and left them to freshen up or take a nap before supper. Effective footmen had already brought their luggage upstairs, and maids were unpacking the bags. Angel waited for them to finish before lying down on the enormous bed to rest for a moment. Despite having been sitting all day, she was surprisingly tired. It was amazing how exhausting it could be to ride in a carriage. She doubted her ability to relax enough to doze off with her nerves frayed with anxiety.

She was wrong, and a few moments after closing her eyes she was fast asleep, wedding nerves or not.

Sitting in the window of her guest bedchamber at Holcombe Hall, Angel stared out into the night, finding comfort in the darkness. A few lights from what she assumed were farmhouses were dotted across the distance. The village was a couple of miles away but in the opposite direction from where her window faced.

The supper served in the large dining hall had been delicious, but she'd only picked at the food, her nervousness making her stomach churn uncomfortably. Nathaniel had turned up in time for supper, but James was adamant about keeping them as far apart as possible before their nuptials the following day.

After dinner, the men had retired for a glass of brandy and a cigar, and she hadn't seen them since. Jessica had done her best to make her forget about the impending wedding, but in the end, she had opted to retire early, hoping to get a good night's sleep. Yet here she was in her room, all ready, but unable to sleep.

Sitting in her modest white nightgown with her hair in a long braid down her back, she wondered if Nathaniel felt even a smidgeon of the same nervousness that she did. Everything was just changing so quickly. She was moving to a new house, with a new family... *and she would share her bed with a man.* A wave of mixed excitement and worry travelled through her.

What could she expect to happen? It was all a big mystery, and that might be the most distressful bit. The not knowing. Some married couples didn't share a bedchamber, but something told her Nathaniel would not be the type of husband who slept separately from his wife.

As she continued to fret about what might or might not happen, a hesitant knock sounded at the door. Surprised, she called out, "Come in."

The door opened, and James stepped inside. He looked rather ill, like he'd eaten something rotten. Closing the door behind him and taking a deep breath, he walked over to sit on the bed. He was silent for a moment, taking several more deep breaths before finally looking up to meet her worried eyes.

"I thought I should come to speak to you," he said hesitantly and patted a spot on the bed next to him.

Puzzled, she left her seat by the window and walked over to sit down by her brother. "What did you wish to speak to me about?"

"Well…" He looked decidedly uneasy with whatever he was about to say, and for a moment, she feared Nathaniel had called off the whole thing. "I realise that the evening before a young woman gets married, her mother usually sits down to talk to her." He drew a deep breath and then added, "Since you don't have a mother, I thought I probably should talk to you. About what is expected of you as a wife and all that."

She smiled, touched by his concern. "It's all right, James. I've been properly schooled in how to run a household."

"Ah." He groaned, and it surprised her to see his cheeks turn a darker shade of pink. "No, I mean… Ah. In the marriage bed."

"Oh." As she realised what he meant, her cheeks must have mirrored his, and she nodded. "That is very kind of you, James. And I really appreciate it because I know little to nothing about it."

"Right," he said, sounding less than positive. "Well, then."

There was a moment of silence when she waited for him to continue. When he said nothing, she prompted him. "Well?"

He stared uneasily across the room without seeming to actually be looking at anything. Moving his hands to his knees with the palms down, he took a deep breath. "Well... On the wedding night, you will share a bed with Pens—" He cut himself short before clearing his throat and finishing the sentence. "With your husband."

"Yes, I know that much already," she said, a little impatiently. "But... What do you actually do in the marriage bed? There's obviously something, and I assume it's more than kissing... But what is it?"

James's face turned an even darker shade of pink, bordering on red, and she couldn't remember ever seeing him this embarrassed before. She would have felt bad for him, but she was desperate to find out what Nathaniel would expect from her the following night. It might make her worry less. She didn't want to disappoint him.

"I should have asked Mrs Grey to do this," James muttered under his breath before turning his head to look at her. "You know bees and flowers? No, wait... I mean birds and bees?"

She frowned. "Yes," she said hesitantly. "I know of birds and bees."

"Wonderful!" James practically bounced off the bed. "Then you know all there is to it."

Before she could point out that it made no sense whatsoever, he bid her good night and fled the room. Staring at the door he'd closed behind him, she was more confused than she had been before he'd arrived. The birds and the bees? What did they have to do with what happened between husband and wife?

Shaking her head, she tried to get some sleep, but lying in bed she couldn't stop thinking about how she was about to marry a man who didn't truly want her. Not in the way she wanted him.

He's only marrying you to play the hero.

She didn't want to listen to Philip's goading words, but she knew they were true. Nathaniel didn't even deny it. He was attracted to her, but was that enough to base a marriage on? She could only hope so.

Nathaniel closed the door to his room behind him and tugged at his cravat. He had hoped to see Angel again after dinner to bid her good night, but by the time he'd left Gowthorpe and Wortham, she'd already retired for the evening. Not getting to see her put him in a worse mood than he wanted to admit.

Which was ridiculous, considering they would be husband and wife tomorrow.

Shrugging out of his tailcoat, he hung it over the back of a chair. A soft knock made him frown. Had Wortham sent a valet over to help him undress? He opened the door to find the woman occupying his thoughts standing outside. She looked innocent in nothing but a thin, white robe on top of a white nightgown, and her hair tied back in a long, golden braid. Why was she here? If Gowthorpe saw her visiting his room a night too early, there would be hell to pay.

He ought to send her back to her room right now, but instead, he ushered her inside and closed the door behind them after making sure no one had seen her. Running a hand through his hair, he watched Angel take a few steps into the room on bare feet, looking around while nervously tugging at the end of her braid.

"What are you doing here?" he asked, startling her enough to make her whirl around to face him.

"I couldn't sleep." One of her hands tucked a few stray strands of hair behind her ear as she glanced at him. "I keep thinking about tomorrow."

He smiled. He couldn't stop thinking about tomorrow, either. About how he would finally take her to his bed and taste every inch of her body. Taking the steps separating them, he took her hands in his and lifted them to his face so he could place a soft kiss on her knuckles.

"Are you nervous?"

She nodded. "Quite. And worried."

"Don't be worried." He turned her hand over and kissed her palms, one after the other. "The wedding will be over before you know it and we have the rest of our lives to look forward to."

He'd said it to calm her nerves, but as he said the words aloud, he realised he meant them. He did look forward to their shared future. Even if he was guarding his heart, he liked the idea of seeing her every day. Of continuing their discussions. Laughing with her about his sisters' antics.

Her eyes met his, and she worried her lower lip with her teeth. "Are you sure you want this?" she asked quietly. "I fear you are only doing this to save me and will come to regret it. What if you fall in love with someone else but you're trapped in a marriage with me?"

"It won't happen."

"You can't know that." The little line between her brows was back, and he wanted to smooth it out, erase the frown from her face.

"We've had this discussion before," he reminded her. "My mind is set. I am marrying you, and I will remain faithful to you, always."

When she opened her mouth to—most likely—argue with him, he captured it in a kiss. He couldn't give her what she wanted. Couldn't offer his undying love. It was an emotion he had vowed never to feel. Even if she deserved more. She deserved someone who could fully love her with every ounce of their being. He could not be that. But he could be the best husband he knew how to be.

Chettisham had stolen her ability to choose her husband, and as much as she worried about him being forced into this marriage, she was the one truly blocked from other choices. She ought to feel sorry about herself more than she did him. He was getting exactly what he had wanted all along. Her in his bed.

With a soft sigh, she relaxed into his arms, returning the kiss. If his words couldn't convince her of his desire to marry her, maybe his kisses could. With their hands still linked, he brought her over to a comfortable-looking armchair standing in the room's corner and sat down.

Angel looked down at him, her teeth biting that plump bottom lip again. Damn, he wanted her.

"Oh!" she gasped when he pulled her onto his lap, setting her snugly against him with her legs to one side. "Nathaniel!" she whispered frantically, but he could have sworn there was a hint of excitement in there. "What are you doing?"

"I missed you today," he admitted. Burying his nose in the hair at her temple, he inhaled the light scent of her rosewater. "We haven't had much of a chance to speak."

"I missed you too," she said shyly, her hands playing absently with the top buttons of his shirt.

With one arm around her back to keep her steady, he put the other just above her knee and massaged her leg slightly. "So you said you were nervous about tomorrow?"

A slight nod of her head. "Aren't you?"

"I don't know." He placed a soft kiss just below her ear and was rewarded by a shaky inhale of air. She was so sensitive to his touches. "I suppose I am. But I'm also very much looking forward to you being my wife."

"I think I look forward to that too," she whispered, and he placed another kiss a little further down her neck.

Touching her chin, he turned her face towards him. They stared at each other for a moment before their lips met. He kept the kiss soft and playful, enjoying the simple touch, alternating between gentle kisses and nibbling teasingly. It wasn't enough for long. Pulling her a little closer, he deepened the kiss, exploring the soft recesses of her mouth. A low moan at the back of her throat sent a jolt of excitement through him.

Unable to keep his hands still, he followed the outlines of her form from the shoulders down to her hips and back up again. When she didn't protest, he hooked two fingers under the seam of her nightgown at the collar and slowly pulled it down her shoulder. With a slow caress, he pushed the fabric out of the way, baring her skin to his touch. Abandoning her mouth to place a kiss at the tip of her shoulder, he kept one hand on her back while the other untied the lace at the front of her nightgown to loosen it.

Returning to her mouth for another deep kiss, he got the laces loose enough and his hand found its way underneath to caress her breast. She felt amazing in his arms, and he knew he should put an end to this exploration soon, but the little gasps of pleasure as he massaged her spurred him on.

"God, you feel so good," he mumbled against her lips.

"I like it when you touch me." The pinkness of her cheeks as she pulled away from him slightly only made her look all the more sweet and innocent, and when she leaned forward to place a timid kiss on his neck, he knew he must stop this soon or they would have their wedding night a day too soon.

"I'm glad," he said hoarsely. "Because I love touching you. Once we're married, I might not let you out of bed for a week. I will want to make sure I've touched every inch of you at least a dozen times before you get to leave that bed."

He closed his eyes for a moment when her soft lips nipped gently at his neck. It was disconcerting how much he wanted her. The need to carry her over to the bed and make her his right now was overwhelming. With a groan, he forced himself to set her on the floor, standing up in front of her. Craning her neck, she stared up at him, her brows knotted in confusion.

"I think it's best you return to your room," he said, placing his hands on her shoulders and turning her towards the door. "Or I will not be able to resist you."

The pinkness of her cheeks deepened when she must have understood what he meant, and she nodded. He allowed himself one more quick kiss before opening the door and, after making sure the hallway was empty, he sent her away. Closing the door behind her, he leaned against it and cursed the fire burning through his body. The wedding night could not come soon enough.

Chapter Twenty-Three

Dear Diary,
   Have there been any recordings of brides vomiting in church? I fear I might.

The church in Bridlewood was a quaint structure from the 13th century, with fine detailing from the medieval era seen in the beautifully carved stone knots on the chancel arch. The exterior was made of typical English grey stone, flint, and early brick, with a small octagonal church tower. For some reason, Angel had believed her nerves would settle once she got inside the old building, but they did not. Not even a little.

Standing in front of the priest with Nathaniel on her right side and her brother on her left, she felt like she might be sick.

The priest spoke, but she couldn't focus on his words over the loud pounding of her own heart drumming in her ears.

What if I faint? Would they still continue the ceremony if she wasn't able to say 'I will'? Nathaniel looked cool and composed, as if the many sets of eyes watching them weren't affecting him at all, while she kept fingering the cufflinks of her brother's tailcoat. Finally, James moved his hand to cover hers and gave it a gentle squeeze.

A warm rush of embarrassment heated her cheeks. She glanced at her brother, and he gave her a quick, encouraging smile. That calmed her marginally. Which was fortunate, because the priest had just asked the most important question of the day.

"I will." When he answered, Nathaniel's eyes didn't leave hers, and her throat suddenly felt dry.

The priest turned towards her, and she froze. There was no way she could speak the words necessary. Not with everyone staring at her.

"Wilt thou have this man to thy wedded husband, to live together after God's ordinance in the holy estate of matrimony? Wilt thou obey him, and serve him, love, honour, and keep him in sickness and in health; and, forsaking all other, keep thee only unto him, so long as you both shall live?"

Her throat seized, and she worried she might faint before her mouth finally cooperated. "I will."

The relief of having been able to say the words calmed her, but she couldn't quite relax knowing that she still had to get through the wedding breakfast. And the wedding night... There was so much yet to come.

"Who giveth this woman to be married to this man?" the priest asked.

James stirred and gave her over to the priest, whose cold, dry hands on hers had an oddly calming effect. The old man motioned for Nathaniel to come a little closer and then made him take her right hand with his own. His strong, warm hand touched hers and when she looked up to meet his dark eyes, she knew everything would be fine. Her nervousness dispersed like the morning mist on the heaths surrounding Hefferton Place.

They repeated the vows after the priest and during the entire recitation, Nathaniel held her gaze. It made her forget about everyone else in church, the wedding breakfast, and the night to come. All that existed was her and him, and the crisp voice of the priest reading their vows.

The ring Nathaniel had given her after their engagement ball was brought forward, and he gently put it on the fourth finger of her left hand. Breaking protocol slightly, he then raised her hand to his face and placed a soft kiss on the knuckle just above the ring.

Maybe she would faint after all.

"With this ring I thee wed, with my body I thee worship, and with all my worldly goods I thee endow. In the name of the Father, and the Son, and of the Holy Ghost. Amen."

Words that had never meant much to her took on their own special meaning when uttered by Nathaniel. Even when she had made a similar statement a few moments ago, it had not been the same. The priest continued speaking, but she was no longer paying attention. But this time it was because the look in Nathaniel's eyes held her spellbound. Finally, the words she'd been waiting for were heard, *'I pronounce that they be man and wife together...'*

She had never realised how much of the solemnisation of marriage remained after those words, but as she stood beside Nathaniel, knowing she was now his legal wife, it didn't matter that she had to stay in the church a while longer. Once the psalms were sung and the rites said they were asked to sign the register, and she realised with a little nostalgia that this would be the last time she would sign her maiden name on anything ever again.

Outside the church in the courtyard, their family and friends stood on both sides of the path leading down to the gates. Several cheerful shouts of good luck and well done echoed around them, but Nathaniel ignored them as he led her to the open carriage that would take them to Davenhall. After assisting her into the vehicle, he jumped up and sat down next to her. They began moving with a servant at the reins.

"You look beautiful." Nathaniel slid a little closer on the bench to caress a lock of hair that had fallen out of her elaborate hairdo.

"Thank you," she mumbled and her cheeks heated. How was it that she was now a married woman? It didn't seem real.

She ran her hands down the skirt of the wedding dress, smoothing out imagined creases. Mrs Grey had helped her choose the garment, and she was so very pleased with it. While a simple cut, it suited her well. She'd gone for a lovely white, which she had favoured over the blue and silver that were also popular. A red rose had been pinned to the chest on the left side with a few more roses tucked into her hair, which was gathered in a mass of curls and braids at the top of her head.

"It's a pretty dress," Nathaniel said before leaning closer. When he was close enough that she felt his hot breath on her ear, he whispered, "I can't wait until I can take it off."

If she thought her face had been hot before, it was nothing compared to the furnace currently burning her cheeks. She threw a glance at the driver, but he didn't appear to have heard them.

Nathaniel touched her chin and turned her head to meet his gaze. "Has anyone ever told you how adorable you look when you blush?"

"No." Her voice was little more than a whisper as she tried to calm her racing pulse. "And when you do, it makes me even more embarrassed."

He chuckled. "I don't mind. It just makes you more adorable."

"I was so very nervous during the ceremony," she said, hoping to change the subject. "You didn't seem the least bit nervous."

"Oh, I was," he said while playing with a lock of hair at her temple. Every time his knuckles brushed against her, tiny jolts travelled across her skin. "I just hid it well."

"Well enough to fool me."

He smiled at her dry tone but seemed a little preoccupied, looking down at her. "I beg your pardon," he said after a moment. "It seems I am having trouble keeping my thoughts from travelling forward in time."

"How so?"

"I keep thinking about tonight." His velvety chuckle was low and hummed against her skin. "Can't we cancel the breakfast and just be alone already?"

While talking, he'd twisted a little and his arm now rested on the top of the seat behind her. His fingertips traced simple shapes on her neck and nape, sending shivers of pleasure travelling down her spine. She sighed. "You know we cannot do that."

"I know." He gave her a lopsided smile. "But I still wish we could. I want to do nothing but touch you."

"You are touching me," she said, making him laugh.

Bending closer again, he whispered hotly in her ear, "I want to touch you everywhere. I want to take off all your clothes and caress every inch of you."

"Oh." It certainly wasn't the most eloquent response, but she doubted she could have said anything else. She shifted in her seat as warmth spread through her. If hearing him say it made her react like this, what would it be like when he actually did it? Flustered, she made a show out of looking out over their surroundings. "Are we there yet?"

"Soon," he promised with a smile that told her he knew exactly how he affected her. Throwing a glance behind them, he sighed. "And the others aren't far behind."

Davenhall turned out to be lying at the bottom of a valley, surrounded by acres of beautiful parkland and with traditional walled gardens. The manor itself was a brick building enclosed by a medieval moat, with a stone bridge leading across. It was a beautiful estate with wonderful, differently themed gardens they passed through on their way towards the house. She could see a rose garden, an orchard, and an oriental garden. The manor house itself looked enchanting where it stood enclosed by the wide moat, with lush green ivy clinging to its facade.

Crossing the stone bridge, Angel peered over the edge of the carriage into the water. It didn't look entirely clean, but not as stale as she'd have expected of a moat either.

"There is a small stream that leads into it," Nathaniel told her. "So it never runs out of water."

"You have a beautiful house," she said when the carriage pulled to a stop in front of the manor.

"Thank you." He jumped down and offered her his hand. "But it's our house now."

Taking his hand and stepping down, she looked at the ivy growing along the front of the house and smiled. She could see what Jessica meant when she said Davenhall felt like a home. There was something inviting about the house. Comforting and safe. The building was large without feeling imposing, and the romantic gardens surrounding the house made it feel like somewhere you'd want to be.

"Since we're lucky with the weather, Aunt Jane has prepared the wedding breakfast to be served in the formal garden." Nathaniel led her inside the house. "It's in the back, so we have to walk through unless you want to swim in the moat. Which, by the way, I don't recommend since the water gets quite dirty."

They entered a large hallway with a marble floor and cream-coloured walls. A large staircase followed along one wall to reach the next floor, and exits were leading in all other directions to different parts of the house. The servants stood in a line waiting to greet the master's new wife, and Nathaniel quickly introduced them all to her, promising a more in-depth introduction later. They were all fidgeting to get back to the preparations for the breakfast. During the introductions, the guests had arrived, so when Angel and Nathaniel exited the back of the house, their families and most of their friends had already gathered.

The formal garden turned out to be an extensive area at the back of the house. The moat, apparently, only enclosed the front courtyard. A large lawn with beds of flowers and trimmed bushes spread out before them, and Mrs Grey had arranged tables and chairs on the grass where guests could sit and enjoy the meal. Two smaller tables had been set up filled with delicious bread, hot rolls, ham, and eggs. In the middle of the table, a wedding cake had been placed, and Nick was already looking at it like she was planning to steal it and make a run for it.

The guests were mainly Nathaniel's family and people living in the area, as well as a few of his friends from London. The Duke of Ashbrook had appeared but was nowhere near Wortham, who stood with James and the remaining Howertys. Everyone came forward to offer congratulations and best wishes, and the attention made Angel slightly uncomfortable. But she would grin and bear it. This was her wedding day, and she appreciated everyone taking time out of their lives to come and celebrate with them. Once everyone had congratulated them, it was time for the meal.

On the whole, it was a pleasant day with a lot of laughter and not a little bit of ribbing of the newlyweds. In the afternoon, Mrs Grey had arranged for some locals from the village to play music and the lawn was cleared for people to dance. Some chairs were left out for those who would rather sit and chat.

There were only two disturbances during the day, and the first was when Nick and Rain got into a fight—they both had tempers as hot as Nathaniel, Mrs Grey told her with a sigh—and had to be forcefully separated before they could tear each other's hair out.

The second disturbance was when Nick fell into the moat. She'd been climbing out on the limb of a tree growing next to the water and had lost her grip and fallen straight in. Mrs Grey had taken her inside to wash her and get her a new dress before she could return to the party. Angel didn't mind the interruptions, partly because it took some attention away from her, but also because it made her feel a part of a family. Nathaniel had been attentive and charming the whole day, only embarrassing her occasionally with dark, promising looks that reminded her of the night to come.

As the evening dusk settled, Mrs Grey had lights lit throughout the garden, creating a romantic atmosphere that worked very well together with the music and the drinks being offered. Angel sat on a chair watching people dancing when Mrs Grey came to sit next to her. After a quick look to see where Nathaniel was—talking to James and Wortham a short distance away—she smiled at Angel.

"It has been a wonderful day," she said.

"It has indeed," Angel agreed.

"Aside from a few smaller mishaps involving the girls." Mrs Grey threw a disapproving look towards the aforementioned girls, who were now dancing merrily with some boys of a similar age.

"I have heard it's not considered a good wedding unless there are at least two mishaps." Angel smiled teasingly.

Mrs Grey laughed. "That may be so."

"Mrs Grey." Angel took the older woman's hand in hers, meeting her gaze. "You cannot possibly understand how grateful I am to be part of your family." She smiled a little, adding, "Mishaps or no mishaps."

The older woman squeezed her hand. "I'm glad Nathaniel married such a sensible, lovely girl. And please. Call me Aunt Jane. You're family now."

Angel smiled. "Aunt Jane. That will take some getting used to."

"You'll learn soon enough."

The other woman was silent for a moment, looking at the people dancing on the lawn, before turning to her again. "Are you nervous?" she asked. "I know I was a bundle of nerves before my wedding night."

Angel's cheeks heated. "Yes," she admitted. "I am, but I suppose that is to be expected."

"I think so," Mrs Grey said and added with a light chuckle, "Something is probably wrong if you're not at least a little bit nervous."

"Nervous about what?" Jessica asked when she joined them and sat down on Angel's other side.

"Never you mind," Mrs Grey said. "This is something between married women."

Jessica smirked. "I see."

"Why don't you go ask the maids to draw Angel a bath?" Mrs Grey suggested.

"Not very subtle, are you?" Jessica muttered dryly before she hugged Angel and left them alone.

"I thought a bath might help you relax a little. You can retire early to enjoy it in peace. It's allowed to retire a little early on your wedding night."

"That sounds lovely." Angel gave the other woman a grateful smile. "How soon do you think I can escape?"

"Soon, I'm sure. People are quite into their cups by now and will most likely not even notice." She nodded towards a man sitting a short distance away with his chin against his chest, snoring loudly. Nathaniel had introduced him as Squire Barton from the village.

Angel smiled. "I will leave soon then."

"I'll go check on your bath in a moment." Mrs Grey met her eyes. "I know you and Nathaniel have opted to stay here at Davenhall instead of going on a honeymoon. Newlyweds require some privacy, which is not something you'd get with the girls living here, so I've agreed with His Grace that the girls and I can stay at Holcombe Hall for a week."

"That is not necessary," Angel quickly said, feeling bad about the idea of forcing them out of their home for her sake.

Mrs Grey smiled. "I know you don't expect us to, but I think it's good for you and Nathaniel to have some time to yourselves as you settle into married life."

The thought of what married life entailed warmed her cheeks, but she nodded. "Thank you. I appreciate that."

"Besides," Mrs Grey added with a teasing smile. "It is not as if living at Holcombe is an inconvenience."

Angel laughed. "I suppose not."

Standing up, Mrs Grey excused herself to check on the preparations for the night. Angel remained where she was, enjoying being able to sit and watch the guests while they danced and chatted. The bath sounded like a wonderful idea. Some time alone might help calm her frazzled nerves. Sooner than expected, Mrs Grey returned and brought her inside the house.

"The maids are preparing your bath now," she said. "I will show you to the master bedchamber."

Following the older woman upstairs, they walked down the hall to an open door where maids carried buckets of hot water. It was a large room decorated mainly in green and rich cream, with large windows facing the extensive gardens around the house.

A massive four-poster bed dominated the room, and two comfortable chairs had a chessboard on a table between them. Opposite the bed was a large fireplace of white and Siena marble. In front of the crackling fire, the servants had prepared a tub with hot water for her bath.

"The room is at the end of the hallway since Nathaniel decided not to use the original state bedchamber." Mrs Grey sat Angel down on a low stool and started pulling the pins out of her hair. "He found it held too many memories of his parents, so he had a wall erected to turn it into two separate rooms. Two others were put together to create this one."

"It's a lovely room." Staring at her wide-eyed reflection in the mirror, Angel hoped she didn't look as nervous as she felt. The gentle chatter from the older woman was helping calm her nerves somewhat. She felt sad for Nathaniel, who had not been able to face sleeping in his late parents' room. The amount of pain he must have felt to make such large changes to his house to avoid it made her heart ache for him.

After delivering and pouring in the last few buckets of hot water, the maids excused themselves and left the two women alone. Mrs Grey effectively finished undoing Angel's hair and let it fall down her back before she moved over to put her hand in the water.

"Perfect," she said, and then smiled when she must have seen the look of panic on Angel's face. "Don't worry, dear. It's not as bad as you've heard."

"What?" She could barely hear herself think over the racing pulse roaring in her ears. "The bath?"

Mrs Grey laughed. "No. The wedding night."

"Oh. That." Running a hand through her loose hair, she mumbled, "The birds and the bees."

"What was that?" Mrs Grey asked while she put a small stool next to the tub and placed a towel, a bar of soap, and some rose-scented water on it.

"Nothing." Her cheeks burned, but she refused to admit her ignorance. Whatever James had meant to tell her to allay her worries, it had not shed so much as a sliver of light on what was to come.

"Do you need any help getting undressed? I can send one of the upstairs maids."

"No, I should be fine."

"Well, then." Mrs Grey walked over and hugged her. "I will see you in a few days. Welcome to the family, Angel."

She nodded and flashed the other woman a brief smile before watching her leave the room and closing the door behind her. It took a few moments before she could bring herself to stand up and undress. Most of the guests were still outside in the garden, enjoying the festivities, so she should have plenty of time to enjoy her bath and calm her nerves. Folding her dress away, she walked over to the bed.

Something red caught her gaze and she couldn't hold back a smile when she picked up the single, dark red rose lying on the white sheets. A thoughtful reminder from Nathaniel. No matter what, she knew he would be gentle and caring. The night suddenly seemed a little less daunting.

Chapter Twenty-Four

Dear Diary,
 I have tried to make sense of what James
 told me to expect on the wedding night.
 But I simply cannot see what birds and
 bees have to do with it.

It was amazing how quickly wedding guests could disappear after the bride left the scene. Once his aunt spread the word that Angel had retired for the night, everyone dispersed like mice before a cat. Nathaniel had watched in amazement while the guests all took their leave, and within a quarter of an hour, the garden was empty and the house staff could begin tidying up.

Aunt Jane and his sisters had left shortly after, returning to Holcombe Hall with Wortham, where they would spend the week. Something he was profoundly grateful for. But that meant that apart from the servants, he was now alone in the house with his new wife.

This was exactly why he now paced the length of the library while looking at the clock now and then, only to find that only a couple of minutes had passed since the last time he checked.

It had been suggested—not particularly subtly—that he give his wife plenty of time to prepare for the wedding night. He'd been waiting to take her into his arms all day, and knowing she was upstairs in his bedchamber was nothing short of torture. After the second glass of brandy, he decided he had waited long enough. Considering he'd wanted to ravish her since the morning she found him sleeping in her bed, he rather thought he'd shown considerable restraint so far.

Putting his now empty glass on a table, he left the library to walk upstairs, only to find his butler standing at the foot of the stairs.

"Roberts?" he said, raising his brow at the older man.

He was an elderly gentleman who had worked at Davenhall since Nathaniel was a young boy. Always prim and proper, he was dressed in suitable black garb, looking every inch the strict butler.

"My lord," Roberts said. "Mrs Grey asked me to remind you, should you try to venture upstairs before nine, that your bride ought to be given a proper amount of time to prepare for her first night as your wife."

Nathaniel scowled, annoyed at his aunt's antics and unwilling to wait any longer before kissing Angel. "Who pays your wages, Roberts?"

"You do, my lord."

"Very well then."

The butler nodded and stepped out of the way, allowing Nathaniel to continue towards his bedchamber. It was sweet of his aunt to care about Angel enough to want to ensure she had enough time to get ready, but surely his wife had finished whatever preparations a bride did on her wedding night by now.

The bath was exactly what Angel needed to relax. Even with the water having cooled off, she didn't want to get out. She'd taken her time in the tub, washing her hair and rinsing it with fresh water from a bucket, and she supposed she had to get up soon. It would take time to dry her hair in front of the fire and put on the luxurious silky nightgown that had been part of her wedding trousseau. Her eyes widened when the door suddenly opened and her new husband walked into the room.

"Nathaniel!" She grabbed the towel on the stool next to the tub and pulled it around herself, soaking it in the water. "What are you doing here?"

He didn't immediately answer, having stopped just inside the door the moment he caught sight of her, staring as if she'd dropped out of the sky. His gaze moved from her soaked-through towel to her face, and a slow smile spread over his face. The sensuality of it sent off a fluttering inside her stomach.

"I've come to pay my wife a visit." He closed the door behind him.

"Well, you're too early. You must leave and return in an hour."

He chuckled, a low sound that sent off another wave of flutters. "I don't think I could leave even if I tried. I've waited too long for this and I've been downstairs in the library, going mad from wanting to be with you."

"I'm not dressed yet." She was being very reasonable. Why wasn't he leaving?

"I can see that." Something dark glinted in his eyes, and her skin tingled when his gaze swept over her. "That is not a problem. Not at all."

"Nathaniel... Please give me some privacy to get out of the tub and get dressed."

Moving across the room to the bed, he shook off his black tailcoat and waistcoat and threw them on a chair. When he untied his cravat and unbuttoned the top buttons on his shirt, she swallowed with some difficulty. Surely he would not undress right in front of her? He removed his cufflinks and rolled the white shirtsleeves up before looking at her with a smile playing on his lips. Picking up the rose lying on the bed, he sauntered over to her where she sat in the tub. She pulled the towel a little tighter.

"How can I possibly resist you when I find you naked in a tub? In my bedchamber."

"I'm wearing a towel," she mumbled, making him laugh.

"That hardly counts as a piece of clothing, darling."

He crouched on the floor next to her. Heat emanated from his body, even though he wasn't touching her. He placed the rose on her shoulder, using its soft petals to trace a line across her collarbones before following the same path back again. Moving it along her throat and up to her jaw, he followed the jawline until he could touch the velvety petals to her mouth. There suddenly wasn't enough air in her lungs, and she drew an unsteady breath.

Tucking his fingers under her chin, he gently moved her face towards him, tilting it up a little to replace the petals of the rose with his lips. The kiss started softly with only a light pressure of his mouth on hers. He nibbled and teased until she relaxed and he could deepen the kiss, his tongue stealing across her lips. The subtle taste of brandy, and the slow, drugging kisses were intoxicating.

Finally breaking the contact and placing a soft kiss on her neck, he mumbled, "Do you truly wish for me to leave?"

Closing her eyes for a moment, she tried to remember what she was doing in the tub in the first place. She shook her head. "My towel is wet."

"I know." Amusement laced his voice. "That's usually what happens when you wrap it around yourself while still sitting in the tub."

Warmth spread in her cheeks. "You startled me."

"There's another one." He stood and lifted a second towel from the stool. "Here. I'll help you."

"I would rather do it myself." She wasn't sure she was ready to stand naked before him yet.

"Very well. I'll turn my back while you make yourself presentable."

He held the spare towel out behind him. Hesitantly, she rose, still clutching the soaked one, with water dripping down her legs. She quickly snatched the dry towel and swapped them. After making sure Nathaniel still had his back to her, she stepped out of the tub and walked over to the fireplace, where she quickly dried herself off.

She was just wrapping herself in the towel when Nathaniel came up behind her and slid his arms around her waist, pressing her close to him. Placing a hot kiss behind her ear, he moved a hand down along the side of her body, following the shape of her hips and waist.

"You're beautiful," he said hoarsely, turning her around to capture her mouth in a fervent kiss.

The world seemed to spin, and her body burned hotly, but she broke away from him. "I need to get dressed. Even got a special nightgown just for tonight."

"Show it to me another time. I don't want to wait any longer." Before she could answer, he lifted her and carried her across the floor, putting her down on the bed. After another passionate kiss, he straightened to undo the remaining buttons on his shirt.

She held onto the towel since it was the only thing covering her, using it like a shield while waiting for what would happen next. Nervous anticipation warred with desire. She watched in fascination when Nathaniel pulled his shirt over his head, revealing a smooth, tanned chest and muscular arms. She drank in the sight—he was stunning. The muscles in his arms and chest rippled underneath his golden skin when he moved, and it made her fingertips tingle in anticipation of touching him. After removing his boots but leaving his black trousers on, he returned to her on the bed.

"You don't know how long I've waited for this." He placed soft kisses down her throat that set off a fluttering in her abdomen. Moving back to capture her mouth, he touched her face gently, leaning her back against the pillows and half-covering her with his body. While he kissed her deeply, he moved a hand to her knee. He caressed up along her thigh until he met the edge of the towel, leaving a trail of fire in his wake that spread through her, igniting every part of her body and making her crave his touch.

Wanting to feel him too, she hesitantly skimmed her hands over his back. Warm, smooth skin met her fingertips. Nathaniel placed soft kisses on her neck and down below her collarbones while she explored his back and shoulders. It was a heady feeling, being able to touch him anywhere she wanted and knowing it was allowed. When he cupped and massaged her breast through the towel, a jolt of pleasure shot through her, and she gripped him a little tighter.

Every sensation was fresh and both exhilarating and a little terrifying. Birds and bees, what? This was a raging fire that threatened to scorch her until she knew nothing else. When Nathaniel moved to remove the towel, she suddenly panicked and quickly covered his hands with her own. He looked up at her with a brow raised, his eyes almost impossibly dark.

"I... I've never shown myself to a man before," she whispered. His mouth curved into a sensual smile, and her cheeks heated.

"I know, darling." He kissed her softly, enticing her with his lips and tongue until she moved her hands up to bury her fingers in his hair. "But I will have to see you eventually," he murmured against her lips before kissing his way down to the edge of the towel.

It was difficult to focus with her heart pounding wildly in her ears. This was it. The moment when Nathaniel would see her. *All of her.* Her mouth was dry and her fingers flexed in his hair. He stilled and his gaze met hers, waiting for her permission. Torn between wanting to hide and wanting to give him everything she had, she nodded jerkily. With a gentle smile, he parted the edges of the towel, revealing her to him.

Unable to look at him, she fidgeted under his hot gaze. "Can't we put the light out?"

"No, I want to see you. All of you." The heat in his eyes seared her skin. "I want to worship you the way you deserve. Kiss every freckle. Lick every delectable inch of your body."

Something hot and desperate unfurled in her abdomen at his hoarse words, and she whimpered as languid heat pooled between her thighs. Nathaniel's hand brushed gently over her nipples, teasing them to tight peaks that ached for his touch. It was nearly impossible to lie still, and she arched her back to get closer. He smiled and bent down to kiss her neck, his hand finally covering her breast fully. Closing her eyes, her head lolled back as the sensations threatened to overwhelm her. How much more of this could she take? She was heavy and aching, gasping for air.

Warm breath caressed her nipple moments before Nathaniel wrapped his mouth around it, and she almost came off the bed. Molten desire rose from somewhere deep inside her, consuming her, heating her from the inside out. He sucked and licked, first on one, then the other, and she thought she might combust. It was almost too much. Too intense. She wanted to pull him closer. Push him away. Wanted more. But what was more?

Returning to her mouth for a deep kiss, he covered her with his body. Skin to skin, with her breasts pressed against his flat, smooth chest, she forgot her fear. Her nervousness. Nathaniel devoured her with his lips, stoking her need with every brush of his tongue, every teasing nibble. When he shifted, she instinctively opened her legs, letting him settle between her thighs. Something hard pressed against her heated core through the fabric of his trousers, and all the blood in her body rushed to where their bodies met.

Was this it? Was this making love? It was a deeper sensation than anything else she'd felt so far, but it didn't seem right. Nathaniel was still partially clothed. When he rocked against her, the hard ridge between them nudged against the sensitive nub at the apex of her thighs, and pleasure shot through her like a bolt of lightning. A moan broke free of her lips.

"God, Angel... You feel so good." Nathaniel groaned against the sensitive skin below her ear, his voice reverberating through her. Lifting his head, he looked down at her. "Is this all right? Would you mind if I remove my trousers now? I want you, but only if you think you're ready."

Ready for what? She frowned, wishing very much that someone had told her a little more about what to expect. Still, she nodded, because despite her ignorance in these matters, she trusted him and her body burned for him. *Yearned* for him.

He moved away for a moment, leaving her feeling bereft without his body covering hers. With a smile, he shed his trousers, and her eyes widened. What was that? She had nothing like that between her legs. It was so big.

"Angel?" He must have noticed her stare. Possibly, her mouth was wide open too. "Are you all right?"

"I... Yes, I..." What could she say? "It's all just so new to me," she finally managed, too embarrassed to admit she'd not known what a naked man would look like.

Returning to her, he took her in his arms. "We will explore everything together. There is no rush, we'll take it at your pace."

A different kind of warmth spread in her chest. She appreciated that he wasn't rushing her, but she also truly loved touching him. "I do want this. I... I want *you*."

Something flashed in his eyes, and he captured her mouth in another kiss. His hardness pressed against her hip, but she didn't have time to worry about it, too distracted by the soft brush of his lips.

He slid his hand down her stomach towards the junction of her thighs, and she fidgeted. Surely, he wouldn't go any lower? The thought of him touching her somewhere so private was shocking despite the hollow ache low in her abdomen that begged for something more. When his hand trailed further, she gasped and grabbed it just below her belly button, gripping it tightly.

"What's the matter, darling?" He looked up at her.

"I don't know if you should touch me there," she said shyly, bringing back his smile.

"Oh, I absolutely should." He placed a soft kiss on the tip of her shoulder.

"Are you certain?" It seemed far too scandalous, and no one had ever mentioned something like this. But then, the extent of her knowledge started and ended with 'birds and bees'.

"Trust me," he mumbled against her skin. "Let me take care of you. I'll do my best to ensure it's enjoyable for you."

Her cheeks burned hotly. "I suppose... I have enjoyed everything so far."

"I'm pleased."

Was that suppressed mirth in his voice? She frowned. "I just don't know if it's necessary for you to touch me... well, there."

He buried his face against her shoulder for a moment, and she wasn't sure if he was amused or irritated, but then he looked at her again and he was most definitely amused.

"I don't appreciate you laughing at me," she said a little stiffly.

"I'm not laughing at you." He gave her a tender smile. "I just want to make sure you're ready."

"Ready for what?" She narrowed her eyes.

He touched her face with his hand and brushed her cheek with his thumb. "For making love, darling."

"I thought we were already making love."

"We're in the beginning stages of it."

"There's more?"

His warm chuckle washed over her. "Most definitely."

Glancing over at nothing in particular, her cheeks heated with the shame of being so clueless. She didn't enjoy feeling stupid. "I hate not knowing," she grumbled.

"I will show you everything there is to it," he promised with a kiss. "If you trust me to. Let me demonstrate..."

His kiss stole her breath away, stoking the fire in her body, as he explored her with his tongue. Teasing. Demanding. These kisses were nothing like what they had shared before. They were scorching, all-consuming, ratcheting her desire higher and higher with every stroke of his tongue.

"If it gets too much..." His warm gaze met hers. "If you need a moment. Tell me and we will stop."

She nodded, and this time, when his hand moved across her stomach, she made no move to stop him, even as she stiffened a little. When his hand brushed across the dark curls at the juncture of her thighs, she held her breath, waiting for the next step. He surprised her by caressing the inside of her thighs rather than where she had expected him to. Having his hand so close to the heart of her heated passion but not touching was both frustrating and thrilling.

Finally, his hand found her moist heat, and she had to bite her lip to stop herself from moaning loudly. Using his fingers, he stroked and teased her, building her need to a crescendo. When his thumb rubbed over the sensitive nub at the apex of her desire, she writhed underneath him, gasping and whimpering. Nothing could have prepared her for this onslaught of sensations. This desperate need to move. To have something more. There was a hollow ache low in her abdomen that she didn't know how to satisfy.

"Nathaniel, please..." she begged, even though she wasn't entirely sure what she was asking for.

Her plea seemed to be his undoing. He let out a groan, nudged her legs apart with his knee and settled between her thighs. With an arm on each side of her face, he gazed at her with a look somewhere between pleasure and agony.

"I'm sorry, darling. This might hurt a bit."

The frantic beating of her heart nearly blocked out every other sound, but she nodded. "I trust you, Nathaniel."

Slowly, he pressed against her, his hardness sliding into her molten heat. There was a brief stab of pain, but he caught her whimper with his lips. Stilling, he didn't move, allowing her body to adjust to the foreign intrusion. Having him inside her was a strange sensation, but not unpleasant.

His hot breath fanned her neck, his head next to hers. She fidgeted a little underneath him, and he breathed through gritted teeth. "Don't move."

"Why not?" She tried to twist her head to see him, but could only see his tanned neck and his dark hair curling slightly.

He groaned and shifted inside her, the friction making her gasp as the fire inside flared up again. Noticing that she was no longer hurting, he moved in long, deep strokes that wrought moans from somewhere deep in her throat. She soon found the rhythm, meeting his thrusts with her hips, and she was rewarded by Nathaniel's low moan.

His hands were everywhere, sliding up her thighs, following the curve of her hips, gripping strands of her hair. Tension built in her core, winding her tighter and tighter, until Nathaniel slid a hand between them and rubbed her most sensitive area. It pushed her over the edge, and her soul seemed to shatter into a thousand pieces as she came apart beneath him.

"Nathaniel!" It was all she could do to cling to him as the world dissolved around her.

With a guttural groan, Nathaniel buried himself deep within her with a final thrust before collapsing on top of her. She didn't mind the solid weight pushing her down into the mattress. It was comforting and made her feel safe to be so encompassed by him while she got her breathing back under control.

Caressing the damp curls at his nape, she placed a kiss below his ear. This had been amazing. Better than she ever could have imagined, and she struggled to contain her emotions as her love for him threatened to overflow.

Nathaniel raised himself on his elbows to look at her with a soft smile, and she felt that tender smile to her toes. She wanted to spill her heart right then and there and tell him she loved him, but she didn't dare. He had made it crystal clear that this was not a love match. Instead, she raised her head slightly to kiss him and he returned it with a smile.

When he rolled off her, she instantly missed his body against hers. But then he pulled her close to him, pressing her back against his chest. She fit snugly against him, and he held his arm around her waist, securing her there. She felt at home. This was where she was meant to be. No matter what, she had made the right choice. It didn't matter if he didn't love her. He buried his nose in her hair, and she closed her eyes, tired and content in his arms.

Nathaniel lay awake as Angel's breathing slowed and a light snore escaped her. Touching her cheek and caressing the golden tresses of hair away from her face and forehead, he frowned. Making love to his wife had been better than anything he had ever imagined. It had been amazing. She had reacted to his every caress with such sweet abandon that he couldn't imagine ever tiring of touching her.

He had known they would be good together. He just hadn't expected it to be quite this good. This consuming. Closing his eyes, he placed a soft kiss on the top of her head, the light smell of roses tickling his nose. He had to be careful. It would be far too easy to care too much. To fall in love.

His parents had been in love. That love had destroyed his father. Nathaniel had vowed never to fall in love himself. He could not risk reacting the way his father had if he lost the woman he loved. His family counted on him. They needed him.

Pulling his wife a little closer, he enjoyed feeling her warm body flush against his own. This felt too good. He must take care or he risked breaking that vow.

Chapter Twenty-Five

Dear Diary,
  Birds and bees indeed! Did James really
  know what he was talking about?
  I cannot help but wonder...

The first week of marriage went by faster than Angel could have imagined, but she loved every minute. She spent her days getting acquainted with the staff, house, and grounds while Nathaniel was busy reading through correspondence or speaking to his steward about the running of Davenhall and other estates. The rest of the time they spent together, with Nathaniel pointing out places where he'd played with his sisters as a boy while they took long walks through the expansive gardens.

Every night was an adventure and sometimes she had to hide a smile during the days when she remembered some wicked new thing her husband had shown her. The house staff said nothing but nodded knowingly when they saw her blush.

Living at Davenhall turned out to be exactly what she had always wished for. A home where she was wanted and appreciated. She even looked forward to Nathaniel's family returning that evening, longing for the laughter and easy familiarity that had been missing most of her life. The only shadow in her otherwise fairytale ending was the knowledge that her husband didn't love her, and never would. She tried to remind herself that he definitely liked her well enough and most certainly desired her, but she couldn't deny the sting of knowing he did not feel the way she did.

She fidgeted with the picnic basket she carried as she walked towards Nathaniel's study. With the rest of the family returning soon, she wanted to take advantage of their last few hours alone. Wearing a green dress with a scooped neckline and a sage green sash tied below her bosom, she was fairly certain she could coax her husband away from his desk. She had convinced the cook to prepare some food, hoping to take Nathaniel for a small bite in the garden. When she entered his study, he looked up at her from behind his desk and smiled when he saw the basket in her hand.

"Will I never be able to get anything done when I am home?" he asked teasingly with a nod towards her, his dark eyes glittering with amusement.

She smiled and set the basket down on a chair. "I won't disturb you too much in the future," she promised. "But with everyone returning soon, I thought it might be nice to spend some time together."

"Is my wife complaining that I don't spend enough time with her?" He rose from his chair and walked around the desk, taking her in his arms and placing a soft kiss on her lips. Then he smiled down at her, his eyes growing more heated. "I must remedy that. Can't have an unhappy wife on my hands."

"You rogue," she said with a low laugh and extracted herself from his embrace. "You spend plenty of time with me and well you know it. I have no cause for complaint. If you need to work, then I will leave you to it."

"It can wait." He picked up the picnic basket before looking over at her, and the warmth in his eyes made her insides flutter. "And, Angel?" he said, and she nodded. "You will never disturb me."

The fluttering intensified when he offered his arm. She gratefully took it, unsure if she could walk with her knees feeling so weak. The warm summer sun heated her skin when they left the house, and she raised her face to bask in the golden glow. It was a lovely summer's day with a blue sky and just enough of a breeze to keep the worst heat at bay.

"Where are we going?" she asked when Nathaniel didn't stop on the lawn like she expected, but continued through the gardens behind the house towards the forest growing on the hills enclosing the estate.

"You will see." He smiled and gave her a conspiratorial wink. "I hope you're wearing sensible shoes."

"Are we walking far?" She wasn't wearing promenade shoes, so she rather hoped they weren't.

"Not very. You'll be fine. It's the perfect spot for a picnic."

A short while later, after reaching the forest and winding their way between the trees, they reached a clearing where a stream rippled over stones towards the valley. The clearing was small but had enough space to place the blanket in a spot where the sun reached between the leaves of the trees. It was an enchanted little area, with the mossy green ground and the soothing sound of the running water. She'd never realised the woods behind the manor was such a beautiful place. With the lush green ground, she could almost imagine tiny faeries living beneath the protective fronds of the wood ferns.

"This was my parents' favourite place." Nathaniel took a few steps into the clearing. "My father showed it to me a few months before he passed. They used to go here when they wanted some time alone."

She turned away from admiring the possibly faery-infested ferns to look at him. He stared at the stream behind her with a vacant expression on his face and a small line between his brows. Taking the steps separating them, she gently touched his cheek with her hand. His eyes focused on her and she smiled up at him.

"This place is beautiful," she said softly, and he nodded.

"I'm glad you like it. I haven't been here since my father first showed it to me. It's fortunate I remembered the way." He smiled, his humour restored. "It might prove useful once my sisters have returned if we ever want some peace."

She laughed. "You're a wise man."

After sharing the food and drink from the picnic basket, they lay down on the blanket and looked up at the sky. Angel rested her head on Nathaniel's shoulder. The forest was so peaceful; the only sounds were the rustling of the leaves, the bubbling of the stream, and the chirping birds. She could fall asleep like this.

Playing absently with the buttons on Nathaniel's clothes, she opened a few on his waistcoat and then on his shirt, allowing her to slip her hand underneath to touch his warm, smooth skin. She couldn't get enough of touching him, even in the little ways. Fortunately, he never seemed to mind.

"Nathaniel?" she asked after a little while.

"Hmm?" His eyes were closed, and his chest rose and fell slowly.

"You mentioned this is where your parents used to go... and I'm sorry for bringing up a painful subject, but how did you lose them? Was it a long time ago?"

He tensed under her palm, but then he relaxed, taking a deep breath.

"Our mother died when Nick was three years old. Influenza. She just couldn't fight it. Father was never the same after that. He loved her so much that I don't think he could function once we lost her... It's probably why he asked Aunt Jane to come and stay. He knew he wasn't able to care for us the way he ought to." He fell quiet for a moment before he continued. "Father died four years later. They say it was a hunting accident, but... I suspect he simply could not go on without her."

Pain lanced her heart at the sadness in his voice, no matter how much he tried to sound like he was just stating facts. She raised herself up on her elbow to look down at him, her hand still resting lightly on his chest, just above his heart.

"I'm so sorry for your loss, Nathaniel," she said softly. "Losing a parent is awful. Losing both is a grief that stays with you forever."

He nodded slowly. "It's an emptiness no one else can understand." His dark gaze met hers, and the pain in his eyes made her heart ache.

"We do what we can to move on." She pressed her hand a little harder against his chest. "And remember in our hearts that our parents loved us."

The line was back between Nathaniel's brows. "Not enough. My father didn't love us enough. Losing Mother was too much for him. It broke him. We needed him, and he left us." There was a hardness to his voice she had never heard before, but beyond it, she could sense the dark edge of grief she knew so well.

"I'm sure your father did his best."

"It wasn't good enough. After he passed... I swore never to fall in love." Staring at something above her head, Nathaniel refused to look at her as he continued, "I cannot risk finding out if I'm too much like my father if something were to happen. My sisters need me."

Disappointment and understanding washed over her. Understanding because she could see the wound on his soul like it was a tangible thing. How it had festered and grown until he had walled it off to save himself from the pain. Disappointment, because she didn't think she could ever break through that impenetrable shield.

He didn't want to love her. Didn't want to love anyone.

It hurt. But she could understand him, too. Losing her parents had shaped her in many ways, and some she probably didn't even realise, having been so young at the time. She wished she could erase the pain. Hers and Nathaniel's. But she didn't know how.

So she did the only thing she could think of. She leaned down and pressed a soft kiss on his lips, hoping she could somehow put her feelings into it, the words she couldn't say out loud.

His mouth was tense under hers, but a moment later, he relaxed. A low moan escaped him, and he buried his fingers in the hair at the back of her head, holding her in place. The kiss turned deeper, hotter, stoking her desire with every stroke of his tongue, every flex of his fingers at her nape.

Finally, he released her, staring up at her with eyes that were nearly black with desire. "I'm sorry." His hoarse voice made her insides melt in a hot heap of want. "Here I am wallowing about losing my parents when you lost yours too."

She smiled wistfully. "I was so young, I don't really remember them. Sometimes, I think I remember my mother's scent but I don't know if it's just wishful thinking."

"I'm sorry you never got the chance to get to know your parents better." He reached up and tucked a strand of her hair behind her ear.

"Me too."

It was one of the things that hurt most about losing her parents. Never knowing them. Never being able to ask their advice. Would they have loved her better than her aunt and uncle? Would they have approved of her choice in rejecting Philip and choosing to marry Nathaniel? She hoped so.

When neither of them spoke, Nathaniel smiled faintly. "Enough talk of such sombre things. Let's speak of something more pleasant."

"Do you have any suggestions?" she asked, inching a little closer.

"Kissing?" He grinned and rolled her over on her back with him on top. "Yes, I do believe kissing would be a suitable topic for discussion."

With a giggle, she slid her arms around his neck. She loved how light he could make her heart feel. No matter what anyone else might think, *she* approved of her choice to marry Nathaniel. It had been the right one, even if he could never love her.

He leaned down, his dark eyes twinkling. "And I know just where to start..."

His lips were a mere breath from the sensitive skin below her ear when he hesitated. Frowning, she was just about to ask him what was wrong when she heard it. Was that... the sound of someone running?

"Here they are!" someone shouted.

Nathaniel quickly got up. Trying not to blush, Angel looked over to see his youngest sister standing by the edge of the trees with a big grin on her face.

"I thought you said your sisters didn't know about this place?" she mumbled when Nathaniel helped her up from the ground.

"Apparently, I was mistaken. I should have realised this wild one has explored every inch of the forest by now." Running a hand through his dark hair, he turned to his sister. "Nick, what are you doing back already? I thought you weren't coming until later."

"We came earlier."

"Obviously."

Nick only grinned at her brother's disgruntled tone, and Angel had to hide a smile. The girl was so impudent and self-assured, such a contrast to her as a child. It was refreshing to see. Nick didn't back down from anything or anyone. Definitely not her brother.

"You better hurry because Rain is searching too," the young girl said. "Or do you want to make a fool of yourself in front of her as well?"

"What I'd like to know is why my sisters think it's a good idea to interrupt my private picnic with my wife," Nathaniel muttered while redoing the buttons Angel had slipped open earlier.

"We thought you'd be eager to see us after we've been gone an entire week," Nick said, blinking innocently. "You must have missed us terribly."

A chuckle escaped him. "You little imp."

They quickly packed the remains of their late lunch and folded the blanket. Taking the basket, Nathaniel walked over and ruffled his sister's hair. "Come on, then. Let's go back to the house."

A short distance away, they found Rain kneeling on the ground, peering into a rabbit hole. Nathaniel sighed. "Get off the ground, please. You're ruining your dress."

"A good day to you too," Rain said cheerfully, standing to brush the leaves and pine needles off her skirts.

"What were you looking at?" Angel asked.

"I was trying to see if the rabbit had its kittens yet."

"It's a rabbit," Nathaniel said dryly. "It has babies several times a year."

"You're in a lovely mood today, Brother." Rain rolled her eyes, falling into step with them. Nathaniel only grunted.

Angel gave the sisters an apologetic look, but they didn't look the least bit offended by their brother's gruff tone, and she supposed they were used to it. When they reached Davenhall, Mrs Grey and Jessica were in the drawing room, inviting them to share some tea and biscuits.

"Have Wortham and Gowthorpe returned to London?" Nathaniel asked, taking a ginger biscuit and popping it in his mouth.

"Gowthorpe left yesterday," Mrs Grey said. "Wortham mentioned he would wait and travel back with you. I take it you are returning to London as well?"

"Yes." Nathaniel gave Angel a warm look. "Will you go with me? Parliament is still in session, and I really ought to go back for the remainder. It's not for long, but I've already missed a week."

"Of course. I'd love to come with you." She smiled. "And I can see James again."

"You should bring Jessica along," Mrs Grey said, and Jessica's head jerked up. "There is still time this Season for her to look for a husband."

"I don't wish to return to London." Jessica looked between her aunt and brother. "I've had enough of men begging for dances and speaking of nothing but the weather or the latest on-dit."

"But you like gossip!" Nick quipped before stealing what must be her fourth biscuit.

"Not enough to endure London."

Nathaniel smirked. "How else will you find a husband?"

"I'm in no rush to find one."

Rain's eyes were wide as she observed their conversation. "How can you not wish to go to London? If they allowed me to attend balls and parties, I would not miss a moment!"

"Then, by all means," Jessica said dryly, "you can go in my stead."

When Rain turned her cornflower-blue eyes toward her brother to give him a pleading look, he choked on his tea and had to put the cup back on the table. "Absolutely not!"

"But Jessica doesn't want to go!"

"Then she will not go," he agreed. "But that does not mean you can. You're far too young. When you're eighteen, I will take you to as many balls as you can stomach."

She sank back in her chair with her arms crossed and a petulant look on her pretty face. "I still don't see why I can't go now."

"Don't worry, Rain," Nick said happily. "You and I can attend the Season together when I turn eighteen."

"When you're eighteen, I will already be married."

"Not if you wait for me."

After a moment's stunned silence, Rain laughed. Angel smiled behind her teacup. There was no way this young lady would wait an additional year before having her season.

"If Wortham is left alone at Holcombe with his father, I reckon we will see him here soon," Nathaniel mused. "The two of them cannot abide having to speak to one another."

Jessica groaned. "Great. Another visit by Wortham. Can we never escape that vexing man?"

"Now, now." Mrs Grey put her teacup down to refill it. "Wortham is not all bad. Underneath all of his antics, he's a good man."

They all pretended not to hear Jessica's scoff. Angel took a sip of tea before admitting, "The things he says often make me blush. He's very... inappropriate."

"And he will continue to try to shock you for as long as you react," Mrs Grey promised with a little smile. "He is a rogue. There is no doubt about that."

"And a cad, and a rake, and a—" Jessica continued, but stopped when her brother gave her an irritated look. "What? I'm only telling the truth."

"One descriptor is enough, young lady."

She grinned. "But they all fit him so well."

"It would be more polite if you told him to his face and not behind his back."

"Very well." Jessica raised her chin slightly. "I shall tell him next time I see him."

Nathaniel pressed his lips into a thin line, looking like he was about to argue, so Angel decided it was time to intervene before he got into a fight with his sisters.

"Did I not stop you from finishing some correspondence earlier?" she said, and his head turned towards her. A smile tugged at the corners of his mouth. He knew exactly what she was doing.

"Correct. I do have some letters to catch up on." Standing, he gave her a quick kiss before he sketched a bow and disappeared out the door.

Later that evening, while they prepared for bed, Nathaniel looked over at her with a smile.

"Are you planning to always save my sisters from my temper?"

She smiled back at him from her seat at the vanity. "If that's what it takes to keep peace in the house."

Pulling his shirt over his head, he chuckled. "I think you'll find that the Howertys are happiest when they get to fight a little."

Any reply she might have had fled when she drank in the sight of her husband's naked torso. A week of marriage had done nothing to temper her reaction to him, the sight always stealing her breath away. He was an astonishing piece of pure masculinity and she absolutely adored his smooth, sculpted chest and muscular arms. He caught her staring, and the look he gave her was enough to make her mouth run dry.

He walked over to her, wearing only his black trousers, and began pulling the remaining pins out of her hair without breaking eye contact. When her long, golden hair fell down her back, he pulled her to her feet and buried his hands in the blond tresses. His lips found hers, and when he kissed her, she forgot all about siblings arguing, and everything else, her mind focusing solely on the sensation of his touch, his smell, and the spark of desire flickering to life.

Later that night, when they lay in bed, her head on his shoulder and his arm around her back, she was sated and happy, filled with love. Unable to hold back any longer, even while she knew he did not feel the same, she moved her fingernails lightly across his chest, watching the gooseflesh trailing in their wake.

"Nathaniel?" Was he even awake?

"Hmm?" His voice was drowsy, but he pulled her a little tighter against him.

"I..." She trailed off, losing courage.

"Go to sleep, darling." He turned his head to place a kiss on her forehead. "We'll talk tomorrow."

She chewed on her lower lip, uncertain if she should confess how she felt. He had been clear about not loving her. About not wanting to love anyone. But she loved him, and she couldn't quench the hope that while he didn't love her, he felt *something* for her. He was so attentive to her needs, so quick to make her smile when something was wrong. And maybe he could appreciate how she felt, even if he couldn't reciprocate.

"I love you." The words spilt from her before she could stop them. She held her breath, waiting to hear his reply.

Silence.

She frowned. "Nathaniel?" She nudged him gently. "Did you hear me?"

"Yes, yes," he muttered sleepily. "That's nice. Now go back to sleep."

She froze. Her chest constricted and she stared into the darkness of the room. That was his only reply? She knew he didn't love her, but she had not expected him to be so uncaring about her feelings towards him. To brush them off so easily. Scooting away, she turned her back to him, needing the distance between them to collect the shattered pieces of her heart. She stared into the wall on the other side of the room, praying he wouldn't notice her tears.

What did I expect?

She wiped the moisture from her cheek. He had only married her to save her reputation. So bloody honourable and helpful that he couldn't resist a damsel in distress. Of course, he would charge in to help his best friend's sister out of a sticky mess. And she had let him. She buried her face in the pillow. It shouldn't hurt this much. She'd known what she got herself into. And yet it did.

Chapter Twenty-Six

Dear Diary,
 What do a few words mean, anyway?
 Surely I can live without hearing
 my husband say he loves me.

Nathaniel couldn't quite shake the feeling that something was awfully wrong, but he couldn't figure out why. Angel had been more subdued today and while she was as pleasant as ever, it was like she held herself back. But why? Everything had been fine when they went to bed last night. He'd asked her, of course. The reply had been the one he feared most. *Nothing.* Whenever a woman said nothing was wrong, something was definitely wrong. One did not live with an aunt and three sisters without learning that.

With a frown, he watched his wife from across the room. She and Jessica were discussing some books they both read and had an opinion on. He couldn't help but feel a little dismissed since she usually spent her evenings with him. With his family back in the house, he supposed he would have to learn to share her attention. Even if he didn't want to.

He absentmindedly scooted over on the sofa to make space for Rain and a kitten she'd found that morning abandoned by its mother. Maybe Angel meant it when she said nothing was wrong. Perhaps she was simply overwhelmed by having the entire Howerty brood around. She was used to a much smaller, much quieter family.

"Ow!" He glared down at the little kitten, which had just dug its tiny claws into his thigh. The little beast stared up at him with enormous green eyes as if he were a giant awakened from its slumber. Then again, to the kitten, he probably did seem enormous.

"I'm sorry!" Rain quickly scooped up the kitten, which took a moment since she had to detach its claws from the fabric of his trousers.

"Don't worry about it. How many more wounded animals have you got hidden throughout the house?"

"They're not hidden." She scoffed. "I've got them all safely set up in the conservatory."

"Naturally," he remarked dryly. "How many?"

She was quiet for a moment, obviously counting her strays and injured animals in her head, before she said, "About a dozen."

"A dozen?" He didn't even have the energy to be angry about his house being invaded by a dozen critters and small beasts. It was something his sister had done since she was old enough to walk. Wherever they were, every stray and wounded animal would find its way into her arms. He sighed. "Just keep them out of my way."

"I will," she promised with a smile. It was an easy promise, considering he was leaving for London the following day. Finally having extracted the kitten from his clothing, Rain took it into her arms and placed a kiss on its furry head. Bringing it with her, she left the room, most likely to return it to its cohorts, all huddled comfortably in his conservatory.

They were all gathered in the upstairs drawing room for the evening. Aunt Jane sat in front of the fireplace, working on a piece of embroidery, while Nick sat by her feet, regaling her with stories of her daily adventures. Nathaniel had brought a book to read but had been too distracted by his wife and had not read more than half a page.

Roberts entered the room, catching his attention, and he gave the butler a questioning look.

"The Earl of Wortham has come to call," Roberts stated simply, but before Nathaniel had the chance to tell him to show their guest in, the butler stepped out of the way as Wortham stalked past him.

"I've not come to call." He sank down on a chair, practically seething. "I've come to stay the night."

"You know, it's custom to wait for the butler to return and tell you whether you may enter." Nathaniel tried to hold back a smile but wasn't sure he managed. His friend could never spend much time alone with his father before fleeing the scene. It was a miracle he'd lasted a whole day after the Howertys left.

Wortham scoffed. "You've never denied me entry." He waved dismissively towards Roberts. "You may go now."

"I may yet," Nathaniel muttered. "Especially if you keep giving my servants orders." Turning his head to the butler, he added, "You may go now."

Sketching a quick bow, the butler left. Wortham sprawled in his chair, looking quite relaxed, but knowing him for as long as he had, Nathaniel could see the anger and frustration lingering in his facial expression and deep in his eyes.

"So what brings you here so late at night?" he asked casually, closing the book and putting it away on a table.

His friend straightened a little and looked about the room like he only just realised they weren't alone. "Good evening, ladies," he said politely with a nod of his head, then turned his gaze back to Nathaniel. "You know I cannot abide my father's full attention on me. Once Gowthorpe and your family all abandoned me, I simply could not remain."

"Well, you made a valiant effort." Nathaniel chuckled. "You lasted a full day. Must be a record of sorts."

"I think I once managed two. Do you have a guest room to spare?"

"Always."

"Thank you. I suppose it makes it easier to travel to London tomorrow since we no longer need to meet up in Bridlewood." Wortham looked over to where Angel and Jessica sat. "Not busy cuddling the new missus?"

"I have to share her with the rest of the family."

Wortham chuckled. "I'm not sure whether it's a blessing or a curse to have a large family."

"A bit of both," Nathaniel admitted wryly.

His wife and sister came over to sit with them. When his wife chose to sit on a chair close to Wortham instead of next to him on the sofa, Nathaniel knew for certain that something was wrong. As his sister sat down by his side, he tried his damnedest not to scowl

Angel smiled pleasantly at his friend. "I did not expect to see you again so soon."

"Ah, but I simply could not stay away from your lovely presence." Wortham flashed one of his more devastating smiles.

When Angel blushed prettily, Nathaniel fought back a pang of what could only be jealousy. It wasn't that he thought his wife was infatuated with his friend—though most women were—but when he watched her laughing and joking with the earl, he couldn't help wishing she was giving her attention to *him*. Maybe because he had been denied it for most of the day, but he craved her presence. Her conversation. He wanted to be the one she laughed with.

The longer Angel and Wortham kept talking, the darker Nathaniel's mood turned. Even Jessica—who normally avoided the rakish earl—joined in. Needing an outlet for his foul temper, Nathaniel interrupted the conversation.

"Jessica? Wasn't there something you wanted to tell Wortham?"

His sister stopped mid-sentence and turned to stare at him in horror, and he immediately regretted his rash decision. Teasing his sister was something he quite enjoyed, but embarrassing her in front of a family friend was something else entirely. He really must learn to control his temper.

Wortham's smile widened, obviously realising it wasn't a compliment Nathaniel referred to. He turned to Jessica. "What did you want to tell me, sweetheart?"

Turning back to the earl, Jessica's cheeks stained red. "I..." Her words faltered, then her shoulders straightened and, after a quelling look at Nathaniel, she addressed Wortham. "We were discussing some of your finer qualities, and I was simply remarking on your considerable charm."

There was no mistaking the withering sarcasm in her voice. Wortham's eyes glittered and the corners of his mouth twitched. "Oh, so you find me charming?"

She snorted. "Like a snake."

The earl chuckled, leaning back in his chair as if enjoying the show, apparently not particularly concerned by Jessica's thoughts on his charms—or lack thereof.

Having heard the discussion from across the room, Nick stood. "Those weren't the words I remember you using," she said. "And you said you would tell him to his face."

Nathaniel would have clapped a hand over his youngest sister's mouth had she been closer, but the damage was already done. And he had been the catalyst. Jessica stood, her face red and strained.

"Fine!" she snapped. Looking down at Wortham, who grinned up at her, she said crisply, "Jacob Hurst, I think you are a cad and a rake."

"Jessica!" Aunt Jane gasped from the other side of the room.

Without another word, Jessica left, the anger trailing after her almost palpable in the room. Wortham's laughter did little to defuse the situation. Aunt Jane came over and even Wortham sobered at her disapproving look.

"You should know better," she said to Nathaniel. "Why would you bring that up?"

He groaned and raked a hand through his hair. "I'm sorry, Aunt."

"I'm not the one you should apologise to." Aunt Jane shook her head. "She's supposed to be the one with no temper."

His aunt left to follow Jessica, and Angel gave him an unreadable look before following. *Bloody hell.* He had upset everyone tonight.

"I knew it was a good idea to come here tonight." Wortham's eyes glittered with barely suppressed mirth. "You lot always put on a good show."

"Damn it, Wortham. Can you never show some compassion?"

"No," his friend replied simply and stood. "How about a drink?"

"I think I need one."

After sending Nick off to bed, they walked downstairs to the library in companionable silence. Once there, Nathaniel took two glasses and a bottle of brandy from the liquor cabinet and filled them. Taking a deep swig from his glass and feeling the heat of the alcohol burning his throat, he felt a little better.

"I suppose I do owe Jessica an apology," he muttered. Handing his friend the other glass, he sat down in a large, winged leather chair identical to the one Wortham occupied.

"You do," Wortham agreed. "What brought this on? You don't usually torture your sisters in front of me. Not that I didn't quite enjoy it, mind you, but it was an unexpected treat. One I believe Jessica would rather not have been an active participant of."

"I don't know." He shrugged and took another sip of his drink. That wasn't entirely true. "Something has felt off today and it has me on edge."

"With your wife?" Wortham quirked a brow at his shocked stare. He wasn't sure why the question surprised him. His friend was annoyingly perceptive, as long as it involved others. "I did notice there was some... tension there."

"She claims nothing is wrong, yet has avoided me all day!" The words came out in a frustrated explosion. "She would never admit it, but she's found every excuse to spend time with my family rather than me."

His friend considered the admission in silence for a moment, watching the liquid in his glass while he swirled it around by moving the glass in a small, circular motion. "Well," he finally drawled. "Have you told her you love her?"

"What?" A surprised bark of laughter escaped him. "No! Of course not. You know my stance on love."

Shifting his gaze from the glass in his hand to Nathaniel, Wortham smirked. "I do. I also know a fool in love when I see one. So why haven't you told her?"

"I..." He ran a hand through his hair, looking out the window, but could see nothing other than darkness outside. "I don't love her. This is a marriage that was convenient for both of us. I needed a wife, and she needed someone to save her reputation."

"Ah yes, ever the knight in shining armour." Wortham chuckled. "I bet bedding her without the worry of tarnishing your shine was a pleasant bonus. Couldn't risk anyone thinking the honourable Nathaniel Howerty would consider compromising a young lady. This was obviously the best choice for everyone. You could bed her with your precious honour intact and save her from ruin all in one go."

"Do you have to put it like that?" Nathaniel muttered as heat spread up his neck. "Yes, I wanted her in my bed, but—"

A sound outside the hallway made them look towards the open doorway, but it was empty. He frowned. "Maybe one of Rain's strays."

Wortham scoffed. "Keep fooling yourself," he said, standing up and putting his empty glass on a small table. "I think we both know why you married her."

Nathaniel watched his friend leave the library, frustration building in his chest. Wortham didn't know what he was talking about. Love was not for him. Would never be for him. No matter how lovely his wife was. It didn't matter that she brightened the days when she was around him. Didn't matter that he missed her company whenever she was not near. That was not love, it was simply... he appreciated his wife. That was all. It had to be all.

Angel buried her face in the pillow, wishing she had never gone past the library. Only intending to inform Nathaniel that she was going to bed, she had reached the door just in time to hear Wortham tease him about marrying her so he could bed her. Nathaniel's reply had been like a punch to the gut.

Yes, I wanted her in my bed.

The words echoed in her mind until she was ready to shove the pillow over her head to make it stop. How had she not seen it? He hadn't even tried to hide it from her. He had always said there was attraction between them, and she could not deny his desire for her. But he was too honourable to ruin her. All those kisses when she had been lost in his embrace. It had always been he who pulled away, not wanting to take advantage of his friend's sister. *He certainly found a way around that, didn't he?* She laughed bitterly. All he had to do was marry her.

Knowing he could never love her was already a hard pill to swallow. The reality of his rejection still hurt with every breath. But she had believed this whole time that he was making a sacrifice by marrying her to save her from ruin, but in reality, he had done it for his own selfish reasons. She was nothing but another woman he could bed in good conscience without having to worry about his honour. That he got to play the hero by saving her was secondary. All that talk of friendship and how well-suited they were was just that... Talk. Sweet nonsense to convince her to marry him.

His silence after she confessed her feelings last night had left her heartbroken, but she had tried to put a brave face on, pretending everything was all right. But this... Finding out he only wanted her in his bed. It was the nail in the coffin. She loved him, but it was becoming more and more clear that she had been wrong about him caring, and that she meant little to him.

After overhearing the men in the library, she had gone straight to the bedchamber, and by now her head hurt from crying. The hour was growing late and Nathaniel would come to bed soon. She had to pull herself together. The last thing she wanted was for him to see her upset. To see how much he hurt her. He didn't deserve that kind of power over her. Taking a deep breath, she turned onto her back and stared up at the ceiling. Continuing to take slow, deliberate breaths, she calmed down.

Not much later, the door opened and Nathaniel entered. He said nothing but must have seen she was still awake. After undressing, he padded over to the bed and gave her an unreadable look before extinguishing the candle on the bedside table. Crawling into bed, he moved over to her, but when he bent his head to kiss her shoulder, she turned her back to him.

"I have a headache," she mumbled.

She could sense him watching her, unmoving in the bed. "Very well," he finally said, lying down on the opposite side. She wasn't sure whether she was relieved or disappointed that he didn't probe her further.

They lay in silence for a while until Nathaniel quietly said, "I didn't see your valise. Did someone already carry it downstairs?"

Right. She had opened it and flung all the clothes back into the closet with the valise following suit. "I'm not coming with you to London."

The mattress shifted underneath her when he abruptly turned towards her. "What? Why not?"

"I decided I would rather stay here and familiarise myself with the house more. I still have a lot to learn about running it." It was an excuse, but it was as good as any.

"Oh." He settled back down but sounded disappointed. "I wish you'd come with me."

"Why?" The question came out more tersely than she had intended.

A warm hand settled on her shoulder. "Why won't you look at me?"

She closed her eyes, hating the fact that she still loved his touch. It wasn't fair. Turning around to look at him, his handsome face etched in the faint light of the full moon outside their window, she met his eyes. "I see no reason to come to London," she said, steeling herself. "You got what you wanted from me. In fact, I think we should consider separate bedchambers."

A line appeared between his brows. "What are you talking about?"

"You married me. You bedded me." It amazed her that she could say it without bursting into tears. Her sadness had turned into anger, and it burned hotly, fuelling her words. "You got what you wanted."

Even in the dusky room, she could see him pale. "You heard that?"

"I did," she replied stiffly. "So you will excuse me if I don't want to join you in London."

"Hell, Angel." He ran a hand through his hair. "I... That is not..."

She let out a brittle laugh. "No? Are you saying you didn't marry me so you could bed me?"

"It wasn't the only reason."

"Spare me," she snapped, sitting up. He sat up too, and they glared at each other for a moment.

"I thought you knew me better than that," he retorted, his temper flaring. "Surely you can't believe I'd marry you only to take you to bed."

"I heard you say exactly that!" she yelled, only to clap a hand over her mouth. She never yelled.

"Bloody hell!" Nathaniel lunged out of bed. Cursing, he pulled on his riding breeches and black Hessian boots. She watched him in silence while he jerkily pulled on his shirt, noticed it was inside out and had to take it off and wring it before putting it on again.

"Where are you going?" she asked hesitantly while he buttoned his waistcoat.

"To London," he replied shortly.

"Now?"

"Yes." He gave her a dark look. "You obviously don't want me here. I might as well leave."

"But"—she looked out the window—"it's the middle of the night."

"I shan't take up any more of your precious time with my offending presence." Grabbing his coat and pulling it on, he sketched a mocking bow. "I'll see you in a few weeks, Lady Pensington."

The door shut behind him, and with a frustrated yell, she tossed a pillow at it. Irksome, bullheaded man!

"Go to London then," she muttered, lying back down. "See if I will miss you."

But she suspected she would. Because no matter how angry and hurt she was, she still loved him.

Nathaniel cursed when he tripped over a low stool in the dark bedroom. It did nothing to appease his foul temper. Anger and guilt gnawed at him, making him rash. He knew he shouldn't make decisions when angry, but the accusatory glint in Angel's eyes when she'd looked at him was chasing him away better than anything else.

Because she was right. He had done exactly what she accused him of. He was an arsehole and deserved every bit of her ire. The truth hurt. And he couldn't stop the fury burning deep inside him. Fury with Angel for making him feel this bad. Fury at the whole situation. But, mostly, fury at himself.

He tripped over another object, which ignited his temper even more, and he kicked the offending boot across the room. It hit the wall with a satisfying bang. The shape in the bed stirred, sitting up.

"Pensington?" Wortham stared at him. "What the hell are you doing in my room?"

"We're leaving for London."

"What? Now?" His friend glanced at the window. It was still dark.

"Yes. Now." Nathaniel paced the width of the room, refusing to slow down. Refusing to stop to think, because every time he did, he saw the pain and hurt in Angel's eyes. "Are you coming or not?"

With a glare, Wortham slid out of the bed and walked over to his clothes, neatly folded on a nearby chair. "What's the rush?" he asked while he dressed.

"I just want to get to London as soon as possible."

Wortham pulled on his riding boots with a grunt. "In the middle of the night? Even if we end up meeting with highwaymen?"

"They're asleep by now."

"Are you hearing yourself?" Wortham rolled his eyes, but when Nathaniel didn't answer, he grabbed his coat and walked towards the door. "Let's go then."

They were halfway to the village of Bridlewood before Nathaniel finally spoke. "She heard us."

"What do you mean?" Wortham reined in his horse to pull up alongside Nathaniel.

"She heard me say I married her to bed her."

There was a moment's silence while Wortham digested that bit of information. For once, he didn't taunt him or come with a clever retort. Maybe he sensed Nathaniel's volatile mood.

"And you solve that by hying off to London in the middle of the night?" his friend asked carefully.

"I couldn't very well stay there while she looks at me like I'm some kind of monster," Nathaniel muttered, staring straight ahead and refusing to meet Wortham's eyes.

"Of course not," Wortham said sarcastically. "*That* would have been stupid."

Nathaniel glared at him, but his friend only shrugged and said, "You never said I had to agree with you."

"True." Nathaniel groaned before dryly adding, "Maybe I should have."

Wortham grinned. "No, you wouldn't like me as much if I didn't tell you what an arse you are."

"I just... I can't believe she would think that's the kind of man I am." Didn't she know him better than that? They were good together. He might not love her, but he wanted to think she knew he cared for her and he'd never wanted to hurt her.

Wortham scoffed next to him. "Yes, she only heard it from you, after all."

"True, but you know that's not the only reason I married her. She should know that, too."

"God, Pensington! Don't be such an arse," Wortham snapped. "She heard the words from your mouth. Who is she to believe if not you? It's not like you've bothered to tell her otherwise. How can you expect her to know something you have never told her? She's not a bloody mind-reader!"

Nathaniel stared at his friend. The truth was so plain when spelled out and when his temper didn't have the best of him. His entire body deflated. "You're right. I'm an idiot."

"I'm glad you finally realised it. Once Parliament is in recess, you ought to crawl back to your wife and beg her to forgive your sorry arse."

"God, Wortham. You make it sound so appealing." He hated it when his friend was right. He'd been such a fool.

Wortham grinned. "Don't forget to grovel. Now, let's find an inn. Travelling at night is a terrible idea."

Nathaniel took a sip from a glass of punch, watching the guests gathered at the ball his friends had dragged him to, wishing he were somewhere else entirely. Preferably back at Davenhall with his wife. Being in London without her didn't feel right. Having left her the way he did, felt... well, he felt like an ogre. An ogre having a temper tantrum. She had every right to be angry and disappointed in him after what she'd overheard.

It wasn't even true. Three days away from Angel was all he needed to realise he hadn't married her to save her. Or to bed her. Though he thoroughly enjoyed the latter. He had married her because he wanted her in his life. Which was exactly what he needed to tell her. And he probably ought to grovel since he had not handled their argument well at all. He'd allowed his guilt to chase him away because he'd known she was justified in her anger. In her hurt. Of course she had believed his thoughtless statements. Wortham was right; he had given her no reason to think otherwise.

He wrinkled his nose in distaste. It felt wrong to think that Wortham was correct about anything—even if his friend was more often than not. Another annoying habit of his.

"What's with the scowling? You're scaring the ladies away."

Nathaniel smiled grimly when the very person he'd been thinking of materialised as if summoned. Speak of the devil…

"Just ruminating on what an arse I've been," he said.

"Good. I was beginning to think I might have to remind you again." Wortham grinned. "So, what are you planning to do?"

"I don't know. Apologise profusely, I suppose."

"Why not just tell her you love her?"

Nathaniel choked on his punch and coughed. "Have we not recently had this discussion?"

"We have." Wortham gave him a knowing look. "I'm just never satisfied with your response. How long are you planning on deluding yourself?"

"I…" Nathaniel fell silent.

Taking the opportunity, Wortham continued. "Look," he said, sounding almost like he was explaining something to a child. "I don't pretend to know much about love. Lord knows I never loved anyone other than myself and no one has ever loved me. But what I do know is that it's not something you get to decide. It just happens. Whether you want it to or not."

"I didn't know you were such a romantic."

Wortham snorted at the obvious sarcasm. "All I'm saying is that you either love the chit or you don't. It's not a choice. If you were to fall apart at losing her, whether you've admitted those feelings aloud hardly matters."

With those words, his friend moved away, smiling charmingly at a group of young women who had been looking admiringly in their direction. Nathaniel stared after him, lips pressed together. *Damn.* He really hated it when Wortham was right.

Chapter Twenty-Seven

Dear Diary,
 I always used to love solitude. It's odd
 how quickly one can change one's mind.
 Now I miss having someone beside me
 in bed at night.

A hollow ache burned in Angel's chest as she sat in the bathtub in the bedroom she was meant to be sharing with her husband. Not even the warm water or the floral scent of the rosewater tickling her nose could dispel the distinct feeling that something was missing. No, some*one*. Nathaniel. He should have been there with her, not in London alone.

She missed him. Despite her anger and disappointment. Despite her heart practically breaking with the knowledge that he'd married her for all the wrong reasons. His absence left a palpable void, one that grew more pronounced with every passing day.

Closing her eyes, she leaned her head back against the rim of the tub. The last few days had been an exercise in pretence, forcing smiles and light conversation for the sake of his family. Acting like her heart wasn't cracking just a little bit more for every day he didn't return. But in the solitude of her bath, she could finally let the mask slip.

"Foolish man," she muttered to no one in particular, wiping at the bothersome tears threatening to spill.

The worst part was that she still loved him. It was a cruel twist, to love someone so deeply while knowing they didn't feel the same. And not only that. He had not been truthful about his reasons for marrying her. It made her question every memory, every interaction, every smile. Had it all been for show?

'He's only marrying you to play the hero.'

Philip's words rose unbidden in her mind. Maybe she should have known better. She *had* known better. Had always doubted that Nathaniel truly wanted her.

No.

Her heart rebelled at the intrusive thoughts. No matter what, Nathaniel did care for her, even if he didn't love her. It was apparent in his actions whenever they were together. In his kindness and thoughtfulness. Even in his passion, being patient and understanding when her shyness made her hesitate. It couldn't all have been a lie. She refused to believe it.

Lost in her thoughts, she didn't know how much time had passed until the water began to cool. With some reluctance, she rose from the bath, water cascading down her body as she reached for a towel. When she dried herself, a faint sound from outside caught her attention.

Her heart fluttered. Could it be Nathaniel?

Pulling her nightgown over her head, she padded over to the window, peering out into the darkness. The grounds of Davenhall were shrouded in shadows, the moonlight casting an eerie glow over the gardens. Was that a movement she saw by the oak tree, or merely a trick of the light?

A hand clamped over her mouth and an arm snaked around her waist. Her heart leapt to her throat and the icy claws of terror slashed at her insides. Kicking her legs out, she tried to twist out of the grip, but her assailant was too strong. Their grasp only tightened.

"Don't scream," a familiar voice hissed in her ear, and her blood ran cold.

Philip.

Panic fuelled her movements. She fought even harder to wrench free, but his arms might as well have been iron wrapped around her.

"Quit struggling," he grunted. "Or I'll give you something to struggle about."

She stilled in his hard embrace, her mind trying to make sense of what was happening. Why was he here? How? When he set her down and released her, other than a vice-like grip on her wrist, she twisted to face him.

"Philip, please. What do you want?"

His face twisted into a sneer, his eyes glittering with malice in the dim candlelight. "You've ruined everything. You and your marquess. And now you'll pay."

Pay how? The possibilities seemed endless, each one worse than the last. Was he going to kill her? Or Nathaniel? Her new family? A hard swallow freed her mind. She needed to get away from him. Somehow. She opened her mouth to scream for help, but before she could, Philip's hand struck her face with a resounding slap. The force of it sent her stumbling backwards, pain blossoming across her cheek.

"Make another sound," Philip growled, pulling out a pistol and aiming it at her, "and I'll shoot anyone who comes through that door. Do you understand?"

The barrel of the weapon stared at her like some one-eyed demon. She nodded. She couldn't call for anyone.. Not the Howertys. Not the servants. She couldn't bear the thought of any of them hurt because of her.

"Please," she whispered, her voice trembling. "Don't do this. Whatever grievance you have, surely we can solve it without violence."

Philip didn't react to her pleas. Picking up her dressing gown from the bed, he threw it at her. "Put it on," he ordered. "Be quick about it."

With shaking hands, she pulled the robe on and tied it around her waist. What was he planning? She tried to think of a way to escape him, but none appeared. At least none that wouldn't put others at risk.

"Move." He gestured towards the door with the pistol.

As Philip marched her through the quiet house, her heart pounded. Most of the servants had retired to their quarters, and the family had gone to bed. As they passed the library, Angel inhaled sharply at the sight of a sliver of light beneath the closed door. Jessica must still be awake, reading one of her beloved books. So close, yet unreachable. She couldn't risk it. What if Philip made good on his threat?

Just as they reached the entrance hall, the sound of approaching hoofbeats made them freeze. Philip yanked her behind a large potted plant in the darkened part of the room, his hand once again covering her mouth. The sharp smell of gunpowder on his fingers assaulted her nostrils.

Through the window, she saw Nathaniel dismounting from his horse and her eyes widened. What was he doing home? Had he returned to her? As of its own volition, her body moved, like it was drawn to Nathaniel like a magnet.

Philip's grip on her hardened, and his breath was hot on her ear. "Go ahead, try it." His voice was laced with cruel amusement. "Call for him. See who's quicker. Him or me putting a bullet in him. Want to take that chance?"

With a soundless wail that resonated through her soul, she crumbled against her captor's body. She could never risk

Nathaniel. No matter what, she loved him, and the idea of a world without him was unthinkable. When Nathaniel opened the door and entered the house, her body tensed. With her breath in her throat and a prayer on her lips, she watched him ascend the stairs, oblivious to her presence. Tears pricked her eyes. This might be the last time she ever saw him.

Once Nathaniel was out of sight, Philip forced her toward the door. As they stepped outside, the cool night air nipped at her skin, sending a shiver down her spine. The gardens she had come to love seemed alien and threatening in the darkness.

A carriage waited in the shadows, away from the main road, its driver hunched and unrecognisable in the gloom. Philip shoved her inside, following closely behind her. The interior was dark and stuffy, smelling of leather and horses.

As her eyes adjusted to the dim light, she gasped. Sitting across from her, a triumphant smirk on her face, was Marie.

"Cousin," Marie said, her voice dripping with false sweetness. "How kind of you to join us."

Before Angel could process this new shock, could even begin to understand Marie's involvement, the carriage lurched into motion. As they pulled away from Davenhall, from safety, from Nathaniel, she drew a shaky breath.

Turning to look out the window, she watched her home recede into the distance. *Nathaniel.* A tear slid down her cheek.

I'm sorry.

It was late when Nathaniel arrived at Davenhall. He had travelled since early morning, wanting to make the trip in one day, and while he was tired, he wanted nothing more than to see Angel. Maybe he should have waited for Parliament to break up for the summer, but the need to apologise to his wife and make everything right was stronger than even his dutiful spirit.

Taking the steps two at a time, he ascended the stairs to the first floor. A light shone under the door to the upstairs drawing room, so he peeked inside. Jessica sat on a sofa next to a lit candle and looked up from her book.

"Nathaniel!" She smiled. "We did not expect you back so soon."

"I came early." He cleared his throat, not wanting to seem rude, but unwilling to waste time. "Has Angel retired for the night?"

"Yes, everyone has. She might still be awake. I believe she was planning to have a bath."

He nodded. "Thank you. I will see you in the morning."

"Good night."

Closing the door behind him, he continued down the hallway to the master bedchamber. He stopped outside, hesitating. What if she didn't want to see him? They hadn't left things on the best of terms. Swallowing, he knocked carefully.

"Angel?" he called out, trying not to wake anyone else. Silence. She might be asleep. Leaning closer to the door, he listened but couldn't hear anything from inside.

As he opened the door and stepped inside, he hoped he wouldn't be met with something lobbed at his head. The room was empty, the window open to let in a faint breeze. There was no one in the bed, but there was a tub filled with bathwater in front of the fireplace, and a damp towel on a stool next to it. So Angel had finished her bath but had not gone to bed. He frowned. Where could she be?

After checking the adjoining chamber, he returned to the bedchamber with a growing feeling of unease. He was just about to leave when his eyes caught a piece of paper lying on the unused covers of the bed. Picking up the note, he fought back the niggle of fear at the back of his neck. He quickly scanned the scribbled words.

Pensington, I've got your wife. The two of you ruined my life, and you owe me. Pay me 10,000 pounds or you will never see her alive again.

He crumpled the paper in his hand just as Jessica walked past the open door to the hallway. Stopping when she noticed he was alone, she came inside. "Nathaniel? What's the matter?"

"Chettisham," he gritted out. "He's taken Angel."

Jessica's face paled and her eyes widened. "What?"

With no time to spare, he didn't answer the question. His feet were already moving him out the door. "How long ago did she go to her room?" he asked over his shoulder.

Jessica's footsteps followed closely behind him. "Not too long ago."

"Good. They might not be too far ahead. It looks like she had a bath first, so maybe they recently left." He hurried his steps. "I must rouse the footmen and make pursuit."

"But you don't know where they're going!"

"Towards London is the only logical direction. If he believes I will pay him, he will need to leave the country shortly after."

Jessica made a noise behind him he could only interpret as alarm. "Please be careful out there. It's dark and the roads are still muddy after two days of rain."

"I must follow, Jessica." He looked at her over his shoulder, and the anguish he felt was mirrored in the strained lines of her face.

"I know," she said. "All I ask is that you're careful. We have lost enough members of this family already."

He nodded tersely. "Agreed, but Angel is one of us now."

Chapter Twenty-Eight

Dear Diary,
 I remember meeting Philip once when
 I was a child. He wasn't a very pleasant
 boy even then. I don't know why I thought he'd change.

Angel watched the shadowy landscape pass by the carriage window in the late summer evening. Tentatively flexing her hands resting in her lap, the ropes cut into the skin of her wrists, and she grimaced. At least her feet weren't bound. Not that it made much difference.

Resigned to her current circumstances, she turned her head to give her travelling companions a cold look. No one had spoken since the carriage started moving. Marie and Philip both sat quietly on the bench facing her.

"I must admit to being surprised to see you," she said coldly to her cousin, tired of the eerie silence. "That Philip would want revenge doesn't surprise me, but I never expected to find you here. But then you always did play dirty. What's in this for you?"

Marie's blue eyes flashed angrily. "You always did underestimate me," she sneered. "Perfect little Angel, never doing anything wrong. Always the one with the biggest room and the prettiest toys. Everyone catered to you because you're the viscount's sister."

That was hardly an answer to her question, but Angel didn't argue. It was clear their memories of their life growing up together were wildly different. She may have had the biggest room but only because she already lived there when Marie and her parents moved in. Had they been able to shift Angel into another one without James noticing, she had no doubts they would have. Her cousin sounded jealous... but of what?

Aunt Christine certainly had found fault in plenty of things during their time together. Enough to make Angel doubt her own worth and consider marrying a man like Philip.

But she was no longer that scared girl who bowed under her aunt's oppressive comments. Nathaniel and his family—even James—had helped her find her voice. To stand up for herself and her own wants. She would cower no more.

"Why are you doing this?" she asked. "You've always disliked me, but to commit a crime... It is a step further than I would have expected, even for you."

"The marquess should have been mine!" Marie snapped. With a frustrated toss of her dark hair spilling down her shoulders, she continued, "I don't know what you did to make him marry you. Seduce him, I suppose. But it should have been me."

Angel could do little but stare. Marie had always coveted anything Angel had and had resented any time she could not have the same—or better yet, take Angel's. But this was a human being they were talking about. Her husband.

"Nathaniel showed no interest in you." She tried to keep her tone calm and reasonable.

"He did." Marie shook her head, unwilling to consider otherwise. "You're lying. He was ever so polite any time I sought him out, and I just know he would have been mine if you had not interfered. You always take everything from me."

"What?" Angel glanced at Philip to see if he would help her make Marie see reason, but he sat quietly with his arms crossed, his cold eyes disinterested in their conversation. Unsurprised, she turned back to her cousin. "Marie, I have never taken anything from you."

"You stole my parents! Then the man I intended to marry. And you already had one lined up!" Marie's arm flung out to indicate Philip, hitting him in the chest and eliciting a grunt. "Why would you discard a perfectly suitable match for you, if not to take something I wanted out of spite?"

The conversation was making less and less sense. Lifting her bound hands to rub her aching temple, Angel tried to understand her cousin's twisted worldview. "I didn't take your parents, Marie. Mine passed away, and you and your family moved in so I wouldn't be alone. You can hardly claim that Aunt Christine and Uncle George cared much for me. Their attention was still fully on you."

"But they were wholly mine before then." Marie crossed her arms, her blue eyes burning with scorching hate. "My earliest memories are having to share my parents with a whiny child who never spoke. Who cried any time she was left alone in a room. They had to be with you at all times while I was left on my own."

"I..." Angel frowned, remembering what James had told her about the period after their parents passed away. "I don't remember those days," she admitted. "But you must understand, I didn't do any of those things to take your parents from you. It wasn't out of spite. I was devastated after losing my parents in an accident."

Marie only scoffed.

"I'm sorry." Angel felt sad for the child Marie had once been. It must have been a big change for her as well, moving from their more humble cottage in the Midlands to Hefferton Place, and seeing her parents suddenly taking care of another child. A child who could not be left alone. "It must have been difficult for you, but I never intended to take your parents from you."

For a moment, Marie's countenance softened and hope sprung in Angel's chest, only to be swiftly dashed when Marie's eyes hardened again. "But you do not deny taking the marquess?"

"Nathaniel is my husband, but I did not take him from you." Angel shook her head. "He was never yours."

"He would have been," Marie insisted.

It was time to change the subject. They were getting nowhere. Angel looked over at Philip, who remained quiet, brewing in his resentment and ill will.

"What brought the two of you together?" she asked.

"We understand each other," Marie replied. "We have the same priorities in life."

Why wouldn't Philip speak? He hadn't uttered a word since he took her from her home. She was still wearing nothing but her nightgown and dressing gown, and the chill of the evening was seeping into her bones in the drafty carriage. Had Nathaniel noticed she was gone? Or was he still angry and would sleep in another room? If he did, no one was likely to notice her absence until the morning.

With her heart sinking, she looked out the window. They were going quite fast, judging by the speed at which the trees and landscape swept past in the darkness. A sliver of fear travelled down her spine when memories of another time in another carriage after dark surfaced. Needing a distraction, she turned back to her captors.

"What are you planning to do with me?"

"Philip left a note behind. If your dear husband doesn't pay us a hefty price for your safe return, he will never see you again."

"What happens if he doesn't pay?"

A smirk contorted Marie's pretty face. "I almost hope he doesn't."

The fear was now less of a niggle and more of a biting, snapping beast threatening to engulf her. Angel's bound hands gripped the fabric of her nightgown and held on as if it would somehow anchor her in the storm. Through the loud beating of her heart, she could hear Marie continue to ramble on, apparently needing to gloat and prove how ingenious their plan was.

"With the money, Philip and I will travel to America," her cousin continued. "We can make a good life for ourselves there. I would have preferred to stay in England…" She chuckled to herself. "But when they find the marquess dead, that just won't be possible anymore, will it?"

Angel's attention snapped back. "Dead?"

"Yes." Marie stared at her with shining eyes. "When the marquess comes to where we will tell him to drop off the money, Philip will shoot him. We can't have any witnesses now, can we?"

"No one takes what's mine," Philip said coldly, choosing that moment to speak.

Panic shot through Angel, and before she could think or consider her actions, she threw herself across the carriage. Her body connected with Marie's with a force she'd not known she possessed. Her cousin gasped for breath. Taking advantage of the stunned shock, Angel scrambled over to the window. The ropes that restrained her wrists cut into her skin, but she gritted her teeth and managed to unlatch the hook. Cold air hit her face when she stuck her head through to get a better look. They were driving along the ridge of a steep hill and were going much too fast on a road still muddy and slippery from excessive rainfall.

"Stop the carriage!" she shouted towards the driver.

"Get back inside!" Philip snarled, and she could feel his hands on her ankle.

"Angel!"

Her head whipped around to see a handful of shadowy figures on horseback following in the distance. *Nathaniel!* Before she could shout a reply, Philip gripped her waist and pulled her back inside, none too gently. Just then, the carriage hit a rut in the road. They fell to the floor, Marie bouncing in her seat. Gritting her teeth, Angel ignored her aching hip and glanced outside. They were picking up speed. The driver must have seen the approaching riders.

When the carriage suddenly listed towards the edge, she inhaled sharply and her insides turned to ice. They hit another rut in the road, throwing the carriage off course. No longer able to find a grip on the slippery surface, the vehicle slid towards the hillside leaning into a river below. They were tossed across the small space with a painful thump as the carriage careened down the hill until it hit an obstacle with enough speed to tilt it, making it tip over and land on its side.

Chilling tendrils of fear grabbed Angel when they fell, all three tumbling over one another, limbs and dresses intertwining. Memories of the last time she'd been in this situation rose to the surface, pushing through the fear. While the carriage carrying her and her parents had turned down a hillside—one much steeper than the one they were sliding down now—her mother had done something desperate that probably saved Angel's life.

Wrapping Angel tightly in a cloak and blanket, her mother had closed her in a compartment underneath the carriage seats. It had been just big enough for a small five-year-old girl and had hindered the worst movements for her, while her parents had been tossed around the carriage as it tumbled down the hill. In the enclosed space and with the protective layers of fabric around her, Angel had made it with only a few bruises.

In the carriage with Philip and Marie, still sliding down the hill on its side, Angel remembered the horror of when the one in her past had finally stopped, and she'd got the hatch open to crawl out of the small compartment.

The sight that had greeted her.

The broken bodies of her parents, their eyes staring unseeingly.

She screamed. She wasn't sure if it was in the past or present. Or both.

The carriage came to a sudden halt, jerking her back to reality. She lay still for a moment, trying to get her bearings. Everything hurt, but she didn't think anything was broken. They were at an odd angle, leaning against a large boulder. Marie must have bumped her head; she sat on the floor with her hands covering her face with dark, wet tendrils trailing down her cheek from a gash by her hairline. The door on the lower side of the carriage was wedged against the boulder and impossible to open, and the other was too high for Angel to reach. Especially with her hands bound.

Philip did not have that problem. He pushed past both of them, shoved the door open, and climbed out.

"Philip!" Marie yelled, but he was gone.

Horses' hooves approached, and men were shouting. The crack of a pistol firing echoed through the night. Claws of icy panic seized Angel's heart.

"Nathaniel!"

There was no answer other than the men shouting indistinctively. She couldn't hear Nathaniel's voice in the mix. Tears streamed down her cheeks, and she tried to use the seats for purchase to let her reach the door, but with her hands still bound before her, it was impossible.

The dull sounds of someone climbing up on the carriage made her look up, and a moment later, Nathaniel's beloved face appeared in the open doorway. Relief washed over her, and her eyes burned as she began crying in earnest. Seeing him safe was overwhelming.

"Angel!" He was pale, with deep lines around his mouth and eyes, and his dark hair stood on end. He looked like he'd been to hell and back. But he was unharmed. "You're alive! Are you all right?" he asked frantically. "Are you hurt?"

"I'm fine." She hiccoughed. "But I can't get out."

Holding her hands up to show him her tied wrists, she saw his eyes darken, and he cursed loudly. Shifting his body further onto the side of the carriage, he leaned his chest on the open door and reached inside. "Take my hands. I'll lift you."

She glanced down at Marie, who stared back glumly. "What about her?"

"We'll get her later."

Not feeling the need to stay in the carriage to keep her cousin company, Angel reached up. Nathaniel grabbed hold of her arms and hauled her out of the carriage. The moment he got her down on the muddy ground, he pulled her close and held her in a grip so tight she could barely breathe, but right then, she didn't mind. She couldn't stop crying, and her hands were still bound, but she was so happy to be back in his arms that nothing else mattered.

Finally, he seemed to realise he couldn't keep squeezing her forever, and he held her out in front of him to get a good look at her. She had no idea what she looked like, but she couldn't imagine it was a great sight. Dark clouds gathered in his eyes as he took in her appearance. His hand came up to stroke the hair from her face, and she could see exactly when he saw the darkening shadow on her cheekbone from where Philip had slapped her earlier.

With a low curse, he helped her up the hillside to the road. Three footmen stood with Philip and a man she assumed was the driver between them. A fourth footman stood with their horses, including the ones from the carriage. Fortunately, the driver had been quick thinking and cut the animals loose before the carriage went down the hill, and they seemed all right if frazzled. But who wasn't?

"A knife," Nathaniel barked, upon which a footman produced one from his boot and handed it to him. After making quick work of the ropes tying Angel, he returned it and said stiffly, "Miss Brown is still in the carriage. Get her out of there."

A footman walked to the ridge, half-walking and half-sliding down the hillside. With only two footmen left by him, Philip turned and ran. Cursing, Nathaniel followed and caught up with him in seconds, the two men falling to the ground in a mass of limbs.

"Damn you!" Philip shouted. "You ruined everything. She was meant to be mine."

"Never," Nathaniel growled, hauling the other man to his feet. "You're not fit to kiss her feet."

"I hope you're enjoying your ice queen," Philip spat. "I should have broken her in for you when I had the chance, maybe she—"

Nathaniel's fist stopped his vile barrage. Philip tried to fight back but had nothing against the sheer fury of Nathaniel's attack. A footman left the driver, who made no attempt to leave, and pulled on his master's arm.

Stepping away and letting the footman grab Philip, Nathaniel asked, "Did you really think you could get away with this, Chettisham?"

Philip glared at him and wrestled free of the footman's grip. "I hoped so," he said coldly. "After you and Gowthorpe let everyone know of my financial status, no one will marry me and my credit has gone bad. I was desperate for money."

"So you resort to kidnapping and ransom?" Before anyone could react, Nathaniel's fist connected solidly with Philip's chin, sending him sprawling to the ground. "Go to hell, Chettisham. Don't let me see your face again."

The other footman returned from the carriage with Marie, and using some of the rope that had bound Angel, they tied Philip's hands behind his back.

"My lord," a footman said. "Take your wife back home. It's cold and dark. We will deal with these three."

Returning to Angel's side and taking her in his arms, Nathaniel nodded tersely. "Bring them to the constable and explain what happened."

Angel shivered. The bottom of her nightgown was already soaking up the wet mud they stood in, and her slippered feet fared no better.

Noticing her distress, Nathaniel's face softened. "You must be freezing in that gown. Here." He shrugged out of his riding coat and helped her into it. While much too large, it warmed her and smelled of him, making her feel safe.

Lifting her up on his horse, he sat up behind her and draped her across his lap before turning the horse back home towards Davenhall. She leaned her head against his shoulder and put her arms around his waist, focusing on nothing but the heat from his body and the pulse racing under her ear. They rode in silence, his posture stiff as if still seething with rage, while she was too tired to talk. Once the danger had passed, all the energy had been sapped from her body and she only wanted to sleep.

She must have nodded off, because when Angel next looked around, Nathaniel was halting the horse outside Davenhall. Before his feet even touched the ground, the door burst open and his sisters poured out, followed by Mrs Grey and several servants.

"You found her." The Howertys' aunt looked at them, her eyes suspiciously moist. She turned to the servants. "They are both cold and muddy. Please prepare a bath immediately. We need to get them cleaned and warmed up."

A flurry of movement sent the servants scurrying to do as they'd been asked, leaving only the Howertys outside. Nathaniel helped Angel off the horse, and she was thankful for his strong arms around her while they walked inside. His sisters were shooting off questions in rapid succession, their voices overlapping, creating a cacophony of sounds.

Standing in the entrance hallway, Nathaniel kept an arm around her, probably a little tighter than necessary. It was like he didn't want to let her go for fear she might disappear again. His movements were stiff, and he hadn't said a word, despite the constant chatter and continued questions from his siblings.

Mrs Grey's voice cut through the young women's queries. "Enough girls," she said, and her clear voice brokered no argument. "Angel has been through quite an ordeal tonight and I am certain she and Nathaniel would like to clean up and get some sleep. You can find out all the details tomorrow."

"But—" Nick began, but immediately silenced after a look from her aunt. "Yes, Aunt Jane."

They each hugged Angel before walking up the stairs to their bedchambers. Mrs Grey lingered for a moment, her eyes taking in their appearances. Taking Angel's hands, she squeezed the cold fingers between her warm ones.

"I am so very happy to see you safe. We've had warm water prepared for when you return, so I imagine your bath will be ready any moment."

"Thank you." Angel smiled softly, grateful for the small favour. Getting out of her muddy clothes and cleaning up sounded wonderful.

Mrs Grey glanced up at Nathaniel, who had remained silent, and simply nodded. "We will speak in the morning." She received a terse nod in response.

Taking Angel's hand, Nathaniel led her up the stairs to their bedchamber. When they arrived, two maids with buckets in their hands left the room, having just finished filling the tub, and he closed the door behind them. Looking at the inviting tub with steam coming off it, Angel moved towards it, but Nathaniel's hand gripped her tightly and wouldn't let go. She turned around to look at him and was shocked to see him shaking.

"Nathaniel? What's wrong?"

He took a deep breath. Then another. When he didn't seem to get enough air but was gulping like a drowning man, she reached up to touch his face. It seemed to bring him to his senses, and he pulled her close, circling her in his arms and burying his nose in her hair.

"I thought I'd lost you." His arms held her a little tighter, but he lifted his head to look down at her, fear still tinting his eyes. "Hell, Angel... When that carriage started down the hill, I thought I'd lost you forever. I've never been so scared in my life."

Her eyes were burning again, and she wiped away a stubborn tear. He slid his hands down her body as if needing to make sure she was still there.

"I never want to lose you, Angel. I don't know if I could handle it."

"You won't. All I could think about tonight was getting back to you. Even when the carriage went down the hill and I remembered my parents' accident, it was all I wanted. I didn't panic because my need to get back to you was greater than my fear."

He looked down at her, his dark eyes suspiciously moist. "I'm sorry for being an arse." His voice thickened with every word. "I should never have left that night. It wasn't you I was angry with, it was myself. For hurting you. For not being everything you deserve."

"What?" She shook her head. "Nathaniel, you're everything I want."

His hands came up to cup her face. "Angel, I..." He sighed. "I have been an arse. Letting my worries take over. I didn't want to admit to loving you, even to myself, because I worried that if I lost you, I would handle it no better than my father. But the truth is that it doesn't matter. I love you, Angel, and I don't want to lose another day that I can spend loving you. And I pray I will never have to find out if I'm stronger than my father was."

Trying to calm her beating heart, she stared up at him. "You love me?" she whispered, almost afraid to believe it.

"So much. And I hope you might care for me, too."

She blinked. "You don't remember?"

"Don't remember what?"

"Nathaniel, I told you I love you before you went to London." Was the man daft? She clearly recalled the conversation and his soul-crushing reply.

"You did?"

"Yes. It was late at night after we..." She trailed off, her cheeks heating.

A smile tugged at the corners of his mouth. "Are you certain I was awake?"

"You responded." He had been tired and his voice slurred. A light dawned, and she stared at him. "You didn't hear me," she whispered. "You were sleeping, responding with no idea what I had said."

He nodded. "Yes. Because trust me, I would have remembered if you told me you loved me." Lowering his head until his mouth was a mere inch from hers, their breaths mingling, he whispered, "Tell me again?"

Threading her fingers through the dark hair at the back of his head, she smiled. "I love you, Nathaniel."

His lips crashed into hers, instantly igniting the fire between them as he pulled her close to his body, warming her with his heat.

"You're the best thing that's ever happened to me," he mumbled against her lips. "And I will do everything I can to make you happy."

She clung to him like a safe haven in a storm. "Nathaniel, you've given me everything I could ever want. A place where I feel at home. A family. I'm happier than I've ever been."

A devilish smile made her toes curl, and he nipped at her lower lip. "Let's get cleaned up, and then maybe we can see if I can make you even happier..."

She giggled while he unbuttoned the riding coat he'd loaned her, pausing after every button to kiss her. Remembering a thought she'd had while he was in London, she touched his face tenderly. "But Nathaniel... Don't you know that you are stronger than your father? You already proved that."

"What do you mean?" He tilted his head to kiss each of her fingertips.

"You lost both of your parents. And you were strong enough to still be there for your sisters. You continued your life, and you made it a good one. Where your father crumbled at his first great loss, you survived two at a much younger age."

His eyes widened. "I never thought of it like that." A smile spread across his face as if someone had lifted a great weight off his shoulders. "You are absolutely amazing, my darling Angel."

She smiled back at him, her heart light. She truly had everything.

"But Nathaniel?" she said when he led her towards the waiting bath.

He met her eyes, and the love in his gaze warmed her more than any bath could. "Yes, darling?"

"Do you think we could avoid travelling by carriage for a while?"

Bending down to place a kiss on her shoulder, he murmured, "I can agree to that."

Epilogue

Davenhall, England
July 7, 1812

Dear Diary,

I had another letter from Marie today. It was predictably crumpled and stained after travelling such a long distance. She continues to beg my forgiveness and asks Nathaniel to change his demands. Even if I were to consider her request—which I would not—Nathaniel would never agree.

All in all, I believe it was a fair deal to make her and Philip choose between moving to America or being charged with their crimes and risking jail. They made their choices, both in this and when they kidnapped me, and now they must live with them.

EMILY MORGANS

But I do not wish to dwell on this any longer. I am running out of pages, and must bid you farewell so that I may enjoy this special day...

Angel closed her diary and put it to the side before standing up from her small writing desk. Having found out her preference for gazing out the window while writing, Nathaniel had brought the piece of furniture into the upstairs drawing room and set it by the window facing the extensive gardens in the back of the house.

Yet another sign of how thoughtful her husband could be. A year into their marriage, he was still as attentive to her needs as he'd been when they first met.

While she had been hiding in the corners of the ballroom—or behind potted plants—he had sought her out, coaxed her out of her shell, and helped her find the voice she had buried for so long. Her shyness was unlikely to ever fully disappear, but she no longer dreaded speaking up in fear of rebuke.

She could voice her dissenting thoughts without censure, and it was a liberating feeling. Belonging to a family that shared their views openly was a wonderful new world, one she was immensely grateful to be part of.

Leaving the drawing room, she reflected on how quiet the house seemed with everyone gone. Mrs Grey and the girls had travelled to Devon to see the Howertys' uncle Ben, Viscount Lyford, and Nathaniel was visiting the tenants with Davenhall's steward. She rather hoped her husband would return soon.

Today it had been exactly one year since they married, and she wanted to—

Something crunched under her foot.

She stepped to the side and stared down at the item on the floor. *A red rose.*

Someone grabbed her from behind and she gasped, before smiling when she recognised the familiar scent of Nathaniel's sandalwood soap. He placed a kiss on her neck. Her body heated when he pulled her closer against his lean frame and nibbled the sensitive skin below her ear.

"I didn't expect you back so soon," she murmured.

"I missed you." His lips moved over her shoulder to place a kiss by the collar of her dress. "It's our one-year anniversary and I don't want to spend it away from you. Rowlings and I can travel the grounds another day."

She closed her eyes, enjoying the feeling of his hands moving along her side and down over her hips before grasping her waist and pulling her closer to him, the evidence of his desire hard against her soft bottom. Life with Nathaniel was never boring. His passion was infinite, and she couldn't say she minded. He'd awoken a fire within her that never seemed to extinguish, always smouldering beneath the surface, waiting for his next touch.

With a reluctant groan, he straightened and nudged her forwards, and she noticed more roses spread evenly along the hallway, leading towards their bedchamber. Bending down, she picked up the one she had trampled on, before moving a few steps to pick up the next.

When Nathaniel didn't immediately follow, she turned around to look at him. "Are you not coming?"

His dark eyes met hers, and the heat in them fanned her own flame. "In a moment," he said. "I'm enjoying the view."

Ignoring her burning cheeks, she turned back to follow the trail of roses leading down the hallway. When she reached the door to their bedchamber, Nathaniel was only a step or two behind. Walking inside, she fought back the sting of tears in her eyes when she saw the rose petals spread over the white sheets on the bed, and a brand new leather-bound journal with a rose etched on the cover.

She turned around to face her husband.

"I noticed you were running out of pages in your current one," he said, closing the door behind them. "Figured you would need a new one soon."

"You didn't have to do this." She reached up to cup his cheek. "Life with you is the only gift I need."

The ghost of a smile played across his lips. "I will shower my wife with all the gifts I want." He bent and captured her mouth.

Fire burned between them as they kissed. Lips meeting, tongues tangling, and hands moving to undo the lacing and buttons of their clothes. Before long, they were both naked, and a soft breeze from the open window caressed her bare skin. Nathaniel moved the journal off the bed and laid her down in the midst of the rose petals, covering her with his body. She moaned when he dragged his mouth down her chest to capture a nipple between his teeth, sucking and teasing until she writhed in his arms.

Her hands buried in the silky hair at the back of his head, and she revelled in the softness between her fingers. Nathaniel kissed a trail down her torso, tickling her abdomen when he continued lower. She inhaled sharply. When he placed a soft kiss on her nether curls, her grip on his hair tightened, making him look up at her with a devilish smile. Heat unfurled within her, and she boldly made space for him between her legs. His smile widened, and a moment later, his mouth and lips descended on her, setting her world ablaze.

After a year of marriage, she still could never get enough of this. Of him. Of the way their desire never seemed to diminish. Nathaniel was near insatiable, and she couldn't complain. She enjoyed every moment of their time together. She gasped when he flicked his tongue in that deliciously wicked way, and her thoughts dispersed, chased away by the pleasure coursing through her veins. Every lick and nibble intensified her desire until her world exploded in a burst of light.

Covering her eyes with her arm, she focused on bringing her breathing back under control. She could feel the mattress shifting from Nathaniel moving up to lie next to her. She was about to turn to him to continue their afternoon delight when a wave of nausea crashed over her. Throwing herself over the edge of the bed, she spilt the contents of her stomach in the chamberpot. When she looked up, Nathaniel sat in the bed, staring at her.

"That... is not quite the reaction I had hoped for," he said slowly, moving over to her. Cupping her cheek, he met her gaze with a crease between his brows. "Are you all right?"

She nodded, feeling somewhat embarrassed by the whole situation. "Yes. I have been waiting to tell you this until our anniversary, but I guess the cat's out of the bag..."

Nathaniel's eyes widened, and then his lips split into a wide grin. "You're with child? We're having a baby!" He pulled her into a tight hug but quickly released her when she made a small noise. Nausea reared its ugly head again. "Oh, darling. That is excellent news."

Fighting back her rioting insides, she smiled. She rather looked forward to adding another member to the Howerty brood. They were loud and boisterous, but also generous with their love and laughter. And they were hers. Her family. She had everything she had ever wanted, and she wouldn't trade it for the world.

"What are you thinking?" Nathaniel tucked a lock of hair behind her ear. "I can't tell if you're smiling or about to be sick again."

"Maybe a little of both," she said with a little laugh. "I was thinking how lucky I am to have found you."

He leaned down to kiss the top of her head. "No, darling. I'm the lucky one. You helped me see I am a different man from my father, and that loving you did not make me weak. In fact, it makes me stronger because I want to be there for you and our family, every day, forever."

"Even when I'm sick in the chamberpot?"

His warm chuckle reverberated through her body. "Especially then."

THE END

Acknowledgements

This book has been a long time coming, and I wish my grandmother could have been here to see it finally published. She was always my biggest supporter, and I will forever miss her presence and the stories she was always so happy to share.

So many people have been a part of my journey through the years, and I'd like to acknowledge how much I appreciate their help and support.

The Flirties—my wonderful group of fellow writers who have been a huge part of my life the last few years. We've laughed and ranted and supported each other through writing blocks and periods of frantic typing. I wouldn't trade you all for the world.

Sal and Eva—thank you two, especially, for your amazing and on-point developmental and line-editing suggestions. You've helped make this story all it could be.

My WP readers, for cheering me on and showing me that there are people out there who want to read my stories. You will forever have a special place in my heart, and some of your comments through the years have been absolutely amazing!

Lastly, thank you, Robin, for entertaining our Tiny Tyrant when I had to write to hit a deadline and putting up with my stressed-out rambling (and occasional teeth grinding while asleep!). I couldn't have done this without you.

www.ingramcontent.com/pod-product-compliance
Lightning Source LLC
LaVergne TN
LVHW041617060526
838200LV00040B/1320